Operation M

'Wonderfully moving. A book to curl up with.'
Fern Britton

'Enthralling from beginning to end.'
Alan Titchmarsh

'A charming novel full of fascinating detail about
the Second World War, AND a heart-warming
love story. I loved every word of it!'
Katie Fforde

'Well researched and extremely moving.
I really enjoyed it!'
Jill Mansell

'A fresh and captivating tale of secrets and
bravery . . . her contemporary love story is
just as compelling.'
Chloe Timms

'I loved this gripping dual-timeline novel
about a centenarian and her past as an
SOE agent during WW2.'
Nikki Marmery

'I absolutely loved this powerful and haunting
story about World War Two Special Operations
Executive Elisabeth, and the elderly lady Betty
that she becomes.'
Gill Thompson

OPERATION MOONLIGHT

LOUISE MORRISH

PENGUIN BOOKS

PENGUIN BOOKS

UK | USA | Canada | Ireland | Australia
India | New Zealand | South Africa

Penguin Books is part of the Penguin Random House group of
companies whose addresses can be found at
global.penguinrandomhouse.com

First published by Century 2022
Published in Penguin Books 2023
001

Typeset in 11/14.7 pt Palatino LT Std
by Integra Software Services Pvt. Ltd, Pondicherry

Printed and bound in Great Britain by Clays Ltd, Elcograf S.p.A.

The authorised representative in the EEA is Penguin Random House Ireland,
Morrison Chambers, 32 Nassau Street, Dublin D02 YH68

A CIP catalogue record for this book is available from the British Library

ISBN: 978–1–529–16042–0

www.greenpenguin.co.uk

To my gran,
the original Betty Shepherd

OPERATION MOONLIGHT

1

2018

A sallow moon shines through the bedroom window. Watching her. Sleep will be elusive tonight, Betty knows. Always the way when it's a full moon.

She really ought to close the curtains, but it would make no difference. The moon will still be there, whether she can see it or not.

A monthly reminder; as if she could ever forget.

From across the landing, she can hear Tali's rumbling snores. Her carer would have slept through the Blitz, Betty has no doubt. Lucky girl.

Sighing, she hoists herself up in the bed, reaching for her glasses on the bedside table. Yesterday's *Times* lies folded next to them, half read. She'll try the cryptic, see if that'll send her off. The moon's light is enough to see by, if she squints.

She rummages in the pockets of her bedjacket, but instead of the pencil she expects to find, she unearths a used tissue, a rusty hatpin, and a strange key whose lock she cannot recall. She peers at the key, an oddly shaped thing made of thick, twisted wire, turning it over in her palm. How had it come to be in her pocket?

From his basket at the foot of the bed, Tosca whines softly.

'What do you make of this, boy?' Betty asks her elderly Scottie dog. Lately, trying to recall things has been like stumbling around the house in the dark, hands fumbling for a light switch or a door handle. This key, for instance. Where had it come from? Its sudden appearance is a mystery.

She turns the metal object over and over, her brain grinding with the effort of remembering. An image flickers, and she thinks she has it, but no. She tries again, searching the shadowy recesses of her mind, tripping over memories long forgotten.

The dog emits a low growl.

'What is it, eh?' Betty pushes herself further up the pillows, and as she does so a vaguely familiar, smoke-hoarse voice comes clear to her across the years.

'A skeleton key'll open almost anything.'

There, in the far corner of the bedroom, all but invisible in the shadows, stands a figure. As it slowly approaches, Betty's fingers tighten around the key. She knuckles her glasses up her nose, trying to bring the man, for it is a man, into focus. He's nearly at the bed when recognition pierces the blackness of her memory; it is a man she knows only as 'Mr Smith the lock-picker'.

Betty's heart stutters. Is she hallucinating?

She hasn't seen her security instructor Mr Smith since 1944. Yet here he is, looking exactly the same as he did back then, wiry as a ferret, greasy-haired, wearing the same threadbare brown suit. There is a sudden waft of Woodbines, a smell that takes Betty straight back to Wanborough Manor, Special Training School No. 5.

Think of it always; speak of it never.

He can't be real.

He is surely long dead.

'How did you get in here?' she demands. If this apparition is indeed Mr Smith, the question is redundant, she knows. A rumour had circulated at Wanborough that their instructor had been sprung from Wormwood Scrubs for his unrivalled knowledge of breaking and entering. Mr Smith could get in or out of anywhere, apparently. Whatever the truth, he certainly knew his locks.

The man grins, revealing blunt, tobacco-stained teeth. 'What sort of a welcome is that, young lady?'

Betty snorts at the thought of anyone, even a ghost, thinking her young. She lets the key drop on to the newspaper and takes off her glasses. But even after polishing the lenses on the frayed hem of her bed-jacket, it makes no difference. He's still there, practically close enough to touch, though the outline of his body is a little smudged now, as though he's someone's unfinished sketch.

A memory of Wanborough returns; watching Mr Smith demonstrate how easy it was to break into a sash window. 'Could use a jemmy,' he'd sniffed. 'Not that you'll have one. Could stick brown paper covered in treacle to the glass, then smash it with a hammer. Bloody faff, if you ask me. Nah, the quickest, easiest way is to slip your knife into the gap here, like so, and you're in.' With a flick of his wrist, he'd sliced the catch, and the window was open.

Betty clears her throat. 'Can I help you?' Perhaps he's come for his key? The thought is ludicrous, a small part of her conscious brain acknowledges. But she's been brought up to be respectful, even to the dead.

Especially to the dead.

'Just wondered if you'd heard,' the lock-picker smirks.

'Heard what?'

Mr Smith gestures at the newspaper on Betty's lap. 'Something on page twenty you'll want to see.'

She's loath to take her eyes off the man for fear that if she does so he'll vanish. He's a bit of company, after all. The nights can be so lonely, even with Tali in the room next door. But Mr Smith is gesturing at the *Times* impatiently.

Betty unfolds the newspaper, turns to page twenty. The obituaries. Of course.

With half an eye on her strange visitor, she begins to read the first entry.

Mrs DORIS BONE née WATERS, 101, died peacefully following a short illness on 27 January at her home in Oxford.

Betty's breath lodges in her throat, but she forces herself to read the whole obituary.

Her dearest, oldest friend was gone. It didn't matter that she hadn't seen Doris since the war. They'd written to each other every Christmas, and never forgot a birthday. She's kept those letters from Doris, every single one of them. In Doris's last communication, she'd been planning to visit Betty in Guildford.

You and I can enjoy tea together at last and reminisce.

The realisation that she will never see Doris again brings tears to Betty's eyes. She blinks them away as the lock-picker drifts back into the shadows. Tali's snores resonate through the wall. Betty rubs her temples, fighting the weariness that sweeps through her; a dark tide that grows stronger each day. Death is inevitable, claiming everyone eventually, she knows this. But still, she'll miss Doris. She'd been one of a rare breed; a fellow SOE survivor. There weren't many of them left.

And now her friend was gone.

It gets us all in the end, whispers Mr Smith.

Betty searches the shadows, but the man is no longer there.

The long, lonely hours of the night stretch before her.

*

The next morning, settled in her armchair in the sitting room, Betty waits for Tali to return from the shops. She watches an extended family of sparrows squabbling on the bird-feeder, scattering seed on the scrubby lawn. She can hear them arguing even through the closed window. She'll have to ask Tali to put some more bird food out later. A fat pigeon descends from nowhere in a flurry of feathers, gate-crashing the avian picnic, sending the little brown birds darting into the bushes.

'You big bully,' Betty murmurs, her fingers tight-ening on the arms of her chair. She lifts her gaze beyond the bird-feeder, staring down the narrow garden to the slice of river at the end, the water glinting in the low winter sun. When had she last swum in its cool, green depths? Or walked along its peaceful banks? She can't remember. A long, long time ago, when she was young and free.

Her knees and shoulders ache. Everything aches.

Old age is like a prison, Betty thinks. She's largely housebound now, only venturing out to visit the doctor, wholly reliant on Tali for her shopping and the upkeep of this house. These days, she is no more able to control the course of her life than a piece of flotsam can expect to steer the river.

She sniffs.

Enough of this.

She will ask Tali to take her to Doris's funeral, so she can pay her respects to her friend, if it's the last thing she does.

At her feet, Tosca wakes and emits a wheezy bark, hauling himself up on his stumpy legs. A moment later, the front door slams.

'*Je suis de retour*, Madame Betty!'

Betty peers at her watch, dangling loose from her bony wrist. Its glass face is cracked, yet it still keeps perfect time, even after all these years. It's now twenty past eleven. Tali had left for the supermarket before nine; what had taken the girl so long?

She can hear her carer crashing about in the hall, no doubt divesting herself of garments. To Betty's bemusement, Tali insists on dressing for Arctic conditions regardless of the weather.

Tosca waddles out to the hallway, tail wagging.

'*J'arrive*, Madame Betty!' There comes the clunk of a heavy bag dropping on the hall tiles, followed by a breathless Creole expletive.

Closing her eyes in concentration, Betty follows her carer's movements by sound, as Tali blunders into the kitchen, mumbling to the dog as she goes. The tap gurgles as the kettle is filled, the hinges of the larder door squeal and then, a moment later, comes the unmistakable pebbly rattle of too much dog kibble being poured into Tosca's bowl. Listening carefully, Betty pictures Tali moving about her little kitchen, and the image cheers her. When at last the young woman appears in the sitting room doorway, her cheeks are glowing, and her unruly dark curls have come free of their clips and are falling in her eyes.

'You will never believe it, Madame Betty,' Tali exhales, hands on her ample hips. 'No flour or eggs in Aldi! I had to walk all the way to Sainsbury's.' She tucks a clump of hair behind an ear and plonks herself down on the settee. If anyone had asked Betty to describe her live-in carer, she would have called her 'wide-beamed'; 'well-built'; 'colourful'. Today, Tali is wearing some mismatched outfit of skirt, sweater and tights, in a glaring clash of reds and oranges, with a scarf of canary-yellow wrapped around her neck. The whole ensemble is too vibrant, in Betty's opinion, for a woman the wrong side of thirty.

'Never mind,' Betty says. 'I have something to show you.' She passes Tali the newspaper, folded open at Doris's obituary.

Tali reads the paragraph slowly. 'Interesting lady,' she says, looking up. 'You knew her, Madame Betty?'

Betty dips her head, swallows a lump in her throat. Doris would not have wanted tears. 'The funeral is on Friday.' She absently strokes the skeleton key in her lap. The scent of Woodbines lingers in her nostrils, and she wonders if her carer can smell it too. 'I want to go.'

'OK.' Tali smiles, her eyes flicking to Betty's lap. 'What is that you have?'

After a moment's hesitation, Betty hands Tali the key, watching her carer's face as she studies its odd shape.

'What is this, Madame Betty?'

'A skeleton key.' There, she's told the truth.

Tali frowns. 'What is a skeleton key?'

'You must have them in Mauritius. They open any lock.'

'Thieves and robbers use them?'

'Not exclusively.' Why did everyone always assume the worst?

'You were a thief or robber once, Madame Betty?' Tali grins.

Betty sighs inwardly. *If only you knew, child.*

Tali heaves herself to her feet. 'Do you want lunch now?'

'*Je n'ai pas faim*, Natalia.'

'Not yet, maybe. But when you smell my *bouyon brede* ...'

Betty's favourite.

'I'm not hungry.' This was true, but it's not only Doris's death that has robbed Betty of her meagre appetite.

'The soup will take a little time, anyway,' Tali says, making her way to the door. 'When you smell it, you'll be hungry then.'

8

With Tali gone, the room instantly reverts to mono-chrome once more. Betty's gaze drifts to the cluttered sideboard; amongst the detritus of her life sit two framed black-and-white photographs. One is of herself and Fred, taken on the River Wey in 1967. They're sitting in Fred's tiny rowing boat, the *Jenny Wren*, which he'd built himself out of scrap wood.

Occasionally, if she stares at this photo for long enough, she can breathe the scent of the river that day, feel the brief caress of sun on her face. She'd been happy, out in that little boat with Fred.

The other photograph, the one her eye keeps snag-ging on lately, is of her son, Leo, plump and scowling from the depths of a Silver Cross pram. He'd been a fractious, colicky baby. They'd tried their best, she and Fred, but Leo had not been an easy child to love.

She thinks of the airmail that arrived from Australia a few days ago.

Mother, I'm coming home.

Betty closes her eyes. When she opens them again, her carer is calling from the kitchen.

'Lunch is ready!' A moment later, Tali appears in the doorway carrying a steaming bowl of soup on a tray. She sets it down carefully on Betty's lap, and the aroma of herbs and chicken is so rich, Betty's stomach growls.

'Thank you, dear.' She smiles.

'My Nani's recipe,' Tali says, modestly. 'Without too much spice.'

Tali brings her own soup through from the kitchen, then sits on the settee opposite Betty, balancing her bowl on her knees. Tosca wanders back into the room, a hopeful look in his eye.

For a while, there is only the tink of metal on china, as both women scoop up broth and blow on their spoons.

'I have something to tell you,' Betty says at last, swallowing a final mouthful of dumpling. 'But don't fly off the handle.'

Tali's forehead furrows as she stares at Betty's spoon. 'What fly on your handle ...?'

'I mean, you mustn't be angry that I haven't told you before now.'

'Told me what?' Tali's shining brown eyes remind Betty of a kitten Fred once bought for Leo's birthday. 'A companion for the boy.' Being an only child could be lonely. Betty had known that well enough herself.

Betty rubs her brow. 'Would you fetch my big handbag, Natalia dear? It's in my wardrobe.'

Minutes later, Tali returns from Betty's bedroom, hefting a leather bag in her arms. 'What have you got in here, Madame Betty? The kitchen cupboard?'

'Sink,' Betty corrects, as Tali sets the bag down gently on her lap. For years, Betty has only used this handbag to hide things in. The burgundy leather is cracked and dusty and her arthritic fingers fumble for a moment with the stiff clasp, but at last she manages to prise it open. She remembers shoving the letter in the bag; out of sight, out of mind.

Delving deep, Betty's fingers touch something hard and she draws out a small dagger, tucked in its worn leather sheath.

'You have *un couteau* in your bag?'

Betty glances up, surprised by her carer's shocked, accusatory tone.

A knife should always be carried … Betty hears the voice of the instructor at Arisaig as clearly as though he stands before her. *A knife is capable of being used either as a utility or offensive weapon.*

'You never know when you might need a sharp blade,' Betty mutters, tucking the knife back in the bag. She pulls out a small pocket torch next.

Followed by a compass on a string.

Then a length of silk cord, wrapped in a loose ball. *This*, the officer intones in Betty's head, *may be used for any purpose, from tying a man up to preparing a booby trap.*

Half a packet of cough lozenges next, stuck with old fluff from the bottom of the bag.

And lastly a box of matches. *Always carry a full box, because a half-empty one rattles and might give your location away.*

'Are you smoking, Madame Betty?' Tali's voice has taken on a reproachful tone.

'What if I am?' Betty snaps. A cigarette was hardly going to kill her now.

Where is that damn letter?

She can feel Tali's eyes on her, as she roots one last time in the bag and finally draws out the airmail. 'This came the other day.'

It doesn't take long for Tali to read the letter. She looks up, her face unusually pale. 'Your son, he is coming home?'

Betty gives a terse nod.

Tali bends her head to the short letter again. 'He writes here—'

'Pay no attention to that,' Betty interrupts. 'I have no intention of going anywhere. And neither are you.'

For a time there is silence, both women deep in their own thoughts. At last, Tali passes the airmail back and rises. 'I will wash up, now.'

Alone, Betty contemplates the return of her son, and a feeling of helplessness sweeps through her. She hasn't always been weak and decrepit, she reminds herself. There was a time – a long time ago, granted – when she was strong. When she was brave.

Could she be brave again?

But that was almost seventy-five years ago, in a world long gone.

The threat she faces now is a very different beast.

2

February 1944

Elisabeth peered through a slit in the blacked-out window, as her train wheezed into Waterloo Station half an hour late. The platform seethed with military personnel, harried commuters, and weary Londoners clutching their scant belongings. Tightening the belt on the black peplum jacket she'd borrowed from her mother, Elisabeth stepped down from the train and was swept towards the exit in a stream of bodies.

Incomprehensible tannoy announcements echoed in her ears as she negotiated a path through the crowded main concourse, heading towards what she hoped was the right exit. A poster on a wall caught her eye: *Is Your Journey Really Necessary?* The question burned in her mind as she hurried out into the freezing drizzle in search of a bus stop.

The first bus Elisabeth attempted to board was rammed full, but the next offered limited standing room. She forced her way down the packed aisle, breathing shallowly, the air thick with the stench of grime and soot and unwashed bodies. Clutching a hanging strap, she braced her legs as the bus lurched out on to the main road. The steamed-up windows ran with condensation, blurring Elisabeth's view of her journey as the bus trundled on, swaying round corners. Her stomach swayed with it.

For the first time since leaving home, she wondered if she was doing the right thing. It was a risk coming into London, and all on the basis of a single letter, even if that letter was from the War Office. She fingered the envelope in her coat pocket.

Dear Miss Ridley,

I would be obliged if you could attend a meeting with me at the Hotel Victoria, Northumberland Avenue, London, on 20 February, to discuss the recent photographs you kindly submitted to the Admiralty. I apologise for the short notice. Please come alone, and hotel reception will direct you.

Yours sincerely,
Captain Porter

Elisabeth had been both disconcerted and intrigued by the lack of detail in the letter, but her mother, Florence, was suspicious when she'd shown it to her at breakfast yesterday.

'What does this Monsieur Porter want with you?' Florence had demanded.

'*Je ne sais pas,*' Elisabeth had answered. 'But I can't very well ignore it, Maman. It's from the government.'

As the bus rumbled over Westminster Bridge and on towards Northumberland Avenue, Elisabeth stared through a patch of window that a passenger had wiped clear. Bomb-damaged buildings slid past beyond the glass, and she glimpsed shattered roofs and collapsed walls, broken furniture piled in the streets like matchwood. The bus lurched on, past a short parade of sandbagged shopfronts. Dazed Londoners loitered on the wreckage-strewn pavement, waiting to be fed at a Salvation Army mobile canteen.

Elisabeth shuddered at the unfurling scene of horror. Her initial sense of excitement at leaving Guildford had long since dissipated, replaced now by a feeling of sick dread. What on earth had possessed her to come here?

Before the war, she'd loved visiting London, only an hour from home on the train. She and her mother had sometimes gone window-shopping along Oxford Street, and once Mr Farr, her boss at the solicitors', had organised a Christmas staff outing to see a show at the Apollo Victoria. Elisabeth had never forgotten her first experience of the art-deco theatre, the huge domed ceiling and gleaming organ pipes reaching to the roof, the stage lights morphing as if by magic from emerald green to mauve to burnished gold. That night, she'd been transported to a fantastical underwater world, a wondrous mermaid's grotto, and the memory had stayed with her ever since.

But on this freezing grey February morning, she struggled to reconcile her memories of the city with the dispiriting, frightening reality unfurling beyond the streaming window.

By the time the bus turned on to Northumberland Avenue, she'd convinced herself she'd made a grave mistake. She had no more scenic photographs of France, if that was what this Captain Porter – whoever he was – wanted. Well, there was one other photograph, but she wasn't going to relinquish that one as it was the only picture she had of her parents together, enjoying their honeymoon on a beach in Normandy.

The bus was slowing before a looming brownstone building, sandbags piled around its entrance.

'Hotel Victoria!' the conductress yelled.

The bus shuddered to a stop, and Elisabeth pushed her way down the steps and out on to the rain-slick pavement. Straightening the hem of her tweed skirt, she took a deep breath, gazing up at the soot-streaked edifice before her. As she'd made it this far, she may as well go in.

Massive glass and mahogany revolving doors led to an ornate, grey-and-ochre marble foyer beyond, echoing with voices. Elisabeth paused inside the entrance, observing the knot of people gathered at the reception desk. Most wore the various uniforms of service personnel. She watched a couple of porters pushing trolleys teetering with suitcases and boxes across the foyer, Messenger Service boys flitting amongst them like minnows.

She drew in another steadying breath, counselling herself sternly. It had taken her a damn long time to get here, and no doubt the journey back home would take even longer, so she may as well find out what this Captain Porter wanted. And the sooner she saw him, the sooner she could go, as she really didn't want to be caught out if an air-raid siren went off. The prospect of taking shelter in the London Underground turned her guts to water. She'd heard horror stories of what went on down there.

She waited her turn at the reception desk, handing her letter to a clerk for inspection. 'Room 238 is on the fifth floor,' the woman informed her. 'The lift's broken.'

The fifth floor, when she reached it, was bustling with more military personnel, but no one paid her any heed as she hurried along a carpeted corridor. Arriving at room 238, she hesitated again.

Qui ne risque rien, n'a rien. Her mother's favourite saying came into Elisabeth's head. *Nothing ventured, nothing gained.*

Elisabeth rolled her tense shoulders, smoothed her damp hair, and knocked on the door.

A man's voice issued from beyond. 'Come in!'

Elisabeth stepped into a small, plain room, a desk, two chairs and a filing cabinet the only furnishings. A sandy-haired man in perhaps his forties was reading a document at the desk, and he glanced up as Elisabeth entered.

'Can I help you?'

'Captain Porter? I'm Elisabeth Ridley. You wrote to me.'

'Ah, yes!' The man rose and came around the desk. 'You got here all right, then.' He gave her hand a brief shake. 'Thank you for taking the trouble.' He blinked, extracted a folded handkerchief from his trouser pocket, and violently sneezed into it. 'Apologies,' he sniffed. 'I can't seem to shift this cold.'

Elisabeth waited politely while the man blew his nose. The room smelled of stale tobacco, and she eyed the narrow, closed window, the glass so grimed with soot and pigeon dirt it was practically blacked out.

'Please, take a seat.' Captain Porter gestured to the vacant chair, and Elisabeth perched on the edge of it, pocketing the now crumpled letter. Her fingers were clammy and she surreptitiously wiped them on her skirt as she smoothed it over her knees.

'Never a spare pen when you need one in this place,' Captain Porter mumbled, rooting in a desk drawer. With his reddened nose and watery eyes, he looked unwell to Elisabeth. She hoped his cold wasn't catching. While the officer hunted in the drawer, Elisabeth took the opportunity to scan the room.

Something wasn't quite right about the place, but the bare walls yielded no information, and when she turned her attention back to Captain Porter she found, to her alarm, that he was staring at her. For the space of one breath, two, three, they faced each other across the desk. It took an effort of will on Elisabeth's part, but she held his pale blue gaze.

She was beginning to seriously consider making her excuses and leaving, when he cleared his throat.

'This interview must seem rather odd to you,' he said, twisting his mouth in what Elisabeth presumed was an attempt at a smile. She smiled hesitantly back. She hadn't realised this was an interview.

'It's not ideal, of course,' Captain Porter said, fumbling again in the desk drawer. 'But needs must.' After a brief search, he brought out a pipe and a pouch of tobacco, placing them next to an overflowing ashtray on the desk. His hand trembled slightly, Elisabeth noticed.

'Now, first things first,' Captain Porter sighed. 'You are Elisabeth Ridley?'

'Yes,' she answered.

'Elisabeth spelled with an "s"?'

She nodded.

While Captain Porter wrote something on a pad of paper, Elisabeth studied the man's face; the crescents of grey beneath his eyes told of heavy responsibilities or lack of sleep.

He looked up suddenly and caught her eye, and Elisabeth felt herself redden.

'Your parents,' the captain said, switching to French. 'Tell me about them.' He spoke with only the barest of English accents.

Elisabeth tried to gather her thoughts. Was he testing her knowledge of French? If so, why not just ask her if she spoke the language?

And why on earth did he want to know about her parents?

She hesitated, yet there was something in the man's eyes, his moist gaze steady and direct, that seemed sincere.

Captain Porter reached for the pipe, packed the bowl with tobacco and lit it, leaning back in his chair. 'Your parents?'

'They met in France in 1916,' Elisabeth began slowly. Her French came naturally, but she chose her words with care.

'They are both French?' Captain Porter pressed.

'My mother is, but my father was English.' Elisabeth's heart clenched at the use of the past tense.

'Go on, please.'

'Papa was injured fighting in the last war. He met my mother while he was recuperating in a hospital in Paris where Maman was a nurse.' Elisabeth remembered fondly her father's tale of falling in love with Florence; his very own Florence Nightingale, he used to joke.

'I knew immediately that I'd found the woman I wanted to spend the rest of my life with, Lisbeth.'

Captain Porter sneezed again. He blew his nose, flapping his free hand at Elisabeth to go on. She wished he would open the window.

'They married as soon as Papa was well enough,' she went on. 'They lived with Maman's parents and had me in 1918.'

'Your father worked in France after the war?'

'He drove omnibuses.'

'Please, go on.'

Elisabeth gave a brief account of her early years growing up in the countryside outside Paris. After Elisabeth's maternal grandparents died, Papa had moved the family to Guildford to live with his elderly, infirm mother. Every summer, they would return to the Continent to visit their few remaining French relatives, and to Elisabeth it always felt like coming home.

'And where are your parents now?' Captain Porter asked.

'Papa volunteered as an air-raid warden. He was too old to be called up this time.' By the way he was looking at her, Elisabeth had the uneasy feeling that the captain already knew all this.

'He ... he was killed in an air raid two years ago.' Her eyes misted and she clenched her jaw. The night of his sudden, violent death was forever seared on her memory, his absence a wound in her chest that had never fully healed.

'My condolences,' Captain Porter murmured, squinting at her through a haze of smoke. 'Your mother? She's alive?' He spoke French confidently, Elisabeth noted. But he wasn't French-born, she felt sure.

'*Oui.*' Maman was definitely alive and well. Elisabeth tried to picture what her mother was doing at this very moment. Florence Ridley had left nursing and was now a leading member of the Women's Voluntary Service (Women of Various Sizes, as Elisabeth thought of them, having read it somewhere once and finding it suited her mother's mixed bag of colleagues).

Since Papa's death, Maman had been busier than ever, filling her days volunteering in all manner of ways. Every day she rose at dawn, barely pausing for breakfast before she was out collecting books and clothing and other useful things from scrap heaps or jumble sales across Guildford, and redistributing them to church refuges and the army barracks at Stoughton. Once or twice a week she attended 'jobbing classes' at the local village hall to learn how to unblock a drain or change a fuse or put up a shelf, all tasks that Elisabeth's father had once done. At home in the evenings she would knit for orphans, or darn socks, or write letters. Sometimes, she would persuade Elisabeth to join her at a local WVS talk on family health or women's rights.

Once, Elisabeth had asked her mother if she intended at any point to slow down, to put herself first for a change, rather than always thinking of other people.

'*Jamais*,' Florence had answered. 'What did your father used to say? A woman's work is never done.'

'And what about you, Miss Ridley?' Captain Porter asked, breaking into Elisabeth's thoughts. 'Do you work?'

'*Oui*,' she answered. 'I'm a secretary, and I volunteer with the WVS at the weekends.'

She thought fleetingly of her colleagues at Lawson and Farr Solicitors in Guildford. Her best friend Josie and the other girls in the office all belonged to the Women's Voluntary Service too, which enabled them to keep their jobs.

The officer puffed smoke and fixed her with a look as if to say *I know all this*.

There came a knock at the door, and a young woman poked her head into the room. 'Tea, sir?'

'Ah, yes, tea would be superb,' Captain Porter smiled. 'And perhaps you could rustle up some of those garibaldi biscuits?'

'I'll see what I can find, sir.'

Elisabeth's throat was parched, and when the tea materialised a few minutes later, she gulped down a cup, scalding her tongue. There were no garibaldi biscuits, apparently, but the girl had managed to get hold of half a tin of digestives. Elisabeth's stomach rumbled as she took one.

'You sent some photographs to the Admiralty,' Captain Porter said, biting a biscuit in half and scattering crumbs down his shirt front. 'Tell me about that.'

'There's not much to tell,' Elisabeth replied. 'I saw an advert in the local paper asking for pictures of the French coastline, and I knew Maman had some

22

photographs of me as a little girl playing on the beach at Deauville, so I sent a few in.'

She hadn't donated all the photographs of course, suspecting she wasn't going to get them back again.

'I've told you all I know,' she said, reverting to English. 'Now please would you explain why I've been asked to come here?'

'Well may you ask that,' Captain Porter continued in French.

'Your letter was very vague,' Elisabeth pressed, still speaking English, not caring that she sounded blunt.

'If you'll allow me to explain, Miss Ridley,' Captain Porter replied. He held her eye a moment and appeared to decide something. 'You've been identified by Special Operations Executive as potentially helpful to the war effort.'

Elisabeth's spine stiffened. 'I'm sorry, I don't understand.'

'How do you feel about the war, Miss Ridley? If you could wave a magic wand, would you eradicate all Nazis from the face of the earth?'

What a ridiculous thing to ask.

'Well, of course the Nazis deserve annihilation,' she answered. 'But it's not as easy as that, is it?'

'Interesting,' Captain Porter murmured, scribbling on the notepad. His next question was even odder. 'Can you ride a bicycle?'

Elisabeth stared at him, as a childhood memory surfaced. An older cousin in France had once tried to teach her to ride, but she'd never really got the hang of it.

'Yes,' she lied.

'Would you be willing to leave the country, for a time?'

Elisabeth considered the question. As a child, she'd left England every summer to visit family in France. But her mother had always been with her. She'd miss Maman if they were parted for any length of time. But Florence was barely at home these days, so taken up was she with war work, and she had many friends; she was not someone who complained of loneliness.

'It would depend where,' Elisabeth answered. 'And for how long.'

The captain gave a wry smile, as though he had expected this response, and offered her the tin of biscuits. She accepted another digestive, wishing she hadn't drunk all her tea so fast.

'Do you have any personal commitments, Miss Ridley?'

Elisabeth was glad she had a mouthful of biscuit, taking her time to think of a polite answer as she swallowed. 'If you mean, Captain, do I have a boyfriend, then no, I do not.' She held his eye, and Captain Porter had the grace to drop his gaze, shuffling his papers unconvincingly.

'Would you be prepared to undertake dangerous work?' he asked next, still speaking French.

'What sort of dangerous work?'

'For reasons of security, I can't tell you precise details, I'm afraid.' Captain Porter relit his pipe. 'All I can say is, if you agree to work for us at SOE, you'll be putting yourself in harm's way.'

Captain Porter fell silent. From beyond the door came the faint beat of footsteps hurrying along the corridor.

Elisabeth's mind raced with them. This meeting wasn't what she had expected at all.

'We need honest, single-minded women, with nerves of steel, to undertake missions in France,' Captain Porter forged on. 'We're looking for intelligent people who will obey instructions. People who are confident, and not risk-averse, but neither are they reckless. Women, like yourself, who would carry on with their mission, however hopeless the situation might seem.'

Elisabeth took a sudden breath. 'Captain Porter, are you recruiting me as a spy?'

'In some ways, what we're asking people to do is very similar to spying,' Captain Porter said. 'Our agents undergo special training before being sent into enemy-occupied territory to undertake particular tasks. This section is concerned with France, where we're trying to make things as unpleasant and difficult for the Nazis as we can.' He paused, letting his words sink in. 'Sabotage is our main concern.'

He gave a phlegmy cough. 'Naturally, the Germans don't appreciate our efforts to blow up their troop trains and such like,' he went on. 'They react violently and brutally. Hence the need to recruit the right people to undertake this sort of thing.'

'And you think I might be one of these people?'

'Well, the first qualification we look for in a potential agent is their ability to pass as a native of France. You speak fluent French, you're small and dark-haired, and all told you have the look of a Frenchwoman.'

That's because I'm half-French, Elisabeth wanted to snap.

'You have a family connection to France,' Captain Porter continued. 'And although I haven't questioned you on this matter, I'd wager you're sympathetic to the French Resistance and their fight for freedom.'

Elisabeth made no reply, but the officer seemed not to be expecting one. 'Finally,' he said, 'a potential agent should possess courage and initiative, which you have shown this morning by coming here alone.'

Elisabeth's mind whirred, trying to make sense of what the man was saying. *Was* he recruiting her to be some sort of spy? All she knew of spies came from novels; *Kim* by Rudyard Kipling was one of her favourites, along with Buchan's *The Thirty-Nine Steps*.

Did this man really think she was special-agent material? But she was only a typist, for goodness' sake. Since Papa's death, she'd tried to stay as safe as possible with her mother, rarely venturing further than town, minding her own business. But what, she thought to herself now, if everyone had that attitude? Her father was dead, her mother busy with her own affairs. She had no siblings, only a handful of French cousins whom she hadn't heard from since the start of the war. There was nobody in her family who was capable of fighting for the freedom of France. Perhaps the time had finally come to do her duty, for the sake of her family across the Channel, and to avenge her poor Papa's death.

She did want to help, she realised.

'If you accept, you'll be sent for training,' Captain Porter said, 'and assessed as to your suitability for the kind of work we have in mind. If you're deemed unsuitable, you'll be debriefed and simply return to your normal work.'

Elisabeth pictured her current existence: the cramped, fourth-floor solicitors' office, and her infernal typewriter under its leatherette cover. Its clattering keys were the bane of her life.

'There are risks, naturally,' Captain Porter continued. 'As there always are in times of war. But in this case, once an agent is in France, the risks for them will be considerably higher.' He cleared his throat. 'An agent's chances of survival may be as low as fifty per cent.'

Elisabeth suppressed a shiver.

'You don't have to give me an answer immediately,' Captain Porter said. 'But I must warn you, for reasons of security you're forbidden from discussing this interview with anyone, even your mother.'

That would be difficult, Elisabeth thought. Though she rarely saw her mother for more than half an hour at dinner these days, and the conversation always revolved around the latest WVS initiative, Florence would still want to know how her daughter's visit to London had gone. She'd just have to invent a story on the journey home, something that would convince her mother that nothing of importance had occurred. She would have to lie.

Elisabeth looked at the officer. *Think.* What questions should she be asking him that she wasn't?

'You will receive a letter soon,' Captain Porter said, rising from his chair and extending a hand. 'This will inform you of the next stage. If you choose to accept, you must tell your family and friends you have taken a job working as an interpreter for the War Office.'

Elisabeth rose on numb legs, and shook the captain's proffered hand. She felt slightly sick. There came a knock on the door. It was the young woman who had brought the tea and biscuits.

'Ah, Mavis, excellent. Could you please see Miss Ridley out?'

Elisabeth followed Mavis back down the stairs and across the foyer, and found herself standing on the damp, bustling pavement again, the real world crashing back in a blur of noise and motion.

The last hour had been the oddest of her life, Elisabeth thought, as she stumbled to the bus stop. Really quite peculiar. She longed to tell someone about her strange 'interview'; she could just imagine Josie in the office pouncing on the details, desperate to know more. But Captain Porter had been quite firm; she must keep this meeting a secret.

Two hours later, back at her desk at Lawson and Farr, she pretended to be suffering from a headache. In truth, her head did feel stuffed full of wet wool. To her relief, Josie and the other girls left her alone for the most part, and for what remained of the afternoon she trudged her way through a stack of typing, working like an automaton, her mind still in that stuffy little room with Captain Porter.

The longer she thought about it, the more she realised he was offering her a way out of this tedious, dead-end job. As for the question of danger, well, that was surely an exaggeration on Captain Porter's part?

Excitement rippled in her belly, a sensation she hadn't felt in a very long time.

*

Three days later, she received a second letter from the War Office, inviting her to attend a translating course at a place called Wanborough Manor, near Guildford. Elisabeth read the letter out to her mother, all but the final line. Florence was suitably convinced that her daughter was doing something official for the war effort, and was happy for her to go.

'Haven't I always told you, to speak more than one language is a blessing,' Florence said. 'Only promise me: *sois prudente.*'

The night before she was due to leave for Wanborough, Elisabeth packed a small suitcase, then read the letter through once more, checking she hadn't missed any instructions. She would be collected by car from the back entrance of Guildford train station at noon. The driver would ask for her name. She was to answer 'Elise'.

But it was the final line that made her blood tingle. *Tell no one.*

3

March 1944

'You're the third one I've ferried to Wanborough this week,' the driver told Elisabeth, as she travelled down the Hog's Back the following day.

'Am I?' Elisabeth stared through the Austin's window at the bare trees and rolling hills of the North Downs Way. She'd only been along this road a couple of times before, by bus. She felt like royalty in the back of this car.

'Strange goings-on there,' the driver said, glancing at her in his rear-view mirror. 'I reckon it's a secret military base. You one of them WAAFs, are you?'

'Just a secretary,' Elisabeth replied, with an innocent smile. It wasn't a lie.

On the short journey through Wanborough village, Elisabeth tried and failed to reconcile Captain Porter's talk of dangerous missions with this benign, picturesque little place.

'Nearly there, miss.' The driver slowed as they neared a large timbered tithe barn, beyond which sat a neat Saxon church.

'Welcome to Wanborough Manor,' the driver announced, turning into a carriage drive and pulling up before a red-brick mansion.

As the driver unloaded Elisabeth's case from the boot, she gazed up at the manor's grand frontage, trying not to feel intimidated by the gabled chimneys and shining diamond-pane windows bearded with thick ivy. It was like something out of an Agatha Christie novel. She could hear faint shouting coming from somewhere in the grounds behind the house.

'Best of luck, miss,' the driver said, with the hint of a wink.

Belly churning with nerves, Elisabeth climbed the stone steps to the mansion's front door. What was she doing here? Her mother and Mr Farr had both accepted her lie that she was on a fortnight-long translating course. Only Josie had questioned her story. Her friend had an uncanny knack of sniffing out fibs.

'But how did the government even know you can speak French?' Josie had asked, on Elisabeth's last day in the office.

'Do you remember that advert I showed you, ages ago?' Elisabeth had replied. 'The one in the *Surrey Ad* asking for photographs of France to be sent to the Admiralty?'

'You sent some, didn't you?'

'Yes, and then they wrote back to me,' Elisabeth explained. 'They said they needed French translators, and I thought, well, I could do my bit for the war ...'

Josie had frowned, but before she could ask more questions, Mr Farr had sent her off to make coffee.

31

How she wished Josie was with her now.

She rang the bell pull, and a moment later the door was answered by a soldier in General Service uniform. Elisabeth gave her false name, Elise, as directed in the letter, and the soldier admitted her into the oak-panelled hallway.

The place smelled like her old school: leather and dust and furniture polish. Directly facing her was an impressive, curving dark wood staircase. Men in khaki uniform were bustling up and down it, and Elisabeth wondered if the driver had been right, that this place was indeed some dubious, underground military organisation.

'Please follow me, miss.' The soldier led the way up the stairs and along a luxuriously carpeted corridor, rapping on a door at the far end.

A woman's muffled voice called, 'Come in.'

The soldier turned to leave. 'I'll tell Officer Stewart you've arrived, miss.'

'Thank you.' Elisabeth pushed open the door, revealing a bright, sun-warmed room containing two single beds. The walls were papered in a pretty, pale blue flower pattern that put her in mind of a nursery or a child's bedroom. A young woman was sitting cross-legged on the bed nearest the window.

'Oh hello,' the woman said, rising and crossing the room. She was perhaps a year or two older than Elisabeth, slim-figured, with styled, dark-blonde hair framing a face Elisabeth instantly judged as photogenic.

'I'm so pleased you're here,' the woman said. 'I thought I was the only one. The only girl, I mean. There's plenty of army chaps everywhere, and I've seen a few FANYs dashing about, but I was getting really worried that I was going to be all on my own ...' She smiled, revealing teeth like pearls. 'I'm Doris Waters, by the way.' She stuck out her hand. 'Though we aren't allowed to use our real names, apparently. I'm Dominique while I'm here.' She pulled an exaggerated face of disgust, and Elisabeth couldn't help but laugh.

'It's a bloody awful name, isn't it?' Doris sighed. 'I'll never remember to answer to it, I'm sure. What's your name?'

'My real name?' Elisabeth wavered for a second, but Doris's forthright gaze was too hard to resist. 'Elisabeth Ridley. But I'm Elise here.'

'So neat and elegant.' Doris gave Elisabeth an appraising look. 'Suits you.'

Elisabeth felt her cheeks warm.

'That's your bed, over there,' Doris indicated. 'I hope you don't mind, but I chose the one by the window. I like a smoke.' She grinned, and a dimple appeared in her left cheek.

Elisabeth shoved her suitcase under the bed, then gave the mattress an experimental press. It felt softer than her bed at home. She looked around the room. Against one wall stood a large walnut wardrobe and matching chest of drawers. The remaining furniture comprised a washstand complete with jug and ewer, and a single wooden chair, currently half hidden beneath Doris's open suitcase.

Elisabeth crossed to the window and looked out over the grounds at the rear of the mansion. Manicured lawns stretched down to a kitchen garden, with regimented rows of vegetables and a shed tucked behind a hedge. Behind this were farm buildings and a field of cows, a meadow beyond dotted with grey military tents, and what looked like a troop of soldiers marching in a circle. Further fields and woodland stretched away into the distance.

She turned back to Doris. 'What exactly is this place?'

Doris extracted a cigarette from a pack of Player's. 'A training school, of sorts.' She waved the packet at Elisabeth, who shook her head.

'Did the War Office write to you?' Elisabeth asked. Had Captain Porter interviewed this woman too?

'We shouldn't discuss our real lives, apparently.' Doris blew smoke out of the window, then gave Elisabeth a frank look. 'But what the hell. A couple of weeks ago I was working on reception at the Grosvenor, and this chap booked in. He must've overheard me talking French with another guest, because he asked me if I'd be interested in doing some translating for him. He took me for a drink, after I'd finished my shift, and then he started on about working for the government. I was a bit suspicious at first, I won't lie, but he turned out to be kosher, and here I am. What's your story?'

'I answered an advert in the newspaper,' Elisabeth began, only to be interrupted by a sharp rap on the door. A tall woman in her late thirties, with tightly curled red hair, dressed in an officer's uniform, strode into the room. Behind her came the soldier Elisabeth had met earlier, carrying a pile of clothing which he deposited on top of the chest of drawers before retreating.

'Welcome to Special Training School number five, ladies,' the woman said, in a strong Scottish accent. 'I'm your conducting officer, Margaret Stewart.' The officer gestured to the heap of clothing. 'These are your uniforms: drill jacket, skirt, shirt and beret.' She brandished one of the khaki hats, on which was pinned a circular badge encompassing the Maltese Cross, the insignia of the First Aid Nursing Yeomanry, the FANYs.

'Ah, nearly forgot these.' From her satchel, Stewart extracted two neatly coiled belts, the leather polished to a chestnut shine. The sight of the Sam Browne belts reminded Elisabeth of her father and his Air Raid Precautions uniform, and she swallowed.

'Do we have to wear this?' Doris asked. 'I would have brought my ATS dress if I'd known we'd be in uniform.'

'The Auxiliary Territorial Service forbids women from carrying guns,' Stewart replied briskly. 'But the First Aid Nursing Yeomanry is a civilian corps, and therefore exempt from this rule. While you're here, you'll earn three pounds a week as a FANY ensign.'

Elisabeth thought of the three pounds six shillings she had earned typing at Lawson and Farr. It was a job she hated, but at least she could wear her own clothes. This rough, unflattering uniform was not what she had expected.

Stewart moved to the doorway. 'I'll leave you to get dressed and see you downstairs shortly.'

'Excuse me, ma'am,' Doris persisted. 'Why do we need to wear a uniform at all?'

Elisabeth couldn't help but admire her room-mate's courage in the face of this formidable Scottish officer.

'Here at Wanborough, you're an honorary member of the FANY,' Stewart said, enunciating her words slowly, as though she were addressing a simpleton. 'You're required to wear this uniform for security purposes. This is ostensibly a military establishment, and the military appearance must be consistently maintained. That way, questions may not be raised as to the nature of some of our activities here.' Stewart paused, and Elisabeth remembered what the taxi driver had said about strange goings-on.

'Secondly, wear and tear,' Stewart went on. 'Many of your activities here will take place outside and involve boisterous, physical effort. By wearing a uniform, you'll save your own civilian clothes.'

Doris opened her mouth, but Stewart cut her off. 'Downstairs in five minutes, ladies.' She shut the door and Elisabeth saw the notice pasted there: *Careless Talk Costs Lives*.

'Stuck-up bitch,' Doris snorted.

'We'd better do what she says,' Elisabeth said, unbuttoning her coat. 'She rather scares me.'

Doris winked. 'I can see you're going to be trouble.'

*

As promised, the conducting officer was waiting for them down in the hall.

'The other students in your group arrived the day before yesterday,' Stewart said, ushering Elisabeth and Doris into a small anteroom. 'I'm going to bring you up to speed, so you can enter the fray from the off.'

36

Doris gave a brittle laugh. 'You make it sound like we're preparing for battle.'

'In a sense, you are,' Stewart replied. Her sharp gaze moved from Doris to Elisabeth, and her frown softened. 'Don't look so worried, Elise.'

Elisabeth unclenched her hands in her lap.

'First, some rules,' Stewart began briskly. 'Incoming mail must be addressed to you by first-name alias only, at PO Box 55, Wanborough. Any outgoing mail must be handed in at the Administration Office, and must not reference your location or activities here.'

Elisabeth thought of her mother back in Guildford. She hadn't told Florence the precise address of Wanborough Manor, but had promised to write to her as soon as she could. How would she explain her alias to her mother without arousing her suspicion?

'No incoming telephone calls are permitted,' Stewart went on. 'If you wish to make a call yourself, you must complete a form for approval by myself and the commandant, Major Ward. He's going to give an address to all the new students shortly.

'I'll tell you when and where your various lectures will take place. Breakfast is at eight fifteen, lunch at twelve forty-five. Tea is taken in the dining room at sixteen thirty, and supper in the lounge at nineteen hundred hours.'

Elisabeth wished she had a piece of paper to note all this down.

'Punctuality is requested,' Stewart continued. 'Any questions?'

'Yes,' Doris said quickly. 'Can we leave the manor in the evenings? If we wanted to go for a walk, you know, or something?'

Stewart shook her head. 'I'm afraid not. For the next two weeks, your world is this wee house and its grounds, and nothing else. Believe me, you'll be exhausted by the end of the day, and longing for your bed.'

After their briefing, Officer Stewart directed Elisabeth and Doris to a drawing room to wait for the commandant's address.

'That woman's so regimental,' Doris whispered as soon as the officer was out of earshot. 'She makes my teeth ache.'

Elisabeth tried to smile as a shudder swept through her.

What on earth was she doing here?

The commandant, Major Ward, was a stout, solemn-faced ex-Coldstream Guard. Elisabeth hoped his opening address would be brief, as her mouth was dry with nerves and she was desperate for a drink of water. She glanced at the dozen or so people gathered in the manor's stately drawing room. Apart from herself and Doris, they were all men, all dressed in khaki uniform. Several of them cast glances at Elisabeth and Doris, and one man in his late twenties with dark curly hair caught her eye and smiled. Elisabeth smiled shyly back.

'Welcome, gentlemen and ladies,' Major Ward began, his gaze roaming over the assembled group. 'I hope your short time here will be productive. You should prepare yourselves for a period of intensive instruction. The NCO instructors are ready to put you through your paces, assisted by the Field Security branch of the Intelligence Corps, who will assess and record your progress.

'You will attend daily lectures, as well as partake in physical exercises, map-reading lessons, weapons training, and wireless Morse code practice. At meal-times you must only speak French. We require of you the highest standards of physical endurance, technical expertise, and security, because when you eventually embark on active duty, it will not only be your own life at stake but the lives of your comrades.'

Elisabeth glanced at the young man who had smiled at her, but he was staring intently at Major Ward.

'The main purpose of this organisation is subversion and sabotage,' Ward continued. 'If we can damage or destroy the enemy's machines, their means of communication and production, we will have gone a long way towards hampering Hitler's efforts to win this war.'

He went on to describe at length how the Germans were desperate for men to put into the field, but if sufficient numbers were diverted to provide sentries, police, and so on, their main force would be thereby weakened.

'One final thing,' Major Ward said, drawing himself up to his full height. 'During this course, we will teach you all the skills of a special agent. What we cannot do is guarantee your safety once on enemy territory, but your chances of being captured will be much reduced if you follow our instructions diligently. Remember, the best agents are never caught.'

Dismissed until tea time, the students were free to relax. Elisabeth and Doris headed back upstairs to their room.

'Do we have to wear this uniform all day?' Elisabeth wondered, tugging at the stiff, scratchy tunic.

'This is ostensibly a military establishment,' Doris mimicked Stewart's Scottish accent, 'and the military appearance must be consistently maintained.'

Elisabeth blew out her cheeks and lowered her voice, imitating Major Ward. 'It will not only be your lives at stake, but the lives of your comrades!'

They both burst out laughing.

*

A buffet tea was served in the manor's imposing dining room, and Elisabeth and Doris joined a throng of people clustered by the oak double doors. Amongst the FANY orderlies and General Service staff were the fellow students Elisabeth had seen earlier at the commandant's address, as well as several officers. The conversations were all in French, and Elisabeth remembered Major Ward's instruction: only French was to be spoken at mealtimes.

A number of trestle tables had been set up around the room, each laden with food the likes of which Elisabeth hadn't seen in months, if not years: tureens of onion soup, fresh bread rolls, boiled eggs, sliced ham and beef, fat-roasted potatoes. She and Doris helped themselves to soup and rolls, and took their places at the long, polished oak dining table. Elisabeth found herself sitting next to the young man she'd exchanged smiles with during Major Ward's address.

'I feel like I'm in the hull of a great galleon,' the man remarked in fluent French.

'Me too,' Elisabeth replied. She lifted her eyes to the vaulted ceiling, wooden beams like whale ribs arching overhead. For the briefest of moments, the hubbub of voices diminished, the clash of cutlery quietened, the scrape of chair legs on the parquet floor ceased, and Elisabeth was back in the hush of the Apollo Victoria theatre, under the sea.

She blinked, and the noise of the room surged back.

As she drank her soup, lifting the bowl to her lips in the French style, as she observed everyone else on the table doing the same, the man next to her spoke again.

'I haven't introduced myself.' He offered Elisabeth his hand. 'Gilbert Donoghue.'

She wiped her lips on a napkin, and shook the man's hand, noticing that his thumb was rather flattened, his fingernails stained black. 'Elisabeth Ridley,' she replied, without thinking. 'I mean, *Elise*.' She took a gulp of water, hoping the officers across the table hadn't overheard her faux pas.

'My grandmother used to add a splash of red wine to the dregs,' Gilbert said, indicating Elisabeth's near-empty soup bowl. 'There's wine here, want some?'

'But it's not even five o'clock,' she laughed.

'Never too early.'

'Perhaps later.' However relaxed things seemed here, she needed to keep her wits about her.

The first course over, she returned to the buffet tables and piled a plate with beef and potatoes, relishing the chance to eat her fill. Rationing barely

41

supplied enough to keep body and soul together, and although she'd continued to tend her father's vegetable beds, she was heartily sick of cabbages and leeks. The longer the war had dragged on, the hungrier Elisabeth had grown, so much so that sometimes she resorted to smoking, just to dull the ache in her belly.

'Do you like to swim?'

She almost missed Gilbert's question, so intent was she on savouring every bite of the juicy meat.

'Pardon?'

'There's a pool here,' Gilbert said, his voice low. 'In the grounds.'

'I haven't swum for a while,' Elisabeth admitted.

'It's in a beautiful spot,' Gilbert said. 'Under some trees, tucked away. Henry and I found it yesterday. This is Henry, by the way.' He nudged the man next to him, who raised his head, fork suspended halfway to his mouth.

'Henry, meet Elise.'

'*Bonjour*,' Henry mumbled. He was slight, with short black hair, his dark eyes framed by wire-rimmed spectacles, giving him the mole-like look of a bank clerk.

Elisabeth discreetly elbowed Doris, interrupting her conversation with an officer sitting next to her.

Doris turned. 'Hello,' she smiled at the two men as Elisabeth introduced her. 'Have you chaps been here long?'

'Since the day before yesterday,' Gilbert replied, wiping his plate clean with a hunk of bread. 'We've done a bit of drill, haven't we, Henry. Some rudimentary map-reading. Not much else.'

'And that bloody awful cross-country run this morning,' Henry said, with a shake of his head. 'My legs are still aching.'

'A run?' Elisabeth echoed.

'Every morning it's either exercises on the back lawn, close-combat training, or a long run.' Gilbert poured more wine into his glass.

'Close-combat training?' Doris wrinkled her nose. 'That sounds painful, and I bruise like a peach. I think I'll give that a miss, thank you very much.'

'You don't have a choice,' Henry said. 'It's all part of the course. These officers from the Intelligence Corps, they're watching us to see if we're good enough. If we don't meet the required standard, we're out.' He started on his pudding, spooning prunes and custard into his mouth.

'I hate tests,' Doris muttered.

'Anyone failing the course is sent to the Cooler,' Gilbert added.

Elisabeth frowned. 'Sounds sinister.'

'It's sort of house arrest somewhere remote,' Gilbert explained. 'They keep ex-agents there until presumably what they've been taught is no longer of any use to the Germans.'

Elisabeth exchanged a glance with Doris.

'I'm having some pud,' Gilbert announced, pushing back his chair. 'Want some?'

Prunes and custard were Elisabeth's favourite, but she shook her head. She no longer had any appetite.

After tea, Elisabeth and Doris followed the other students to a lounge, in the corner of which a make-shift bar had been set up. Alcohol was freely available, they were told, and they could drink as much as they liked.

'They'll be watching to see if we get tipsy,' Doris warned Elisabeth.

It wouldn't take much, Elisabeth thought. She hadn't had a drink since her father's funeral. While she sipped a ginger ale, half listening to Doris enthuse about a film with James Cagney she'd recently seen, she covertly studied the four other students in her group. There appeared to be no physical blueprint for a secret agent, she concluded: Gilbert was rangy and tousle-haired, with Celtic pale skin and deep brown eyes. Henry was compact, with neatly combed hair and a studious air about him. John was tanned and broad-shouldered, in his late forties. And Terrence, somewhere in his thirties, Elisabeth guessed, was thin as a whip with a slightly dazed expression, as though he hadn't slept properly in days.

'I don't really drink spirits,' Elisabeth protested weakly, when Doris returned from the bar with two large whiskies.

'Think of it as liquid courage,' Doris whispered, before continuing her conversation with Henry.

'All this drink,' Gilbert said, enjoying another large glass of red wine. 'It's like I've died and gone to heaven.'

Elisabeth hardly knew how to reply. This wasn't her idea of heaven at all, surrounded by strangers in a secret military establishment, about to embark on a gruelling fortnight of physical tests and mental assessments.

'What do you do, in your normal job?' she found herself asking him.

Gilbert leaned closer, and she caught a hint of sandalwood. 'We aren't supposed to talk about our real lives,' he said, his eyes teasing. 'How do I know I can trust you?'

'You'll just have to take the risk,' Elisabeth replied. She took a gulp of her whisky. It burned a trail down her throat, making her cough.

'I'm a compositor,' Gilbert told her. 'I work for a printer near London.'

Elisabeth hadn't realised a compositor was a reserved occupation. But it explained his ink-blackened finger-nails. What had brought him here to Wanborough? she asked.

'My boss, he's got contacts in the government,' Gilbert said. 'The War Office were looking for French speakers, and so my boss suggested me. He knew my father was French and I grew up there …'

Elisabeth nodded.

'So that's my story,' Gilbert said, leaning a little closer. 'Now what about yours? How's a girl like you end up in a place like this?'

'What do you mean?'

'Well,' Gilbert cocked his head. 'You look like a very attractive secretary, and yet here you are, training to be *un assassin*.'

'*Un assassin?*' Elisabeth snorted, the whisky heating her face.

'OK then, *un terroriste*.'

'What are you talking about?'

'That's what we're here for, isn't it?' Gilbert drained his wine glass. 'To train to be terrorists.'

It was on the tip of Elisabeth's tongue to tell him not to be so silly, when Captain Porter's words came back to her.

If you agree to work for us at SOE, you'll be putting yourself in harm's way.

Was Gilbert right? In deciding to do her bit for the war effort, had she signed up to be trained as a terrorist?

She met Gilbert's eye, and something crackled between them, a radio transmission through the ether. And all at once she knew it was true.

4

2018

The lightbulb on the landing has blown again. Tali
blunders her way downstairs, clinging to the loose
banister, muttering Creole swearwords under her
breath. The steep, uneven stairs are treacherous
enough without having to negotiate them in the dark.
Madame Betty's whole house is a death-trap.

'*Merde*,' Tali gasps, as her slippered foot catches on
a ruck halfway down the stair carpet. She clutches the
banister, wondering not for the first time how Madame
Betty has avoided plummeting down her own stairs.
Tosca, following Tali like a little shadow, chooses that
moment to push past her legs, unbalancing her again.

'*Tou, tou!*' she gasps. The dog ignores her.

At least there are no longer stacks of newspapers
piled up the stairs, or random single shoes lying about
waiting to trip a person. It's taken months, but Tali
has gradually restored a semblance of order and clean-
liness to Betty's house, ridding the place of as much
junk as the dustmen are willing to cart off each week.

Tali's favourite room is the narrow kitchen at the
back of the house. As the sun rises over the river, it

fills the kitchen with light, lifting Tali's spirits like the first shot of rum. She misses the hot Mauritian sun more than she misses her family, truth be told. But not as much as she misses Zezette.

Don't think of her, she tells herself.

She lets Tosca out into the garden, then begins to prepare breakfast, moving about the kitchen with fluid familiarity. She sets Betty's breakfast tray on the twin-tub washing machine that doubles as an extra worktop when not in use. She hates using the twin-tub; it has a mind of its own. The last time she'd shoved it full of dirty washing, she'd set it going then quickly visited the loo, only to return minutes later to find the machine had worked its way halfway along the kitchen, the electric lead on the brink of wrenching the socket from the wall.

She fills the kettle at the butler sink, then searches for the box of matches to light the gas stove. Sometimes, she finds the matches in weird places, like on a shelf in the rattling old fridge, or in a tin pail under the sink. It's a little unnerving. This morning, the matches are in the dresser drawer, hidden amongst Betty's vintage cutlery.

The gas stove is temperamental, its sputtering flame unpredictable and weak. Wonky shelves hang above it, laden with pots, pans, and grimy glass jars filled with desiccated herbs and dusty spices of dubious heritage.

Tali has been surreptitiously emptying these jars out, one by one, and refilling them with fresh turmeric, coriander, cumin. She's determined to wean Madame Betty off her bland diet of corned beef, boiled potatoes, bread and butter. Gradually, she's introducing her to more interesting food, more exotic dishes. Meals with *flavour*. Sometimes, it feels like force-feeding a reluctant tortoise.

Although the kitchen is ancient and shabby, Tali loves its old-fashioned Englishness, its quirky individuality. It's like Madame Betty herself: small, unfussy, enduring. But Tali most loves the fact that, unlike the rest of the house, it's always warm in here.

She opens the larder door, revealing marble shelves and a faint whiff of nutmeg and cinnamon. Tali has never been able to work out where this smell comes from, as all that's stored in here are rusting tins of corned beef, peaches in syrup, prunes and sardines. She selects a tin of sardines, then lights the grill for Madame Betty's toast. As she works, her mind turns to her family back in Mauritius. Every week for the past four months she's texted her parents to let them know she's well.

So far, she's received no reply.

They're punishing her, she knows.

As for Zezette ... A pain throbs in Tali's chest and once again she clamps her mind shut.

She cuts up the sardines and drops a scrap into the dog's bowl. 'Don't tell anyone, *tou tou*,' she mutters to Tosca, who has returned from the garden. The dog sniffs the fish suspiciously, then slowly begins to eat it.

'You think I poison you?' Tali tuts. She turns back to Madame Betty's breakfast tray: mashed sardines on a slice of toast, a cup of tea, and a small glass of apple juice. The woman eats like one of those *petits moineaux* always pecking on the bird-feeder. She wants some flesh on her bones, in Tali's opinion.

She's about to head upstairs with the tray, when the dog gives a growling bark. Seconds later, the letterbox in the hall rattles. How the dog can detect the postman's approach from the kitchen is a perpetual mystery to Tali. The postman must smell really strong, because the dog is practically deaf.

Lying on the doormat is a flyer from a pizza restaurant in town, and a single white envelope. It's the first proper letter delivered to Weyside since Tali moved in, and hope surges in her breast as she snatches it up.

But it's not for her. The envelope is addressed to *Mrs E. Shepherd*, the handwriting looped and neat. Tali trudges on up the stairs.

The curtains in Betty's room are already open, and Tali finds her propped up with pillows in bed, peering at yesterday's newspaper. Betty's wrinkled face is softened by sunlight streaming through the window, her sparse hair a silver halo. She doesn't look up as Tali enters.

'*Bonjour*, Madame Betty.'

'Oh Doris, I'm stuck on six down,' Betty sighs, tapping the newspaper with a crooked finger. The page is folded at the cryptic crossword. 'Hips that can move quickly. Seven letters.'

Tali sets the tray down on the end of the bed. 'You know I am not good with these clues, Madame Betty.' Had Betty just called her Doris? She's never done that before.

Perhaps she's still processing her friend's funeral yesterday, Tali thinks. It had been a huge, flamboyant affair. Tali recalls the hundreds of mourners gathered at St Lawrence Church, the British Legion standard-bearers flanking the hearse, and Doris's oak casket draped in a Union Jack and the Tricolore of France.

For most of the service, Betty had sat stiff-backed and dry-eyed, Tali weeping helplessly beside her. But when the military attaché from the French Embassy in London had stood up and spoken – *We owe brave women like Doris for the freedom of our country. It is thanks to people like her that we can live peacefully today* – Tali had sensed Betty trembling. But despite her obvious emotion, she'd refused to attend the wake afterwards, insisting they go straight home.

Betty gives a loud sniff, breaking into Tali's thoughts. 'They must have a different fellow setting the clues,' she says. 'Can't catch his drift at all ...'

'Look, I made you sardines.' Tali gently shunts Betty's newspaper to one side, and sets the breakfast tray on her meagre lap.

'Hips must be an anagram,' Betty mutters, still peering at the paper. 'Ah, of course – *ship*.'

Ignored, Tali studies the handwriting on the envelope again. Who is writing to Madame Betty? Not her absent, faraway son, she feels sure.

'So,' Betty is talking to herself. 'A ship that can move quickly. Seven letters, fourth letter G.'

'Someone has written to you.' Tali waves the letter.

'Frigate!' Betty cries. She lowers the paper, then fishes a set of flesh-pink dentures from a glass of cloudy water on the bedside table. Inserting them into her mouth with a slurp, she flexes her jaw, and Tali marvels at the ability of the false teeth to alter the entire shape of Betty's face.

'Shall I open the letter for you, Madame Betty?'

Betty picks up her fork and prods a sardine. 'Can't think who'd want to write to me ...'

Tali's long nails make short work of the envelope.

'*Dear Mrs Shepherd,*' she reads aloud. '*You are cordially invited to join the Century Society, a social club that's exclusively for Surrey residents who have reached their first century—*'

'Is it a flyer?' Betty interjects. 'Throw it away if it is! I'm not buying anything ...'

'It looks more like an invitation.' Tali reads on. '*The club meets monthly on a Saturday afternoon between 1.30 and 4 p.m., at the community centre, in Guildford.* That is near here, isn't it?'

'How did they get my name?' Betty snaps. 'How do they know I'm going to be a hundred?'

'*Je ne sais pas,*' Tali shrugs. 'Perhaps your son?'

'*Leo?* What on earth makes you say that?'

'Let me read the rest,' Tali says quickly. '*The society was launched four years ago by Bridie Ayling, inspired by a project she discovered whilst visiting her daughter in New Zealand. The society brings centenarians together to create memory boxes, decorated to reflect their lives. The boxes are then filled with special objects for their families and loved ones to treasure ...*'

'Filled with junk, more like,' Betty mutters.

'*The club,*' Tali ploughs on, '*enables its members to share their unique experience of being the oldest people in Britain ...*'

Betty sniffs. 'Nothing to be proud of.'

'... *and chat openly about death and end-of-life matters* ...'

'Huh! As if we don't think about that enough.' Betty takes a shaky sip of apple juice, spilling some down her nightdress.

'*The memory boxes are eco-friendly, and made from re-purposed wood.*'

'Chipboard.'

'*The society,*' Tali forges on, '*sometimes invites experts from the funeral industry to visit and answer questions* ...'

'I don't want to speak to any damn vicar ...'

'*... and is open to all centenarians. Come along and make your own unique memory box, to celebrate the treasure trove of your life. Kindest regards, Alison Trumble. Community Geriatric Liaison Officer.*'

Tali looks up from the letter. 'That is interesting, *n'est-ce pas*, Madame Betty?'

'Treasure trove of my life? I've never heard anything so ridiculous.'

'There's a meeting next Saturday,' Tali says, her mind whirring. Apart from her short daily walks along the river, dragging a reluctant Tosca on his lead, and a twice-weekly visit to town for provisions, Tali goes nowhere, sees no one. It would be good for both of them to get out, meet new people; they could take a taxi to the community centre, it wasn't far.

'I think we should go, Madame Betty. It might be fun.'

Betty stares at the window, toast crumbs on her chin.

Had she heard her? Tali clears her throat and tries again. 'It might be fun, Madame Betty ...'

Betty looks at Tali, her expression firm.

'Over my dead body,' she says.

*

That evening, after she's made Betty a cup of *chocolat chaud*, warmed her sheets with a hot-water bottle, and tucked her into bed, Tali retreats to her own room. There, she opens the wardrobe door, wincing as the ancient hinges squeal an alarm. A smell of mothballs hits her as she burrows amongst a mound of shoe-boxes, and pulls out a bulging shopping bag filled with chocolate bars, cans of gin and tonic, and various shop-bought cakes.

Plastic crackles as she sinks on to the bed, cradling the bag in her lap. One bite, she tells herself. That's all she needs.

She tears open a packet of doughnuts.

The sweetness of the jam explodes on her tongue, and she eases back into the pillows, waiting for the sugar to work its numbing magic and help her forget for a little while how cold and lonely she is. The British weather is so fickle; this morning there was sun, now it's raining and windy. And so, so cold.

Through her bedroom window, Tali can see the cemetery on the other side of the road; an army of grey headstones flanked by looming yew trees beyond a stone wall. It's a bleak view, even when the sun shines. She compares her view with Betty's, whose bedroom at the back of the house looks out over the garden and down to the river.

Tali likes the garden, though it's sloping and narrow and difficult to keep neat. A dilapidated shed at the bottom is stuffed with antique tools that might have belonged to Betty's grandparents. There's a green-house missing more panes of glass than it has whole ones; a death-trap that Tali has yet to venture into. Stretching along the right-hand side of the garden are abandoned vegetable beds, the soil choked with weeds.

The one area that Tali tries to maintain is the patch of grass under the willow tree down by the river's edge. Using an ancient push-along lawnmower she found in the shed, she keeps the grass mown. Some-times she sits on the bench to enjoy the tranquillity of the river, and when the sun glitters on the water it helps remind her of home.

Tali stuffs the rest of the doughnut in her mouth, as drops of wind-whipped rain splatter against the bedroom window. In her mind's eye, she pictures coconut palms swaying in a warm breeze, their verdant green fronds sharp against a cerulean sky. She fantasises she's with Zezette on La Cuvette beach, lying in the blessed shade of a palm, and Zezette turns to her with a smile so sweet …

Tali sighs. What was Zezette doing right now? Had she erased Tali completely from her mind, her life? Tali expects she has.

She licks sticky jam from her lips, and reaches for another doughnut.

*

During the following week, Tali brings the Century Society into her conversations with Betty as often as possible: what it might be like; who might be there; how good it will be to meet new people.

But Betty refuses to discuss the society at all, insisting instead that Tali start clearing out the spare bedroom in preparation for her son's forthcoming visit.

By Thursday, Tali has emptied the little boxroom of all Betty's old clothes, extracting bin bags full of skirts, blouses, shoes, handbags, belts and costume jewellery. Beneath a mound of clothes in the corner, Tali unearths a boxy object that Betty identifies as a gramophone.

'A record player,' she explains. 'You wind it up here, do you see?'

Betty doesn't know where any of her old records are any more, so she can't demonstrate how the thing works. Even so, she wants it out of the spare room. Tali hefts the contraption downstairs to the sitting room and makes space for it on the cluttered sideboard. She takes a moment to wipe the dust off the big trumpet horn; its shape reminds her of the daffodils that have begun springing up in Betty's garden and along the pavements lately.

By Friday, there are bags and boxes piled everywhere, and Betty instructs Tali to store some of them in the cellar.

'I haven't been down there for years,' she tells Tali. 'There's a trapdoor in the cupboard under the stairs.'

But the cupboard is so chock-full of junk, Tali decides instead to access the cellar from the back garden, easily breaking open the rusted padlock on the warped wooden doors.

The roof of the cellar, barely five feet high, forces Tali to stoop, and she wrinkles her nose at the smell of damp earth and mould. The dank space stretches the entire length of the house, and is so dark that Tali is glad she discovered a torch in a dresser drawer earlier. As she edges further into the cellar, the torch's beam picks out a pair of striped deckchairs, a rotting parasol, the sooty remains of a coal heap, and a collection of rusting garden implements leaning against the far wall. The tools look as if they haven't been moved, let alone used, for years.

Bag by bag, Tali lugs the contents of the boxroom down into the cellar. She's dumping the last load, when her torchlight reflects off the tarnished metal clasp of a suitcase, tucked in the shadows. The case is covered in dust and cobwebs and Tali peers closer, gingerly touching the dark brown fabric of the case.

It's none of her business, she knows, and it's probably locked anyway, but what harm can there be in having a quick peek? Perhaps Betty's gramophone records are inside? Or it might be full of mementos Betty could take to the Century Society.

She hefts the suitcase up by its frayed rope handle, and carries it outside into the light. To her surprise, both metal catches flick open at her touch, and she prises the lid up to reveal a loose, jumbled heap of envelopes, postcards, letters. She lifts a postcard resting on the top, notes the Canadian stamp. The handwriting is tiny, and she can barely make out the words.

Dearest E, she reads. *Matt and I have arrived safely, despite the efforts of the weather to blow us off course ...*

It's obvious the suitcase hasn't seen the light of day for years, and therefore neither have the contents. Would Betty like to be reacquainted with them?

Tali closes the case up again, deciding to keep it in her bedroom for now, until she's sure of Betty's mood.

*

'It looks like a prison,' Betty remarks, as the taxi drops them outside the community centre, a grey block of a building in the middle of a litter-strewn car park. She's not wrong, Tali thinks. Has she made a mistake bringing Betty here?

'If it's terrible, we will just have a cup of tea and leave again,' Tali promises.

The entrance foyer, to Tali's relief, is more welcoming, filled with glossy-leaved pot plants and bookshelves crammed with jigsaw puzzles and second-hand paperbacks for sale. Pinned to a noticeboard are cheerful posters advertising various social activities from evening yoga classes to a children's Easter disco.

'Look,' Tali says, drawing Betty's attention to an eye-catching neon poster. 'Bingo every Thursday night. Do you like to play bingo?'

'I'd rather boil my head,' Betty replies. 'I'm only here now because you forced me to come.'

'I didn't force you,' Tali corrects, suppressing a sigh. 'You agreed to try it once ...'

At the front desk, a girl in her late teens offers Tali and Betty a smile full of metal braces. 'Can I help you?'

'We have come for the Century Society,' Tali says. 'Madame Betty had an invitation ...?'

'The oldies club?' the girl says bluntly. 'It's just through those double doors. The woman who usually runs it is ill, so someone else is doing it while she's away.'

'*Merci*, thank you.'

With Madame Betty clinging to her arm, Tali pushes through the doors. They find themselves in a large, plain hall with a raised stage area at one end, cluttered with an assortment of stacked chairs and nursery equipment. At the other end of the room, half a dozen tables have been arranged in a loose circle, around which eight people are sitting and chatting.

Betty tugs on Tali's arm. 'We're in the wrong place.'

Tali suppresses another sigh. It's been like dragging an unwilling toddler to nursery, getting Betty this far. No way is she going to let her back out now.

'The girl said it was in here, Madame Betty. Let's just say hello, shall we?'

A Black man in his thirties wearing a crisp white tunic rises from one of the tables. 'Hello, hello,' he says, coming to greet them. His smile is wide and warm. 'Welcome to the Century Society. I'm Abeo.'

'Hello,' Tali returns the man's smile gratefully. 'I'm Tali, and this is Madame Betty. It's our first time here.'

'Yes, yes,' Abeo nods, as though he's been expecting them forever. 'Come. Meet the club.' He leads them

59

over to the tables. 'Everyone, please welcome our new member, Betty. And this is her friend, Tali.'

Tali smiles around at the group, four of whom are obviously of Betty's age. Everyone is staring at them, and Tali can feel Betty's nails digging into her arm.

One by one, Abeo introduces the members of the club, starting with the frailest of the centenarians, a bone-thin woman with silvery tufts of hair who puts Tali in mind of a sugar-cane flower.

'Violet Johnson is one of our longest-standing members,' Abeo says. 'One hundred and two years young, aren't you, Violet?'

Violet shakes her head, frowning. 'Margaret's the oldest,' she corrects Abeo. 'She's a hundred and ten.'

'My apologies!' Abeo says. 'Of course, dear Margaret. I was forgetting, but we haven't seen her for some months—'

'Hilda Clarke,' interjects the elderly woman sitting opposite Violet. A surprisingly strident voice for such an ancient person, Tali thinks.

'Retired headmistress,' Hilda adds.

That would explain it.

'Sit down, here,' Hilda instructs Betty, indicating the seat next to her. Despite the woman's grand age, Tali can well imagine Hilda commanding a room of unruly students. With uncharacteristic obedience, Betty does as she's bid. Tali takes a chair nearby.

'Things are slightly unusual this month, I should warn you,' Hilda goes on. 'Bridie, our founder, isn't well. Her friend, Jo, is taking the club today. Jo will be back in a minute,' she adds.

'This is Olive,' Abeo continues his introductions, gesturing to Hilda's carer, a plump, middle-aged woman with pink-rimmed eyes and a fuzz of pale brown hair. She reminds Tali of a guinea pig. 'Olive is an expert knitter,' Abeo informs Tali. The guinea pig dips her head in greeting, her needles clicking without pause. She's knitting what looks to Tali like a tiny, bright-pink cardigan.

The remaining club members are both men. 'Alfred Sharpe,' the first introduces himself. The flesh of his cheeks is sunken, but his watery brown eyes twinkle. He extends a hand in greeting and, as Tali tentatively shakes it, she feels the bones in his fingers shift and grind.

'I was a catch-pole for fifty years,' Alfred tells Tali. 'Do you know what that is, girl?'

Tali shakes her head.

'Tax inspector,' Alfred supplies. 'During my lifetime, I've seen twenty-one different prime ministers come and go.'

'Who was the biggest bastard, Alf?' drawls a heavy-set young man in boardshorts and a T-shirt sitting next to him. Canadian, Tali guesses from his accent.

'Language, Duncan,' Hilda chastises.

'When I retired,' Alfred goes on, ignoring Duncan's question, 'I was invited to have afternoon tea at Number Ten with Margaret Thatcher.'

'But I thought you were a staunch Labour supporter?' Hilda says.

'I told her I was Labour when she tried to sweet-talk me,' the old man replies. 'I said, "Don't waste your breath, lady. I'm Labour."'

'What did Thatcher say to that?' Hilda asks with a sniff. 'The old witch.'

'She said, "Well, that's a shame, let's have a cup of tea."'

'It's three thousand, five hundred days ago today that my Nelly died,' a rusty voice declares.

Everyone turns to look at the last member of the club, a man dressed in a grey suit, his collar creased, brown tie a tangled knot. Tali longs to straighten it.

'Is that so, Robert?' Abeo says softly. Robert nods but has nothing more to add, it seems, and the conversation moves on.

'Where on earth has Jo got to?' Hilda says. 'I don't have all afternoon to waste ...'

Alfred winks at her. 'Think of it as another day wrested from the geriatric ward.'

'Don't wish your life away,' Abeo admonishes.

Alfred puffs out his narrow chest. 'I've got another decade in me, young man, you wait and see.'

Duncan glances up from his mobile. 'Remember Bridie's rule,' he pronounces solemnly in his Canadian drawl. 'No one's allowed to die at Century Society.'

'Perfect place to pop your clogs, if you ask me,' Alfred quips.

Their conversation is interrupted by the squeal and clash of the hall doors opening. Tali looks over to see a slight woman about her own age, her arms laden with newspapers and paint pots. She is dressed in combat trousers and a baggy white T-shirt, her short dark hair windswept. Where is her coat? Tali wonders. She must be freezing!

'Jo's here.' Abeo hurries over and takes some of the art equipment from her.

As Jo reaches the tables, Tali sees she's wearing black, clumping, steel-capped safety boots that look too big for her feet.

'Cheers, Ab,' Jo says, as Abeo starts spreading newspaper on the tables. 'I'll just bring the rest of the boxes in from the van.'

'I can help,' Tali finds herself offering.

Jo brushes her messy fringe from her eyes and flashes Tali a smile. 'Thanks.'

Ignoring Betty's panicked frown, Tali accompanies Jo back out to the car park and over to a battered transit van. Jo grapples with the stiff lock on the van's rear door, opening it to reveal a stash of tools and paint pots and what look like wooden shoeboxes. These must be the memory boxes, Tali thinks. As Jo pulls the nearest boxes out, Tali can't help but notice her lean, toned arms; the woman might be small, but she gives off a physical confidence that Tali envies.

'If you could carry these two, please ...'

'*Oui*, yes, of course.' Tali accepts the surprisingly heavy boxes, admiring Jo's ability to balance four of them on her arm while locking the van again. Jo catches Tali's eye and smiles. 'I'm used to lugging tree trunks around all day,' she explains. 'This is nothing.'

Returning to the hall, Tali does her best to ignore Betty's frigid glare. Abeo and Duncan distribute the boxes, while the centenarians don aprons. Tali can see now that each of the boxes is in various stages of decoration. Painted on the lid of Hilda's box is a remarkably lifelike portrait of Elvis Presley. Duncan catches Tali looking.

He smirks. 'All hail the king.'

'It's very good,' Tali finds herself saying. 'Did you paint it yourself?' she asks Hilda.

The centenarian gives her a piercing look. 'Of course.'

'You could paint someone on your box, Madame Betty,' Tali ventures.

Betty responds with silence, her lips pursed in an expression Tali's brother Rozo would describe as a cat's arse.

'Thanks for your help.' Tali turns to find Jo smiling shyly at her. Jo's face is flushed, her hair ruffled where she's run her hands through it, and Tali finds herself transfixed by her eyes, a striking blue-green shade Tali has never encountered before. To her dismay she feels the heat of a blush.

'I'm sorry, I didn't even ask your name,' Jo apologises. 'Bloody rude of me.'

'That's OK.' Tali swallows, and introduces herself and Betty.

'We'll get you started on your memory box in just a sec, Mrs Shepherd,' Jo says. 'I'll grab some paper and we can jot down some ideas …'

She reaches for a satchel hanging on a chair, flapping the hem of her T-shirt, revealing a flash of toned stomach, and Tali has to look away.

While Jo talks to Betty, Tali helps Robert with his box. 'Have you belonged to the society for a long time?' she asks him, in an effort to make conversation. Too late, she realises she's inadvertently insulted him, but Robert makes no indication he's noticed.

'A goodly while,' he tells her. 'Esther brings me, then goes off and does her shopping or whatever. Suits us both fine.'

'Is Esther your daughter?'

He nods.

Robert's memory box is covered in photographs of military planes. Tali recognises a Spitfire, but can't name any of the others. He was a former pilot in the war, Robert tells Tali proudly. 'Always wanted to fly, so I joined the RAF.'

Tali listens, rapt, as Robert describes how he shot down Hitler's V1 rockets over the Channel.

'Doodlebugs, we called them,' he says. 'Four hundred miles an hour they went, sounding like an asthmatic motorbike.' He coughs. 'My job was to blast them out of the sky.'

'That must have been frightening,' Tali says.

'It was if you ran out of ammunition.' Robert gives a dry laugh. 'Happened to me once. My Tempest was only a whisker faster than the rocket I was chasing, but I got alongside it somehow, and then I couldn't shoot the damn thing. So do you know what I did?'

Tali shakes her head, enthralled.

'Positioned my wing so it tipped the underside of the rocket's fin. Rolled it, sent it crashing into the sea.'

'You must have been very brave,' Tali says, struggling to picture the crook-backed old man chasing down enemy rockets in the sky.

'We were playing with fire,' Robert replies. 'Or rather, fire was playing with us.' He meets Tali's eye. 'Every time we flew, we stared death in the face.'

Tali can only nod, unable to think of an adequate response. She turns to Betty on her other side. 'Monsieur Robert fought in the war, Madame Betty.'

Betty stiffens.

'Did you serve in the war, Mrs Shepherd?' Jo asks. Tali sees that her pad of paper is still blank.

'Is it time to go yet?' Betty asks Tali, as though Jo hasn't spoken.

'We've only just got here, Madame Betty.'

Betty sighs, her face a closed book.

Why was she being so taciturn? Tali is wondering this, when Abeo announces he is making refreshments for everyone. Betty visibly brightens at the prospect of a cup of tea.

There is no more talk of the war.

*

Back at Weyside, Betty retreats to bed soon after dinner, claiming exhaustion. In contrast, Tali feels energised in a way she hasn't felt in so long. Jo's cyan eyes haunt her, and she can hardly bear it that she won't see her again for another month. In an effort to distract herself, she kneels and drags the old cellar suitcase from its hiding place beneath her bed. Perhaps there's something inside Betty might want for her memory box.

A damp smell wafts out, as Tali sifts through yellowing letters and receipts, marriage, death and birth certificates covered in faded copperplate hand-writing, and several little booklets filled with coloured coupons. Ration books from the war, Tali presumes.

As she delves deeper, rooting amongst the papers, her fingers touch something hard and cold.

She lifts away the layers of envelopes and postcards, and suddenly she can't breathe.

There, buried at the bottom of the case, is a gun.

5

March 1944

The next morning Elisabeth was wrenched from sleep by a loud rapping at the door. Rubbing her eyes, she struggled up in the bed with a groan. Sunlight leaked through a gap in the curtains, and she winced. How could it be morning already when she'd only been asleep five minutes? Across the room, rhythmic snores emanated from Doris's bed. Elisabeth envied her room-mate's ability to sleep through such persistent knocking. Whoever was on the other side of the door wasn't giving up.

'OK, OK, I'm coming.'

She tugged on her dressing gown and opened the door, entirely unprepared for the sight of Officer Stewart, brandishing her clipboard.

'Good morning, Elise,' Stewart greeted her briskly.

Elisabeth's mouth felt dry as ashes. 'Morning, ma'am,' she croaked. *How much had she drunk last night?*

'It's seven o'clock,' Stewart said. 'PT on the lawn in fifteen minutes.'

Elisabeth rubbed her brow, her head pounding. 'We are just getting dressed, ma'am ...'

From behind her came a long, sonorous snore. Elisabeth met the conducting officer's eye. Was that a glint of humour?

'PT in fifteen minutes,' Stewart repeated. 'Get a move on.' The officer turned on her heel and was gone.

Elisabeth leaned on the door jamb, her legs suddenly weak. Physical training? She could barely stand.

'Who was that?' Doris groaned from her bed.

'Stewart,' Elisabeth replied. 'She wants us outside in fifteen minutes.'

'What on earth for? It's not even morning. God, my head ...'

Elisabeth stumbled back to her bed, the room spinning. She lay down and closed her eyes, as fragments of the previous evening began to surface. She remembered someone playing a piano at one point, everyone singing along to Cole Porter tunes. But there were alarming gaps in her memory too. She never usually drank alcohol; it was far too expensive, and her mother was teetotal, so predictably it hadn't taken much to tip Elisabeth over the edge. Now she thought about it, all evening her glass had miraculously refilled itself, despite her efforts to stay sober. Her throat burned; she could still taste the whisky.

Without warning, a wave of nausea surged through her. She dropped to her knees on the rug, scrabbling for the thankfully empty chamber pot under the bed, and retched into the bowl.

Oh God, she felt awful. She wiped bile from her lips with the back of a hand, longing for a glass of water. Gradually, the nausea passed and she forced herself up on rubbery legs.

'Come on.' She gave Doris's shoulder a shake. 'Or Stewart will have our guts for garters.'

'I *hate* that woman.'

'What am I going to wear?' Elisabeth worried. 'I've only got one spare blouse.'

Doris turned over in bed. 'If Stewart thinks I'm doing bloody PT at this time in the morning, she's got another think coming.'

'Doris, you have to get up, she wasn't joking.'

'I don't feel well,' Doris mumbled, pulling the bedsheets up to her chin. 'Be a love and tell the Gestapo I've got women's trouble.'

'I'm not telling Stewart that. She'll never believe me, anyway. Do you actually want her to come and drag you out of bed?'

'Let her try.'

I give up, Elisabeth thought. If Doris was prepared to face the wrath of Margaret Stewart, then she was a brave woman indeed.

*

A dozen men in shorts and vests were gathered on the front lawn, jogging on the spot and slapping their bare arms. Several looked wan-faced and hungover. Elisabeth shivered in the chill dawn air, self-conscious in her flimsy blouse and a pair of shorts she'd borrowed from Doris. She returned the silent nodded greetings of Henry, John and Terrence, and joined Gilbert at the edge of the group.

'Morning,' he muttered. 'Sleep all right?'

70

Before Elisabeth could reply, a squat, barrel-chested sergeant appeared and began issuing orders. 'Right!' he bawled. 'Let's get you miserable lot moving!'

He had them limbering up, running on the spot, performing press-ups on the dewy grass. Light-headed, Elisabeth struggled to keep up with the men. Next to her, Gilbert puffed and moaned. 'Christ, I need a fag.'

'Come on, you duffers!' the sergeant shouted. 'Lift those arms! Move those legs! Bunch of girls, the lot of you!'

The exercises dragged on, the warming rays of the rising sun burnishing the tired, haggard figures labouring on the lawn. At last, the sergeant declared they were done, and Elisabeth almost collapsed on the grass with relief.

'Get some breakfast down you,' the sergeant ordered, dismissing the group.

'Where's Dominique?' Gilbert asked, as they made their way back inside.

'Still in bed.' Elisabeth stifled a yawn. 'Where I should be.'

'Must say, I'm impressed you're up and about after last night,' Gilbert grinned, as they crossed the hallway. 'I've never seen anyone dance the Charleston like that before ...'

Elisabeth froze at the foot of the staircase. 'What?'

'Extremely entertaining,' Gilbert winked. 'You'll have to give me a lesson some time.' He was away up the steps before Elisabeth could think of a response.

She made it back to the bedroom, to find Doris lying on her bed, grey-faced, and half dressed.

'How was it?' Doris muttered, fumbling with her tunic buttons. 'Sorry you had to go on your own, but my head …'

'Did I dance the Charleston last night?'

'What?'

'Gilbert said I danced the Charleston. But I wouldn't have done that, I just couldn't have …'

'He's pulling your leg,' Doris laughed. 'You were a mouse in the corner all night, far as I can remember.'

'The rotter,' Elisabeth muttered. Stiff-limbed, she washed her face and under her arms with a flannel, then slowly donned the FANY uniform. 'Did Stewart give you a black mark on her clipboard?'

'That cow's got it in for me,' Doris replied. 'Told me if I missed class again, I'd be out.'

'I'm not going to let that happen,' Elisabeth said, pulling Doris to her feet. 'Come on, we need a cup of tea.'

The dining room was busy with officers and students, and Elisabeth spotted Henry, John and Terrence already tucking into hearty breakfasts. To her surprise and delight, there was a bowl of sugar on the buffet table. She hadn't had sugar in her tea since before the war, and within seconds of drinking a cup she felt the sweetness surging through her veins, reviving her. Ravenous, she tucked into a generous bowl of porridge, liberally sprinkled with more sugar. Alongside her, Doris nursed a mug of black coffee.

'You should try and eat something,' Elisabeth said, remembering to speak French at the last moment. She drank down a second cup of sweet tea.

'I don't think I could manage anything,' Doris whined in English.

'*En français!*' snapped an officer from across the table. Doris glared at him.

'The porridge is actually quite good,' Elisabeth said. 'I'll fetch you a bowl.' There was no point being annoyed with Doris, she realised. They were in this together, and right now her friend needed her support.

A movement at the door caught her eye; Gilbert had arrived. She wanted to tell him off for teasing her about last night. But when he smiled at her, warmth bloomed in her chest, and she found herself smiling back.

As they left the dining hall, Elisabeth and Doris were met by Stewart, checking to see they had both eaten enough. 'Today is going to be long, and we don't want you fainting.'

The officer escorted them through the house, to a living room at the rear that had been transformed into a temporary classroom. Sofas had been pushed against the walls, and half a dozen school desks were set out in two rows. At the front was a blackboard on wheels. This room, Stewart informed them, was where all their lectures would be held. The practical elements of the course would take place outside.

'After this lecture on security,' Stewart said, 'you'll be in the barn for wireless training and Morse coding.'

Elisabeth sat with Doris in the front row of desks, and gradually the other students filed into the room and took their seats. The security instructor was a sharp-faced, greasy-haired man, dressed in a shabby brown suit. He introduced himself as Mr Smith, his tobacco-stained fingers fiddling with a Woodbine tucked behind one ear. His eyes roved over the small audience and came to rest on Doris, lingering on her chest a second too long.

'I'm going to teach you the rudiments of house-breaking,' he began, his voice a rasp. He proceeded to describe silent and covert lines of approach and retreat, how to use lawns and grass borders, whilst avoiding gravel, flower beds, stones and mud.

'If there's a dog present,' he said, 'you can use aniseed as a decoy, or kill it with poisoned meat.'

Elisabeth exchanged a look with Doris as the instructor talked on.

'It's best to break into an open window,' Mr Smith said with a smirk. Was he trying to make a joke? Elisabeth wondered. No one was laughing. 'But if you can't find an open one, then you can cut and break. Just make sure you break the glass first time. One crash will wake 'em up. Two will get 'em out of bed.'

From his pocket, Mr Smith took a piece of folded black cloth, opening it to reveal a handful of different-sized keys, and a twist of thick wire.

'This here's a skeleton key,' he told them, handing the wire round for inspection. 'It'll open most simple locks.

'Once you're in, that's only the start,' he went on. 'If you're casing a joint, you gotta leave no trace.' He described how to move through a house undetected. 'Act like you're stepping on eggshells,' he advised.

'I reckon Smith's done time,' Doris whispered to Elisabeth later, as she grappled with a hairpin, trying to release the handcuffs cinched around Elisabeth's wrists. 'He's a crook, for sure. I reckon the War Office pulled some strings, got him let out of prison just to train us.'

'Or perhaps he's just an experienced locksmith who's volunteered for a very irregular job?' Elisabeth whispered back. 'Slow down, remember what he told us about *feeling* the lock.'

'Damn thing,' Doris muttered. Suddenly, something inside the mechanism clicked, and the handcuffs fell open.

'Bravo,' Elisabeth said, rubbing the faint red marks on her wrists. She glanced across the room, where Mr Smith was demonstrating to the men how to jemmy open a window. The security instructor certainly possessed the pallid skin and fidgety eyes of an ex-prisoner, Elisabeth thought. But who better to learn underhand ways from than a criminal?

*

Following a brief lunch, the students were taken to a draughty barn in the grounds behind the manor. Here, they would learn how to assemble a radio transmitter, send and receive Morse code, and cypher simple messages using the one-time pad system. The instructor was a retired signals sergeant, his once-dark hair streaked with grey like a badger's pelt. Elisabeth watched closely as the instructor dismantled a transmitter set on a trestle table. She'd never seen inside a radio before, and was intrigued to discover how a mass of wires and dials could produce sound sent from miles away.

The instructor patiently described the four main components of the wireless set: the receiver box, with its tuning knob and scale readout; the transmitter, with its switches, coils and power cord; the seventy-foot-long aerial wire; and the tiny but crucial crystals.

'Transmitters are tuned with slices of quartz,' he explained, showing the students a little rectangular Bakelite box, inside which a piece of crystal not much bigger than a postage stamp had been mounted. A pair of prongs enabled it to be inserted into the set. 'This quartz crystal has been cut to a precise wavelength, which determines the frequency the set transmits at.

'Radio sets must be plugged into the mains or a car battery,' the instructor went on. 'You'll probably be transmitting from a barn, or maybe even a field, so I'll show you how to modify a car battery to run a wireless off it.'

Once the students could name the parts of their transmitters, and reassemble one from scratch, they were then taught the one-time pad system.

'It's an uncrackable encryption technique,' the instructor explained, showing them a notebook-sized pad made of silk, each sheet printed with rows of letters. 'A plaintext message is paired with a random secret key, as printed on your one-time pads, like this one. The key must never be reused. Each time you send a message, you must destroy the relevant page.'

After a short tea break, the students were given a sheet on which was written the alphabet in Morse code. They were then put into pairs, and Elisabeth found herself partnered with Gilbert. She hoped he'd know what to do, as the amount of information was overwhelming her.

'The length of a "dit" is one unit,' the instructor intoned. 'A "dah" is three units. So the letter "A", for instance is dit dah. The letter "B" is dah dit dit dit.'

'I'm never going to remember this,' Elisabeth whispered to Gilbert.

'It'll come with practice,' he reassured her. They were shown how a Morse key worked, then each pair practised sending dummy messages to each other, one tapping a short Morse message, the other scribbling the letters down on a piece of paper.

Gilbert offered to tap out a message first. 'I'll go slowly,' he promised.

Pencil poised over a sheet of paper, Elisabeth tried to concentrate on discerning the dits from the dahs, as Gilbert tapped on the Morse key. At last he stopped, and Elisabeth contemplated the string of letters she'd transcribed.

Y. O. U. C. A. N. D. O. T. H. I. S.

She glanced up to find Gilbert smiling at her.

*

The following morning began with a run around the estate. The instructor was the same sergeant from the day before. He'd marked out a five-mile loop, he informed the students gathered on the lawn. Shivering in shorts and a thin blouse, Elisabeth eyed the low, heavy clouds. She could taste rain in the air. Next to her, Doris shifted from foot to foot, grumbling under her breath.

'I've tied a few ribbons to trees,' Sergeant Morton said, 'so you shouldn't get lost. If you're quick, you might not get wet either.'

Wearily, the group set off through the gardens and past the small farm that was attached to the estate. Elisabeth and Doris soon lagged behind the men, and Sergeant Morton jogged back and forth amongst the straggling group, barking threats of cold baths if 'you duffers don't put some bloody effort in!'

A chill rain had begun to fall by the time the two women staggered back to the manor, Elisabeth practically dragging Doris the final half-mile. They were the last to arrive, and the men had already disappeared inside.

'You've got fifteen minutes to clean yourselves up and get down to breakfast,' Morton barked.

Upstairs in their room, Elisabeth collapsed on her bed, legs aching, plimsolls crusted with mud.

'We're being tortured,' Doris sighed, peeling off her sodden socks.

Elisabeth was inclined to agree, but feared the truth was far worse: they were being prepared.

*

Weapons training took place in the middle of a meadow on the estate, beneath the broad shelter of an ancient oak tree. Elisabeth looked on as, one by one, the small-arms instructor held up and named the bewildering array of weapons spread over a pair of trestle tables – *Tommy gun, Colt automatic, Browning, Luger P08.*

'The Sten,' the instructor said, wielding a simple, lightweight machine gun, 'is made of three pieces, the barrel, body and butt.' He proceeded to dismantle the gun.

The men, Elisabeth noticed, seemed unfazed by the lesson on weaponry. John was standing with his arms nonchalantly crossed, and Elisabeth recalled him mentioning something about gamekeeping once.

'You may have had previous pistol training, in the old style,' the instructor continued, selecting a handgun from the table. 'You can forget all that. The aim is to turn out good, fast, plain shots.' He held the Colt pistol up for all to see. 'First, check it's not loaded.' He manipulated the gun with practised ease. 'Now it's safe.'

The pistol was duly passed around the group. Elisabeth felt the solid heft of it, how the gun fitted neatly in her palm, the weight evenly balanced.

'Get it out of your mind that your gun is a weapon of self-defence,' the instructor continued. 'It's not. It's a weapon of attack, and has a very short range. Not only will you need speed, but you must be able to kill from any position and in any sort of light, even at night.'

While the students took turns handling the gun, the instructor described various scenarios they could be faced with. 'Your safe house might be raided,' he said. 'Chances are, you can't escape. When you're faced with the enemy, without a second's hesitation, you must fire and kill him before he has a chance to kill you.'

Elisabeth could sense Stewart watching her, and forced herself to stand straighter.

'There's no time, in a fight, to compose yourself,' the instructor went on. 'Hold the gun close, pointing directly at your target. It moves with you, an extension of your body. No locked arms, no two-hand hold, no lining up of sights. Just point and fire. Bullseye.'

The students were issued with a handgun each. For the next two hours, Elisabeth practised loading and unloading her Colt pistol, and firing at wooden posts set at various distances. It surprised her how quickly she mastered the weapon, hitting her mark nine times out of ten.

'You've done this before, haven't you?' Henry asked her, when at last they broke for tea.

Elisabeth shook her head. She didn't like to admit she'd never held a gun in her life, never dreamed she'd be shooting at targets in a field, nor how much she was enjoying it.

'Could have fooled me,' Henry said.

*

As the days passed, the training steadily intensified. The instructors made no concessions for the women, and Elisabeth found it a constant struggle to keep pace with the men. At the end of the second week, the students faced a final test, one that would force them to draw on all the knowledge they'd gained so far on the course. Alone, they were to break into a mock-up of an enemy-held house in nearby woods, and 'kill' the armed occupants inside.

'I don't feel ready for this,' Doris confessed to Elisabeth, as they followed the instructors, Stewart and the other students into the woods beyond the manor. Though the weather was overcast with a chill wind, Elisabeth was sweating in her khaki overalls.

'Me neither,' she admitted. In truth, she was terrified; Stewart had told her that if she failed this test, she would be sent to the Cooler, to be kept under house arrest until her knowledge was no longer relevant.

The path led through the woods to a clearing, where the students were ordered to wait by a pile of logs while the officers decided who would face the trial first. Elisabeth shared a cigarette with Doris, trying to contain her nerves.

Please God, don't let them pick me, Elisabeth prayed silently.

Her prayer was answered. Gilbert was the first to be called forth.

'Wish me luck,' he said, pinching the smouldering end off his fag and handing the butt to Henry. 'Keep it warm for me.' He raised his chin, and Elisabeth's heart stumbled as she watched him walk away, flanked by two officers.

With Gilbert gone, an uncomfortable silence fell. Elisabeth smoked her cigarette to a stub, tensing as a volley of gunshots echoed through the trees. Was Gilbert all right? It surprised her that she cared so much.

God, let this be over soon.

Long minutes passed, and at last Gilbert returned, pale-faced and tight-lipped.

'Thanks,' he muttered, as Henry relit his cigarette for him.

'What happened?' Terrence pressed. 'What's the set-up?'

Gilbert pulled deeply on his fag and exhaled. 'I'll tell you this,' he said. 'You'll need your wits about you.'

Before Elisabeth could ask him for more details, it was her turn.

Accompanied by Stewart, she followed a winding path through the trees, emerging into another clearing. Here, a single-storey house of rough timber stood on its own, the glassless windows and bullet-peppered front door lending it an abandoned, sinister air.

The sergeant briefed Elisabeth on what she was about to face. 'There's a "charging man" target,' he explained, 'controlled from a hidden bunker, which runs on a wire straight through the doorway and out. When you approach the door, the target will be released.'

Elisabeth eyed the building warily. Although she knew this was a simulation, that there weren't actual Nazis hiding inside waiting to kill her, still she felt afraid. She could all too easily imagine the enemy holed up behind those dark, curtain-less windows.

The sergeant handed her a loaded pistol and a couple of spare magazines.

'Two shots must be fired at each target,' he reminded her. 'If the first shot doesn't fell it, the second will.'

'Good luck,' Stewart said, patting Elisabeth on the shoulder. 'Do your best.'

Taking a steadying breath, Elisabeth slowly approached the house, the gun raised before her. Just as the instructor had warned, she was only a few feet from the door when it suddenly opened with a terrible clang and a human-shaped piece of metal hurtled towards her. Instinctively, she dropped into a crouch, firing twice, the bullets ricocheting off the metal, making her ears ring. The target flipped to the side, and the doorway was clear.

She rose again, legs shaking now, but there was nothing for it. She had to carry on.

The ground floor of the house appeared to be one large, open-plan, unfurnished room. Through a doorway on the right, rough wooden steps led down into darkness. Cautiously, Elisabeth descended into a low-roofed, narrow passage, a pale light visible at the far end. As she moved towards the light, a metal bullseye target flipped down from the ceiling with a jarring clank. Reacting on instinct, she fired twice and the target collapsed, controlled by some invisible pulley system.

She stumbled on along the passage, down some more shallow steps to a chamber, the earth-walled room dimly lit by a Tilley lamp hanging in one corner. With a metallic screech, a cut-out half-figure of a man sprang from the left-hand wall. Elisabeth lurched backwards, stifling a scream. Without thinking, she fired once, twice, three times in quick succession, and the figure swung back against the wall with a rusty squeal.

Fingers shaking, Elisabeth fumbled to reload the gun, trying to ignore the voice in her head screaming at her to *get out, get out, get out.*

She turned, and something in the darkest corner snagged her eye – a human shape, slumped on a chair.

Oh God, she was caught!

The figure wasn't moving. She stepped closer, gasping when she saw it was only a straw dummy dressed in khaki uniform. Nobody had mentioned dummies. Was she meant to 'rescue' it?

Breathing deeply, she heaved the dummy on to her shoulder and began to stagger back up the steps, along the passageway and finally out into the blessed fresh air.

'Well done,' the sergeant said, lifting an eyebrow at Elisabeth's swift reappearance. 'And with the dummy too.'

Stewart lowered her clipboard, as Elisabeth dropped the dummy at the officers' feet. She stepped back, waiting for Stewart to acknowledge her.

'Good job, Elise,' Stewart said at last, rewarding her with a rare smile.

Elisabeth flushed. 'Thank you, ma'am.'

Relinquishing her pistol, she followed Stewart back to the waiting group, her galloping heartbeat gradually returning to normal. She gratefully accepted a cigarette from Doris, and only then did she allow herself a moment of self-congratulation.

She'd done it.

6

2018

She's been waiting for Betty to come out of the downstairs lavatory for twenty minutes. It feels to Tali like twenty hours.

'Madame Betty?' Tali calls through the door. 'Do you need help?'

From inside the cloakroom comes the clanking gush of the toilet's ancient flushing system, and Tali winces. She lives in perpetual fear that Betty will pull the chain too hard one day, causing the whole wobbly cistern to fall off the wall and flatten her.

She checks the time on her phone; the Century Society will be starting in ten minutes. The sound of running water has diminished to a faint dripping – Betty is surely nearly finished. Taking a deep breath, Tali reminds herself she must be patient with her; the more she tries to rush her, the slower Betty seems to go. But she really doesn't want to be late to the club. She pictures Jo's face, those gorgeous eyes of hers, and—

From out on the road comes the toot of a car horn. Their taxi has arrived. At last, the toilet door opens

85

and Betty shuffles out. Tali longs to hurry her on, but bites her tongue. She knows from experience that Betty can be as immoveable as a mini boulder when she wants to be.

'I think that's our taxi—'

'I'm not deaf, girl,' Betty snaps. 'Don't hassle me.'

Tali stifles a sigh as she helps Betty into her coat. *Why are you behaving like a toddler*, she wants to cry. Lately, everything Tali has suggested – a game of cards in the evening, a little walk down the garden to feed the ducks on the river – has been rejected. Persuading Betty to attend the Century Society today feels like nothing short of a miracle.

Within seconds of the taxi doors closing, the heavens open and rain pelts on the roof of the car. It sounds to Tali like distant applause, as though the weather is congratulating them for making it out of the house. She helps Betty fasten her seatbelt, but instead of thanking her, Betty stares through the rain-streaked window, hands clasped tightly in her lap. What is she thinking?

As they head towards the community centre through the driving rain, Tali finds herself recalling, again, the dreadful incident with the gun. At first sight, the matte-black pistol with its hatched wooden grip had reminded her of something from a gangster movie. She'd lifted the weapon gingerly from its bed of paper, careful to keep the muzzle pointing at the carpet in case it was loaded.

After her initial shock had abated, she'd decided to show the gun to Betty.

I found this in a suitcase, Madame Betty, she'd said.

Tali had never seen colour drain from someone's face so quickly. Betty had remained frozen for so long, Tali had honestly thought she'd died, sitting bolt upright in her armchair.

She'd reached for her hand. *Madame Betty?*

Her touch had jolted Betty from her trance. As though a switch had been thrown in the old lady, she'd suddenly become disturbingly agitated, shouting at Tali to *get rid of it!*

You want me to take this away, Madame Betty?

Throw it in the river! Betty had cried. *In the river!*

Shocked at Betty's terrified reaction, Tali had stumbled out into the dark garden. A voice in her head was telling her not to do it, and halfway down the path she'd faltered and looked back. Betty's crooked silhouette was framed in the lighted kitchen doorway, and Tali knew that she would not be allowed back in the house again if she didn't obey.

Standing at the river's edge, Tali had hurled the gun into the ink-black water. It had disappeared with a muted *plosh*, barely disturbing the hush of the night.

The incident hadn't been mentioned again since, and all Tali's questions – where had the gun come from? Why was it in the suitcase? Why did it terrify Madame Betty so much? – remained unspoken.

*

The Century Society is in full swing by the time Tali and Betty arrive at the community centre. Tali slips Betty's arm through hers, and leads her reluctant charge into the hall. She looks around for Jo, but there's no sign of her, though she's relieved to see the same four centenarians from their previous visit. All are busy tending to their respective memory boxes, and Tali feels her spirits lift at the tranquil scene.

Alfred's carer, Duncan, is lolling on a chair, playing with his phone, and Hilda's companion, Olive, is knitting what looks to be a blue blanket. Olive glances up, red-rimmed eyes blinking diffidently as Tali and Betty approach the tables, her needles continuing to move as though independent of her hands.

'Hello,' Tali says.

'You're late,' Hilda remarks, and Tali blushes.

Abeo comes to greet them. 'It's so good to see you again,' he beams, enveloping a stiff Betty in a hug, and pumping Tali's hand. 'How have you both been?'

Abeo exudes a hot energy, like the sun's rays, and Tali wants to bask in his orbit for a while. It's such a contrast to the frigid environment she's had to endure at Weyside lately.

'Good, thank you,' Tali lies. 'How are you? Everyone looks very busy.'

'We are a hive of industry,' Abeo says, guiding Betty to an empty chair. At the next table, Hilda is bent over a sheet of paper scattered with dried flowers, carefully applying glue to the petals and sticking them along the edge of her box lid.

'Are they real flowers?' Tali asks her.

'Of course,' Hilda replies. She straightens up with an audible click of her spine. 'Each one represents a hike. I used to love hiking through the countryside.

88

Seems a shame to keep them hidden between the pages of a book.'

The hall doors open, unoiled hinges emitting their customary squeal, and Tali looks over to see Jo approaching, her arms laden with art materials.

'Hi,' Jo smiles at Tali, who has to catch her breath before she can return the greeting. Jo deposits her load on a table and turns to Betty. 'How are you, Mrs Shepherd?'

Betty eyes the pots of paint and brushes with a frown.

'Have you thought any more about your project, Mrs Shepherd?' Jo asks, setting a plain wooden box before Betty.

Tali gives silent thanks for Jo's tact. 'Project' is a good word, she thinks.

'We can do some more mind mapping if it helps,' Jo says. 'I'll just fetch my bag, I think I left our notes in it from last time ...'

Tali watches Jo hurry away, and feels a pinch on her arm.

'Where's she going now?' Betty scowls up at Tali. 'Busy as a bee in a foxglove, that one. She wants to relax.'

It's the most Tali has heard Betty utter all day.

'Good afternoon, ladies,' Alfred calls from the table he's sharing with Robert. 'Couldn't keep away from my scintillating company, eh?'

Alfred is pasting a sepia newspaper clipping to the lid of his box. Tali glimpses a photograph of a young man holding a sports trophy above his head.

'Oh, do be quiet.' Hilda waves her glue stick at Alfred in a mock threatening manner. 'Ignore him, Betty. Thinks he's God's gift, that one.'

Betty sniffs. Tali hides a smile.

At a neighbouring table, Violet is humming softly to herself as she peruses a small pile of cat photographs.

'My babies,' she says, showing Tali a slightly blurred image of two large ginger cats curled together on a chintz sofa.

'What are their names?' Tali asks politely. She's never been keen on cats; something about their aloofness has always made her wary of them.

'Norman and Nancy.' Violet sighs, and suddenly gives a hacking cough, dropping the photo as she fumbles for a handkerchief in her cardigan sleeve. Before Tali can ask Violet if she needs anything, a glass of water perhaps, Abeo appears with one.

Jo returns, and places a sheet of paper and a marker pen before Betty.

'I can't find our notes from before,' Jo apologises. 'I'll just switch the urn on, then we can jot down some ideas.'

'I can do that for you,' Abeo offers. 'Duncan, will you help with the tea things?'

To Tali's surprise, Duncan agrees, pocketing his phone and following Abeo to the kitchen.

'What do you think, Madame Betty?' Tali offers her the marker pen.

Betty folds her arms. 'I haven't had a cup of tea yet.'

'I'll get you started,' Jo says. 'I know what it's like to need tea.' She draws a large circle on the paper, with half a dozen lines radiating out from it, like a child's rendition of the sun. In the middle of the circle she writes BETTY.

'OK,' Jo says. She looks at Betty, and Tali waits for her to say something more, but she seems lost for words.

Alfred comes over to Betty's table, taking the vacant chair next to her. He plucks the pen from Jo's unresisting fingers. 'Mind maps,' he says, shaking his head. 'New-fangled nonsense. What you need, dear lady,' he addresses Betty, 'is a good old-fashioned chat.'

Good luck, Tali thinks.

Thankfully, Abeo and Duncan reappear bearing tea trays, and everyone downs tools. The conversation over tea centres on various deaths and funerals that have occurred over the past month. Hilda's cousin died recently in Spain, she tells the group. Her cousin hasn't spoken to the rest of the family for years and years, so Hilda doubts the funeral will be well attended.

'Miserable woman,' Hilda says with a sniff. 'I'll not be going.'

Tali offers to wash up the tea things, and her stomach flips when Jo says she'll help.

In the kitchen, Jo runs hot water into the cavernous sink. 'Abeo said you're from Mauritius?' she says, snapping on some industrial rubber gloves. 'What's it like there?'

Tali opens drawers at random, searching for tea towels, trying to think. Being on her own with Jo is having a scrambling effect on her brain.

'My family live in the capital, Port Louis,' she says at last. How best to describe that hot cauldron of a city, boiling with people from all over the world – India,

China, Europe, Madagascar? 'It's like the whole world in one place.'

'I don't know much about Mauritius at all,' Jo admits, passing Tali a teacup to dry. 'But I did read a book about the island once by Gerald Durrell.'

'I love to read too,' Tali says. 'But all my books are at home.'

'You've no books?' Jo stares at her, soap suds dripping from her gloves. 'Doesn't Mrs Shepherd have any you could borrow?'

'Too many,' Tali laughs, picturing the hundreds of old paperbacks stacked in every corner of Betty's house. 'Charles Dickens, Daphne du Maurier, Agatha Christie. She says her son will throw them all out when he comes, so I should read what I want now.'

'She has a son? Does he live nearby?'

'Australia.' Tali carefully sets the dried teacup on a shelf. 'But he's coming here soon.'

'Tell me more about Mauritius,' Jo says. 'I'm imagining palm trees and beaches, but I've no idea what languages are spoken, or who the prime minister is or anything. Do you speak other languages, apart from English?'

'French is my mother tongue,' Tali replies, accepting a dripping saucer from Jo. 'Then English – that's government language. Then Creole, which is what I speak with my friends and family. But most people speak French.'

'Do you have a big family?'

'You could say,' Tali laughs. 'There is not much room in our house even now that my three brothers have their own places. Nani and Dada, that's my mother's mother and my father's father, both live with us also.'

'That must be … interesting,' Jo says. Tali waits for more, but Jo says nothing as she rinses soapy froth off a spoon.

Tali takes a breath. 'You have a family?' She braces herself for Jo's answer. She must have a husband, or at least a boyfriend, though her slight figure doesn't show any evidence of bearing children.

'No, I'm not married,' Jo replies, running fresh hot water into the sink. 'My parents are both dead. I've no siblings. No kids either. I've had … had relationships, you know, but I live on my own now.' She turns and gives Tali a sad smile, and Tali notices a flush of colour has crept into Jo's cheeks.

Tali rubs a saucer dry, and hears herself express sorrow that Jo's parents are gone.

'It's all right,' Jo says, dunking and rinsing the last of the cups. 'I mean, it's not all right, but it happened long enough ago now. But tell me more about Mauritius …'

Beneath the harsh strip lights of the functional, beige-painted, communal kitchen, Tali does her best to conjure her homeland. She tries to describe how the towering sugar cane marches for miles and miles across the island, a forest of green. She trawls her mind for English words to portray the stunning golden beaches, the dazzling aquamarine lagoons, the coral reefs teeming with sea life, the cascading waterfalls.

And then, somehow, she finds herself trying to describe Sega, the music of Mauritius. 'It's a mix of flavours,' she says. 'Like a cocktail.'

'I've never heard of Sega,' Jo admits, pulling off the washing-up gloves and draping them over the edge of the sink.

Tali knows this is the moment she should return to Betty, but she finds herself hoping for a few more precious minutes with Jo. 'Let me show you,' she says, fishing her mobile from her skirt pocket. She scrolls through the clogged memory, finds a video, presses Play. Rhythmic drumming issues from the phone.

Jo comes to stand close. On the screen, a small group of men and women are playing musical instruments and dancing on a beach by the light of a campfire. The amateur video is wobbly and grainy, but the music pulsates and Tali notices Jo tapping her foot. There are five female dancers dressed in colourful skirts and bikini tops, and one man in a long white shirt and trousers. The musicians are all men: two are beating hand drums, one is striking a large metal triangle, and the last is keeping time with a box shaker. Tali lets the music wash over her, tugging her back home like the tide.

'What are they singing about?' Jo asks.

'It's a love story,' Tali explains. 'The man,' her long nail taps the screen, 'is telling this woman how much he loves her.' The video was filmed more than three years ago, and Tali was substantially slimmer back then. She wonders if Jo will recognise her.

Jo stares at the phone but says nothing.

Tali wants to ask her what she's thinking, but she hasn't the courage. The faces of the dancers are sheened with perspiration, their skin glistening in the firelight. Tali can almost feel the heat now, as the tempo of the song begins to speed up, faster and faster.

'It reminds me a bit of Bollywood dancing,' Jo says. 'I really admire people who can move so naturally to music.'

It takes many years of practice, Tali wants to tell her. She thinks of all the evenings she used to spend dancing Sega with Zezette and her friends, performing for the tourists on the beaches.

Suddenly, an overwhelming urge to dance comes over her. She hands Jo the phone, then begins to roll her hips, moving her body in time to the tinny music issuing from her mobile, twining her arms through the air in the way Zezette had once taught her. She watches Jo, her mesmerised gaze fixed on the screen, and Tali doesn't have to look to know that the man and woman in the video are dancing closer and closer, their movements flirtatious and ecstatic.

'Oh, la, la, eh, la, la!' The singing is growing louder. 'Oh, la, la, eh, la, la!'

The drumming is intensifying, the clash of the triangle striking the beat in a frenetic rhythm. Jo is transfixed, and Tali slows her dancing and comes to stand next to her again.

The music is building to a crescendo now.

Orgasmic, Zezette pronounces in Tali's head.

Gathering her courage, she turns to Jo. 'Will you dance with me?'

Jo glances up. 'I can't,' she stammers, blanching. 'I dance like an elephant with a hernia.'

'You are a very small elephant,' Tali smiles. Before she can change her mind, she holds her arms out, beckoning. Zezette's voice in her head is shouting at her to *stop, you idiot*.

Jo hesitates, but then, to Tali's surprise, she sets the phone down on the countertop and moves towards her. 'I really can't dance,' she repeats.

'You can,' Tali says, ignoring Jo's tense expression. 'Relax and move your hips, like so.' Tali sways her body, flowing with the music, gently pulling Jo with her. She smiles encouragingly, as Jo tries to copy her. As the music plays out, Tali manoeuvres them around the kitchen, trying not to collide with the counters. She can't believe she's actually dancing; she's missed it so much.

She nudges Jo playfully with her hip and Jo stumbles. They collapse in breathless laughter, just as the musicians give one final, decisive bash on the goatskin drums and triangle, and the music and dancing stops.

Tali touches her phone screen and the video disappears.

'That was incredible,' Jo gasps. 'So much feeling and emotion.'

'You danced really well,' Tali fibs.

'Don't be silly.' Jo's cheeks are blooming and she grins. 'But I don't care, that was so much fun.'

Tali's heart is tripping over itself, and her knees are shaky. The last time she danced like this was several years ago.

The door opens, and Abeo bursts into the kitchen.

'You must come!' he cries. 'Betty has fallen!'

For a moment, Tali stands frozen, Abeo's words making no sense. And then Jo is tugging her hand, and she finds herself in the hall again, and there is Betty's small, crumpled figure, lying on the floor. Tali drops to her knees next to her with a muted cry. Betty's eyes are closed, but her chest is faintly moving.

Tali feels a wave of guilt engulf her. She shouldn't have made Madame Betty come today; she shouldn't have left her while she danced with Jo.

'*Je suis désolée*, Madame Betty,' she chokes. '*Je suis désolée.*'

'Abeo's calling an ambulance,' Jo says, gently slipping a folded cardigan under Betty's head. 'At least she's breathing. Perhaps she fainted ...'

A blanket is found and draped over Betty's body.

Tali looks up and catches Duncan's eye. 'What happened?'

'She was coming to find you,' the young man tells her. 'And she just fell down.'

*

The hospital's accident and emergency department is frighteningly busy, and Betty is left on a trolley in the corridor for a long time. Perched on a plastic chair next to her, Tali watches Betty's sparrow chest fluttering beneath the thin blanket. From somewhere down the corridor a man is shouting obscenities, and a child begins to wail. Tali's bladder aches, but she can't leave Betty alone.

'I don't know what happened,' Tali repeats to each medic she encounters. 'One minute she was OK, the next she was falling on the floor.'

'Are you a relation of Mrs Shepherd's?' a nurse asks, keying Betty's address into an online form.

'I'm her carer.'

'Does she have a son or daughter you can contact?'

Tali hesitates. 'She has a son, but he's overseas.'

The nurse taps on her screen, tight-lipped, but offers no suggestion as to what Tali should do.

Eventually, just as Tali is beginning to fear her bladder will explode, Jo appears.

'I'm so sorry,' Jo gushes. 'I couldn't find a parking space anywhere.'

'You're here,' Tali breathes. She wants to hug her, but first she needs the toilet.

When she returns, she finds Jo alone, Betty's trolley bed nowhere to be seen.

'They took her away,' Jo says, swallowing. 'They're going to keep her overnight. Run some tests. The nurse said we should go home and come back in the morning.'

'Oh.' Tali's thoughts are broken and tangled.

'I'll drive you home.'

Tali stares at Jo. 'I can get a taxi,' she says weakly.

'Don't be silly.'

'Then I will cook dinner for us.'

*

It's strange returning to Weyside without Betty. The central heating never quite reaches the bones of the house, but the place feels even colder than usual to Tali.

Tosca gives them an enthusiastic welcome, and Tali gratefully accepts Jo's offer to walk the dog round the block. Once Jo is gone, she hurriedly switches all the lights on downstairs, and turns on the gas fire, then starts to prepare a simple stir-fry.

'You really don't need to cook for me,' Jo says, on her return. Her eyes settle hungrily on the carrots Tali is peeling.

'But I want to,' Tali says. 'Please will you stay?'

'I'd love to.' Jo's smile is like a sudden slice of sun on a cloudy day, and Tali feels a warm fizzing sensation in her chest. With Zezette, she'd fallen in love gradually, unwittingly, like a moon drawn towards a planet. In contrast, Jo's smile makes her heart blaze hot as a comet.

She tries to concentrate on chopping carrots and onions, but she can sense Jo watching her and it makes her clumsy. 'Do you live in Guildford?' she asks, desperate to fill the silence.

'On the river,' Jo replies. She describes her narrowboat – *Thyme*, named after the herb – moored at Stoke Lock, and Tali realises she must have passed it on many occasions walking Tosca. How has she never noticed Jo and her boat before?

'What do you do as a job?' Tali asks, deftly adding spices to the vegetables sizzling in the pan.

'I work for Bridie's husband, Choppy,' Jo replies. 'He's a tree surgeon. Choppy and Bridie were friends of my parents, I've known them all my life. That's why I'm helping at the club, until Bridie's better.'

'You cut down trees?' Tali remembers something Jo had mentioned when she was unloading the van, something to do with lifting tree trunks.

'Choppy does all the high rope work, up in the canopies,' Jo replies. 'I stay on the ground, sorting things down there.'

'It must make you very fit,' Tali says, pouring more oil in the pan.

Jo shrugs. 'I suppose so,' she replies. 'It makes me hungry, I know that much. God, this smells good ...'

Jo's warm compliment melts Tali's tension away.

After dinner, Jo insists on helping Tali wash up. All too soon, the last plate is dried and the kitchen tidied, and in an effort to prolong the evening, Tali offers to make them some hot chocolate.

'Madame Betty loves my *chocolat chaud.*' Tali warms milk on the stove and fetches a bar of dark chocolate from the fridge. 'I hope she's OK ...' She breaks off a chunk of chocolate, stirs it into the milk.

They take their drinks into the sitting room and Tali perches on Betty's armchair while Jo sits on the sofa. Through the window, the evening sky is freckled with faint stars and a crescent moon floats low over the river.

Without warning, Tali feels a sickening lurch as she pictures herself standing at the bottom of the garden, hurling the gun into the water.

'Have you lived with Betty long?' Jo asks, breaking into Tali's thoughts.

'Six months,' Tali replies. 'It sometimes feels longer.'

Jo nods and takes a long swallow of her chocolate, pronouncing it the most delicious she's ever tasted. She smiles at Tali, and Tali's heartrate ratchets up a notch.

'Betty is so lucky to have this house, right on the river,' Jo says. 'It's so peaceful.'

'Madame Betty hardly goes out to feed the birds now,' Tali finds herself telling Jo. She has a sudden mental image of Betty in her hospital bed, wires and tubes emerging from the blankets.

They are quiet for a time, and Tali longs to ask Jo if she'll stay the night. In the spare room, of course. Just to keep her company.

'It's getting late,' Jo says. 'I should really be heading back soon.'

In the hallway, Jo fumbles in her pockets for her van keys, and again Tali resists the urge to embrace her, to hold on to her for a bit longer.

'Here they are.' Jo waves the keys. 'Thanks for dinner. I'll pick you up at eight tomorrow, shall I?'

'Are ... are you sure?'

'Totally,' Jo smiles. 'Oh, we'd better swap mobile numbers, in case.'

This they do, and then Jo is backing down the steps, and the chance to hug her is gone.

*

For some time after Jo leaves, Tali stands in the hallway, her chest tight. She feels exhausted, but also strangely restless. Frightened, almost. She can't remember the last time she spent a night entirely on her own in an empty house. Tosca nudges her calf, as if to remind her she isn't alone.

Upstairs, she digs out a packet of millionaire's shortbread from the bag in the wardrobe, dismayed to find only a few crumbly mouthfuls left.

She tries to tell herself that if she can survive this night, she'll be fine. She's a big girl, after all. As her mother often reminded her.

But she's so cold.

Jo's river-green eyes and shy smile haunt her.

To take her mind off the lack of shortbread, and the lack of Jo, she decides to continue investigating the contents of Betty's old suitcase. Sliding out of bed with a shiver, she clicks open the case and scoops up a handful of papers. Back in bed, blankets wrapped tight again, she settles down to read.

As she opens a booklet with *Carte D'Alimentation* stamped on it, a folded piece of paper falls out, and Tali finds herself reading a handwritten letter dated April 1944.

War Office
London

Dear Mrs Ridley,

Thank you for your letter. I understand how troubling Elisabeth's silence must be. Please try not to worry. I can tell you that, to my knowledge, your daughter is safe and well.

I want you to know that we are truly grateful to Elisabeth for her hard work. Her role is very important to the war effort, and you have every reason to be proud of her.

Yours sincerely,
Flight Officer L Watkins

Tali scrutinises the faint, old-fashioned handwriting, questions swirling in her mind.

7

April 1944

Having passed the initial phase of training, Elisabeth and the other students were sent to Arisaig on the far north-west coast of Scotland. Here, in a remote area requisitioned by the military, Elisabeth embarked on a gruelling three-week period of paramilitary training, learning skills she never dreamed she'd need.

Stationed at Garramor, a large, isolated house taken over by SOE, Elisabeth practised handling a plethora of weapons, from Colt pistols to Sten sub-machine guns. On the moors beyond Garramor, she learned to navigate in all weathers, and how to survive and find food and water in the breathtakingly beautiful yet harsh and unforgiving Scottish landscape.

'You might find yourself hiding with the French Maquis in the wilds,' the fieldcraft instructor told the students. 'Or forced to escape across the Alps or the Pyrenees.'

Elisabeth tried to imagine herself living rough, subsisting on berries and rainwater. The prospect scared her, and she tried not to dwell on this worst-case scenario.

On Camusdarach Beach – rippled, golden sand stretching away for miles, the rugged blue peaks of the isles of Rum and Eigg visible across the Sound of Sleat – the students were taught how to blow things up. Lengths of old railway track had been dumped on the windswept shore for this purpose, and Elisabeth learned how to prepare plastic explosives, set a charge, light a fuse, and then calmly walk away.

During the second week, a pair of ex-Shanghai policemen introduced the students to a technique of close combat called 'silent killing'. Elisabeth learned how to strangle a person efficiently and easily, how to throw someone from a window or down a flight of stairs without falling with them, how to tie a person up using the Highwayman's Hitch with a few yards of parachute cord, a lamp wire or some curtain string, and how to protect herself with nothing more than her hands and her wits.

At the end of the course, Elisabeth was given a small compass, a pocket torch, and a sleeve dagger. She strapped the lethal blade in its leather sheath to her wrist.

She was now a skilled terrorist, just as Gilbert had predicted. But as she and the others headed south again to embark on the dreaded parachute training at Ringway Aerodrome, the realisation left her conflicted. What sort of person had she become?

*

As the army truck approached the airfield, Elisabeth's guts churned. At Manchester train station earlier, she'd been on the verge of confessing her terror of heights to Stewart. She'd rehearsed in her head how best to broach the subject:

I really don't think I can do this next part of the training. Can't I be sent into France by boat or submarine perhaps?

But, despite Elisabeth's intentions, there'd been no chance to speak privately with Stewart, and the moment had passed. Now, the officer was ensconced in the front cab with a staff sergeant and the driver, and Elisabeth was stuck here in the back of this bloody lorry.

She felt Henry trembling next to her. His face was grey and drawn in the gloom of the truck, and it struck Elisabeth that he was as terrified as she was.

At last they reached Dunham House, the men's accommodation for the week. Situated a short distance from the airfield, the mansion was set in substantial grounds, cloaked in trees and positioned far enough from the main road to deter prying eyes. The place was owned by a Major Singleton, a keen sportsman who also bred Alsatians. Singleton had converted the stables behind the house into a shelter for his dogs, and employed a kennel manageress, Miss Abbott, who lived in a cottage nearby. It was with her that Elisabeth, Doris and Stewart were to board for the week.

Major Edmondson, the commander of Dunham House, and Group Captain Newbury, the chief training officer, welcomed the students into the grand residence.

'Good afternoon, everyone,' Captain Newbury began without preamble. 'We've got one week to train you to be parachutists. One week to teach you how to safely drop from a plane over enemy territory, and not kill yourself.'

A murmur rippled through the group, and Elisabeth bit her thumbnail, drawing blood.

'Gentlemen, you'll complete four jumps in total,' Newbury continued. 'Two from a fixed barrage balloon, one from an aircraft in daylight, and one from an aircraft at night.' His gaze came to rest on Elisabeth and Doris. 'Women are not required to perform the night exercise,' he pronounced.

Elisabeth exchanged a look with Doris – should they feel relieved or insulted?

'Listen carefully to everything the instructors tell you,' Newbury went on. 'The techniques they will teach you are tried and tested, and designed to equip you with all the knowledge you'll need to execute the perfect jump. As with any operation involving flight, there is always the risk of an accident. But our success rate here at Ringway is high, you'll be pleased to hear, with very few casualties in the past year. Our aim, over the next week, is to turn you into skilled parachutists, with every chance of landing safely.'

The training, he concluded, would commence at first light.

*

Elisabeth slept poorly that night, waking at dawn to the sound of barking coming from the kennels. Miss Abbott had already breakfasted and left the cottage by the time Elisabeth and Doris had washed and dressed in the khaki overalls that Stewart had sourced for them. In the kitchen, Elisabeth forced down a few spoonfuls of porridge, but her stomach was clenched tight as a clam, and she felt sick with nerves.

At the aerodrome the students were taken to an empty hangar, where they met their principal instructor. Warrant Officer Brown was a muscular man with a no-nonsense air. For their first test, he set the group performing push-ups, and Elisabeth was soon sweating despite the chill of the hangar. Alongside her, Doris gasped out curses under her breath.

'Pair up!' Brown yelled. 'Fifty sit-ups each! Hold your partner's ankles. Go!'

Elisabeth gripped Doris's slender ankles, anchoring her friend's feet to the floor.

'Christ,' Doris wheezed, as she strained up and tapped her bent knees with her elbows. 'How many did he say?'

'Fifty. Don't stop,' Elisabeth urged. 'It's worse if you stop.'

At last, Doris was done, collapsing back on the floor, breathing hard. 'I think I'm going to die.'

Now it was Elisabeth's turn. She completed the set with mechanical swiftness, her stomach muscles taut and burning; the exercises in Scotland over the past few weeks had helped prepare her for this.

After a brief lunch, the group was hustled off to witness the work of the parachute packing department. In a vast hangar, filled with long tables, scores of women dressed in Women's Auxiliary Air Force uniform were busy untangling lengths of silk cord and folding what looked like acres of parachute material. Printed in yard-high white lettering along the back wall of the hangar were the words:

REMEMBER: A MAN'S LIFE DEPENDS ON EVERY PARACHUTE YOU PACK.

'Is that supposed to reassure us?' Doris whispered to Elisabeth. The concentration on the WAAFs' faces was more comforting, Elisabeth thought. No one was chatting, and barely any of the women glanced at the audience of wide-eyed students, even when the foreman encouraged them to handle the parachute fabric.

'Each chute is twenty-three feet in diameter,' the foreman lectured, 'with twenty-eight rigging lines, each of them over twenty feet long.'

Elisabeth tried not to think about all that material and cord getting tangled in the pack.

'When your life's hanging by a thread,' the foreman concluded cheerfully, 'you'll be all right if it's eighty yards of this silk thread. Any questions, ask away.'

'What if a hole gets ripped in the chute?' Henry wanted to know.

'Valid question,' the foreman replied. 'The canopy might appear flimsy, but if you look closely you'll see that it's not one single piece of material, but lots and lots of smaller sections of silk all stitched together. So if one section is torn, the other sections will hold firm. Which is just as well, as you have to put all your trust in it.'

'Have you jumped yourself?' Gilbert asked.

The foreman flushed. 'No,' he said with a forced laugh. 'I go to pieces up a ladder.'

At last, the day's training was over, and the students were trucked back to Dunham House and the cottage.

That evening, after dinner, Miss Abbott invited Elisabeth, Doris and Stewart to join her for a nightcap in the snug lounge. Over glasses of wine, the kennel mistress entertained her guests with tales of scent-hounds she'd worked with that could sniff out a man hiding in the deepest depths of the woods.

'You look exhausted,' Stewart said to Elisabeth, when Miss Abbott had left the room to hunt down more wine, and Doris had stumbled off to the bathroom. 'Why don't you turn in? Long day tomorrow.'

Elisabeth's throat constricted, as she met the officer's eye. 'I don't think I can do it.' The words were out before she could stop them.

'Do what?'

'Jump.' The word sounded so small. So innocuous. So utterly terrifying.

Elisabeth waited for Stewart to say something. Anything. From outside in the darkness came the mournful sound of a dog howling.

'You'll feel differently in the morning,' Stewart said at last. Moments later, Miss Abbott returned, brandishing another bottle of wine, and Elisabeth knew then that no one would save her.

*

Early the following morning, Elisabeth struggled out of bed, her whole body tense and aching. It was an effort to pull on her rumpled overalls from the day before.

'Feels like I've been punched in the guts,' Doris groaned, rubbing her ribs. 'It hurts to breathe.'

'Me too.' Elisabeth thought of Gilbert. Was he suffering too? She felt a sudden longing for him.

Downstairs, Stewart had found a bottle of aspirin from somewhere, and Elisabeth and Doris took some with their porridge. By the time the truck was rumbling on to the airfield, Elisabeth was feeling a little more human. But the tablets did nothing to dispel the fear crouching in her chest, clawing at her heart.

'It's like putting a coat on,' Officer Brown told the group, as he demonstrated how to fasten a parachute harness. Elisabeth watched closely, as Brown deftly tightened the straps across his chest and between his legs.

'The static line is attached to your parachute cover,' Brown went on, showing them the all-important length of webbing. 'The other end is clipped to an anchor cable in the plane. When the line's pulled taut, it will yank your parachute cover off and release the chute automatically. Takes just a few seconds for all the knots and strings to snap open.'

A few seconds of free-fall. It didn't bear thinking about.

Trussed in her parachute harness, Elisabeth followed the others over to the cannibalised fuselage of a Whitley bomber. The wingless, tailless carcass had been raised several feet off the ground on a specially constructed wooden platform. Here, they were to practise exiting from the plane.

A hole the size of a trapdoor had been cut in the floor of the Whitley's fuselage. The instructor, an older man with a pronounced limp, referred to it as the 'Whitley Hole', and explained how, in an actual flight, this opening would be their means of exit. Elisabeth climbed after the others into the fuselage, and waited while the instructor took them, one by one, through the exit procedure. Elisabeth's turn came, and she approached the hole. A curved rim had been installed around the opening, reminding her of her mother's hip bath but without its rusty bottom. A thin, sagging mattress had been positioned on the ground, six feet below the opening, to cushion her fall.

'Drop your legs through the hole,' the instructor said.

Elisabeth did as he ordered.

'Good girl.' The instructor placed his hand, warm and heavy, on her thigh and left it there. Elisabeth looked at him. The man gave a sly grin and slowly released her leg, pointing to a pair of lightbulbs mounted on a board. One bulb had been painted green, the other red.

'See these?'

Elisabeth nodded.

'When the red one goes out, and the green one lights up, the dispatcher will shout "go", and you drop. Got that?'

Elisabeth nodded again.

'Just drop straight down, don't push off too hard or you'll end up ringing the bell.'

'What bell?' She looked around.

The man's lip curled. 'You'll bash your nose on the other side of the hole.'

'Oh.' *Why didn't he just say that?*

'Ready?'

She tensed. Below her, the mattress looked even further away.

'And if you can, keep your legs together,' the instructor added. He leaned close and she smelled garlic on his breath. 'Though I know it's hard for you ladies.'

Elisabeth resisted the urge to spit in his face, and dropped through the hole.

*

The platform tower creaked and swayed in the breeze, the afternoon sun glinting off the metal scaffolding soaring fifty feet into the sky. Elisabeth gaped up at the zip line attached to the highest point of the tower, the beast of fear clawing its way up her throat now.

Before ascending, the students were shown 'proper landing attitude'.

'Keep your feet together, your toes pointing slightly downwards,' Warrant Officer Brown instructed. 'Grasp the parachute straps, like so, bend your knees on impact, and roll forwards.' With the skill of an acrobat, he performed a front somersault and jumped to his feet again.

'Easy as falling off a log,' he grinned. 'Up you go, then.'

The breeze grew stiffer the higher Elisabeth climbed. Terrence and Henry were above her on the ladder, Henry's progress so slow that Elisabeth had to watch that her hands didn't get caught under his boots. The rest of the group were waiting their turn on the ground.

The instructor at the top of the tower was smoking a roll-up. 'Welcome to my office,' the young man grinned, flicking his cigarette butt into the ether.

'What a view!' Terrence exclaimed. 'You can see for miles ...'

Elisabeth's body was clammy with cold sweat. Light-headed, she gripped the barrier, her knuckles blanching. She'd never realised before how fear could be so physical. Henry was visibly shaking, his face a sickly shade of grey. Elisabeth wondered if he was about to pass out.

Terrence, opting to jump first, was already donning a padded helmet and clipping his safety line to the zip wire. Elisabeth watched as the instructor checked his harness, then led him to the edge of the platform.

'Ready?'

Terrence gave a thumbs-up. 'Ready.'

'On the count of three, then. One. Two. Three!'

Sour bile flooded Elisabeth's mouth as Terrence disappeared over the edge.

Moments later, a faint cheer drifted up from below.

The instructor turned back to Elisabeth and Henry. 'Who's next?'

Elisabeth looked at Henry, expecting him to step forward. But he was sinking to his haunches, shaking his head.

'I can't do this,' he gasped.

'Henry?' Elisabeth crouched next to him. 'What's the matter?'

'Come on,' the instructor said. 'Which one of you is next?'

'You go,' Henry breathed. 'I just need a minute ...'

Oh, God.

From far below came the shriek of Officer Brown's loudhailer. 'Get a move on, ladies!'

Elisabeth clenched her fists. *Bastard.*

Her failure to jump would prove this really was a male-only domain.

Breath held, heart beating backwards, Elisabeth got to her feet. Her hands were shaking so badly the instructor had to fix the safety line for her. The young man's grip was firm on her elbow, as he guided her to the edge of the platform. Between her and the ground yawned fifty feet of nothing.

'Don't look down,' the instructor said. 'On the count of three, you're going to launch yourself off.'

Elisabeth inched closer to the edge. She was going to be sick. 'I really don't think—'

'Three!'

She felt a pressure against her back, and before she could react she was dropping over the side, speeding down the wire. Seconds later, she reached the ground, barely hearing Officer Brown's shouted orders as she came in to land. 'Legs together! Legs together and roll!'

She hit the coconut matting and tumbled over, the impact knocking the air from her lungs. Breathless, she lay for a moment, wondering dazedly if she'd broken anything.

Hands helped her up, and she staggered to the side. 'Here,' Doris said, passing her a lit cigarette. 'Well done, girl.'

'Thanks,' Elisabeth managed, drawing smoke into her lungs and letting it out again in a shuddery breath. She glanced up at the platform, and saw a figure descending the ladder. Henry was climbing back down.

'Refusing to jump.' Officer Brown shook his head. 'He'd better have a bloody good excuse.'

*

'It's the barrage-balloon jump this morning, ladies,' Stewart announced the next day at breakfast. 'And you've the perfect weather for it.'

'Is it right we're not going to get our wings?' Doris asked.

'What do you mean?' Elisabeth stirred her bowl of porridge, doubtful she could eat much of it.

'The men get four practice jumps,' Stewart explained. 'Their fifth is into France. Once they've done five, they get their wing badge. But you're only doing three jumps. Two today from a balloon, then one tomorrow from a plane. Your fourth will be into France. But you need five to get your wings.'

'I hadn't realised,' Elisabeth admitted.

'Can't you say something?' Doris asked Stewart. 'It's not fair.'

'It wouldn't make any difference,' Stewart sighed. 'I didn't get my wings either.'

'I didn't know you'd jumped.' Elisabeth widened her eyes at Doris. Stewart had kept that quiet. But then again, the officer hadn't told them much about herself at all.

The students were driven to nearby Tatton Park, where they joined a group of instructors and WAAFs gathered beneath an enormous metallic-grey barrage balloon floating several feet in the air. A large basket with a canvas roof hung below the balloon, attached by metal cables.

Elisabeth, Doris and Terrence were to ascend first, accompanied by Officer Brown. Elisabeth was seized by an urge to prostrate herself at the officer's feet, and beg the man not to send her on what was surely a suicide leap. Instead, somehow, she forced herself to climb into the basket.

'Stand back from the hole and clip your static lines to the safety bar,' Officer Brown instructed.

The order was given to hoist, and the basket jolted as the blimp was winched slowly higher. Elisabeth gritted her teeth, her stomach lurching.

'Think of it as a fairground ride,' Doris suggested with a sympathetic smile.

Elisabeth couldn't reply, nor could she drag her gaze from the gaping hole in the floor of the basket, through which she could see the ground receding. Soon, the aerodrome resembled a patchwork quilt of brown, grey and green, the cluster of hangars and vehicles below reduced to the size of a toy town.

'You'll go out in single file,' Officer Brown said. 'Ladies first.'

Elisabeth had feared this would happen. She remembered Gilbert mentioning how the female agents were made to jump first, to show the men up and force them to jump too. It was a dirty trick, in her opinion. She thought of poor Henry, back at the main house. There was a rumour he'd be sent to the Cooler.

All too soon, the required height was gained. Doris offered to go first, and under Officer Brown's direction, she dropped through the hole, disappearing like a magician's assistant through a trapdoor.

Next, it was Elisabeth's turn.

Knees weak, eyes clenched shut, she forced her toes over the edge of the opening. She felt Brown's hand on her back.

'Ready ... Go!'

Suddenly she was plummeting, her heart in her throat, a scream on her lips. Seconds later, the safety line jerked, releasing the parachute. Elisabeth opened her eyes just in time to find the ground surging up to meet her. She landed awkwardly, but somehow managed to roll, reducing the impact on her ankles. By some miracle, she'd remained in one piece.

*

The final day of training arrived, and Elisabeth knew that – despite everything she'd faced so far – this first real jump from a plane would be the greatest test of her courage.

'I don't give a damn any more about gaining my wings,' Doris said, as they clambered aboard the waiting aircraft. 'I'm just thankful I don't have to jump again tonight.'

'You ladies dodged a bullet,' John replied grimly. 'That's for sure.'

'What'll happen to Henry?' Elisabeth wondered. He hadn't been seen since the aborted tower jump.

Gilbert and Terrence shrugged. It seemed that no one knew.

Crouched uncomfortably in the dark, narrow fuselage, Elisabeth remembered the air crew's nickname for the Whitleys – Flying Coffins – and thought how apt it was.

The aircraft climbed steadily higher, and as the pressure built, Elisabeth's ears began to ache. She swallowed once, twice, and the pain receded. She sat in silence, shaking with cold and fear, and when Gilbert reached for her hand and gave it a squeeze, his gesture of reassurance almost undid her.

The plane began its circuit over Tatton Park, and one by one the students jumped, first Terrence, then John, Gilbert, and Doris.

Last to drop, Elisabeth approached the opening. The dispatcher clipped her static line to a hook and gave it an experimental tug. 'Ready?'

She couldn't speak.

The plane juddered, and the dispatcher said something else, but she couldn't hear the man for the blood throbbing in her ears.

The red lightbulb flashed once, twice, Elisabeth's signal to stand by. The dispatcher held her arm as she sat, lowering her feet through the hole.

'Keep looking at me!' the man shouted, his voice barely audible over the roar of the engines. Elisabeth stared up into the man's eyes. Was this stranger's face the last face she'd ever see? The flashing red bulb cast an eerie light over the man's features, turning him into a leering Satan.

The dispatcher raised his arm in the gesture Elisabeth had been dreading. She kept her eyes on his, willing him to keep his arm up, even as the plane's dull purr dipped to a low warning rumble.

And then the red light winked out.

'Don't look down!' the dispatcher shouted. 'Keep your eyes on my arm!'

Elisabeth's heart thrashed in her chest. Never before had she been so painfully aware of the beat of her life.

The green light flashed on. The dispatcher's arm swooped down.

Elisabeth closed her eyes, took one final breath, and fell.

8

2018

In the depths before dawn, Tali lies awake, listening to the lonesome clatter of a train travelling into Guildford. The railway tracks ran along the back of the cemetery; when she had first moved into Weyside, she'd frequently been woken by the haunting sound of the night trains. Over the months, she's grown accustomed to their schedule, and now they rarely disturb her.

But not tonight.

She turns over in bed, cocooning herself in the sheets and blankets. If she weren't so cold, she'd cry. She briefly contemplates altering the thermostat on the landing; she's been cranking up the central heating while Betty's been in hospital. But she can't bring herself to leave the meagre warmth of the bed. And besides, the clunking, ancient, air-locked radiators have so far proved a poor defence against the permanently chilly atmosphere in the house.

She tugs the blankets more tightly round herself, dislodging an empty can of gin and tonic concealed in the bedding. It rolls with a faint thunk on to the floor, and Zezette's voice comes to her.

What's the matter, sugar? You used to be able to sleep through an earthquake.

The drink might numb Tali briefly, but it's failed to wash Zezette's voice from her head.

Ever since she found that suitcase in the cellar, she hasn't been sleeping well. If only she'd left it alone. In her search for something to put in Betty's memory box, she's unearthed a mystery.

Where had the gun come from? Who had hidden it in the suitcase? Why did the sight of it upset Madame Betty so badly? Why, *why* had Tali thought it a good idea to show the gun to Betty at all? Now the thing is lying at the bottom of the river, and Tali can't get it out of her mind.

Guilt burns in Tali's chest; all this is her fault. There's a clear correlation in her mind between her desire to see Jo again, and Betty's accident. If she hadn't selfishly insisted Betty go back to the Century Society, Betty wouldn't be in hospital.

The sound of the train melts away into the night, and an eerie silence falls. There's a charged vibe in the air, like the ominous lull between lightning and thunder. Tali peers into the shadowy corners of the room, trying to ignore her prickling skin, an unnerving sensation warning her there's something, some presence, in the bedroom with her.

Mauvais air. Her mother's voice this time.

Outside, the wind abruptly rises, gusting through the yew trees in the cemetery. Rain lashes the bedroom window as though someone is throwing stones at the glass, and Tali shivers.

She gropes for her phone on the bedside table, switches it on. The last text was from Jo, earlier that afternoon, checking Tali was OK and asking when Betty might be home.

Thinking of you. J xx

If Jo only knew how often Tali thought of her.

She scrolls back through their text exchange, counting the kisses at the end of each of Jo's messages. Always two. How much significance should she read into them?

Tali's fingers hover over Jo's last message, wishing she could text Jo now or, better still, phone her and hear her voice. But it's three in the morning. No one in their right mind is awake at this ungodly hour.

The dark wood wardrobe looms, a hulking black shape against the far wall. Tali closes her eyes briefly, trying to imagine Betty on the other side of the wall, sleeping in her room. But she can't fool herself. The wind is battering at the windows now, the thin glass rattling in the warped wooden frames, and Tali's stomach knots. Lying in the dark, alone and fearful, brings back a vivid memory of when she was eight years old and a terrible cyclone wreaked havoc across Mauritius.

She'd never discovered why her parents chose to stay in Port Louis during that lethal storm. Later, she'd found out that friends in the south of the island had offered them refuge, but for some reason her parents had refused to take it. She remembers her father boarding up the windows of their house with scavenged planks, her mother stockpiling huge canisters of drinking water and tins of food. Tali needed to be a brave girl, her parents had told her.

Tali had tried so hard to be brave, but she was only a little kid, and the furious roar of the wind had terrified her. With the house under siege, and her parents battling to stop parts of it being blown away, Tali had climbed into her parents' wardrobe, huddling amongst the shoes and the dust and the spiders. Her brother Rozo, seven years older, had tried to coax her out, regaling her with some fantastical story about the storm being a dopey old dragon come looking for its gold.

But despite her brother's attempts, she'd refused to come out, and in the end Rozo had joined her in the wardrobe. She'd curled up with her ear pressed to Rozo's warm chest, the measured whoosh of her brother's heartbeat drowning out the dragon's fury, gradually soothing her to sleep.

If only Rozo was here with her now.

*

The storm blows itself out towards dawn, and at last Tali falls into a restless slumber. She sleeps through her seven o'clock phone alarm, waking over two hours later to the sound of Tosca scratching at the bedroom door. Thick-headed, Tali drags herself out of bed.

'Oh, *tou tou*,' she mumbles to the dog. '*Je suis désolée.*'

When she'd first started working for Betty, Tali had been wary of Tosca. Dogs were not generally kept as pets back home in Mauritius, and Tali had initially found it strange to be sharing living space with a pampered ball of smelly, off-white fur that slept for most of the day.

But though it's taken months, she's gradually warmed to the dog, and this week she's found herself grateful for his bumbling presence in the house while Betty's been gone.

Tosca gives her a baleful look and pads back out of the room.

Tali dresses with clumsy haste, wrangling her unbrushed hair into a scrunchy, and hurries downstairs. Tosca is whining at the kitchen door to be let out into the garden.

'OK, *tou tou*. I'm here.'

All week the dog has been unsettled, padding from room to room, sniffing for Betty, barely interested in his food. Tali decides to mix a sardine with his dry kibble this morning. The treat makes her feel a bit less guilty for abandoning him while she visits Betty at the hospital later.

As she's grilling toast for her own breakfast, the letterbox clangs. On the mat lies a postcard with Australian stamps, a photograph of Brisbane skyscrapers on the front. Tali can't help but read the message.

Mother,
I'll be with you by the end of the month.
Leo

Tali's fingers itch to rip the card up. What sort of son writes such a brief line to his ninety-nine-year-old mother, whom he hasn't seen for so long?

She shoves the postcard in her coat pocket. She'll wait and see how Madame Betty is feeling today, before she shows it to her. No sense in upsetting her if she can avoid it.

The bus drops Tali outside the hospital, and she hurries inside. At the kiosk in the foyer, she buys a *Times* newspaper and the biggest bar of milk chocolate available.

'Mrs Shepherd didn't have a very good night,' the nurse tells Tali as they make their way down the aisle to Betty's bed. 'She woke everyone up in the early hours, shouting in French. At least we *think* it was French. No one could work out what she was crying about, and we had to give her a sedative to calm her down. She might be a bit confused, but that's normal,' the nurse continues. 'Sedatives can have that effect on the very elderly.'

'Can I still take her home today?' Tali asks. The doctor had visited Betty yesterday and declared her well.

'Yes, but you'll have to wait for the DO to see you.'

'Who?'

'The Discharge Officer,' the nurse explains. 'Mrs Shepherd won't be mobile for a while, so she'll have to sleep downstairs, if she hasn't got a stairlift fitted. The DO will discuss that sort of thing with you.'

Tali hasn't considered mobility issues. If Betty can't get up to her bedroom, the only other option is for her to sleep in the front room downstairs. Tali pictures the unused, sunless, permanently chilly room, full of dusty, dark wood furniture. It will take some work to make it comfortable.

The nurse parts the curtains around the last bed, revealing Betty awake and sitting up, her spun-wool hair unbrushed and standing out from her skull in tufts. The skin of her face is sallow, her eyes sunken, and she looks every one of her ninety-nine years. But as Tali greets her, tenderly taking her cold fingers in her own larger, warmer hands, Betty's eyes brighten.

'Natalia,' she breathes.

'Good morning, Mrs Shepherd,' the nurse chirps, bustling about straightening the bedsheets and inspecting the vital-signs machine beeping in the corner. Betty ignores her, gripping Tali's hands with surprising strength.

'I brought you a present, Madame Betty.' Tali perches on the edge of the bed, trying to keep out of the nurse's way. She gently extracts her hand from Betty's, and pulls out the newspaper and chocolate from her bag.

'*Merci*, Natalia.' Ignoring the chocolate, Betty fumbles to open the newspaper, searching for the crossword. She jerks her head up. 'Tosca? *Comment va-t-il?*'

'*Bien*,' Tali smiles. 'He's fine.'

The ward telephone is ringing, and the nurse hurries away, the curtain swinging shut behind her.

Tali notices the water jug on the bedside table is empty. Madame Betty must be thirsty.

'I'll be back in a minute,' Tali says.

Betty peers at the crossword, mumbling to herself in French, and doesn't respond.

Tali is halfway through filling the jug at the sink at the end of the ward, when her phone rings in her pocket. The sight of her brother's number on the screen sends her stumbling out into the corridor.

'Tali?'

'Rozo, hi ...'

'Tali, can you talk? We need to talk ...'

Her brother's voice is drowned out by a loud screeching sound. A hospital porter is pushing a trolley full of bedding along the corridor. Tali waits for the man to pass her and the squeak of wheels to diminish.

'Can you hear me? Tali? Where are you?'

'I'm in hospital—'

'What? Shit, what's happened? Are you all right?'

'I'm fine, there's nothing wrong. Madame Betty, she had a fall. But she's fine. I hope. She's coming home today.'

'Whoa. What? Who's Madame Betty?'

'She's the lady I'm caring for. She's nearly a hundred, Rozo, but she's tough, like Nani.' Tali swallows as a sudden image of her beloved grandmother flits into her head.

She waits for her brother to reply, but there's only silence from the phone. Further along the corridor, someone starts whistling tunelessly.

'Nani cries every day, Tali.'

'Rozo ...'

'No, listen to me. You have to come home, OK? No running away any more. Just buy a ticket and come home.'

'But—'

The line cuts off.

'Rozo?'

Tali stares at her blank phone screen. Rozo's never cut her off like that before. He's always been there for her, prepared to hear her out, fight her corner.

She pockets her phone again, her mind numb, oblivious to the hospital staff and visitors passing by. A familiar churning starts in her guts, a toxic mix of guilt and grief she recognises well. The hospital porter with a now-empty trolley is coming back along the corridor. As he draws level with Tali he gives her a friendly nod, but she can barely muster a smile.

She returns to Betty's bedside, and is pouring two cups of water when a young woman clutching a folder and an electronic tablet pokes her head through the curtains.

'Good morning,' the woman greets Tali and Betty with a smile. 'I'm Gillian Hill, the Discharge Officer. I hear you're escaping today, Mrs Shepherd.'

Gillian is wearing a short-sleeved blouse, revealing arms covered in vibrant tattoos, and Tali finds herself transfixed by the bright green snake twining its way down Gillian's left arm, its fangs encircling the woman's slender wrist. On her right arm is a large faded red rose, and a bird with very long tail feathers. It's an exquisite work of art, and Tali wonders what her own parents would say if she came home with tattoos inked all over her body. They'd disown her immediately. Her arranged marriage would be off ...

'Are you Mrs Shepherd's granddaughter?' Gillian's soft Irish lilt interrupts Tali's hopeful daydream.

Tali tears her eyes away from the woman's arms. 'Oh no,' she stammers. 'I'm her carer. I live with Madame Betty.'

'Ah, that makes things a whole lot easier,' Gillian smiles.

'*Fleur de peau,*' says Betty.

'What was that, honey?' Gillian turns back to Betty, but Betty's lips are a thin line.

'Everything is on the surface of the skin,' Tali translates, gesturing at Gillian's tattoos.

'Oh,' Gillian says after a pause. She smiles. 'I forget I have them sometimes.' She makes a show of consulting her tablet. 'OK, so just some bits and pieces to check, and then we can get you sorted to go home, Mrs Shepherd. Is this date of birth right? Are you nearly a hundred?'

'A hundred years young,' Tali confirms, smiling at Betty.

'*J'approche de ma date d'expiration,*' Betty mutters.

'Don't say that!' Tali rolls her eyes at Gillian, who gives her a blank look. Tali wants to explain that although Betty might *appear* to be nearing her expiry date, she actually has a will of iron and a mind as sharp as a swordfish.

'Did you serve in the war, Mrs Shepherd?' Gillian asks. Tali tenses.

Betty mumbles something in French that Tali fails to catch and refuses to look up from the crossword in her lap. Tali glances apologetically at Gillian Hill. She wishes she could explain Betty's rudeness.

Was it something to do with the sedatives Betty had been given last night? Or had the fall shaken her brain perhaps? Or was Betty just being awkward?

'You did work in the war, Madame Betty,' Tali prompts. 'First-aid work, you told me.'

130

'A nurse?' Gillian asks.

Betty gives a dismissive snort.

'My granddad was in the war,' Gillian chats on. 'He never liked to talk about it much, but I remember once asking him why he fought, when Ireland was supposed to be neutral, and he told me something I've never forgotten. He said he didn't understand how anyone could sit back and allow Hitler's evil, brutal regime to triumph. People's freedom was at risk, and once it had gone it would never come back.'

Betty lifts her head and Tali tenses, waiting for her to say something inappropriate, but Betty looks past her, as though Tali isn't there.

'Course, the family made him suffer when he got back, by all accounts.' Gillian sighs. 'Treated him really badly, which is why he never spoke about it, except when he'd had too much of the Guinness.' She swipes her tablet screen. 'Do you have family, Mrs Shepherd? Any children?'

Tali waits for Betty to answer, but Betty remains silent, pencil trembling over the crossword. Noises filter through the curtain: the rhythmic squeak of a nurse's rubber-soled shoes; the rattle of the approaching drugs trolley; the persistent ringing of an unanswered phone.

'*Mon fils est un salaud,*' Betty mutters at last.

'Madame Betty!' Tali gasps. To call her own son a bastard, in front of a stranger – had the old woman lost her mind? She suddenly remembers the postcard in her pocket. 'Madame Betty has a son, in Australia.'

'OK,' Gillian says, tapping her tablet. 'Has he been informed that his mother is in hospital?'

'He's flying here soon,' Tali replies.

'But he's happy for you to arrange things in his absence?'

Tali assures the woman all is fine, the lie slipping from her lips as smoothly as air. 'Madame Betty can come home today?'

'Oh yes, we're pretty much done here now. You'll soon be free to go, Mrs Shepherd.'

Before she leaves, Gillian gives Tali the contact details of a local company that provide special equipment for people recuperating at home.

'If you ring them now and explain the urgency, they'll sort a bed out for you,' Gillian says. 'You can borrow a wheelchair from the hospital.'

Tali thanks her, and as she tucks the leaflet in her coat pocket, her fingers brush the postcard from Australia. What is Monsieur Shepherd going to think when he finds out about his mother's fall? Will he hold Tali responsible?

She realises Betty is speaking to her.

'*Si je pouvais lire dans tes pensées.*'

Tali manages a nervous smile. She wouldn't be at all surprised if the old lady really could read her mind.

'I was thinking about Tosca,' Tali fibs. 'He'll be so glad when you are home again.'

*

To Tali's surprise and relief, the rehabilitation equipment company have a cancellation and are able to install a bed that afternoon. While Betty rests in her armchair by the fire, Tosca lying like a hairy sandbag at her feet, Tali braves the frigid front room. She will do her best to transform it into a warm, welcoming temporary bedroom. She's still not sure how she'll get Betty upstairs to the bathroom, but in the meantime there's the little downstairs cloakroom she can hobble to, and Tali can give her bed baths as needed.

By six o'clock, Betty is happily ensconced in her new electric, ergonomic bed. A flush of colour has returned to her face, her cheeks the soft velvet of a pale pink rose. She would have been quite a beauty in her day, Tali thinks.

'I don't know what I would do without you, Natalia,' Betty says, gripping Tali's hand. 'I never thought I'd end up sleeping in here. Maman will be turning in her grave.'

Tali can't help but gape at her; it's the first time Betty has spoken English since before her accident.

Betty's focus shifts to the bay window, and Tali follows her gaze, half expecting to find someone staring in. The glass is obscured by net curtains, and the flint wall of the cemetery opposite is a greyish blur in the gathering dusk. It gives Tali the shivers to think that Betty's whole family are probably buried on the other side of the road.

'It's only for a short while, Madame Betty,' she says, switching on the Anglepoise lamp. Its warm glow suffuses the room, and Tali feels a sudden pang of homesickness for the hot Mauritian sun.

'Oh, I nearly forgot ...' Tali hurries out to the hall and retrieves the postcard from her coat. 'This came for you.'

133

Betty scans the card, then hands it back to Tali with a sigh. 'Put the kettle on, will you, dear?' she says.

Later, as she's getting into bed, Tali's phone pings, announcing a text.

Was it Rozo again? Or her parents, demanding she come home? She has to force herself to look.

She breathes out in relief to see Jo's name on the screen.

Hey, how's Mrs S doing? Hope you're OK? xx

Two kisses.
She will send Jo three.

Hi, all is OK, *merci*. Mme Betty very
tired. But glad to be back home.
Xxx

Great! Will Mrs S come to the next
club? I can't wait to see you again.
Xxx

Three kisses.
Tali's thumb trembles over the phone screen. At last she taps:

Oui, I can't wait to see you too. xxxx

Four kisses. What will Jo make of that?

Great! See you then. Night night. Xxxx

'*Bonne nuit*,' Tali whispers, and kisses the phone.

A train rumbles by beyond the cemetery, and Tali wonders if Jo can hear it too, alone on her narrowboat. She pictures Jo on the deck of *Thyme*, gazing up at the night sky. Was she thinking of her too?

Unable to sleep, Tali searches for distraction, but none of Betty's dog-eared novels appeal. At last, she retrieves the cellar suitcase from under her bed.

The familiar smell of the past wafts out as she lifts the lid. She stares at the messy contents for a moment, and a shudder runs through her as she remembers the gun. A corner of a photograph snags her eye, and she pulls out a folded French identity card, dated 1944. There's a black-and-white photo of a pretty young woman attached to it. Tali peers closer. The woman has Madame Betty's eyes and nose, and the date of birth printed on the card is the same as hers: 10 June.

But the name inked below – *Elise Ricard* – is a stranger's.

9

April 1944

On their last evening at Ringway, Elisabeth and Doris joined the men for a celebratory dinner at Dunham House. Elisabeth found herself sitting next to Gilbert in a grand dining room, trying to hear what he was saying over the tumult of voices around the enormous table. Drink flowed, and the mood was buoyant.

'I'm glad this week is over,' Gilbert confided to Elisabeth, leaning close enough for her to smell his familiar sandalwood scent. 'Are you?'

'I honestly didn't think I'd make it,' Elisabeth admitted, hoping no one else could hear over the chatter. 'I feel rather strange, as though I'm walking on air.' She kept to herself the fact that the whole world appeared in sharp focus, including Gilbert. Especially Gilbert.

'I'll tell you why that is,' Gilbert said. 'You've cheated death. We've all cheated death.'

He was right, Elisabeth thought. They'd survived falling out of a plane, and the miraculous fact of that made everything more vivid for a time.

*

Before her final training was to start, down in the New Forest in Hampshire, Elisabeth was granted two days' home leave. Though sad to leave Doris, she found to her shock she was even more reluctant to be parted from Gilbert. She would miss his gentle teasing, the secret smiles he gave her when no one was looking.

She endured a long, uncomfortable train journey back to Guildford, finally reaching Weyside by the early evening, to be met with tears of joy from her mother. Much had happened in Elisabeth's absence, she discovered, including the fact that her mother had taken in a lodger, a young soldier from Stoughton Barracks called Frederick Shepherd.

'He has a shrapnel wound in his leg,' Florence explained as she made them tea. 'He needed somewhere *pour sa convalescence*. His rent has been helpful.'

Frederick was duly called down from the spare room, and Elisabeth found herself shaking hands with a slim, sandy-haired man a little older than herself, whose friendly, rather bashful smile immediately endeared him to her.

'Your mother's told me all about you,' Frederick said, when Florence had bustled off to the kitchen to make more tea.

'Oh Lord, has she?' Elisabeth laughed nervously. What on earth had Florence been saying?

'All lovely things,' Frederick stammered, blushing. 'Truly, lovely things.'

'It's good to know Maman has company while I'm ...' Elisabeth faltered '... away.' Frederick opened his mouth to say something, but to Elisabeth's relief her mother returned at that moment with a fresh pot of tea, and the conversation moved on.

That evening, Florence cancelled her WVS commitments to cook Elisabeth's favourite meal, boeuf bourguignon. As the three of them sat down to eat, Elisabeth was shocked to see how little food was on her mother's plate.

'You've given me half your portion, Maman,' she protested, thinking of the enormous servings she'd enjoyed whilst training.

'You need it more than me, *chérie*,' Florence replied.

'But Maman ...' Elisabeth hesitated. Her mother had aged alarmingly over the past few weeks. There was no flesh on her at all, her bones prominent through wan skin. The years of rationing were taking their toll, and Elisabeth felt another stab of guilt. 'I'm eating perfectly well, Maman,' she said. 'You really don't need to feed me up.'

'There's nothing of you,' Florence argued. She sighed. 'Frederick has plans to extend your father's vegetable patch.'

'If you don't mind, of course.' The young soldier's face reddened as he glanced at Elisabeth, and she gave him an encouraging smile.

'I'm so glad you're home, *ma chérie*,' Florence chattered on. 'Mr Farr, he knows you're back? He's kept your position open, I hope ...'

Elisabeth chewed a lump of gristly meat, unable to meet her mother's eye. 'I can only stay until Wednesday,' she said at last.

'*Mercredi?*' Florence stared at Elisabeth across the table. '*Je ne comprends pas.* Mr Farr will surely be expecting you back?'

'The War Office still needs me.'

Florence wiped her mouth with a napkin. 'I've had enough of this War Office *absurdité*, Elisabeth.'

Frederick's knife clattered on his plate. Elisabeth forced herself to meet her mother's eye.

'Tell me the truth,' Florence said, 'and I will never ask you again. What exactly are you doing? I've been so worried about you.'

'I *am* working for the War Office, Maman, I promise you.' *The best lie is a half-truth.* 'Typing and translating, that sort of thing. *Pas grand-chose.*'

Florence looked as though she was about to ask more, when a familiar haunting wail came from outside: the air-raid sirens had started up.

Elisabeth set her fork down and made to rise. 'Is the cellar unlocked?'

Florence and Frederick remained seated. 'We don't bother going down straight away any more,' Florence said, her voice flat. 'Finish your dinner.'

For a fleeting moment, Elisabeth considered arguing, but she could see her mother's mind was made up. And really, Florence was right. What were their chances of surviving in the cellar if the house collapsed on top of them? She dutifully scraped up the last of her stew, thinking how annoyed the brass at SOE would be if she were to die at the hands of a German bomber before she'd even set foot on French soil.

Frederick rose and began collecting the plates up, limping away to the kitchen, leaving mother and daughter alone. The sound of him washing up reminded Elisabeth of her father; he'd always cleared up after a meal, too.

'When will you be home again?' Florence asked.

'I honestly don't know, Maman.' The training had been so arduous and exhausting, she'd barely had the energy to miss home. But now she was back at Weyside, doubt swept through her, as she realised she was all her mother had. What would happen to her if she didn't come back?

Florence took a crumpled handkerchief from her sleeve and dabbed at her eyes. 'You will write to me,' she said, her voice cracking. 'Every week.'

Elisabeth swallowed. Lying to her mother made her feel sick. 'I'll try my best, Maman, but we're kept so busy I may only manage a postcard sometimes.'

'As long as I know you're alive and safe.' Florence began to cry quietly.

'Oh, Maman!'

They held each other then, and Elisabeth breathed in her mother's unique scent, a blend of violets and carbolic soap. She longed to bottle it, to keep her mother's essence with her for always. She hugged her tighter, feeling the latent strength in her mother's slight frame. 'I'll be back soon,' she whispered. 'I promise.'

*

Two days later, she bid a tearful farewell to her mother and Fred, and took the train to Brockenhurst in the

New Forest. At the station she was reunited with Officer Stewart and Doris, who pulled her into an embrace. 'Here we go again,' Doris said, and Elisabeth managed a smile.

Stewart drove them through the village of Beaulieu, towards Special Training School No. 31. Elisabeth stared out of the window, thinking of her mother and how she would love this quintessentially English village with its pretty flowers, honey-stone cottages and tranquil river. She hoped Maman had stopped crying by now. One thing at least gave Elisabeth a little comfort: her mother wasn't alone; she had that sweet soldier for company.

Alongside Elisabeth on the back seat, Doris was quiet, lost in her own thoughts. Elisabeth hadn't asked her friend how the brief time with her family had gone; there had been no need. Both women had sensed each other's private pain. Elisabeth found herself reflecting on her own reasons for leaving everything she knew and loved at home. The SOE training she'd received so far had been an education beyond anything she could ever have dreamed of. She had skills now that ordinary people simply didn't possess. And she couldn't deny that she felt a certain romantic thrill at being part of a secret elite.

What surprised her the most, however, was the urge for adventure that had grown over the last few weeks.

'Here we are,' Stewart announced, as the car turned off the road and crunched up a sweeping gravel drive flanked by sprawling rhododendrons, verdant lawns and clipped shrubbery. At the end of the drive stood an impressive three-storey manor house, climbing roses framing the ground-floor windows, the grey stone walls covered in twining wisteria.

'Another stately 'ome,' Doris remarked with droll humour, as they heaved their suitcases from the boot. 'Didn't the Prince of Wales meet Mrs Simpson here?'

Elisabeth gazed about her. 'Hobnobbing with royalty, who'd have thought it?'

'Chance'll be a fine thing,' Doris quipped, as Stewart hurried them on.

An elderly housemaster welcomed the women into a vast foyer, busy with soldiers and FANY orderlies, the atmosphere one of restrained urgency. Once Elisabeth and Doris had been shown the room they were to share, and had freshened up, they returned downstairs to wait for Stewart.

When they entered the hall, they found Gilbert, John and Terrence were already there. On seeing the women, the men broke into spontaneous applause.

'We were just taking bets on whether you two had bailed, weren't we, lads?' Terrence teased.

'You cheeky devils,' Doris laughed. 'Where's Henry?'

John shook his head. 'Gone.'

'What? You don't mean ...?' Doris faltered.

'The Cooler?' John finished. 'Reckon so.'

'It's good to see you again,' Gilbert smiled at Elisabeth, his eyes holding hers.

'You too,' she replied.

He leaned closer, and for one heart-stopping moment she thought he might kiss her.

'I missed you,' he said, his voice low. 'Did you miss me?'

Of course she'd missed him. She'd missed him beyond words, she wanted to say. But to admit this would not be wise, she feared. Once their training was over and they were sent to France, there was a high chance they would never see each other again. She was spared having to answer by the arrival of Stewart, who informed the group that the commander of Beaulieu was waiting to address them in the lounge.

Captain Warrington was a large man with thick black hair and a piercing gaze.

'Welcome to Beaulieu,' he began. 'I hope your short time here will be beneficial to you. The staff will inform you of the housekeeping rules, but it's my duty to set out the ground rules. The non-negotiables, shall we say.'

The captain's stance on security was strict, and the students were effectively cut off at Beaulieu. Each large house on the estate was separated from its neighbours by high fences and bushes, and the students were not to stray. As the officer droned on, Elisabeth thought of her mother and Frederick and her friend Josie at work. All must be forgotten, and she shivered at the prospect of disappearing from her life once again.

*

That afternoon, in one of the ornate drawing rooms, their final training commenced.

'These last lectures are the most important,' their instructor, Corporal Barnes, began. 'From now on, only French is to be spoken, at all times.' He switched to heavily accented French to prove his point. 'You must only call each other by your *nom de guerre*.'

He was interrupted by a knock at the door. A female officer came into the room, followed by a gaunt man in a baggy, ill-fitting suit, leaning on a cane.

'Officer Watkins,' Barnes greeted the woman. 'I wasn't expecting a visit ...'

'Jack returns to London today,' Officer Watkins replied. 'I thought it would be helpful if he spoke to your students before he left.'

A chair was found for Jack, and Officer Watkins spoke privately to him, before leaving the room.

Jack was an agent, the students learned, who had been working with a group of Maquis for the past two months, living rough, deep in the wilds of the French countryside. As the students listened, he began to describe the terrible conditions in France, how the feral Maquis were growing desperate, existing on wine and bravado and not much else. 'They're suspicious of everyone, even the English,' he said. 'They want arms, not interference.

'You must never relax,' the agent warned. 'Never fool yourself into thinking the enemy aren't watching. A single, simple mistake could mean the end of you.' His voice was hoarse, his eyes unable to settle. 'And not just for you, but for the entire operation you'll be undertaking.'

Many changes had occurred in France during the Occupation, Jack continued. 'One example,' he said, 'is that French women are no longer entitled to a cigarette ration.'

Elisabeth heard Doris swear under her breath.

'Some wives share their husbands' tobacco rations,' Jack added. 'But no woman smokes in public.

'There's no milk for coffee,' he went on. 'So asking for a *café noir* will raise a few eyebrows, as nobody would expect milk anyway. Some foods are only available on certain days of the week. *Jours sans* are days when you can't buy alcohol. You need to be aware of these changes, because to make even a small error will mark you out.'

Jack told them how male agents must carry their photo identification card, ration card, work permit, and the medical certificate showing their exemption from forced labour in Germany at all times.

'But you,' Jack said, looking first at Elisabeth, then at Doris, 'you'll only need your identity cards. But don't think you won't be stopped and searched. Because you will.'

As Officer Watkins returned to collect him, Jack shared a last piece of advice:

'If you remember only one thing, remember this,' he said. 'Trust absolutely no one.'

*

The following day, a costumer from the West End arrived at Beaulieu. Effete and extravagantly conspicuous in a shiny blue suit and silver cravat, Mr Bollinger had been hired to share his expertise on disguises.

'Your ability to assume an entirely different persona is vital,' he counselled the students. 'Your survival may well depend on it.'

Mr Bollinger had brought with him a wardrobe of clothes and paraphernalia such as false hair-pieces and different styles of hats. 'But really, you don't need greasepaint or false moustaches, or anything of that nature,' he told the students. 'Merely dressing your hair differently, or wearing glasses when normally you don't, is often enough to fool people.'

After lunch, the students learned they were to be sent on a mission, and told to dress in their civilian clothes. Elisabeth chose her favourite grey tweed skirt and a moss-green wool jumper that her mother had knitted. She looped a cotton scarf around her neck, thinking it might come in useful as a disguise.

'You'll take the bus to Southampton,' Corporal Barnes briefed the students. 'There, you'll separate and conduct your business around town. Your descriptions have been given to the Southampton police force, and they will be on the lookout for you. They've been told that some parachutists have been dropped in the area, thought to be German agents. Your task is to elude capture, and return here by seventeen hundred hours.'

Barnes then gave each of them a slip of paper with a telephone number written on it, to be divulged to the police only as a last resort, if they were arrested and their cover story wasn't believed.

'Remember, in France we can't do much for you if you're caught,' Barnes warned. 'So don't get caught.'

Elisabeth felt a heady sense of freedom at being released from the confines of Beaulieu, if only for a few hours. But as she boarded the bus with the others, she reminded herself this was no game. Could she evade capture by the police for hours?

'Fancy sticking together?' Gilbert asked, as they disembarked at Southampton. 'The police won't be looking for couples.'

Elisabeth hesitated, weighing up the options. She'd planned to go it alone, and yet she'd never been to Southampton before, and with Gilbert there was less chance of becoming hopelessly lost. The others had already scattered, vanishing into the crowd.

'OK,' she agreed. 'But we're not a couple.'

'Of course not.' Gilbert's lips twitched.

The razed buildings and rubble-strewn streets were dispiriting to witness after the tranquil, cloistered safety of Beaulieu. When Gilbert tucked Elisabeth's arm into his, she didn't object, glad of his warm, solid presence.

They found a Co-op serving tea, and sat at a table in a shadowy corner, sipping their drinks, trying to make them last. Elisabeth kept half an eye on the door, tensing every time someone came into the café, but Gilbert seemed relaxed. She was grateful for his attempts to take her mind off the ordeal, asking her about the music she enjoyed and the authors she admired.

'Have you ever been to the Astoria?' he asked, pouring a second cup of tea. Elisabeth had to admit she hadn't.

'I saw Benny Goodman play there a few months back,' Gilbert said. 'And Tommy Dorsey.'

'I love Tommy Dorsey!' Elisabeth allowed herself a moment to imagine dancing with Gilbert, somewhere far from here. Somewhere safe.

'When this damn war is over, I'm going to take you to the Astoria,' Gilbert promised.

Elisabeth smiled. 'I'd like that very much.'

Eventually, they were forced to leave the café. A chill rain had begun to fall, and Elisabeth tied her scarf about her head, pulling her coat on. There were four more hours to kill.

'We could try and find a library,' she suggested, as they walked arm in arm along the street.

'I've got a better idea,' Gilbert said, and steered her into a nearby Woolworth's.

Elisabeth began to browse the dispiritingly empty shelves, but Gilbert led her down the aisles, towards the rear of the shop where a photobooth was tucked in the corner.

'I want a memento of today,' he said, grinning at her.

'A photo?' Elisabeth said. 'But you know that's not allowed ...' They had been warned right at the start of their training to keep as low a profile as possible, to avoid leaving any trace of their presence.

'Who's going to know?' Gilbert said. 'Come on, you know you want to.'

Elisabeth had never used a photobooth before, and eyed the curtained cubicle warily. Did he expect her to go in there with him?

Before she could object, Gilbert grasped her hand and tugged her into the booth. Inside was a round stool, and Gilbert sat down, pulling Elisabeth on to his lap.

'What are you doing?' She tried to rise again, but Gilbert held her gently but firmly around her waist, his breath warm on her ear.

'It'll only take a minute,' he promised. He drew the little curtain across, plunging them into shadow. The backs of Elisabeth's knees tingled.

'Gilbert, we shouldn't,' she said weakly.

'Just one photo, that's all I ask.'

How could she resist?

When at last they emerged from the booth, Elisabeth blinked in the shop lights, grateful to see no other customers nearby. Gilbert held up the strip of photos, four tiny black-and-white images of their faces, pressed close together.

What they'd done was stupidly reckless, highly illegal, Elisabeth knew. If Stewart found out what she'd done ... it didn't bear thinking about.

But when Gilbert carefully divided the photos in half, handing her the top two images to keep, she slipped them in her skirt pocket with a smile.

On their return to Beaulieu, Gilbert was called into Captain Warrington's office. Elisabeth waited nervously for her summons, ready with an excuse for her misdemeanour. *It was a silly mistake; she'd never do anything like that again.*

The summons didn't come. Later, when she joined the others in the lounge for evening drinks, Gilbert was nowhere to be seen.

'You've been very quiet since we got back,' Doris remarked, pressing a whisky into Elisabeth's hand. 'Did something happen in Southampton?'

'No,' Elisabeth replied, a little too hastily. She took a sip of her drink, ignoring Doris's raised eyebrows. 'I'm just tired.'

That night, as Elisabeth and Doris were preparing for bed, John tapped on the door.

'Sorry to disturb you, girls,' he said. 'Just thought you'd want to know. Gil's gone.'

Elisabeth could only stare at him. *What did he mean?*

'He's been deployed?' Doris asked. 'Already?'

John nodded. 'He said to tell you goodbye.'

*

Elisabeth jerked awake, a shadowed figure looming over her. Before she could cry out, rough hands ripped away her warm blankets and hauled her out of bed.

The bedroom light snapped on, and she raised a hand to shield her eyes against its glare, only to have it slapped down. 'Keep your hands by your sides!'

She stood frozen in shock, utterly confused by the presence of Corporal Barnes and two other men in the bedroom. She recognised the signal sergeant, but the third man she'd never seen before. Most confusingly, all were dressed in the sinister grey-green uniform of the German SS.

'You're to come with us,' Barnes said in his rough French.

'Elisabeth?' Across the room, Doris had woken. 'What's happening?'

Even in her bewildered state, Elisabeth knew her friend had made a grave mistake in speaking English.

'Silence!' Barnes yelled at Doris.

Elisabeth gasped as the officer seized her arm and dragged her from the room. Already it was dawning on her that this must be the mock interrogation. Stewart had warned them it might happen; she just hadn't expected it to be so soon. She wasn't ready.

Barnes dragged her along the corridor and down a back staircase, to a sparsely furnished room lit only by a single, flickering bulb. In the centre of the room stood a desk on which had been placed an electric lamp, currently switched off, and a metal tray of disturbing-looking medical implements. Two wooden chairs completed the ominous scene. Elisabeth's eye snagged on a bulky object in the corner: the disconcerting yet unmistakable form of a dental chair, its armrests looped with buckled leather straps.

'Sit.' To Elisabeth's relief, Corporal Barnes shoved her down on an ordinary chair before the desk. The sergeant and the other man stood behind her, beyond her line of sight.

Barnes glared down at her. 'What's your name?'

Elisabeth's mouth was dry, her voice hoarse. 'Elise, *monsieur*.'

'Elise what?'

For a terrible second, she couldn't remember her cover name. 'R-Ricard, *monsieur*.'

'Put your hands on your head!'

Slowly, Elisabeth did as she was told, desperately trying to recall the last lecture they'd had on Gestapo interrogations.

The first interrogator is usually the 'bully' type who will try to make you either angry or frightened, she remembered. *He will impress on you the terrible power of the Gestapo. He may threaten you, or throw things.*

'Tell the truth!' Barnes shouted.

The best lie is a half-truth.

'It … it is the truth,' she stammered, ensuring she still spoke in French. Her arms were already beginning to ache. Barnes switched on the desk lamp, angling the light so that it shone directly in Elisabeth's eyes.

He's only trying to intimidate you, she told herself, clenching her eyelids shut. *Just hold on.*

'Open your eyes!'

Barnes lit a cigarette, blowing smoke in Elisabeth's face. 'Where were you born?'

The best lie is a half-truth. 'Paris.'

'Speak up!'

'Paris, *monsieur*.' She shuddered at a draught of chill air against her bare legs. The room was freezing, and she was only wearing a thin nightdress.

'Whereabouts in Paris?'

'Val-de-Marne.'

'You lie!'

'*Non, monsieur.*'

'Stand up!'

Before she could comply, her arms were seized by the two men behind her, and she was yanked to her feet.

'Hold the chair above your head.' Barnes blew a stream of smoke towards Elisabeth, and she coughed.

'P-pardon, *monsieur*?'

'You heard me!'

Slowly, she lifted the wooden chair up, hoisting it above her head. Her nightdress fluttered around her knees, her arms trembling, and she was suffused by a wave of self-consciousness. The men could surely see her body through the flimsy material. With an enormous effort of will, she straightened her arms and locked her stance. In her head she began to count.

A minute passed, the longest sixty seconds of her life.

'Now, I'm going to ask you again,' Barnes said. 'What is your name?'

'Elise, *monsieur*,' she gasped. 'Elise Ricard.'

'Tell the truth!'

She gritted her teeth. 'Elise Ricard.'

Another minute passed. Her vision started to blur, arms shaking so much she was on the verge of dropping the chair.

Footsteps and low voices behind her; one of them a familiar Scottish burr. Stewart was here.

'Where were you born?' Barnes asked again.

'Paris, *monsieur*.'

He glared at her. The bastard was enjoying this.

'Enough.' Barnes motioned for Elisabeth to lower the chair. 'Sit down.'

Elisabeth sank on to the seat. Despite the frigid temperature of the room, she could feel sweat sliding down her back. She wiped her brow with the back of her hand, aware she must look a sight, but too exhausted to care.

The questions went on and on, until Elisabeth's head pounded. Soon, she had entirely lost track of time. When at last Barnes paused his interrogation, an hour could have passed, or three, Elisabeth had no idea.

Corporal Barnes came around the desk to stand directly over her. She braced herself for another attack.

'You did well,' he said, speaking English now with his soft Welsh lilt. He looked over Elisabeth's head, nodding to someone behind her, and then Stewart was at her side. 'Take her back.'

Upstairs again, while Stewart disappeared in search of a stiff drink, Elisabeth collapsed on her bed.

'What did they do to you?' Doris asked, clasping Elisabeth's shaking hands.

'They ... they asked me the same questions over and over ... waiting for me to slip up ...'

'Christ,' Doris breathed, reaching for her cigarettes.

'I didn't think I could hold out.'

'But you did,' Doris said. 'You did.'

*

After breakfast, Elisabeth was called to Captain Warrington's office. She was alarmed to find Corporal Barnes and Stewart also present. She could barely look at the instructor, knowing he'd seen her practically naked.

'You coped admirably last night,' Captain Warrington congratulated Elisabeth.

She raised her eyes and encountered Warrington's steady gaze. 'Thank you, sir.'

'God forbid you should be interrogated for real. But at least if you are, you'll be a little more prepared.'

'Yes, sir.'

There was a long silence.

'You're ready to be sent into the field,' Warrington said at last.

Elisabeth blinked. She must trust his judgement, though she felt far from ready. All she knew for certain was that this world she had entered was one of secrecy and deception, risks and danger, and, even if she walked away now, her life would never be quite the same again.

'A mission has come up, in northern France.' Warrington cleared his throat. 'We think you are the perfect fit.'

'Sir?'

'With regards to this particular assignment,' Warrington said, 'time is in short supply.'

Everything was in short supply in this bloody war, Elisabeth thought. Except fear and heartbreak.

'If you accept,' Warrington said, 'you will be deployed immediately.'

Elisabeth caught Stewart's eye. The officer's face bore an unfamiliar, almost pitying expression.

Elisabeth turned back to Captain Warrington. He was expecting her to refuse, she realised. But she'd come too far, endured too much to back out now. She thought of her beloved father, killed by the Nazis. She thought of her mother's ongoing grief and stalwart endurance.

She thought of Gilbert, no doubt already in France. There really was no choice.

'I accept, sir,' she said.

10

2018

Tali manoeuvres Betty's wheelchair through the community-centre foyer and into the hall. The Century Society is in full swing, and there are two new people Tali doesn't recognise; an elderly lady in a wheelchair like Betty's, and a small, middle-aged woman with a glossy black bob who Tali presumes must be the old lady's carer. Tali spots Jo, head bent over Robert's memory box, and something flips in her chest.

'How are you, Betty?' Abeo greets them. 'How is the hip?'

'Bruised, not broken,' Betty replies. 'Natalia has taken care of me, she's an angel ...'

Tali feels a blush creep up her neck, as the members of the club all pause in their work and look at her. Jo catches Tali's eye and grins.

'I'm not an angel—' Tali protests.

'There's someone you must meet, Betty,' Abeo interrupts. He gestures at the stranger in the wheelchair parked next to Hilda's table.

'This is Margaret Stewart, our oldest member,' Abeo introduces. 'And Margaret's companion, Juliana.'

The carer leaps from her chair and shakes Tali's hand, then Betty's. '*Kamusta*,' Juliana says, nodding and smiling. 'Nice to meet you.'

'*Kamusta*,' Tali replies, recognising Filipino.

'It's good to have Margaret back with us,' Abeo says. 'You've been unwell for some time, haven't you, Margaret? But you're better now.'

Margaret Stewart stares at the hall doors, silent. Tali notes the woman's noble features. The years have carved deep ravines down the sides of the super-centenarian's nose, and the powder-filled creases of her face are like pink seams fissuring a rock face. Margaret's long legs are folded sideways, her heels on the cusp of falling off the footplates. If she stood up, she would be tall, Tali reckons.

Tali's gaze drops to Margaret's lap, where her crooked hands rest. The folded corner of a silk handkerchief pokes from one cardigan sleeve and, despite Margaret's advanced years, she exudes a faintly imposing aura. Tali suspects she was quite formidable in her day.

Tali feels a pinch on her forearm, and glances down to find Betty's bony fingers digging into her flesh. She tries to free her arm, but Betty tugs her lower. '*Je la connais!*' she hisses into Tali's ear.

'You know Madame Stewart?' Tali whispers back in English.

'*Oui, je la connais!*'

'Where do you know her from, Madame Betty?'

Betty stiffens, her fingers gripping Tali's arm like a vice, but she makes no reply. Tali exchanges a look with Juliana, who blinks back at her, helpless.

'Would you like a cup of tea or coffee, Margaret?' Abeo asks, diffusing the awkward moment in his usual way. 'Hilda has brought some shortbread for us today.'

Juliana stoops to shout into Margaret's ear. 'Coffee and shortbread, Mrs Stewart: your favourite.'

A faint smile hovers on Margaret Stewart's lips.

'A small coffee only,' Juliana tells Abeo. '*Salamat*. Thank you.'

Tali feels Betty's grip on her arm relax. 'I'd like a cup of tea,' Betty says quietly, still staring at Margaret Stewart's impassive face. What history did these two women share? Tali wonders.

'We will all have tea and coffee,' Abeo beams. 'And Hilda's delicious shortbread. Energy for our work ahead.'

'I can make the drinks,' Tali offers.

'You're an *angel*,' Duncan drawls sarcastically from his chair.

'I'll help,' Jo says, laying down her paintbrush. Tali longs to hug her.

'Make sure you put the shortbread on a plate,' Hilda's voice follows them. 'Don't leave it in the tin …'

'Promise you won't laugh?' Jo says, as they reach the kitchen. 'But I've decided to learn French.'

Tali fills the kettle with fresh water, unsure how to respond to Jo's announcement. Why did Jo think she would laugh?

'I failed French at school,' Jo says. 'Well, I failed all my exams, if truth be told. But I've decided to do something about it at last.'

'If you like, I could help you,' Tali says, before she can stop herself. *'Je peux t'apprendre lentement.'*

'Was that French?'

'Oui,' Tali smiles. 'I can teach you slowly,' she translates.

'Oh, that would be so helpful, thank you.' Jo drops teabags into a teapot. 'Could you grab the sugar? I think there's some in that cupboard.'

Tali retrieves a crusty bag of Tate & Lyle, then arranges Hilda's shortbread on a plate. The kettle begins to steam, and she wills it not to boil, so she can stay out here with Jo as long as possible.

'Can you believe Margaret Stewart's a hundred and ten?' Jo says, spooning coffee into mugs. 'Abeo reckons she's the fifth oldest person in the whole of Britain.'

'Madame Betty says she knows her,' Tali replies. 'But she's been saying bizarre things since her fall.'

'Maybe they worked together once?' Jo muses. 'Margaret has dementia, poor woman. Bridie told me she won the George Medal in the war.'

Tali wonders how Margaret won the medal, but Jo doesn't know. She flits around the kitchen, pouring milk into a jug, wiping down the countertop, and it soothes Tali to watch her. Though small, Jo exudes a robust energy, her natural smile weakening Tali's knees. With a start, she realises Jo is speaking to her.

'I don't suppose you're free for dinner tomorrow?' Jo asks, hesitantly. 'If you are, I could cook something, and you might help me with some French verbs? If you aren't busy, of course. It wouldn't be anything fancy. The dinner, I mean. I'm no good at cooking, really. But I can fry a sausage ...'

160

Tali contemplates the weekend stretching before her; she's supposed to be sorting out the spare room before Leo Shepherd's arrival, and there's a pile of dirty laundry that needs dunking in the dreaded twin tub. Tosca is due a worming treatment, and at some point she'll have to do a grocery shop.

But the chance of spending time with Jo pushes everything into insignificance.

She finds herself grinning. 'I'd love to.'

*

Gradually, Betty's 'project' takes shape. Tali gives the box an undercoat of cream paint, while Jo attempts to prise out some ideas to add to Betty's still largely blank mind map. But Betty is resolutely unhelpful.

'I wish Bridie was here,' Jo confesses to Tali quietly. 'She's so good at asking the right questions. You know, finding out about people's lives.'

'What about the river, Madame Betty?' Tali suggests. She can feel her patience waning. 'You've lived by the river all your life, haven't you?'

Betty gives a grunt, and Jo takes this as affirmation. She begins to sketch a river scene on the lid of the box. 'Shall I draw a couple of swans here, Mrs Shepherd?' Jo points to a corner of the lid, and Betty nods.

'And ducks,' Tali says. 'Don't forget the ducks.'

With swift strokes of her pencil, Jo produces a river scene complete with various wildfowl.

Tali is impressed. 'You're very good,' she offers.

'Thanks,' Jo replies modestly. 'Bridie's the real artist, though.'

Tali can't take her eyes off Jo's hand, moving so fluidly, the shape of a moorhen emerging from the tip of her pencil as if conjured by magic.

'Will you be seeing Bridie soon, Jo?' Hilda calls from her table. 'Only, I have that recipe book to give back to her ...'

'I'm having dinner with her tonight, actually,' Jo replies. She smiles at Tali. 'Choppy cooks the most amazing toad-in-the-hole.'

Tali blinks at her. '*What*-in-the-hole?'

'Toad.' Jo's grin widens.

'*Toad?*' Jo can't mean a frog, can she?

'The toad is a sausage,' Jo tries to explain. 'I don't know why it's called toad-in-the-hole, it's really only sausages in a Yorkshire pudding batter.'

'I thought the batter was the toad,' Alfred interjects.

'Don't be ridiculous,' Hilda scoffs. 'The batter is the hole. Obviously.'

'I don't see why,' Alfred argues.

'Toad-in-the-hole,' Tali says weakly. She knew the English were eccentric, but this?

'Sparrows,' Betty says, jabbing a finger at her box. 'I want some sparrows.'

'Good choice,' Jo nods. She begins to draw a sparrow sitting on a branch. 'I love those tough little birds.'

Madame Betty was like a sparrow, Tali thinks. 'Your drawing looks so real,' she remarks, watching Jo pencil whorls and ridges of bark. 'You are very talented.'

'Oh, no,' Jo replies shyly. 'I just ... notice details.' She flexes her fingers. 'What do you think so far, Mrs

162

Shepherd? The river scene just needs painting now, so you might like to start thinking about what to put in your box ...'

'Shoes,' Betty says, deadpan.

'Shoes?' Tali says.

'It's a shoebox, isn't it?'

'Well, the idea is to create a treasure box of memories,' Jo says, exchanging a glance with Tali.

'What about crosswords?' Tali ventures. 'You love your crosswords.'

'That's a good idea,' Jo says. 'We could draw a cross-word grid on the underside of the lid, and then write cryptic clues only you know the answer to all around the edges ...'

Betty stares at her, snowy brows raised, watery eyes piercing.

'You don't like the idea?' Tali asks.

'I didn't say that,' Betty mutters.

'Do you have any photos of your dog, Mrs Shepherd?' Jo tries. 'A collage of animal photos can look good.'

'How do you know I have a dog?' Betty asks.

'Jo has met Tosca,' Tali reminds her. 'When you were in hospital.' A memory of drinking hot chocolate with Jo sends a little quiver through Tali's heart.

'You could put some photographs of Tosca on your box maybe, Mrs Shepherd?' Jo suggests.

Betty makes a non-committal noise.

'Or family photos perhaps?' Jo forges on. 'Look at Violet's project, it's covered in her grandchildren and great-grandchildren.'

Tali tenses, and tries to shoot Jo a warning look, but Jo is bent over Betty's box lid again, adding feathery details to a sparrow on a twig.

'The river is enough,' Betty says at last.

To Tali's relief, Jo doesn't press her for more.

*

The following afternoon, Tali prepares to visit Jo on her narrowboat. She's kept herself busy all day bathing Tosca, tackling the laundry, preparing Betty's tea for later. The guilt she feels about leaving Betty alone for the evening has been steadily eclipsed by a rising excitement, bubbling in her veins like shaken lemonade.

'I've put a salad in the fridge for you,' Tali tells Betty as she settles her in the armchair with a blanket and a cup of tea. 'Don't forget to eat it, will you?'

'Where are you going?'

'I told you,' Tali says, biting back a sigh. 'I'm having dinner with Jo on her boat.'

'What do you mean, on her boat?'

'She lives on a boat,' Tali says patiently. 'You know this, Madame Betty. It's down the river, at Stoke Lock. You know Stoke Lock?'

'Of course I know Stoke Lock, girl.'

'Well, that's where Jo's boat is,' Tali says. 'So not far. I won't be late. I'll put the radio on for you.' Not for the first time, Tali wishes Betty had a television. Instead, there is only a battered little transistor radio on the windowsill, permanently tuned to Radio 4.

'Don't forget the salad, Madame Betty,' Tali says, and is through the door and gone before Betty can respond.

Clutching a bottle of wine in a plastic bag, Tali makes her way to the towpath and follows the river towards the lock. The dark green water reflects the afternoon sun, rippling and flashing with gold. A couple of boys skid past her on their bikes, surprising her with their cheerful call of 'thanks, miss!' as she hastily steps out of their way. Further on, a dog walker with three huskies straining on their harnesses stumbles past, closely followed by a red-faced, generously proportioned jogger in figure-hugging Lycra. Tali can't help but stare at the woman as she pounds away down the towpath. She's never understood people's urge to run.

Tali soon reaches the footbridge that crosses over the lock, and pauses to marvel at the two pairs of huge wooden gates holding back the river. Six boats are tied up, one behind the other, along the far bank, and she picks out Jo's royal blue narrowboat easily. Three ducks and a single lonely swan are busy feeding on the water by the boats, but instead of being soothed by the peaceful scene, Tali finds her throat tightening with apprehension.

She takes a steadying breath, then crosses the little bridge over the lock. Ignoring the sign that says PRIVATE: KEEP OUT, she hurries through the front garden of the lock-keeper's pretty, ivy-clad cottage. Jo had told her she was allowed to do this, but still Tali expects to be shouted at for trespassing. To her relief, no one comes out of the cottage to challenge her.

Jo is waiting on the bank next to her boat.

'Hi,' Jo grins, and Tali stiffens in surprise as she pecks her on the cheek. 'Welcome to my home.' Jo sweeps her arm over the narrowboat. Tali reads the name painted along the side of the vessel in flaking red lettering: *Thyme*. 'She needs a lick of paint,' Jo says, hopping with practised ease on to the stern deck. 'Come on board.' She offers her hand, and Tali steps gingerly from the bank.

'I've never been on a boat like this before,' Tali confesses as they stand close together on the gently rocking deck. Tali gazes down the boat's thirty-foot-long roof, the surface covered with neat coils of rope, a bicycle strapped on its side, and a collection of flower pots filled with herbs tumbling over their rims.

'Come on inside,' Jo says, heading down the shallow steps into the boat. 'I did try and tidy up.'

Tali follows Jo, ducking to avoid smacking her forehead on the overhanging hatch cover. The interior of the narrowboat is nothing like she imagined, and she's momentarily struck dumb. She's stepped into a house, but in miniature. Tucked in the corner on her immediate right is a neat wood-burning stove, its thin metal chimney extending through the roof. Stacked next to the fire is a small pile of logs. To Tali's left is a bench seat with navy blue cushions, above it a shelf packed with folded maps and books. Alongside this is a brass porthole window.

Further into the boat, she can see a kitchen area, and beyond that a tiny table and more bench seats. Curtains frame the windows, patterned in the same blue material as the cushions.

If she stretched her arms out sideways, Tali could practically touch both walls. Whenever she's tried to picture Jo on her boat, she never imagined something so cute.

Jo says something, and Tali nods absently, her mind drifting as she fantasises about living in this cosy, floating nest.

Jo's touch on her wrist jolts her from her daydream. 'What would you like to drink?' Jo repeats.

'Pardon,' Tali stammers. *Rum, she'd love some rum.* '*Thé, s'il vous plaît.*'

'Coming up.' Jo moves to the galley in the middle of the boat, and sets a copper kettle on the stove. 'You can sit down, you know,' she smiles, cocking her head towards the benches in the bow. As Tali squeezes past, she remembers the wine. 'This is for you.' She meets Jo's eye, and there's something in her river-tinted gaze that sends a tremor through Tali's body.

'My favourite,' Jo says, unwrapping the bottle. 'How did you know?'

Tali can't think of an answer. She'd had no idea whether Jo even drank wine.

'Oh, *très belle,*' Tali says, feigning interest in a little cushion with a bright green duck stitched on it. She can feel her face growing hot, and she flaps the collar of her blouse.

'Bridie made that for me,' Jo says. 'A moving-in present from her and Choppy.'

'Your boat is very ...' Tali dredges her mind for the English word. 'Snug. But where do you sleep?' Jo may be petite, but even she would struggle not to fall off these seats, surely?

'There's a wooden board under the bench here that slots between them to make a big bed,' Jo explains.

'Oh.' Tali's blush deepens, as she pictures herself lying with Jo on the cushions. 'That's clever.'

'Yep.' Jo grins. 'She's got everything I need: fridge, cooker, sink. There's even a loo.' She opens a door behind her, revealing a tiny compartment with a toilet inside.

'I wonder,' Tali muses, as Jo pours tea into two enamel mugs, 'why boats are called "she"?'

'Because they're fickle,' Jo answers without hesitation. 'And it takes a lot of paint to keep them looking good.'

Tali sips her tea, meeting Jo's eye. Was she joking?

'And they need a good mate to handle them,' Jo adds. 'Otherwise they're uncontrollable.'

Tali takes another swallow of tea. A good mate. What did Jo mean? Friend or partner?

'Are you hungry yet?' Jo asks.

Tali is perpetually hungry, and could eat all day if only she didn't put weight on so easily. 'A little,' she fibs.

'I'd better get the toad sausages on, then,' Jo says with an exaggerated wink, making Tali laugh.

Tali eyes the gas oven. It's so small that she doubts Jo could bake a real toad in there. She thinks of Betty and the salad she left for her, hoping she'll eat at least some of it. She's wasting away.

'I can cook extra sausages,' Jo says. 'If you want to take some back for Betty?'

'Are you a *treter*?' Tali gasps. 'Can you read my mind?'

'What's a *treter*?'

'A witch doctor,' Tali explains.

'Oh,' Jo laughs. 'Not to my knowledge. Let me get these bangers on, and then we can go outside. It's a lovely evening.'

Up on the bow deck, Tali spies more logs stacked under a tarpaulin. 'I get a free supply from work,' Jo tells her. 'One of the few perks of being a tree surgeon's slave.'

Tali settles herself in a camping chair, as Jo lights a couple of candles in jars. On a folding table is a package wrapped in brown paper.

'This is for you,' Jo says, handing Tali the package. 'I found it in the second-hand bookshop in town.'

Tali unwraps the paper, revealing a French edition of *Alice in Wonderland*. 'Oh,' she says, surprise and delight robbing her of speech.

'I thought about keeping it for myself,' Jo says, 'to help me learn French. But then I changed my mind. I want you to have it. Perhaps you could read some to me? I love listening to proper French.'

She comes to sit next to Tali, so close that Tali smells her familiar aroma of strawberries and freshly cut wood.

'*Proper* French?' Tali teases, flicking through the book, admiring the black ink illustrations. 'What if I'm fake French?'

'You know what I mean,' Jo says, nudging Tali's shoulder. Her touch sends a flicker of electricity through Tali's body. 'Read to me?'

Tali clears her throat and turns to the first page. '*Chapitre premier*,' she begins, her voice a little husky.

She clears her throat again. '*Au fond du terrier.*' Down the rabbit-hole.

Tali begins to read aloud, self-consciously at first, but soon the story draws her in and she relaxes. By the time she reaches the end of the chapter, the sun is dipping below the treeline, the light leaching from the sky.

'Look,' Jo whispers, pointing out small black shapes flitting over the water. 'Can you see the bats?'

'Bats?' Tali is distracted by Jo's leg, lying warm against her own.

'There, do you see?' Jo leans closer, pointing.

'Ah, *oui.*' *These tiny flakes of ash are bats?*

Tali thinks of the fruit bats on Mauritius, so much bigger than these English dots. She would love to take Jo home to show her.

The temperature drops as the sun sets, and they retreat back into the boat to eat. Afterwards, Tali washes up and Jo lights the wood-burner. They sit together before the fire, Jo's legs tucked up beneath her on the narrow bench seat, Tali trying not to take up too much space. She wishes she could stay here on *Thyme* for ever, but she can't leave Madame Betty alone much longer. She swallows her wine and opens the book again.

'*Chapitre deux. La mare aux larmes,*' she reads. The pool of tears.

'This is where the dodo appears, isn't it?' Jo says.

Tali had forgotten about the dodo.

'I read once that dodos lived on Mauritius,' Jo adds, 'but they became extinct in the nineteenth century. The birds couldn't fly, so were an easy target, and they were all shot dead.'

Tali shudders, as a sudden image of the gun in the suitcase comes into her mind.

'Are you cold?' Jo's gentle voice brings her back. 'I can put more wood on the fire ...'

Tali shakes her head, longing to tell Jo about the gun, confess what she's done, but the words won't come. Jo's hand settles on Tali's arm, her kind face close, and Tali is overcome with the urge to kiss her.

Without thinking, she lets her eyes close and leans forward, and her mouth meets the soft warmth of Jo's lips.

Jo gasps and jerks back. 'What ... what are you doing?'

'Please ...' Tali begins, with no idea what she wants to say.

Jo rises, and they stare at one another for a long, awful moment.

At last, Jo breaks the silence. 'I'm really sorry, Tali ...'

'Please,' Tali stammers again. I didn't mean to do that, she wants to cry. Except she did.

'I've got an early start in the morning ...' Jo says, staring at her boots.

Ice trickles along Tali's spine as she realises Jo is asking her to leave.

Throat dry, Tali mumbles an apology. On numb legs, she manages to climb the few steps up to the deck. Jo doesn't follow her, and Tali is left standing on the dark bank alone.

She waits, but Jo doesn't appear, and a weight settles on Tali's heart as she realises Jo won't, no matter how long she stands here.

On legs that barely support her, Tali stumbles back past the lock-keeper's cottage and across the bridge over the yawning abyss of water. The towpath stretches away into the darkness, the path swathed in shadows. But Tali is oblivious to any danger. All she can think about is the huge error of judgement she's made. Her friendship with Jo has been snuffed out, the brief, hopeful flare of a new relationship extinguished.

How can she have got it so wrong?

She somehow makes it back to Weyside. As she fumbles Betty's front door open and staggers inside, she trips over an obstruction in the hall. It's a large suitcase, an Australian airline sticker wrapped around the handle.

Tali slumps against the wall.

Merde.

As if the evening couldn't get any worse.

Leo Shepherd has arrived.

11

May 1944

The operation was on. Early the following morning, a car arrived to take Elisabeth to the SOE offices in London. There was no chance to say goodbye to the others, only Doris and Officer Stewart were witness to her abrupt departure.

At the car, Doris wrapped Elisabeth in a hug, gripping her shoulders as she released her. 'You take bloody good care of yourself, do you hear me?' Doris's voice cracked.

'You too.' Elisabeth swallowed. 'I'm going to miss you ...' She couldn't finish the sentence. The knowledge that she might never see her friend again brought the sting of tears, and she wiped at her eyes roughly with her sleeve.

'I'll miss you too.' Doris pressed a kiss on Elisabeth's cheek.

'Best of luck,' Stewart said, as she shook Elisabeth's hand. 'You're one of the best agents I've known.'

'Thank you, ma'am.'

It wasn't until Elisabeth was in the car that the relevance of the officer's words hit her: Stewart had used the past tense.

*

As the car approached the suburbs of London, the sky grew overcast and a sooty rain spattered the windows. Elisabeth stared through the glass, shocked anew at the streets of bomb-damaged buildings, roofs blasted open like huge, gaping wounds. The pavements were littered with mounds of smoking rubble, desperate people searching the debris, salvaging what they could. Elisabeth felt a terrible sorrow for their plight. She couldn't imagine how it must feel to have your home smashed to brick dust.

At last, the car reached Orchard Court and the SOE offices, where Elisabeth was met by a dark-suited man, introducing himself simply as 'Park'. He took her suitcase and led her up to a spacious, elegantly furnished room on the third floor.

'Please wait here,' Park said. 'Officer Watkins will be with you shortly.'

Left alone, Elisabeth breathed in the restful silence and tried to relax. The room was painted pale green, with floral brocade curtains swathing the window. Three leather armchairs had been arranged around a low table, and she took the nearest chair facing the door.

Soon, Park returned bearing a tray of refreshments.

'Is there a convenience I could use, please?' Elisabeth asked, as the man set the tray down.

'Indeed, miss.'

Park led her along the corridor to the most opulent bathroom Elisabeth had ever seen. Jet-black glass tiles covered the walls, an onyx toilet sat alongside a matching bidet, and gold taps sparkled on the ornate sink. Elisabeth's shoes sank into the thick pink carpet, and as she dried her hands on a linen towel, she wondered who this luxurious room had been designed for. Visiting dignitaries, perhaps? Certainly not for lowly little agents like her. How Doris would squeal if she saw this! Thinking of her friend, left behind at Beaulieu, made her eyes prickle.

There was no sign of Park when she returned to the room. In his place was a tall, dark-haired woman with a familiar face. The woman was dressed in an officer's uniform, a folder tucked under her arm.

'Lena Watkins,' the woman introduced herself, shaking Elisabeth's hand. 'Welcome to Orchard Court.'

It came to Elisabeth where she'd seen the woman before: Watkins had brought the agent, Jack, to Beaulieu.

'Oh good, Park has made tea,' Watkins said, inviting Elisabeth to take a seat. 'And he's even found some sugar. We *are* honoured.' She gave a brittle laugh and Elisabeth dutifully smiled. Watkins was clearly trying to make her feel at ease, despite the strange, tense situation, and for that Elisabeth was grateful.

'So,' Watkins said, pouring the tea. 'We have a few final tasks to complete before your transferral to the airfield later today.'

Elisabeth's throat tightened; she hadn't realised her mission would begin so soon.

'If there's anything you need,' Watkins said, 'anything at all, you are only to ask.'

Elisabeth took a gulp of tea, feeling like a murderer on the eve of her execution, granted her last wish.

'Firstly,' Watkins said, 'the paperwork.' She pushed the tea things to one side, opened her folder, and took out a French identity card. Affixed inside it was a photograph of Elisabeth.

'A good likeness, I think,' Watkins remarked.

Elisabeth had a sudden flashback to when the photograph was taken at Wanborough, however many weeks ago now. With a flush of guilt, she thought of the other, illicit photo of her and Gilbert, hidden in her skirt pocket.

She scanned the personal details inked on the identity card. 'Elise Ricard,' she read aloud.

'That's your cover name,' Watkins asserted. 'Your field name is Marie. That's what your Resistance colleagues will know you as. And your code name for use in messages to London is Librarian.'

Elise Ricard; Marie; Librarian. Easy enough to remember.

'We've kept your cover story as close to the truth as possible,' Watkins continued. 'As you can see, you were born on the tenth of June 1916, in Péronne.'

They'd made her two years older. And why had they chosen Péronne? She'd never lived there.

'The place suffered damage during the battle of the Somme in July 1916,' Lena Watkins explained. 'A dreadful fire raged through the *mairie*, and all records were lost.'

'Oh, I see. That's convenient.'

'Indeed.'

From her folder, Watkins produced a fake birth certificate, a forged marriage certificate, half a dozen French food ration cards, and a counterfeit travel pass. 'Have a good look at them,' Watkins urged. 'They're yours.'

Elisabeth studied each document closely; the attention to detail was astonishing.

'Our forgery department is the best in the world,' Watkins said. 'We know only too well how one tiny mistake can be all it takes ...' She broke off to sip tea, her eyes never leaving Elisabeth's face.

Elisabeth returned to the marriage certificate that bore her new name and that of a complete stranger.

'Your husband, Edouard, is a prisoner of war in Germany,' Watkins supplied.

Also convenient, Elisabeth thought.

'Do you have a ring?' Watkins asked.

'Pardon?'

'It would be good if you wore a wedding band,' Watkins explained. 'A curtain ring will do, if you have nothing else.'

Elisabeth shook her head.

'Never mind,' Watkins muttered. 'Edouard, *conveniently*, was also born in Péronne. In 1916. You can invent the rest.'

Elisabeth set the marriage certificate back down on the table, her mind racing.

'Now,' Watkins said. 'The mission itself.' She handed Elisabeth a single typed sheet of paper. 'Take your time. Read it carefully.'

You will be parachuted into the North of France, Elisabeth read, *during the present full-moon period.*

A reception committee will be waiting for you. They will ask for your field name: Marie. They will take you to a temporary safe house, where you can stay for one to two days.

You will then find lodgings, and notify London. As soon as possible, you must establish contact with the Lion-trainer circuit in Rouen, using the password we have given you. You will follow the orders of your circuit chief, and those sent by London.

You will be given a micro-camera.

You will be given 20,000 francs to use at your discretion.

You will continue to be paid £300 p.a. as a FANY ensign.

Elisabeth placed the sheet back on the table and looked up at the officer. There was a moment of silence, broken only by the receding clang of a fire engine's bell as it passed along the street far below.

'Do you have any questions?' Lena Watkins said at last, her expression a mixture of concern, empathy and dispassionate professionalism. Like a doctor who'd just bestowed a grim diagnosis, Elisabeth thought.

'It's a lot to take in.' She couldn't believe it was all happening so quickly. 'How do I make contact with the circuit?'

'Le Petit Café, in Rouen, is a letterbox. The *patron* is in contact with the chief of the circuit. He can be trusted.'

'How will he know me?'

'There's a password,' Watkins replied. 'You must ask him: *Y-a t-il une librairie près d'ici?*'

Is there a bookshop near here?

'He will reply: *Oui, juste au coin de la rue.*'

Elisabeth nodded, her mouth dry despite the tea.

Lena Watkins began tidying the documents together. 'I trust that's all clear.' It wasn't a question.

Elisabeth wanted to ask what the emergency plan was, if for instance the café's *patron* didn't respond correctly to the password, but the officer had produced something else from her folder.

'You'll need this,' Watkins said, handing Elisabeth a Minox miniature camera. 'It's ready to use.' The camera was so small it fitted easily into the palm of Elisabeth's hand.

'Guard it with your life,' Watkins said.

Elisabeth could only nod.

With the officer bearing witness, Elisabeth drafted her last will and testament on a single piece of paper. It didn't take long, as she owned few personal effects. In the event of her death, Elisabeth wrote, she would like her War Office salary to be paid to her mother, her only next of kin.

As she scrawled her signature, it occurred to her this might be the last time she ever signed her real name. She couldn't quite hide the tremor in her hand, and when she glanced up she caught Lena Watkins's eye. The woman's shrewd gaze told Elisabeth she knew full well how frightened she really was.

'Cigarette?' Watkins drew a silver cigarette case from her pocket and Elisabeth gratefully accepted a Player's.

'Once you're at the airfield, you'll only be allowed to smoke French cigarettes,' Watkins said. 'Have you smoked French tobacco before?'

Elisabeth shook her head.

'It's harsher than ours,' Watkins warned. 'But even your breath must smell French if you're to pass.'

Elisabeth drew on her cigarette, head swimming as the nicotine hit. 'Do you think I'll be flying tonight?' she asked.

'With luck,' Watkins replied. 'The weather looks to be calm this evening, but as the moon period extends over several days, if you don't fly tonight, you could fly tomorrow or the next day.'

They smoked in silence for a time, and Elisabeth thought of her mother, ignorant of her daughter's imminent departure to enemy-occupied France.

Oh, Maman, what have I done?

But there was no time for regrets. Lena Watkins stubbed out her cigarette, rising to her feet. 'Time presses,' she said. 'Once the tailor's finished with you, we'll leave for the airfield.'

Elisabeth followed Watkins to an office on the floor below, where a diminutive man in a waistcoat measured her for a set of French clothes. As he circled Elisabeth with his tape, Watkins asked after his team of tailors and seamstresses hidden away beneath the police station in Savile Row.

'All hours, they work!' the tailor replied. He jotted Elisabeth's waist measurement on a scrap of paper. 'Night and day, making the suits and the shirts and the dresses, and still they want more!'

'I never realised French clothes were so different,' Elisabeth remarked. The tailor shot her a look of such incredulous disdain, she regretted opening her mouth.

'The seams, the cuffs, the collars,' the tailor ticked each off on his fingers. 'Everything is different.' He sighed. 'Take off your skirt and blouse,' he ordered.

Elisabeth hesitated, looking round for Watkins, but the officer had somehow slipped from the room.

'No time to be shy,' the tailor snapped.

'But I've already picked the laundry marks out,' Elisabeth stammered. She'd also rubbed off the brand name inside her shoes with sandpaper, but she didn't have a chance to tell him that as he was already ushering her behind a screen in the corner.

'Hurry up, please,' the tailor called, as Elisabeth fumbled to remove her clothes. She could hear him rattling metal hangers, searching through the rails of French clothes. A pair of grey slacks and a pale blue blouse were thrust around the side of the screen. 'Put these on.'

From her skirt pocket Elisabeth took out the half-strip of photos taken in the booth in Southampton. Gilbert's face smiled out at her. She tucked the photograph inside her bra, not caring that she was breaking the rules. Just knowing it was there gave her a tiny grain of courage.

Lena Watkins reappeared, just as Elisabeth emerged wearing her new outfit.

Watkins looked her up and down approvingly. 'Good choice for your drop into France,' she said. 'But as soon as possible, pack the trousers away again, and be mindful when you wear them.'

In the room next door, Elisabeth repacked her suitcase with entirely French garments: woollen underclothes, a set of faded burgundy pyjamas, a grey tweed skirt, a spare blouse, a couple of pairs of stockings, a blue silk headscarf and a pair of French-style walking shoes. Amongst the clothes, Elisabeth tucked her powder compact, a tin of French toothpaste, another of shoe polish, a slim notecase containing blank sheets of paper, two pencils, a hairbrush and comb, a housewife sewing kit, and lastly the skeleton key she'd been given in Scotland. Her dagger was strapped to her wrist, concealed in the sleeve of her blouse.

In a separate holdall Watkins added a Michelin map of Normandy, a small torch and spare battery, a basic first-aid kit, a water bottle and a folding spade. These items would all be carried on Elisabeth's body, in the pockets of her flying suit.

'What about my gun?' Elisabeth asked. She'd been issued with her own Colt at Beaulieu, along with several magazines of ammunition.

'Carry it with you tonight,' Watkins advised. 'But once the danger of the actual landing is over, I'd advise you to hide it. Your chances of being searched will far outweigh the risk of having to fight yourself out of a corner. A gun will only betray you, when otherwise you might have a chance of bluffing your way out of trouble.'

The packing complete, Watkins took Elisabeth to another room. Here, three WAAF clerks were busy sorting documents. Identity cards, ration booklets, photographs and letters were spread out on tables around the room. After speaking with one of the WAAFs, Watkins handed Elisabeth a creased photograph of a man in his late twenties, with a dark moustache and kind eyes. 'Your husband, Edouard,' Watkins said.

One of the WAAFs left the room, returning a few minutes later with an envelope.

'Your emergency fund,' Watkins told Elisabeth, handing her a thick wad of francs. 'Don't lose it.'

Elisabeth's palms were beginning to sweat. With each passing minute, her fear was mounting.

'I'll find you a money-belt,' Watkins said. 'Carry as much concealed cash on you as possible; sew it into your coat lining, inside your underwear, everywhere you can think. You might need money at short notice to bribe someone, or fix a bicycle puncture, anything.'

Finally, Watkins took Elisabeth down to a room on the ground floor, where a barber was cutting soldiers' hair. Outside in the corridor, a line of men in uniform were waiting their turn, but Watkins spoke quietly to the barber and he agreed to attend to Elisabeth next.

Afterwards, she studied her new haircut in a hand mirror. The barber had styled and pinned her hair at the front, in the French fashion, and somehow succeeded in transforming her into her mother.

'You look older,' Watkins remarked, as she escorted Elisabeth out.

I *feel* older, Elisabeth wanted to cry.

A station wagon was waiting to take the two women to Tempsford Airfield, near Bedford.

'It's known in the SOE as Gibraltar Farm,' Watkins confided to Elisabeth. 'The buildings and runways are disguised as a cattle farm.'

Dusk was falling by the time the car drew up outside a large cottage near the airfield that served as a base for aircrew and agents. Watkins warned Elisabeth that the place was likely to be busy. 'Several planes will be flying tonight.'

Elisabeth hauled her suitcase and holdall from the boot, and followed the officer into a dim hallway smelling of cigar smoke and fried food.

A man in a peaked cap and a dark blue airman's uniform appeared, greeting Watkins with a warm handshake. 'Back so soon, Lena?'

Elisabeth noted the squadron leader rank slides on the man's sleeves.

'It's been a busy week, Archie.' Lena Watkins smiled wryly. 'I've brought you another bod.'

'So I see.'

As she shook the squadron leader's firm hand, Elisabeth wondered how many other agents Watkins had delivered to him.

'You've brought the good weather again, Lena,' the squadron leader remarked, leading the two women into a room dominated by a large wooden table strewn with maps and charts. A fire was smouldering in the hearth, and on the opposite wall a giant map of France had been tacked up, stuck with red pins. At a desk in the far corner, a man was talking intently into a phone.

'Don't jinx it, Archie,' Watkins chastened.

Elisabeth was shown her impending flight path on a chart, along with a grainy black-and-white photograph of the field where she would be landing in a few short hours. She couldn't help but ask how on earth the pilot was supposed to find such a tiny speck of land in the pitch black of night, from hundreds of feet up in the air?

'He'll use various landmarks, like the rivers, to navigate by,' Watkins reminded her. 'They'll be lit up by the moon.'

'We don't call our pilots the "moon men" for nothing,' the squadron leader said.

Moon men. Was the name meant to sound romantic? To Elisabeth, it only served to illustrate how lunatic this whole endeavour was.

Once the squadron leader had finished briefing Elisabeth, Watkins took her to a supply store where she was issued with half a dozen packets of Gauloises cigarettes, a couple of boxes of matches, and a small tin of emergency rations.

While Watkins went off in search of a money-belt, Elisabeth waited at a corner table in the dining room. An orderly served her a fried egg on toast, and she tried to eat it, but could only manage a few mouthfuls. To her relief, the dozen or so airmen eating and smoking at the neighbouring tables paid her little heed. She tried unsuccessfully to distract herself by reading a battered copy of *Blighty* magazine that someone had left, but the words swam before her eyes.

She glanced at her wristwatch: five minutes to nine.

Watkins returned with a money-belt, and Elisabeth stowed her documents and francs in it, then wrapped it round her waist under her blouse. She accepted a Gauloises from the officer, despite her rising nausea.

'Are you all right?' Watkins asked, her voice low.

Just then, a WAAF appeared with a message from the squadron leader. 'Air Ops in London have called,' the young woman reported. 'The second BBC message went out on schedule.'

The cigarette shook in Elisabeth's hand, ash scattering on the table.

'Relax,' Lena Watkins murmured. 'Everything's proceeding as planned.'

From her tunic pocket, the officer took out a small phial of blue pills. 'Benzedrine,' Watkins explained. 'If you feel completely done in, take one of these. It will keep you going for a couple of hours.'

'Now, this one,' Watkins said, producing a capsule encased in rubber, 'is a wholly different kettle of fish.' The L-pill, as the officer called it, was filled with a lethal dose of potassium cyanide. 'Swallowed whole, it should pass straight through you,' Watkins said. 'But one hard bite, and it will all be over.'

Elisabeth stared at the officer as her words sank in, but already Watkins was pressing something else into her hands: a lipstick holder made of brushed gold.

'We give all our agents something to remind them of home,' Watkins said. 'You can always hock it, if you need money in a hurry.'

'Why are you giving me a lipstick?' Elisabeth couldn't think of anything less useful.

'Open it,' Watkins urged.

Elisabeth did as she was bid, and found the lipstick holder was empty.

'The perfect place to conceal a message ... or something else,' Watkins said. Realisation dawned, and Elisabeth took the L-pill and slipped it into the tube. For a moment, neither woman spoke.

'I have every faith you can do this,' Watkins said at last. 'We wouldn't have chosen you if we didn't think you were capable.'

Elisabeth wanted so much to believe the officer, but she felt swept out of her depth. 'I'm scared,' she confessed.

'I'd be surprised if you weren't,' Lena Watkins replied, her gaze almost tender. She sounded so like Florence, who always instinctively knew where the pain was, that Elisabeth had to bite her cheeks to stop herself sobbing. She took a deep breath, looked up into the officer's discerning eyes. She would *not* cry. She was doing this for Papa, and he would want her to be brave.

*

Shortly before ten o'clock, a truck arrived at the cottage to drive Elisabeth and various other aircrew to the departure hut. The full moon shone down, its pearly light transforming the airfield into a surreal film set.

The truck deposited Elisabeth and Watkins at a corrugated metal Nissen hut. Inside, the air was thick with the smell of burning oil from a stove in the centre. An orderly found Elisabeth a green and brown camouflage flying suit small enough to fit her. He called it a 'striptease suit', as it had a long zip down the front for easy removal. The suit was covered in zipped pockets, and into these Watkins stashed the items from the holdall. Finally, the tiny crystals for Elisabeth's wireless set were wrapped in cloth and tucked in her trouser pocket, where she hoped they would remain intact.

It would be cold in the plane, so Watkins found Elisabeth a pair of leather gloves to wear, then helped her put on a padded helmet, followed by the bulky parachute itself. Trussed up in the straps and buckles, Elisabeth felt as though she were bound in a strait-jacket.

A WAAF knelt at Elisabeth's feet, tightly bandaging each of her ankles to protect them from any impact damage. When she'd finished, Watkins offered Elisabeth a nip from her flask, and rum burned a path to her stomach.

At last, she was ready.

'*Bonne chance*,' Lena Watkins squeezed Elisabeth's hand. 'May God be with you.'

There was nothing more to be said.

*

A Halifax bomber, its bodywork painted matt black, loomed on the tarmac. Elisabeth gaped up at it, unable to believe that this huge plane was solely for her. The pilot was already on board, making his final checks, and it was the dispatcher, a lanky, bright-eyed young warrant officer called Bryant, who helped Elisabeth into the aircraft. As she climbed into the fuselage, she couldn't help but notice the chipped paintwork indicating damage from machine-gun fire.

'Welcome aboard the Lunar Express,' Bryant said with youthful cheeriness. 'Moonlight all the way!'

The windowless plane stank of hot engine oil, and as there were no seats Elisabeth was forced to sit on the floor on an old sleeping bag. With her para-chute pulling on her back, she struggled to find a comfortable position, watching Bryant as he secured the last of the cargo.

To her left came the cooing and rustling of homing pigeons in their little wire cages. Stacked at the rear of the plane, over the bomb bay, were half a dozen large black cylindrical metal containers, each a foot in diameter and six feet in length. They reminded Elisabeth of coffins, but instead of bodies inside, she knew from her lectures at Ringway that they contained all manner of supplies for the Resistance: bicycle-repair kits, torches, batteries and bandages, first-aid kits, soap, boots, water-purifying tablets, blankets, toilet paper, jemmies and wire cutters. Some of the canisters were packed with food: sugar, tea, coffee, tins of sardines, biscuits, powdered egg, jam, oats, chocolate and tobacco; others filled with sabotage equipment, guns and knives. The containers would be dropped before her, most destined for Resistance circuits she would likely never meet.

With her back braced against the wall of the plane, the straps of her parachute digging into her shoulders, she tried to relax. On a signal from the pilot, Bryant sealed up the trapdoor, then turned off the interior light, plunging them into gloom. The engines thundered louder, and Elisabeth sensed the plane start to move, gathering speed along the runway.

Bryant reached behind Elisabeth, attaching a static line to her parachute. The other end of the strap he clipped to an overhead wire. Her life depended on this thin length of webbing, Elisabeth knew. She prayed it wouldn't break.

'Barley sugar?' Bryant bellowed, presenting a sweet on an oily palm.

Elisabeth took it gratefully.

The engines roared, the walls of the plane thrumming as the Halifax rose higher, higher. Elisabeth's ears began to ache and she sucked on the sweet, thinking of the lipstick holder in her pocket.

One hard bite, and it will all be over.

The thick stench of aviation fuel was making her nauseous, and the higher the plane climbed, the colder the air grew. Soon, she couldn't feel her feet. Bryant, she noticed, had turned up the fur collar of his leather flying jacket, but apart from that he didn't seem to be affected by the temperature at all.

Only a short while ago she'd been warm and safe on the ground, surrounded by people she trusted. Now she was on her own, flying into the darkness, soon to be dropped into a country controlled by a ruthless, deadly enemy. All her training seemed suddenly, ridiculously, inadequate.

If she survived the night, it would be a miracle.

An hour passed. They were zigzagging across the Channel, Bryant informed her. Elisabeth thought of the stretch of sea below, both connecting her to home, and at the same time separating her from all she knew and loved.

'Have a kip!' Bryant yelled after a while. Surely rest was impossible, yet she must have dozed, for some indefinable time later she felt a tap on her leg, and opened her eyes to find the dispatcher holding out a flask of coffee.

'Over the Seine now!' Bryant shouted, the roar of the engines almost drowning out his voice. He switched on a little handheld torch, negotiating the boxes and containers, and knelt by the trapdoor. As he lifted the boards away, Elisabeth felt a gust of warm air. Her stomach rolled, bile mixing with the bitter trace of coffee in her mouth. She tried not to look at the trapdoor, concentrating her gaze on Bryant instead as he tightened straps around bundles of paper.

'Leaflets!' he shouted, tossing the bundles, one after the other, through the hole. They disappeared in an instant, sucked out into the ether.

The homing pigeons were next to be expelled. Their compact wire containers made an odd whistling sound as they hit the plane's slipstream.

'Hope some of 'em fly home!' Bryant yelled. 'There's a questionnaire in the box with 'em, but I reckon most of 'em will end up eaten!'

Elisabeth mustered a weak smile.

'Your turn soon!' Bryant gave her a thumbs-up.

It took every ounce of Elisabeth's willpower to drag herself to the trapdoor. She sat on the edge, legs dangling through the hole, wind tugging at her boots. Risking a glance down, she could see a dark swathe of land below, a blur of fields and farms and woodland. Wisps of cloud streamed past beneath her feet, and between feathery ribbons she glimpsed a river twining like a silver snake through the landscape. She was startled to see a parachute float past, followed by another, and another. It took her a moment to realise Bryant had jettisoned the canisters from the bomb bay.

Oh God, that meant she was next.

She tried to summon her courage.

You've trained for this.

Bryant was back next to her, checking Elisabeth's suitcase and the length of webbing that attached it to her harness. The case would drop with her, to be released just before she landed. Her wireless set was packed in a foam- and rubber-lined bag, and would be sent out immediately after her, attached to its own miniature parachute.

The plane abruptly dropped several feet, and Elisabeth's stomach dropped with it. She focused her attention on Bryant's face, eerily lit by the red light on the panel on the wall.

'Nearly there!' Bryant yelled. He was leaning over the hole, searching for the torch lights marking out the landing site, five hundred feet below. The reception committee would flash a prearranged Morse letter, but it was hard to make things out so far up.

Elisabeth began to count in her head, but as each second passed it felt as though her brain was shutting down, and she could think no further than ten. She was barely aware of her hands gripping the straps of her harness, her feet swinging in the void. Warm air from the engines rose through the trapdoor, but she couldn't stop shivering.

Bryant grasped her shoulder. 'Get ready!'

Elisabeth squeezed her eyes shut, heart hammering, every single molecule in her body contracted to this one moment.

She forced her eyes open again. *I'm not ready!* she wanted to scream.

But the red light had winked out, and now the green light shone. As if in slow motion, Bryant's arm was swooping down, the signal for her to jump.

'Go! Go! Go!'

And suddenly she was dropping through the hole, her stomach in her throat, plummeting into the void.

12

May 1944

Wind blasted Elisabeth's body, battering the exposed skin of her face, penetrating the very roots of her teeth. Eyes clenched shut, she braced herself for the impending impact.

Please, let it be over quickly. Let it be painless.

Seconds later, the static line jerked taut with a distinct snap, followed by a muffled crack like a giant sheet flapping on a washing line. The parachute had deployed, arresting her fall, and above her billowed a canopy of lifesaving silk.

Thank you, God, thank you.

She glanced back down at her feet, to find the dark earth surging up at such a speed she had no time to prepare. Crashing to the ground, her right ankle twisted painfully, tearing a curse from her as she was dragged several yards by the parachute. Hauling on the risers, she battled control of the canopy, until at last it deflated like a lung emptied of breath. She collapsed gasping in the mud, the metallic taste of blood in her mouth.

High above her in the night sky, the Halifax dipped its wings once in farewell. The rumble of its engines faded away, and an uncanny silence fell. After hours of constant roar, the hush was deafening.

Blood beat in Elisabeth's ears, and a terrible iciness gripped her. This was not an exercise. There were no longer instructors assessing her every move. Stewart and her clipboard were gone.

She was completely alone. The knowledge made her stomach swoop in terror. All she could think was: *one single misstep and I'm dead.*

Struggling to her knees, she managed to untangle the parachute cords from around her legs and release herself from the harness. Tugging off her leather helmet and gloves, she peered around. The field she had crashed in was bordered on all four sides by thick hedgerows and copses, the landscape bathed in silvery moonlight. Relief washed over her at the sight of her suitcase, lying in the dirt nearby. By some miracle it was intact.

But her precious wireless set, dropped separately in its padded bag, was nowhere to be seen.

Despite studying the map at Tempsford, she couldn't orientate herself at all. There were no landing lights that she could see, no light at all apart from the moon, and yet the pilot must have spotted something, surely?

The starry sky arced above, the Halifax a distant, black speck.

Where the hell was the reception committee she'd been promised?

She fought against the fog of panic and terror threatening to engulf her.

Stay calm. Stay calm.

Gradually, she remembered her training. First task after landing: hide the parachute.

Arms shaking with adrenalin, she started to haul in the chute. The silk material felt unusually heavy, but at last she gathered it all in.

She must bury the lot, and fast.

Using the folding spade, she began scraping at the stony earth at the edge of the field; it felt like she was digging her own shallow grave. A few inches beneath the surface, the ground became stonier and harder to dig, but desperation lent her enough strength to excavate a hole just deep enough to contain the bundled parachute. Working quickly, she covered it over with a loose layer of soil.

Kneeling in the mud, she listened keenly to the noises of the night; some small creature was rustling in the hedgerow behind her, and an owl's distant hoot floated on the breeze. The harness, flying suit and helmet were too bulky to bury, and she was just wondering what the hell she was going to do with them when a waft of cigarette smoke made her stiffen. She caught the low murmur of men's voices coming from beyond the hedges to her right. Holding her breath, she waited; it was all she could think to do.

The voices grew louder. Elisabeth's hand stole to her trouser pocket, fingers gripping the loaded pistol. She strained to make out what language the men were speaking – French or German?

Crouching low, she slid the Colt out, eyes trained on the hedge twenty feet or so away. Suddenly, two shadowy forms appeared through a gap in the foliage. Elisabeth tensed, readying the Colt for the crucial double tap: the first shot to disable, the second to kill. But which man to shoot first? One German she could handle but, faced with more, her chances of escape were slim.

'It came down here,' she heard one of the men say in French. His voice was deep, with a rough smoker's edge.

A match flared in the darkness. 'You'd better be right.' His companion sounded impatient, irritable, and Elisabeth's nerves stretched taut as bowstrings. They might be French, but could she trust them?

If they weren't her reception committee, what were they doing out here in the middle of the French countryside in the dead of night?

The men still hadn't seen her crouched in the narrow moon shadow cast by the hedge, but they were coming closer now and would discover her any second. She made the split decision to take a risk and reveal herself. With the pistol gripped at her side, she cautiously stood up.

At the sight of her, both men froze. The taller of the pair lifted a torch, aiming its beam at Elisabeth's face. She tried to shield her eyes, but the light was blinding.

'Marie?' the taller man said.

Elisabeth exhaled, her fingers relaxing around the gun at her thigh. '*Oui*,' she answered hoarsely.

The torch was lowered, and Elisabeth rubbed her eyes, her night vision slowly returning. The two men were dressed like farmers or workmen, she now saw, in baggy jackets and thick leather boots.

The taller man took a step closer, peering at her. 'We were waiting for you over there.' He jerked a thumb towards the field on the other side of the hedge.

Elisabeth pocketed the Colt, deliberately allowing the men a glimpse of the gun.

'The wind blew me off course,' she replied. She hadn't the energy or the time to explain the vagaries of parachuting to these strangers.

'We've got to move, Raoul,' the second man said.

Raoul grunted and before Elisabeth could react, both men turned away, heading back through the hedge.

'Wait!'

Raoul glanced back at Elisabeth's hissed call.

'I have to find my other case.'

Raoul muttered a curse. After a brief debate, the men agreed to help Elisabeth search the field. Elisabeth's ankle throbbed as she stumbled over the rutted ground, questions crowding her brain: what would she do if she couldn't find the wireless? How could she contact London? How could she ever get home again?

Raoul noticed her limping. 'Are you hurt?'

'No,' she lied. It was only a sprain, she told herself.

At last, the radio set was found caught in the lower branches of a tree some way across the field. The padded bag had split open, but the suitcase inside was intact. Elisabeth offered up a silent prayer of thanks.

She limped back across the field, following the Frenchmen, biting her lip against the pain, the wireless in its case dragging on her arm. Raoul collected her other suitcase and parachute equipment, then led Elisabeth through a gap in the hedge.

In the neighbouring field, a small group of men were hauling one of the canisters dropped from the Halifax towards a nearby copse of trees. Greetings were muttered, but there was no time to talk. Elisabeth worked alongside the men, helping to haul a second canister over to a lorry parked under the trees, trying to ignore her aching ankle. Adrenalin surged through her as she toiled, heightening her senses. The sound of a distant engine made her tense, but the men ignored it, working swiftly, focused entirely on the task at hand. As soon as the canisters were emptied, the food and weapons safely stashed beneath sacks in the back of the lorry, the group bid Raoul and his colleague goodbye, and the lorry rumbled away.

'Come,' Raoul said. He took up Elisabeth's suitcase, but his younger companion made no effort to help her with the bulky wireless case.

She followed the Frenchmen along a narrow track that twisted through a wood. They walked in silence for perhaps half a mile, the moonlight barely penetrating the thick canopy. At last, they reached the boundary of the wood. Beyond the treeline lay a farmstead, the buildings steeped in shadow.

As Elisabeth followed the men across a muddy yard, she tried to gather herself. From now on she was Marie. She must never drop her guard.

They came to a farmhouse, and Elisabeth found herself in a limewashed kitchen lit by oil lamps, an aroma of dried herbs and roasted acorns in the air. Seated at a scrubbed wooden table was a small, middle-aged woman wrapped in a shawl, darning something on her lap. As Raoul ushered Elisabeth forward, the woman set her needle down, rising to her feet, her eyes wary.

'Our bird has landed, Mathilde,' Raoul said as he took off his cap and heavy coat, slinging both on a chair in the corner.

Elisabeth nodded a greeting at the woman, not trusting her voice.

'The girl from the sky,' Mathilde said. 'You must be tired and hungry. Come, sit.'

'*Merci*,' Elisabeth managed.

As Mathilde bustled about the kitchen and the two men smoked, dissecting in rapid French the night's events, Elisabeth took the chance to study the three strangers. Raoul, she guessed, was in his fifties, with the weathered face of someone who spent their life outdoors in all seasons. His colleague, whose name she discovered was Louis, was perhaps a decade younger, with collar-length dark hair, a long nose, and watchful eyes that put her in mind of a wolf.

Mathilde, Raoul's wife, brought a pitcher of water to the table, and noticed Elisabeth rubbing her ankle.

'You're hurt?' the Frenchwoman frowned.

'I'm fine,' Elisabeth lied again. She felt far from fine. 'Just a sprain.'

Mathilde looked unconvinced as she retreated to the stove. 'You were gone a long time,' she said to her husband, as she stirred the coffee.

'It took longer than it should've,' Raoul muttered. He stared at Elisabeth as he rolled another thin cigarette. 'Our lights were in the wrong place, apparently.'

'Am I the first "bird" you've received?' Elisabeth asked, swallowing her irritation. Mathilde poured coffee into bowls and the smell of grilled barley made Elisabeth's stomach growl. To her surprise, the Frenchwoman produced a jug of creamy milk and a loaf of crusty bread.

Raoul broke off a chunk of the loaf with strong brown fingers. 'First female bird,' he replied.

Mathilde wiped her hands on her smock-apron, casting worried glances at Elisabeth, who mustered what she hoped was a reassuring smile. But the fact remained; she was a stranger who'd quite literally blown in from the night.

'Eat,' Mathilde said, pushing a plate of bread and butter towards Elisabeth.

'*Merci, madame.*'

The men helped themselves to more bread and bowls of coffee, and as they ate and drank, Elisabeth learned that Raoul had taken over the farm from his late father-in-law, though he was a railway engineer by profession. He and Louis had both worked as *cheminots*, before the war.

Time passed, and Elisabeth's eyelids grew heavy. Sleep tugged at her, but the Frenchmen wanted to know what was going on across the Channel, and pressed her on news of when the Allies might launch an attack.

'Everyone's working very hard,' Elisabeth replied, stifling a yawn.

'Not hard enough,' Louis said, kicking back his chair with such sudden force that Elisabeth flinched.

'Louis.' Raoul's voice rumbled with warning.

'There are plans,' Elisabeth heard herself say. 'We just have to be patient ...'

'Patient?' Louis seized his jacket and tugged it on. 'I'm done with being patient. The fucking Boche are killing France, and no one's doing anything about it.' He strode to the door.

Elisabeth stared after him, shock rendering her speechless.

Raoul rubbed his brow and sighed.

'Sit down, Louis,' Mathilde said wearily. She appeared unperturbed by his outburst, and Elisabeth wondered if he often lost his temper like this.

Louis ignored Mathilde, wrenching open the door. With a final glance at Elisabeth, he disappeared into the night.

Elisabeth met Raoul's eye. 'We *are* doing something,' she said. 'That's why I'm here.'

*

Mathilde led Elisabeth across the dark courtyard, to a looming, ramshackle barn. Cows were stalled at the far end, the sound of their chewing and belching loud in the silence, a stench of manure in the air.

'I can hide your luggage in the house,' Mathilde offered. Her eyes flashed in the sallow light from her lamp, and Elisabeth wanted so much to trust her.

'It's better they stay with me, *madame*,' she replied. '*Merci*.'

Mathilde handed over the oil lamp and two thick woollen blankets, promising to wake Elisabeth in a few hours. The moon was fading, night leaching away, and soon it would be dawn.

Hauling her suitcases up the rickety ladder into the loft, Elisabeth collapsed on the soft hay. Her ankle throbbed, and she wearily prised off her boots, then unpeeled the muddy bandages. Exhausted, she barely registered the skitter of rats crossing the beams above her head. Concealing the two cases as best she could in the hay, she took her Colt from her pocket and placed it within reach, then extinguished the lamp and wrapped herself in the blankets. Her hand stole to the torn strip of photos tucked inside her bra. Where was Gilbert? Was he thinking of her too?

*

She woke to daylight and for a brief, floundering moment had no idea where she was. She lay still, breathing in the heady smell of hay and cow dung, as everything flooded back: the plane journey, the terrifying jump, Raoul and Louis leading her through the darkness to this place.

Reality hit her, a punch to the gut: she was in Nazi-controlled France.

For so many weeks she'd been hidden away in country mansions with only censored, out-of-date newspapers to keep her informed of what was happening across the Channel.

Now, she was actually here. Alone.

She sat up, alert to the silence, and it dawned on her that the cows must have been let out to pasture. Why hadn't she heard them leave? Berating herself for sleeping too heavily, she massaged her aching ankle. The pain had lessened, but she'd have to be careful on it for a day or two. She quickly changed out of her trousers and pulled on a skirt, slipping on the French-style shoes she'd brought with her. Then she tugged a brush through her hair, and dragged her cases back down the ladder.

She emerged from the barn, squinting in the bright sunshine. The sky was an intense blue, promising a day of warmth to come. Raoul and his wife were in the kitchen, Mathilde frying eggs on the stove, Raoul fixing what looked to be some sort of animal trap on the table. Of Louis, there was no sign.

'You sleep deeply,' Mathilde said by way of greeting, setting a bowl of milky coffee before Elisabeth. 'How is your foot?'

'Still aching a little,' Elisabeth admitted. The coffee's bitterness was tempered only slightly by the milk, but she drank deeply.

'Once you've eaten, I'll drive you into Chounoît,' Raoul said. 'My aunt has a spare room.'

Elisabeth's heart lifted. The prospect of trawling the streets looking for somewhere safe to stay had been preying on her mind. But should she blindly accept this offer?

'We'll tell her I picked you up on the road,' Raoul added. 'You have a story ready?'

'My husband, Edouard, has been a prisoner of war in Germany for a year,' Elisabeth recited. 'I can't bear the stress of life alone any more, so I'm moving nearer to family.' She watched his face closely. Did her story sound plausible?

Raoul nodded his approval.

'Remember to renew your ration cards at the local *mairie* each month,' Mathilde reminded Elisabeth, sliding a plate of eggs in front of her. 'And be careful of Madame Couly next door. We've heard rumours she's a collaborator. Stay out of her way.'

*

Raoul had converted his truck to run on charcoal, he proudly informed Elisabeth. 'The bloody Germans can stick their rationed fuel up their arses.'

The pungent smoke from the engine stung the back of Elisabeth's throat as they chugged their way slowly and noisily away from the farm. The surrounding fields and scattered woodland reminded Elisabeth of the countryside around Guildford. Would she ever see her home again?

The narrow, cobbled streets of Chounoît were largely deserted. Elisabeth glimpsed one or two Nazi flags hanging from windows, and someone had chalked a crude swastika on a wall. The truck rumbled towards a quartet of German soldiers striding along the pavement, sub-machine guns slung over their shoulders, and Elisabeth found herself holding her breath; this was the closest she'd yet come to the enemy, and the proximity of the Germans sent her stomach plunging.

The soldiers stared at the truck as it passed, but to Elisabeth's relief they made no attempt to stop it. Raoul kept his eyes on the road, muttering a curse under his breath. A little further on, he turned down a side street signposted Rue Vincent, and brought the truck to a shuddering halt outside a half-timbered building. It was an ironmonger's; cast-iron pots and cauldrons were piled haphazardly on the pavement.

Elisabeth climbed awkwardly down from the cab, lugging her cases after her. The flying suit, helmet and harness she'd left with Mathilde who'd promised to hide them. She glanced along the empty street, noting signs for a *boucherie*, a *charcuterie* further along, and beyond that a *boulangerie*.

She followed Raoul inside the ironmonger's, and found herself in a large room cluttered with tools and farm implements stacked against the walls, cooking pots hanging from hooks in the ceiling. The place smelled of damp and rust, like a dungeon. Raoul called out a greeting, and eventually an elderly woman dressed in dusty black appeared in a doorway at the rear of the shop.

'*Tante*,' Raoul greeted the woman gruffly. 'How are you?'

'Starving to death,' Madame Blanc replied. 'I hope you brought cheese. I'm wasting away.'

Elisabeth suppressed a smile. Raoul's aunt was built like one of her cauldrons; what she lacked in height she made up for in girth.

'Mathilde sends her love,' Raoul said. He gestured to Elisabeth, hovering behind him. 'I picked up this stray cat on the way here. She's looking for a room.'

Raoul's aunt scrutinised Elisabeth as though inspecting a genuine vagrant.

'*Bonjour, madame,*' Elisabeth said politely.

'You want a room?' the old lady snapped. 'For how long?'

'I'm not sure,' Elisabeth replied. 'My home was bombed, and my husband is a prisoner of war ...' She wiped away non-existent tears with her sleeve, and from the corner of her eye she saw Raoul shrug, as if to say, *poor girl, what could I do?*

'I have money,' Elisabeth added meekly.

The old lady's expression softened, her doughy cheeks dimpling as she smiled. 'You're in luck, child.'

Madame Blanc owned the two-room apartment above her late husband's ironmonger's shop, but she herself lived in the house next door. When Raoul had gone, his aunt led Elisabeth up a dark, narrow stairway at the back of the shop, to the sparsely furnished flat. The main room contained a small table, a couple of chairs, a dresser displaying a few chipped plates and bowls, and a stove in the corner. Flaking green wooden shutters opened on to a wrought-iron balcony overlooking the street, the cramped space filled with pots of drooping herbs.

'The bedroom.' Madame Blanc opened a door, revealing an even smaller room containing a single iron-framed bed, a battered metal trunk, and a wash-stand. A tiny closet opened off the bedroom. 'The flush is temperamental,' Madame Blanc warned.

The rent was considerably above what the place was worth, but Elisabeth pretended to be relieved and grateful, and the widow shuffled back downstairs, happily clutching a month's rent to her bosom.

As Madame Blanc's clumping footsteps faded away, a heavy silence descended. Elisabeth sank down at the table. The scratched surface was covered in a thin layer of ashy dust and she brushed away a dead fly. Solitude had never frightened her in the past. At home she was quite used to her own company, and would spend hours of her free time reading, or walking along the river.

But now she was here, alone in this flat, in an unfamiliar French town, she felt like a prisoner placed in solitary confinement.

She craved a cigarette.

Forcing open the stiff shutters, she stood amongst the pots on the balcony and looked down on the street below. Two boys were kicking a rag ball along the gutter, as an old man with a twisted back hobbled past. Elisabeth lit a Gauloises, trying to think of every-thing she needed to do. Her main priority was to make contact with the Lion-trainer circuit, but first she had to get her bearings.

She drew deeply on her cigarette.

Just take each day as it comes and try not to worry. Papa's voice came to her, and she wiped her eyes on the sleeve of her blouse, stubbing her Gauloises out on the balcony railing. Already, she wanted another one.

But there was work to do.

She needed to hide the wireless as a matter of urgency. There were no cupboards in the flat, no nooks and crannies, only the dresser and the washstand, and they were far too obvious. The only place she could think to put the wireless was in the tiny closet.

In the bedroom, she opened her luggage case and took out the photograph of Edouard, her fictitious husband. The young stranger stared out at her with his unfathomable eyes. Why had Lena Watkins chosen this particular man? A sudden thought sent an unpleasant shudder along Elisabeth's spine: perhaps he was a real prisoner of war?

She would leave the photo on display, in case Raoul's aunt snooped. Something told her she would snoop.

Her clothes and toiletries she left in the suitcase, along with her compass and first-aid kit, Michelin map and writing equipment. The Colt she tucked right at the bottom. She could think of nowhere else to stash the gun, and the risk of it being discovered terrified her.

Then she took the bulk of the francs from her money-belt, stuffed the cash in one of her spare stockings, and attached this to the back of an oil painting of a sunflower field hanging by the door. The gold lipstick holder with its deadly cyanide pill rattling around inside she secreted in her now empty money-belt, along with the miniature camera. Instinct warned her to keep the suicide pill close, like a talisman. As long as she had it to hand, she would never need it.

That done, she remembered she must message London and let them know her status.

Locking the door of the flat, she retrieved the wireless from the closet, pulled the shutters closed, and began the laborious process of preparing the radio set for transmission. As she draped the seventy-foot aerial around the room, hanging it over the picture rail and looping it around the door, she tried to push from her mind everything she'd been told in her training about how the Germans triangulated frequencies, tracking radio transmissions down ruthlessly, terrifyingly, using sophisticated detection systems. Instead, she tried to emulate Gilbert's focus and steady fingers.

Never before had she encrypted, tapped and transmitted a message so fast.

LIBRARIAN TO LONDON
ARRIVED SAFELY

She didn't wait for a response, but hurried to gather up the aerial again, then packed away the wireless.

A wave of tiredness swept through her, yet her wristwatch read barely two o'clock. Eating something might revive her. Mathilde had thoughtfully packed her some bread and cheese, and she ate some of this, saving the rest for breakfast tomorrow. She spent the next few hours studying the Michelin map and planning her movements over the coming days. She would have to quickly familiarise herself with the layout of the town, find out where the nearest railway station was, and where any German roadblocks were situated.

The last of Elisabeth's energy dissolved with the waning sun. In the bedroom, slowly undressing, she caught a glimpse of herself in the cracked mirror above the washstand. Her face was grey with fatigue, and her hair hung lank.

She lay down on the lumpy straw mattress, the precious photo of Gilbert clutched tight. The faded chenille bedspread smelled musky and strange, reminding her how far from home she was.

Despite her exhaustion, sleep was slow to come.

13

2018

Tali creeps along the landing, ears pricked for any sound from Leo's bedroom. The scent of his aftershave lingers, but all is quiet beyond the closed door. Leo must still be sleeping. In the four weeks he's been here, he's rarely emerged from his bedroom before ten in the morning, which is practically lunchtime in Tali's opinion.

Yesterday, when Leo had disappeared out for the evening, Tali had succumbed to the urge to nose around in his room, under the pretext of returning his laundry. There wasn't much to discover. His suitcase contained only clothes, mostly checked shirts and beige chinos, and a laptop in a scuffed holdall. There were no photographs on the bedside table, nothing personal at all except a tatty leather washbag and a small pile of boring-looking *Investors' Chronicle* magazines.

All Tali knows about Leo Shepherd is that he's twice divorced, has no children, and is planning to move back to the UK after fifty years in Brisbane.

From tiny clues Betty's let slip, Tali has pieced together a rough history of Leo's life, though with many gaps. Betty's son had left Guildford for Australia in 1968, at the age of twenty-three, and soon after married the daughter of a sheep farmer. Over the years, the marriage and various farming business endeavours had failed, and Betty has loaned her son thousands of pounds. As far as Tali can make out, Leo has yet to repay a penny.

Everything else about Betty's prodigal son is a mystery to Tali, including his relationship with his mother. Leo treats Weyside like a hotel, coming and going at all hours, expecting Tali to cook his meals. He spends hardly any time with Betty. But most strangely of all, Betty herself behaves as though her son is an unexploded hand grenade.

Tali doesn't trust the hand grenade further than she could throw him. Even Leo's accent is suspect, a whining blend of Australian-British tainted with a note of bitterness that bewilders Tali. Betty and Leo are both hiding something, she's certain. On the rare occasions Leo ensconces himself in the sitting room with Betty for 'private chats', Tali is excluded from the conversation, made to feel like a piece of furniture, a settee perhaps, large and soft and functional, and no more worthy of attention.

This morning, Tali welcomes Leo's tardiness. With luck, he won't surface for hours, leaving her free to concentrate on getting Betty ready for the Century Society later.

As she makes her way downstairs, Tosca at her heels, Tali wonders if Jo will be at the club, and her heart twists at the thought of seeing her again.

She taps on the living-room door and enters Betty's makeshift bedroom, to find Betty sitting up in bed, a book open on her lap.

'Good morning, Madame Betty.' Tali crosses to the window and tugs apart the curtains.

'At last,' Betty replies, closing her novel. 'I was about to send out a search party.'

'Search party?'

'Never mind,' Betty says. 'Close the door, I want you to do something for me.'

'You need the lavatory, Madame Betty?'

'In a minute.' She gestures for Tali to come closer. 'I need you to contact my solicitor,' Betty says, her voice low.

'Solicitor?' Tali frowns.

'To check my appointment still stands for four o'clock.'

'An appointment? On a Saturday?' When had Betty organised this? She's never seen her use the dusty telephone hanging in the hallway.

'Four o'clock,' the old lady repeats firmly.

'But, the Century Society ...'

'The taxi can drop us afterwards.' Betty lifts her chin, a gesture of determination that Tali recognises. 'The solicitor's number is in my address book, in the kitchen drawer.'

'I'll ring them at nine o'clock when they open, Madame Betty,' Tali promises. She moves to the door.

'Natalia.'

'*Oui?*'

'*Ne le dis pas à Leo.*'

Tali shakes her head. There are so many secrets in this house, what was one more?

In the kitchen, Tali roots amongst the detritus in the dresser drawers, finally unearthing a battered little address book. Heartbreakingly, the pages are mostly blank, and Tali quickly locates the solicitor's details under 'S': *Lawson, Mason and Farr Solicitors, High Street, Guildford.*

She tucks the address book in her apron pocket, then sets about preparing a pot of tea and feeding the dog, who is scratching at the back door to be let out. She's just sugared Betty's teacup when she senses a movement in the doorway and turns to find Leo Shepherd in a maroon dressing gown and velvet slippers. His thick mop of grey hair is standing up in dishevelled tufts, and Tali finds herself revising her opinion that it's a wig. He has clearly just crawled out of bed.

'G'morning,' Leo yawns.

Tali mumbles a greeting, too thrown by his unexpected appearance to think clearly. 'You want some tea, Monsieur Shepherd?' she manages. 'I made a pot.'

'Coffee,' he replies. 'And some toast. When you're ready.' He turns away and wanders off into the sitting room.

'*Connard,*' Tali curses him under her breath. Did he think she was his personal servant?

Pouring Betty's tea, a sudden thought strikes her: what if Leo insists on coming with them to the Century Society this afternoon?

'Is Leo up?' Betty asks when Tali returns with her breakfast tray.

'*Oui*. I will make him coffee, then phone the solicitor.'

'He can make his own coffee, Natalia.'

'It's OK,' Tali fibs, smoothing the sheets at the foot of the bed.

Betty beckons Tali closer. 'Has he said anything to you?'

Tali hesitates. 'About what?'

'About me.'

Tali gives a quick shake of her head. '*Non*.'

Betty sniffs, takes a sip of her tea. 'You haven't told him about the Century Society, have you, Natalia? He won't want to come. He was never one for group activities, even as a child.'

Tali takes a mug of coffee and a plate of buttered toast through to the sitting room, to find Leo rooting through the contents of the sideboard.

'Where are the batteries?' he blusters. 'My bloody shaver's packed up.'

He's lying, Tali knows. 'I don't think there are batteries in there,' she says. She sets the mug and plate on the table, smiling wryly to herself as Leo gives up his charade of searching for batteries and sits down.

'Is my mother decent?' Leo takes a slurp of coffee and grimaces. 'No sugar ...'

'Decent?'

'Dressed,' he snaps.

'Not yet.'

'Right, well, tell her I'm going out this morning.'

'You are back for lunch?'

'Doubt it.' He flaps a hand vaguely, scattering toast crumbs on the carpet. 'Dinner time, I expect.'

Don't hurry back, Tali thinks, as she returns to the kitchen.

The prospect of seeing Jo at the Century Society that afternoon fills Tali with a mixture of longing and dread. She can't settle to any task, so decides to walk the dog around the cemetery. Perhaps the fresh air and sunshine will calm her nerves.

The graveyard is deserted, so Tali lets Tosca off his lead. The dog loiters behind her, sniffing sun-bleached plastic flowers and weather-worn grave offerings, while Tali peers at headstones. The names and dates inscribed on some of the older, lichen-furred stones are practically impossible to read. On previous dog walks she's kept to the main path, but this morning she finds herself drawn to the more overgrown corner of the cemetery.

She follows a moss-slick path that winds beneath looming boughs of ancient yew trees, reading the names etched on random crumbling headstones. *Mabel White*, *Arthur Johnson*, *Alice Wickham*. The names are so quaintly English, like the characters in Betty's novels. Scattered amongst the graves are creepy stone angels, some small as dolls, others life-size, their unseeing eyes tracking Tali as she passes.

She's making her way back when she spots Tosca nosing around a gravestone set a few paces from the path, its base choked with ivy.

'Come on, *tou tou*,' she calls. But the dog ignores her. She moves towards him to attach the lead, and that's when she sees the inscription:

Frederick Shepherd 1916–1988
Beloved husband and father
Farewell

Tali gasps. Is this Betty's late husband's grave? It's a little unnerving to discover he died the same year she was born.

She kneels in the muddy grass next to the headstone and tries to pull some of the foliage away. But it's too tough and she hasn't any gloves or cutters, and she soon gives up. She'll come back another time with some secateurs and a trowel and tidy the grave up a bit. Then maybe she could bring Madame Betty to visit?

Back at the house, she's relieved to find that Leo has gone out. Betty is napping in her armchair, the cryptic crossword partially completed on her lap. It's not quite time for lunch, so Tali decides to tidy Betty's bedroom upstairs. As soon as Betty can manage the stairs, she will want to return to her room.

Tosca follows Tali up, lying in the bedroom doorway with his head on his paws. Tali is grateful for the dog's company. The disconcerting scent of Leo's aftershave permeates the air up here, as though he's lurking somewhere close by, and it puts her on edge.

Betty's bedroom still smells faintly and reassuringly of her: a blend of Chanel No. 5 perfume and lavender talcum powder. Tali scans the room. The bed needs remaking, the carpet needs a hoover, and the antique dressing table could do with a tidy. Its three spotted mirrors reflect Tali in triplicate, and she grimaces at the heft of her hips, the bulge of her waist. She sucks in her belly, but can't hold her breath for more than a few seconds, and lets it all sag again.

She picks up Betty's silver-backed hairbrush, its soft bristles tangled with fine white hairs. Next to the brush is a powder compact, and an expensive-looking gold lipstick Tali's never seen before. She'll take them down to Betty; she'll want to be presentable for the club.

*

The taxi drops them outside the community centre, and Tali instructs the driver to return at half past three. She helps Betty into her wheelchair, taking deep breaths in a vain effort to suppress her anxiety. If Jo is here, how will she react?

'What's the matter?' Betty asks, sharp blue eyes missing nothing. 'What's the panic?'

'*Je vais bien,*' Tali lies, wheeling Betty inside.

The members of the Century Society are all at work on their projects, and Tali immediately spots Jo helping Violet with her box, but she doesn't look up.

'Ah, Betty, you made it,' Abeo greets them. 'Come, there is space here next to Margaret.'

Juliana, Margaret's assistant, is daubing pungent varnish all over the lid of Margaret's unadorned box. Margaret herself appears to be dozing in her wheelchair.

'She had a bad night,' Juliana whispers to Tali. 'No sleep.' Juliana looks exhausted herself, wan-faced and baggy-eyed, but she smiles cheerfully as she downs her brush and helps Betty settle at the table.

Tali glances across to Jo, busy cutting a photograph from a magazine. Jo looks up, her cheeks flushing as her eyes meet Tali's.

'Hello,' Tali ventures. 'How are you?'

'I'm fine, thank you,' Jo says, running a hand through her tousled hair. She lowers her head again, and Tali's heart slumps.

'I've been published,' Alfred announces, thrusting a newspaper clipping in Tali's face.

Dear Sirs, Tali reads. *I would like to voice my objection to the constant denigration of immigrants. The care industry in this country relies on those so-called 'foreigners' and life would grind to a halt without them.*

'Fat lot of good writing to a paper'll do,' Duncan mutters. Sprawled across two chairs, he stares at his phone, thumbs tapping the screen. Tali wants to smack the mobile out of his fat hands and tell him to help Alfred with his box instead.

'I think it's a wonderful thing you have done, Alfred,' Abeo says.

Tali agrees, passing the clipping back. Alfred carefully tucks it away in an inside pocket of his tweed jacket.

Tali can't stop casting furtive glances at Jo. She is still cutting pictures out, concentrating so hard that the tip of her tongue peeks between her lips. Spare and compact, Jo is the polar opposite of tall, graceful, beautiful Zezette, and yet there's something so honest, so earnest about her, it draws Tali like a bee to nectar.

With an effort of will, she forces her attention back to Betty.

'Have you thought any more about what you want on your box, Madame Betty?'

'Isn't the river enough?' Betty replies.

'The river here is beautiful,' Hilda says. 'Jo lives on the river, did you know?'

Tali stiffens.

'What's your boat's name again?' Hilda calls out to Jo.

'*Thyme*,' Jo replies, studiously avoiding Tali's eye.

'*Thyme*,' Hilda echoes, nudging Tali's arm. 'Lovely name, don't you think?'

Tali forces a smile to her lips. Margaret jerks awake with a muted cry, and Juliana fusses around her, adjusting blankets, talking to her all the while. Margaret gives no indication that she understands her carer. Tali notices Betty staring at her, a strange expression on the old woman's face.

'Madame Margaret won a medal in the war,' Tali tells Betty. 'Do you have anything from the war for your box?'

'No damn medal, that's for sure,' Betty snaps. 'I told them where to stick it.'

'What?' Tali is momentarily taken aback by this disclosure. 'You had a medal?' She is about to ask more when Duncan interrupts.

'What'll you put in yours, Tali?'

'My what?' she stammers.

'Your box. What shit'll you put in it?'

'I-I don't know,' Tali admits. It hasn't occurred to her to make her own box.

Duncan brandishes his mobile. 'I'd put my phone in mine,' he says. 'Then make sure I'm buried with it.'

Hilda straightens up from varnishing Elvis Presley's quiff, her spine audibly cracking. 'What are you talking about?' She glares at Duncan. 'You can't be buried with your phone.'

'Why not? If I'm not dead, I can call my mates. Tell 'em to come and dig me out.'

'I've never heard anything so ridiculous, young man.'

'A conch shell,' Tali replies swiftly. 'To remind me of home.'

Duncan regards her for a moment, as if reassessing her. 'D'you miss the place?'

Tali nods.

Every day.

But she can't go back. If she returns to Mauritius, she'll be forced to marry Noa, and end up living a lie. The knowledge that she can't go home, not for a very long time, makes her eyes burn. She turns back to Betty, hoping no one has noticed her tears.

*

The taxi driver is true to his word, and returns to collect Tali and Betty at half past three. He drops them in town, outside the solicitors' office, and Tali asks him to pick them up again in an hour.

'Leo mustn't know about this,' Betty tells Tali, as they wait in the reception area for the solicitor, Mr Mason, to appear. 'He'll find out soon enough.'

'Find out what, Madame Betty?' Tali doesn't like the sound of this at all.

Betty is staring at a corner of the ceiling, and Tali follows her gaze. There's a damp patch shaped like a large brown banana. 'Seventy-five years, you'd think they'd have painted over it,' Betty mutters.

'Find out what?' Tali asks again.

But now the solicitor has arrived. 'Mrs Shepherd, how are you? It's been a while since we last saw you ...'

Requesting two teas from the receptionist, Mr Mason wheels Betty away to his office.

Left alone, Tali checks her mobile. No messages. For a second, she contemplates texting Jo. But what could she say?

*

To Tali's relief, there's no sign of Leo when they finally arrive back at Weyside. She hopes he stays away until she's gone to bed, then she won't have to lie to his face about where she's been with his mother today.

She clears away the dinner things, and helps Betty settle in her armchair for the evening. The day has been sunny, but now the temperature is dropping, and the creaking radiators barely warm the cold air. Tali switches on the gas fire, then fetches Betty's woollen blanket from her bedroom. She finds herself wondering what Leo had been searching for when she'd caught him nosing in the sideboard earlier. If, as Tali suspects, Leo was looking for his mother's financial paperwork, he won't find anything in there.

A thought strikes her: should she tell him about the suitcase from the cellar?

'I know I shouldn't say this, but it's nice to have the house to ourselves again,' Betty sighs, as Tali tucks the blanket over her legs. 'You look after me so well. You're a good girl, Natalia.'

Tali doesn't know how to respond to this surprise compliment; it's perhaps the kindest thing Betty has ever said to her, even if it isn't true. After the incident with the gun, and the awful fuck-up she's made with Jo, not to mention the dark suspicions she's having regarding Leo Shepherd's intentions, Tali certainly doesn't feel like a good girl at all.

She sinks down on to the settee, staring at the hideous gas fire with its fake plastic logs and feeble flames. Tosca stretches out on the hearth rug and begins to snore.

'Thank you for being my friend,' Betty says. 'When you get to my ancient age, trusted friends are hard to come by.'

'Oh, Madame Betty.' Tali's heart twists.

'Old age is the loneliest place on earth,' Betty sighs. 'Not only have I lost my beloved family – Maman, Papa, Freddie – but over the years I've lost all my friends as well.'

Tali shakes her head miserably, thinking of Zezette, and her family, and Jo. All lost too.

'I can't picture most of their faces any more, or hear their voices,' Betty goes on sadly. 'Nobody is left who knew me when I was young. People only see me as

I am now, ready for the scrapheap.' Her eyes glisten and she fumbles a crumpled hankie from her sleeve to wipe them.

'You have me,' Tali says. 'And your friends at the club.'

The clock on the mantelpiece ticks in the silence. A thought strikes Tali.

'Madame Betty?'

'Mm?' Betty's eyes are closed.

'How do you know Madame Margaret?'

'Who?'

'Margaret Stewart. At the club. You said you knew her.'

'In another life.'

'Another life?' Tali probes gently.

No response.

Betty's eyes remain closed, and after a while Tali wonders if she's dropped off. It's been a busy, tiring day after all.

'Madame Betty?' Tali speaks softly, and Betty's eyes snap open. She shifts in the armchair, dislodging the blanket, which slips from her knees. Tali scoops it up and tucks it back around Betty's thin legs.

'Margaret Stewart and I go back a long way,' Betty says at last. 'I knew her in the war. She was my conducting officer.'

What's that? Tali wants to know.

'She helped me,' Betty replies, 'when I was going through a very challenging time.'

'If she helped you, why don't you talk to her at the club?'

'There's no point,' Betty sighs. 'She's clearly lost her marbles.'

It takes Tali a second to work out Betty's meaning. 'She might still welcome a friendly chat, Madame Betty.'

'Oh Natalia.' Betty gives a mirthless laugh. 'Margaret Stewart was never the chatting sort.'

Tali wants to ask what Betty means by this, but the old woman is talking on.

'Do you want to know the truth?'

Tali finds herself nodding slowly.

'History paints war in a certain light,' Betty says. 'But the truth is not as romantic as people like to believe.'

Tali has a sudden mental image of the gun lying at the bottom of the river. What secrets was Madame Betty keeping?

'You should tell people the truth,' Tali says quietly.

'Sometimes the truth isn't what they want to hear, Natalia.'

Tali can't argue with that.

*

Leo Shepherd returns to Weyside eventually, as Tali knew he would. Betty has long since gone to bed, and Tali is letting Tosca out into the garden for his final wee of the night, when she hears the scrape of a key in the front door. Leo appears in the kitchen doorway, bringing with him a faint waft of stale beer.

'Thought we could have a little chat,' he says, plucking an apple from the fruit bowl on the counter and biting into it.

'A chat?' Tali tries to keep her voice even, but her heart is thud, thud, thudding.

'Yeah,' Leo says through a mouthful of fruit.

'Now?'

'If you don't mind.'

She does mind, of course she bloody minds, but she follows him through to the sitting room.

'Bit of privacy,' Leo says, closing the door, sealing them in. He sinks down in Betty's armchair, and Tali perches on the edge of the settee, hands clenched in her lap.

'I saw my solicitor today,' Leo announces, tossing the apple core down on a folded newspaper by his feet.

Tali stares at him. Of all the things to come out of his mouth, she was least expecting this.

'I'm applying for Power of Attorney,' Leo goes on. 'Do you know what that is?'

Does he think she's an idiot? She gives a terse nod.

'I'm worried Mother's mind is going,' Leo says. 'You know what she's like, she's very forgetful. I don't know how you stay so patient with her sometimes.' He rises and rummages in the bureau, emerging with a half-bottle of whisky and two dusty tumblers. 'Drink?'

Tali would love nothing more. 'No, thank you.'

'We have to be prepared for things to get worse,' Leo sighs. He pours a finger of whisky and downs it.

Tali thinks she knows what he's trying to do, pretending they're in this together. He wants to get her onside.

Her heart slows to a steady tick. 'Madame Betty is OK—'

'She needs to move somewhere much smaller,' Leo interrupts, as if Tali hasn't spoken, 'with no stairs, and no garden to worry about.'

Tali stares at Leo as his words sink in. 'But this is her home ...'

'Home is a relative term,' Leo replies, pouring himself another measure of whisky. 'Mother can't manage the stairs and, more to the point, she doesn't need such a big house.'

Before Tali can think about how to respond, he continues. 'So I've made enquiries, and there's a brand-new care home just been built, near the hospital. Oak Manor. Heard of it?'

Tali can only shake her head.

'Residents buy their own room, and they pay for care on top of that, as they need it. Or not, as the case may be. There's a little communal garden, and a residents' lounge, and they organise regular outings all over the place. Honestly, I'm tempted to move in myself.'

'Aren't you going home?' Tali stammers. 'Back to Australia?'

Leo makes a strange snorting noise. 'I'm staying here for the time being, although actually it's none of your business.'

'But Madame Betty is happy at Weyside,' Tali blurts. 'She's lived by the river all her life ...'

'Mother will be happy at Oak Manor, too. She'll be surrounded by other oldies, in her element, playing bingo and all that guff that old folks love.'

Do you know your mother at all? Tali wants to scream at him.

'But for things to move quickly and smoothly, I need Power of Attorney,' Leo concludes. He fixes Tali with a look that chills her blood. 'And once that's done, you can go too.'

14

May 1944

Early the next morning, before Raoul's aunt had opened her shop, Elisabeth quietly slipped down the back stairs and out into the street. She wasn't early enough. A queue had already formed at the bakery, and she joined the straggling end of it, keeping her scarfed head lowered. Her ankle still ached, but she'd dosed herself with enough aspirin not to limp.

Her forged ration card stated she was entitled to ten ounces of bread a day, but judging from the famished faces of the people around her, Elisabeth doubted anyone received their full quota. She was surrounded by grey-faced housewives, a few skinny children clinging to their mothers' aprons, and a handful of rheumy-eyed elderly men and women. No one spoke to her, but she sensed one or two glances flitting in her direction.

Gradually, the line edged forwards, but when at last Elisabeth crossed the bakery threshold and stood before the counter, there was no bread left.

'Fresh batch at ten,' the baker said.

There was only week-old tripe on offer at the *charcuterie*. At the grocer's along the street, the fare was no better, baskets half full of potatoes soft with mould, and a few mangy cabbages. She bought as much as her ration card allowed anyway, deciding to make soup.

She was back at the *boulangerie* in good time, only to be told that the new batch of loaves had already been sold.

Returning to the flat, she tried to distract her dark thoughts by preparing the soup. She could hear Raoul's aunt clattering about in the shop below, and prayed the old woman wouldn't come up to see how she was settling in. She needed time to gather herself, in private, for the terrifying days ahead.

*

The following day was warm and sunny, and Elisabeth decided to explore a little of the countryside around Chounoît, scouting for potential drop sites she could tell London about. Tomorrow she would attempt the journey to Rouen, and locate the letterbox café.

She packed her money-belt with extra francs, her forged identity card and the Michelin map, then secured her sleeve dagger, filled her flask with water, and wrapped some bread and cheese to eat later.

As she descended the back stairs, she could hear Raoul's aunt talking to a customer. Escaping their notice, Elisabeth slipped out into the junk-filled yard behind the shop. Her eyes fell immediately on a man's bicycle propped up against the rear wall.

What were the chances?

She gave the bike a brief inspection: the frame was rusty in places, the chain in need of oiling, but the tyres felt firm. All at once, something made the hairs on the back of her neck prickle. She turned to find an older, heavyset woman dressed in a grey pinafore, a full basket of washing resting on her wide hip, staring at her from the neighbouring yard. Elisabeth dipped her head in greeting, but the woman ignored her as she set the basket on the ground and began to peg sheets on a line.

Was this Madame Couly, the collaborator Mathilde had warned her about?

Unnerved, Elisabeth turned her attention back to the bicycle. Would Raoul's aunt mind if she borrowed it for a few hours? It didn't look as though it had been ridden in a while. There was a little wicker basket looped over the front handles, and into this she placed her flask of water and the food parcel. She wheeled the bike through the gate, out into the cobbled alleyway that ran behind the shop. At the end of the alley, she mounted the bike and pushed off, wobbling precariously along the street until she found her balance. She could barely reach the pedals. The brakes squealed, but worked well enough if she didn't go fast.

Studying the Michelin map earlier had given her a rough mental picture of Chounoît and the surrounding area. She biked in a north-easterly direction out of the town, passing a couple of weary-looking women carrying bundles of wood on their bent backs, who paid her no heed. To her relief, she encountered no Germans, and was soon out in the countryside.

As she cycled along, she scanned the verges blooming with wild flowers. She thought of the field-craft instructor at Arisaig who had taught her which fungi and plants were safe to eat, and which weren't. An invaluable lesson to which she wished now she'd paid more attention.

After a couple of hours, having explored as far as she dared, the bicycle's basket full of sticks for the stove, she turned back towards town. She didn't notice the roadblock up ahead until it was too late.

Two German soldiers dressed in the grey-brown uniform of the Wehrmacht and brandishing sub-machine guns were guarding a makeshift barrier. There was no time for Elisabeth to back-pedal, no time to abandon the bike and escape into the nearby trees; the soldiers had already spotted her.

'Halt!'

Elisabeth slowly dismounted and wheeled the bicycle the last few yards.

'*Papiers, mademoiselle.*'

Both soldiers were young, barely in their twenties, yet they loomed over Elisabeth, bull mastiffs in their uniforms.

She fumbled in her money-belt for her false identity card, her hand trembling as she passed it over. She could feel the strap of the dagger cinched tight around her sweating wrist. If the soldiers decided to search her … She cut the thought off, staring down at her dusty shoes, trying to emulate a poor housewife, out foraging. If she acted meek and defenceless, perhaps they would take pity on her.

Instinctively, her eyes picked out a large stone on the ground to her right, a smaller rock to her left. But even if she could reach them, she had little hope of overcoming two armed soldiers.

Her heart was beating painfully hard and fast. If these Germans should decide to check her pulse rate as well as her papers, they would surely arrest her.

Stand firm. Stay calm.

'Name?' The soldier's rough French was barely intelligible.

'Elise Ricard.'

'Repeat.'

'Elise Ricard.'

'Address?'

For the space of a heartbeat, her mind blanked. She had no idea what street Raoul's aunt's flat was on.

'Ch-Chounoît,' she stammered, and somehow, by uttering the town's name, her memory unlocked. 'Rue Vincent.'

'You are married?'

Elisabeth stiffened. What concern was it of theirs if she was married or not? *'Oui.* But my husband is away ... working in Germany.'

The soldier who had spoken was staring at her. His colleague sneered, picking at something in his ear.

Every fibre of Elisabeth's being was screaming at her to run, but one tiny rational part of her brain held firm. If she tried to escape, the soldiers would simply shoot her. She could smell the oniony tang of their sweat.

Suddenly, the soldier thrust Elisabeth's identity card back at her. 'You will come with me.'

'P-pardon?'

'Move!' He wrested the bicycle from her grasp and flung it to the ground, sticks scattering over the road.

'Move!' The soldier raised his gun, levelling the barrel at Elisabeth's chest, and fear gripped the back of her knees as the truth hit her: if she didn't act quickly, she would die.

The soldier dragged Elisabeth into the woods to a small clearing, far enough from the road that she knew no one would hear her scream.

'Down!' The soldier twisted Elisabeth's arm behind her back, wrenching with such force she cried out. 'Down!' The guard's sour breath was hot against her cheek.

He wanted her on the ground.

Never go to ground.

She tried to pull her arm free, but the soldier held her fast, forcing her to her knees. '*S'il vous plaît,*' she gasped. 'You're hurting me ...' Sharp stones and twigs dug into the scant flesh of her knees.

'*Ich könnte dich jetzt töten.*' The soldier's words needed no translation. He could kill her now.

She whimpered as the soldier twisted her arm higher up her back, shoulder bones grinding painfully. Her head was close to the ground now, hair hanging loose in her eyes, beetles and forest insects crawling inches from her face. The sleeve dagger on her wrist was useless, as she suddenly felt the cold press of a gun barrel against the back of her neck.

Elisabeth stiffened, barely breathing.

Her mind emptied, and her limbs grew numb.

'Schmitz!'

A shout came through the trees, from the direction of the road. Elisabeth felt the gun shift on her neck.

'Schmitz! *Komm her!*' the guard's colleague yelled again.

'*Verdammt!*' The soldier spat a curse, and hauled Elisabeth round to face him. He pointed his gun at her head. '*Beweg dich nicht!*'

His meaning was clear: *don't move.*

The soldier loped away, disappearing through the trees.

Elisabeth collapsed, gasping. Precious seconds ticked by as she slowly dragged herself to her feet. Numb with terror, she began to stumble through the trees, along a faint deer track that led in what she prayed was the opposite direction to the roadblock. All she could think of was to get away.

An hour later, Elisabeth had eventually made it back to Chounoît and the flat. She'd missed her afternoon 'sked', the prearranged time London expected her to transmit a message, but there was nothing she could do about that. Bolting the door behind her, she sagged against the wood. Without warning, her guts roiled, and she rushed to the closet, retching over the bowl. Clammy sweat beaded her brow and she wiped it away with a shaking hand.

In the bedroom, she took stock of herself; her hair was dishevelled, all her hairpins lost, her skirt was stained with mud, and her blouse was ripped along one seam. But her money-belt was intact, thank God. And she still had her dagger.

Too shaken to undress, she lay on the bed fully clothed, the attack replaying itself in her mind, fragments of images spooling like a film on a loop. She'd come so close to being killed, and yet the fact she'd escaped did nothing to soothe her deep-rooted fear.

*

The following morning she woke early, mouth parched, her tongue a strip of cured leather. Soft sunlight filtered through the window shutters, caressing her face, and for a minute or so all was calm. But as she rose stiffly from the bed, memories of the attack assailed her, and her knees buckled, forcing her to sit back down. She sucked in a deep breath, then another, feeling again the sharp press of the soldier's gun against the back of her neck. How had she survived?

After a while, she felt strong enough to stand. She drank a few mouthfuls of brackish water from the jug, nibbled stale bread and cheese. There was precious little else to eat.

To stifle her hunger pangs, and quell the tremor in her hands, she lit a precious Gauloises. She would have to leave the flat soon to find some food, though the prospect of venturing outside terrified her. The flat was by no means safe, but it was still an island of sanctuary in a hostile sea.

The attack had left her horribly shaken, but now she realised something worse: she no longer trusted herself. Despite all her training, she'd committed the gravest of sins yesterday by bicycling blindly into a roadblock. Hadn't all her instructors warned of the importance of staying alert?

She knew full well that making the smallest of mistakes – accidentally thanking a shopkeeper in English, or asking for milk in a café, or smoking in public – could prove deadly.

But being constantly alert was exhausting. From the moment she left the flat she must be wary not only of the German soldiers, armed and ready to shoot, but she must also avoid being arrested by the patrolling French Milice, the militia, and even worse, the Gestapo, who preyed on resisters and agents and anyone who stepped out of line. And, of course, she must not forget the most dangerous enemy of all, the countless collaborators, like Madame Couly next door, hidden in plain sight.

Everyone was watching everyone.

She lit another cigarette, opening the shutters a crack, looking down on the first stirrings of life in the street below. Two German officers strode past the shop, and Elisabeth shivered despite the sun's early warmth; the sinister clip of the officers' boots on the cobbles would haunt her dreams.

Drawing back into the shadows, she smoked the Gauloises down to a stub. There was no avoiding it, she would have to leave the flat to find food. But what if she ran into her landlady? How would she explain the lost bicycle to her? Elisabeth stubbed out her cigarette. Her need for food was greater than her fear of Raoul's aunt.

Hanging on a hook behind the bedroom door was a crocheted shopping bag, and under the sink she found an empty wine bottle. Tying her headscarf tight, she pulled on her coat and made her way down to the back yard.

There was no sign of the landlady, but in the yard next door Madame Couly was pegging out washing. Elisabeth had exchanged no words with her, and yet there was something about the way Madame Couly's eyes tracked her that was deeply unnerving.

Trust no one.

Elisabeth escaped through the gate, heading for the *boulangerie* first, hoping the shelves hadn't been stripped bare yet; she was so hungry, she'd buy any loaf, however stale.

The queue outside the bakery was depressingly long, and Elisabeth took her place at the end of the line, eyeing the downcast, hungry, enduring citizens of Chounoît around her. The only healthy, well-fed figures she'd seen here were the Germans. The queue crept forward, and Elisabeth's thoughts turned to her mother. What was she doing right now? Was she missing her, wondering why her only daughter hadn't been in contact for days?

Reaching the counter at last, she was met with the stomach-plunging sight of empty shelves. Yet again, she was too late. Her belly ached as she turned to leave, but at the door the baker called her back.

'Luck smiles on you today, *mademoiselle*,' he said. 'I have one loaf left.' He reached beneath the counter and handed her a small baguette.

'*Merci*,' she managed. The bread was still warm.

The baker's words echoed in Elisabeth's head as she left the shop. Luck was arbitrary and unreliable and random. When would hers run out?

*

For the next two days, Elisabeth kept mostly to the flat, her nerves gradually recovering. But time was swiftly passing, and she knew she must make contact with the Lion-trainer circuit soon. The city of Rouen was roughly forty kilometres south-east of Chounoît, which meant she'd have to take the train, even though travelling by rail brought so many risks and dangers.

The next morning she prepared to make the journey. She considered taking her gun with her, until she remembered what Lena Watkins had said. It was better not to carry one, for if she was stopped and searched, its presence could not be explained away. She'd arm herself with the sleeve dagger instead.

The question of whether she should take the wireless was more problematic. It was a risk to leave it in the flat, but if she took it with her and was caught in a spot check, she would doubtless be arrested and imprisoned.

She agonised for a long time, finally deciding to leave the wireless behind. She'd set a trap, though, in case the landlady came prowling while she was out. Raoul's aunt may or may not know what her nephew was involved in, but Elisabeth was taking no chances. Remembering Mr Smith's advice, she locked the door of the flat, then carefully inserted a fragment of folded leaf snipped from the stunted bay tree on the balcony into the keyhole. If anyone tried to unlock the door they would dislodge the leaf, alerting her to the break-in. She hid the door key itself in a gap between the floorboards and the skirting board.

Down in the yard, she glanced over the neighbouring wall, relieved not to see Madame Couly. But as she unlatched the gate, a familiar voice made her spin round; Raoul's aunt was shuffling wheezily across the yard towards her.

'Glad I caught you, girl.'

Elisabeth pasted an innocent smile on her face. 'Good morning, *madame.*'

'My husband's bicycle, it's missing.' The old woman's shrewd eyes held Elisabeth's.

'His bicycle?' Elisabeth made a pretence of gazing around the yard. 'I may have seen it here, but ...'

'So you didn't take it?'

Elisabeth shook her head. 'I never learned to ride properly,' she said. The best lie is a half truth.

Raoul's aunt frowned. 'It was here the other day, and now it's gone.' The accusation was clear.

'I'll keep my eyes peeled for it.' Elisabeth gave her a sweet smile. 'Hopefully it will turn up.'

Before Raoul's aunt could respond, Elisabeth slipped through the gate and away.

At the railway station, she bought a return ticket to Rouen. When at last her train arrived, she found a seat in an empty compartment, wishing she had a book or newspaper with her: anything to distract her nerves. She gazed through the dirty train window, watching strangers passing on the platform, going about their business.

She heard a cough behind her and jerked round to find a tall, broad-shouldered man in a suit filling the doorway. Elisabeth's heart stalled as she glimpsed the bronze tag around his neck depicting the unmistakable eagle and swastika stamp of the Gestapo.

In accented French he demanded to see her papers, his voice as coldly assured as his expression. Giving her identity card a cursory glance, he then asked to see her train ticket. Elisabeth handed it over for inspection.

'What is your business in Rouen?'

Elisabeth's stomach knotted. 'I'm looking for work,' she stammered.

She forced herself to meet the German's eye, and several long seconds passed, until finally he thrust the ticket back at her with a grunt, closed the door and left.

With a belch of steam, the train jolted into motion. Elisabeth turned back to the window. The scene rolling by beyond the glass might as well have been painted on boards, so removed from it did she feel, trapped in this carriage.

She was just beginning to relax, when the compartment door was flung open again and three Wehrmacht officers entered. The Germans spread themselves out on the seats opposite Elisabeth, and one of them, a captain with an iron cross pinned to his collar, dipped his head at her in greeting. His thick leather utility belt was cinched tight around his portly belly, and his face was mottled, as though he'd been running.

Elisabeth forced herself to smile politely back, taking slow, deep breaths through her nose. Memories of the soldier dragging her into the woods, the barrel of his gun against her neck, circled her brain. She concentrated on her hands clasped in her lap. It took everything she had to stay seated.

'Where do you go, *mademoiselle*?'

Glancing up, Elisabeth found the ruddy-faced officer smiling at her. He'd removed his visor cap, revealing a head of thick blond hair. Although this man was much older than the soldier who'd assaulted her, and looked nothing like him, still Elisabeth's chest tightened.

'Go?' she croaked.

The officer repeated his question, enunciating the words in a deliberately slow and patient voice that didn't fool her for a moment.

'Rouen, *monsieur*.'

The officer's two colleagues were conversing in German, and one of them said something to cause the other to laugh sharply, making Elisabeth jump.

'You work there, *mademoiselle*?' The blond captain was still smiling at her.

'I'm ... I'm hoping to,' Elisabeth stammered. *Please God, no more questions.*

The officer nodded slowly, his eyes sharp. Elisabeth couldn't meet his gaze, and instead stared through the window. But he wasn't finished with her yet.

'*Mademoiselle?*'

The German captain was holding out a pack of cigarettes. She longed to take one, but shook her head. '*Non, merci,*' she muttered, as politely as she could. He was trying to catch her out.

The officer frowned at her nicotine-stained fingers, clasped tightly in her lap.

Elisabeth tried to breathe normally, as a blur of trees whipped past the grimy window. If she left the compartment now, it would look highly suspicious. And besides, how could she escape a moving train?

The captain thrust a cigarette at her, and she tensed. Was he going to force her to smoke it?

'You have fire?' the German asked, miming lighting his cigarette.

Elisabeth dug in her coat pocket, handing over her precious box of matches.

'*Danke schön, mademoiselle,*' the officer said, his eyes never leaving hers.

At last, the train reached Rouen, and the German officers disembarked. Elisabeth sagged with relief, waiting until she was sure they'd gone before leaving the train. She joined the stream of bodies heading towards the exit, a tannoy announcement ringing out.

The train has arrived at Rouen.

It will stop for twenty minutes.

Passengers must produce their identity papers and passes ready to be checked.

Do not block the platform.

An engine pulling cattle trucks, belching plumes of sooty smoke, was easing to a halt on the opposite platform. As Elisabeth hurried past, German guards began wrenching open the wagon doors.

The crowd around her had thinned, and Elisabeth found herself staring at a scene she couldn't at first comprehend. The cattle truck nearest her was filled with ashen-faced women and children, huddled on the filthy, straw-covered floor. A terrible stench of human waste wafted out to mix with the smoke on the platform, and Elisabeth stumbled to a halt, covering her mouth in sickened shock.

She'd heard of these death trains, read about them in the newspapers, but the scene before her was beyond her worst nightmares. From the mass of bodies, one woman lifted her head, locking eyes with Elisabeth, and the fear in her gaze was so raw, so intense, Elisabeth was robbed of breath.

She held the woman's gaze as the plaintive cries of the prisoners and the noises of the station subsided to a dull drone inside her head. A German guard further down the platform shouted an order, and his voice snapped Elisabeth back, but still she held the woman's eye. Another guard thrust a bucket of water into the truck, and then the wagon door was slammed shut again, and the woman was gone.

The shrill blast of a whistle close by made Elisabeth jerk. Someone pushed past her, and she found herself stumbling towards the exit once more.

Where was that poor woman being taken?

Never had Elisabeth felt more helpless.

Hold your nerve, Lisbeth. Her father's voice came to her. She staggered on, hoping that whatever small part she seemed destined to play in this war would help someone, somewhere, soon.

Outside at last, she hurried away from the station, along rubble-strewn pavements. The streets of the city were clogged with bicycles and army trucks and wild-eyed, sweat-flecked horses pulling dilapidated carriages. Thin, hollow-eyed people clustered around makeshift canteens in a scene reminiscent of London, except here Nazi occupation was evident in every direction Elisabeth looked, swastika flags flapping from windows, German soldiers swarming everywhere.

A sinister, oppressive atmosphere pervaded the city, and Elisabeth's heart beat double-time as she headed in what she hoped was the right direction. Thankfully, Lena Watkins had told her the address of Le Petit Café, and after asking directions of a street-seller hawking rags from his cart, Elisabeth finally found the place down a murky alleyway.

Remembering her training at the last moment, she walked a little way past the café, crouching to remove an imaginary stone from her shoe. Had anyone followed her? She couldn't be certain, but she didn't think so.

The café was narrow and dimly lit with cracked black-and-white tiles on the floor. Half a dozen small tables lined one wall, every one of them empty but for an old man sitting in the shadows near the counter.

Elisabeth took the table by the door, ensuring she had a good view out to the alleyway. A young waitress with a harelip appeared. 'What can I get you?'

'What do you have?' Elisabeth laid her ration cards on the table. She still found the system confusing, and hoped the girl would know what to do.

The girl pointed to a slate board on the wall: *Les plats du jour.*

Hunger and fear battled in Elisabeth's guts. She ordered a plate of beans and ham and a glass of water.

'Anything else?' the girl asked.

'Just a coffee, *s'il vous plaît.*'

As the girl turned to leave, Elisabeth took a breath and called her back. 'Is the *patron* here?'

The waitress shook her head. 'He's out.'

'Will he be back soon?'

The waitress shrugged. 'Not long.' She gave Elisabeth a suspicious look, and as she walked away

Elisabeth tried to ignore the unnerving prickle in the base of her spine warning her that she'd crossed an invisible boundary.

She ate her meagre meal, taking as long as she could over it. Only one other person came into the café during this time, a woman who looked as though she was related to the waitress. The two spoke briefly, and the woman left again.

Elisabeth was just contemplating ordering another coffee, when she noticed a thickset, unshaven man emerge from the doorway behind the counter. The waitress said something to him, and the man came over to Elisabeth's table.

'Hélène says you're asking for me.'

Elisabeth cleared her throat. 'I'm looking for a bookshop,' she said. 'Is there one around here?' As soon as the words left her mouth, she knew she'd garbled the code.

The café owner locked eyes with her. '*Oui,*' he said slowly. 'There is one just around the corner.'

It was him.

Elisabeth stared at the man; could she trust him? He was a complete stranger to her; she knew nothing about him, not even his name. And yet, if she was to fulfil her duty, she must put her life in his hands.

She glanced at the old man in the corner, but he was seemingly asleep, his head resting on his chest.

'Don't worry about him.' The café owner stepped to the door and flipped the *Ouvert* sign to *Fermé*, then sat down opposite Elisabeth. He was in his sixties, she guessed, and was perspiring heavily, his sparse grey hair plastered to his forehead.

Elisabeth's half-empty coffee cup sat on the table between them. Her mouth had grown dry, but she didn't trust her hands to hold the cup steady enough to drink from it.

'London?' the *patron* said.

She nodded. 'I need to make contact with the Lion-trainer circuit.' She watched his eyes for any flicker, but he held her gaze. 'Can you help me?'

'*Oui.*' Saying nothing more, the man rose and disappeared behind the counter again.

Elisabeth sat, one eye on the old man sleeping in the corner, wondering how long she could safely wait.

Her attention was caught by a movement beyond the café door. Through the glass she saw a man in a long brown leather coat approaching. The man's fedora was tipped low over his eyes, and Elisabeth couldn't see his face. Reaching the café, the man ignored the Closed sign and simply pushed open the door.

Elisabeth's heart seized.

Gestapo.

The café owner had betrayed her.

The coffee cup slipped in Elisabeth's hand, clattering on to the saucer. The man glanced at her, as if noticing her for the first time, and at that moment the young waitress appeared.

'*Bonjour, monsieur.*' The girl showed the man to a table, and Elisabeth tried to breathe, but it was as though all the air in the café had been sucked through the door.

He wasn't here for her.

To Elisabeth's relief, the owner returned, greeting the man in the fedora before coming over to

Elisabeth's table. He scooped up her plate and coffee cup without speaking.

'*Merci*,' Elisabeth croaked. She would have to come back to the café later, and the prospect filled her with dread.

As the café owner walked away, Elisabeth realised he'd left her crumpled napkin behind. She reached for it, and felt the outline of something small and hard tucked in the folds. Lifting the napkin to her lips, she managed to slip the little matchbook into her sleeve.

Hurrying back to the train station, Elisabeth felt a murmur of unease, an animal instinct that warned her she was being followed. A glance over her shoulder revealed no one obvious, but she couldn't rid her mind of Gestapo officers, tailing her.

She tried to recall her lectures at Beaulieu.

If you suspect you're being watched or followed, do not quicken your pace. Abandon your immediate plans until either you're sure you are not being followed, or you can shake your pursuer off. The best way is to lead him through a long, empty street where he's forced to keep his distance, before plunging into a crowd.

The advice was useless to her in this strange, unknown city.

Passing a grocer's, she pretended to inspect some shrivelled carrots in a tray. When she glanced back along the street, there was no sign of any Gestapo officer. But this was no comfort, as all it meant was that if indeed she *was* being followed, they were terrifyingly good at it.

Arriving back at the railway station at last, she headed straight for the public conveniences, locking herself in a cubicle until the panic subsided and she could breathe almost normally again. With shaking fingers, she took out the matchbook the *patron* had given her. A tiny piece of rice paper was tucked behind the matches, the pencilled message faint but legible: *13:00 Church of the Holy Cross. Wednesday.*

15

May 1944

For the next four days, Elisabeth hid in the flat, only venturing into town once for food. On the fifth day she forced herself outside, walking the fields and meadows around Chounoît, searching for potential drop locations. At the back of her mind, she nurtured the unlikely hope that she'd stumble over the bicycle, discarded in a ditch, perhaps.

Identifying one suitable meadow, a short distance beyond the town, Elisabeth relayed the coordinates to London, keeping her transmission as brief as possible. She lived in permanent dread of a knock at the door. Although the transmitter, hidden in the closet, might evade a superficial search by the landlady, Elisabeth knew that the Germans could locate her by radio signal bearings. And if that should happen, even the best of hiding places would be useless.

That evening, Elisabeth prepared for her return to Rouen. As the sun dipped below the rooftops, she bolted the door of the flat, fetched the sewing kit from her suitcase and lit a precious candle. First, she carefully cut up a rag and roughly stitched a hidden gun-pocket inside the lining of her coat. This done, she painstakingly unpicked the hem of her skirt and inserted as many rolled-up francs as she could fit without them showing – a secret emergency fund. She stitched the hem up again, then lifted the insoles of her shoes and tucked more money into the recesses of both heels.

Next, she filled her coat pockets with her toothbrush, the tin of army rations she'd received at Tempsford Airfield, the skeleton key Mr Smith had given her, a box of matches, and her last pack of Gauloises cigarettes; if she found herself trapped in the city, unable to get back to Chounoît, she would need these essentials.

Stowed in her money-belt were her identity card, the gold lipstick holder containing the suicide pill, and the miniature camera wrapped in a stocking. She hoped the circuit chief would enlighten her as to its purpose.

She loaded her pistol next, tucking it away inside her coat, and then, using the base of a ceramic mug, she sharpened the blade of her sleeve dagger, as she'd been shown in Arisaig.

Lastly, she tucked her silk one-time code pad inside her bra, alongside the photo of Gilbert. If the silk code should fall into Nazi hands, then it was all over for her. But they'd have to strip her to find it, and by that time— She cut the thought off.

After much deliberation, she decided to take the wireless transmitter with her. She couldn't bear the stress of leaving it behind again, and would just have to hope she wasn't stopped and searched. If only the damn thing didn't weigh so much. It was a struggle to carry it any distance without straining her arm muscles.

*

Early the next morning, before Raoul's aunt had opened her shop, Elisabeth made her way back to the railway station. Just as before, the train to Rouen was delayed. While she waited, she bought a cheese sandwich from a *vendeur* on the platform, but her stomach was so unsettled she had to force herself to eat the stale bread.

When at last the train arrived, most of the front carriages were full. Elisabeth managed to board a less crowded rear carriage, claiming a seat by the window, remembering something an instructor had told her. When travelling with an illegal wireless set, it was best to stow it as far away as possible, preferably in a neighbouring carriage. If the Gestapo should spring a spot check, then you could feign complete ignorance.

Elisabeth wished the instructor was with her now to witness how difficult that manoeuvre actually was in practice. She took off her coat, wedged the suitcase as far under her seat as it would go, and folded the coat over her lap so that the corners of the case were hidden. It was the best she could do.

She pretended to stare through the window at the countryside blurring past, one eye on the reflections of the other passengers, alert to anyone suspicious. But no one paid her any undue attention, and after a time Elisabeth relaxed sufficiently to rest her head against the smeared glass and close her eyes.

When the train finally wheezed its way into the station at Rouen, Elisabeth hefted the wireless and made her way towards the exit. She could see guards checking passengers' tickets and paperwork, and her palms grew slick with sweat. She spotted a young mother with a squalling toddler, and hurried to stand just behind them in the queue. The child's tantrum would distract attention from her, Elisabeth hoped. The toddler's cries grew more intense as they approached the barrier, and she suddenly tugged her small hand from her mother's grip, darting towards the platform.

'Suzanne!' the mother cried, lunging to catch her child.

With a swift sidestep manoeuvre, Elisabeth corralled the toddler, earning a weary smile of gratitude from the mother. But Suzanne's tantrum was building momentum, her cries drowning out the tannoy announcements. The guards up ahead were glaring in Elisabeth's direction, and she couldn't breathe. Would her gamble pay off? To her relief, the guards at the barrier waved the exhausted mother and her wailing daughter through, along with Elisabeth a step behind, without checking any of their paperwork.

Emerging from the station, into the turmoil and chaos of the city, Elisabeth took a moment to gather herself. An elderly woman in a tattered fur coat shuffled past, and Elisabeth deemed her safe enough to ask directions to the church.

'Shut up since it was bombed,' the woman flatly informed her.

'But can you point me in the right direction, *s'il vous plaît*?'

The woman gestured down the street. 'A kilometre.'

'*Merci, madame. Merci.*'

Elisabeth finally found the neo-Romanesque church down a side street, its roof staved in at one end, shattered wooden beams exposed like broken ribs.

She ducked into the porch, checking the time on her wristwatch. A quarter of an hour to kill. Should she wait here, or keep moving? Blisters were forming on her palms from lugging the heavy wireless. The church felt entirely abandoned, the porch deep and shadowed, so she decided to stay put rather than keep tramping the streets, and sat down on the narrow bench to wait.

At one o'clock precisely, she heard the scuff of footsteps approaching down the path, and a middle-aged man dressed in a shabby black suit and clerical collar appeared. Elisabeth rose to her feet as the man reached the porch entrance. She met his eye, waiting for him to speak, but he only gave her the briefest of glances, before unlocking the church door and disappearing inside.

Was this her contact? Had he given her a sign to follow?

Instinct told her yes, so she waited twenty seconds and then, with one final glance behind her, she slipped through the door after him.

The dark, cavernous church was empty, stripped of most of its furniture apart from a few remaining pews. Elisabeth scanned the shadows stretching away into the heart of the building, but there was no sign of the man. The temperature was several degrees cooler than outside and she shivered, gazing around at the stained-glass windows. One or two panes had been smashed, but most were boarded up. Her footsteps echoed on the stone floor as she made her way slowly down the nave towards the altar.

Where the hell had the man gone? The wireless case pulled on her arm, as she slipped her free hand inside her coat, fingers ready on the pistol. The heel of her shoe crunched on a splinter of glass, and Elisabeth froze.

A light glowed from the darkness ahead, growing steadily stronger. The man in the black suit was coming towards her, an oil lamp swaying at his hip. The lamp cast the man's face in shadow, his eyes hollow pits. Instinctively, Elisabeth's fingers tightened around her gun.

'Marie?' The man's voice was barely a whisper.

'*Oui.*'

'Did anyone follow you?'

Elisabeth shook her head.

'You're certain?'

'As I can be.'

They stood facing each other for several long seconds, Elisabeth hardly daring to breathe.

'Come with me,' the man said at last, and turned away.

Elisabeth hesitated; what if this was her last chance to escape a trap? But the man had known her code name, and had clearly been expecting her. She decided to trust her instincts, and followed the man back down the echoing nave. Halfway along he opened a door, and Elisabeth found herself in a small vestry. Old robes hung from pegs on the wall, and a bureau at the back of the room was piled with calf-bound ledgers and thick wax candles. The dusty, stale air was laced with the reassuring scent of beeswax.

'Please, sit,' the man said. Elisabeth gratefully set her wireless case on the floor, and sank down on a seat whose ragged velvet cushion looked as if it had been gnawed by mice or rats.

'Father André,' the man finally introduced himself. His brown eyes held Elisabeth's, his gaze inscrutable. 'You've brought what's needed?'

'I have a wireless set with me, and a camera,' Elisabeth croaked, the words sticking in her dry throat.

'When did you last contact London?'

'Yesterday,' Elisabeth answered.

'Good.'

'What is the camera for?' She had to know.

Father André frowned at her. 'London haven't briefed you?'

'I was only told to make contact with the Lion-trainer circuit. I know nothing else.'

Father André sighed, running a hand through his grey-flecked hair. 'You know nothing of the operation?'

'I'm afraid not ...'

'I've only known of it myself a few days.' He checked the door of the vestry, then began to speak. He was a cut-out for the Lion-trainer network, he explained. Elisabeth nodded: she had fully expected to deal with an intermediary; it was the safest method of not compromising the whole organisation.

'An unusual amount of rail transport's been travelling north out of Rouen recently,' Father André continued. 'Most of it ends up at the goods yard at Auffay, close to the new construction site at Bonnetot-le-Faubourg.'

'Construction site?'

'The Germans are building rocket launch pads.' Father André rubbed his jaw. 'We know the V1 rockets are ready to be deployed, and the Boche are starting to get them in position.'

Elisabeth thought of the newspaper reports she'd read back at home, of so-called 'ski slopes' appearing across northern France, all pointing in one direction: towards the south coast of Britain.

'How does this connect with my mission?' she asked.

'The Allies are bombing the launch pads,' Father André explained.

Elisabeth nodded. The success of an Allied invasion, rumoured to be mere weeks away now, would rely on the disablement of Hitler's V1s. 'But I still don't understand how I fit in,' she said.

Father André glanced nervously towards the small window on the far wall. Elisabeth followed his gaze. Could someone be lurking just beyond the glass? She rose and drew the threadbare curtains closed. 'My mission?' she pressed.

'Tomorrow night, you're to infiltrate the command post at Rouen Station,' Father André told her. 'Once inside, you'll photograph the monthly rail movement schedule. The RAF need this information to target their attacks on the German rail transport. The V1s must be prevented from reaching the launch sites, but blowing up all and sundry is untenable. There's enough innocent blood on the Allies' hands.'

Questions crowded Elisabeth's mind. 'The command post,' she said. 'How will I get in? Won't it be guarded?'

Father André explained how Rouen train station was in direct contact with all the region's stations, and its *poste de commandement* was never left unmanned. The only chance Elisabeth had to infiltrate the office without being seen was during a particular shift change at midnight, when the transport control officer on duty, a man sympathetic to the cause, would conveniently leave the office unmonitored for a few minutes while he went for his break.

'Our man's next shift is tomorrow night,' Father André said.

'And once I'm in there, where will I find this schedule?'

'Locked in a cabinet. It's too much of a risk for him to leave that open. You can pick a lock?'

Elisabeth nodded, more confidently than she felt.

'All the trains are given codes by the Boche,' Father André warned. 'If there's a sheet of codes with the schedule, snap that too.'

'How long will I have?'

'A few minutes at most.'

Elisabeth thought of Mr Smith, and his lesson on breaking and entering. *You've got to move fast, but at the same time carefully. When you're picking a lock, you've got to feel for the mechanism.* Would her skeleton key, a mere twist of wire, be enough?

'Our boys will set off the air-raid siren if there's Boche prowling too close.'

The oil lamp guttered, the flame dipping and flaring as if blown by a breeze, though the window and door were both closed. Father André tinkered with the lamp and the flame settled once more.

'Tomorrow night, you say?' Elisabeth said quietly.

Father André gave a stiff nod. 'We must contact London. Tell them it's on.'

With Father André's help, Elisabeth proceeded to set up the wireless, working as quickly as she could. There was no electrical socket in the room, no electricity in the entire church, so Father André was despatched to fetch a car battery. While he was gone, Elisabeth took out her silk coding pad and compiled a short message.

'The aerial needs to be hung up, ideally outside,' she told Father André on his return. They both eyed the curtained window. 'What does that open on to?' Elisabeth wondered.

'The graveyard,' Father André told her. The wire was carefully fed through the window.

With Father André watching closely, Elisabeth attached the car battery to the wireless, inserted the tiny crystals, and fired up the transmitter. She adjusted her headphones, flexed her fingers, and proceeded to tap out her message.

LIBRARIAN TO LONDON
CONTACT MADE WITH LION-TRAINER

Waiting for London to respond, Elisabeth visualised the interminable process: she pictured a WAAF wireless operator in headphones, sitting at her desk in a receiving station somewhere in Britain, laboriously noting down the signals as they came through. This wireless operator would then take Elisabeth's message to the cipher clerks for decoding, after which it would be read by someone in Baker Street, then an answer compiled and encoded, and finally transmitted back.

The whole awful performance could take hours.

In the event, an answering message came through swiftly. Elisabeth seized her pencil and pad and quickly took down the dits and dahs travelling through the crackling ether.

PREPARE FOR OPERATION MOONLIGHT

'I'll return tonight with some food and a change of clothes,' Father André promised.

'Clothes?'

'Your disguise.'

Elisabeth wanted to ask him what kind of disguise, but he was already heading through the door. 'I'll be back soon, Marie.'

She stood listening to his footsteps receding, until the silence engulfed her once more, smothering her like a shroud.

At least Father André had left her the oil lamp.

She dragged several gowns off their pegs and arranged them in a pile in the far corner of the vestry, partly hidden by the old bureau. The makeshift bed might not be the most luxurious she had ever slept in, but it was at least soft and warm and the best she could manage in the circumstances.

She hid the wireless in its suitcase deep inside the bureau, shoved behind a clutter of candlesticks, prayer books and wicker collection baskets.

Time slid slowly by.

If only she had a novel to read. She flicked through one of the ledgers, coughing on dust as she skim-read baptism records dating back a hundred years or more. Closing the ledger with a sigh, she listened to the aching stillness. From outside came the distant sound of a blast, followed by a fainter echo a moment later. Father André could be killed, and she would know nothing about it, sequestered in here.

Hours passed, and her bladder began to ache.

Easing open the vestry door, she peered out into the darkness. Gripping the oil lamp in one hand, her pistol in the other, she hurried across the nave towards a small door, set back into the wall, that she'd noticed on her arrival. To her relief, the door was unlocked. Beyond was a cupboard containing boxes, brooms and mops, and in the corner was an empty tin pail. It would have to do.

Father André eventually returned, bringing with him provisions and Elisabeth's disguise. He emptied his satchel on to the floor, passing Elisabeth a set of oil-stained overalls. 'Smallest I could get.'

So she was to disguise herself as a *cheminot*?

She held the overalls up against her body; they'd hang off her.

From another bag, Father André produced a pair of engineer's work boots, the leather scratched and covered in soot, but at least they weren't enormous.

'Shove some newspaper in the toes if they're too big,' Father André advised.

Elisabeth looked about the room. Where was she supposed to find newspaper?

A dirty black beret and a greasy neckerchief were next out of the bag, completing the disguise. 'It'll cover your hair,' Father André said. 'With a bit of grease on your face, no one'll spare you a second glance.'

'You really think so?' Elisabeth muttered. She couldn't help but wonder if she might be better off disguised as one of the homeless who slept in and around the station. No one spared them a second glance.

Father André had brought two bottles of red wine, a flask of water, some bread, cheese and apples. The cheese was so strong it made Elisabeth wince, the dark bread so hard her teeth ached with chewing, but at least it was food. Despite her nerves, or perhaps because of them, she found she was ravenous. While they ate and drank, Father André went through the details of the plan.

'While you're concentrating on the schedule, our boys'll distract the Boche,' he said. 'Give them something to think about.'

The saboteurs would do this by setting off an incendiary device, somewhere along the tracks just outside the station, or on one of the stationary engines.

'While the Boche are busy dealing with that,' Father André said, 'you'll slip into the office, unlock the cupboard, photograph the schedule, then get out again as quick as you can.'

It all sounded so simple, so straightforward, when he put it like that.

London needed the film quickly, but as it contained such sensitive information, Elisabeth would have to arrange a rapid pick-up and take the camera back across the Channel herself.

She'd have to wait for the start of the next full-moon period, though.

'You need this.' Father André unfastened the strap of his wristwatch and handed it to Elisabeth. 'You can't wear your own, it's too feminine.'

The thick leather strap was warm on Elisabeth's skin as she tightened it around her wrist. 'Is this right?' The time was an hour behind her own watch.

'It's French time,' Father André said. 'I refuse to live by German time.'

Elisabeth sympathised, as she wound the watch forward an hour.

'I'll be back in the morning.' Father André buckled his empty satchel, looping the strap over his shoulder. 'Try and get some sleep. I'll lock up on my way out.'

'Goodnight,' Elisabeth managed, though her throat was closing at the prospect of having to spend the night alone in the church. But Father André had already gone.

She dimmed the oil lamp, but didn't completely extinguish it. The deathly silence was terrifying.

Captain Porter's words came back to her.

An agent's chances of survival may be as low as fifty per cent.

She tried to take comfort in the knowledge that she was playing her part, however small, in defeating the Nazis, and avenging her dear Papa's death. A memory of the poor women and children imprisoned in the cattle truck flickered through her mind. The haunted look on that Jewish woman's face brought sour bile to her mouth. She'd witnessed the true horror of Nazi rule right there in front of her, and the experience would stay with her for as long as she lived.

Enough. She must try and sleep.

She barred the door with a chair, then took down the remaining garments hanging on pegs and lay them in a pile on the floor; in the shadows they resembled bodies looming over her, and would only add to her nightmares.

In the silence of the vestry, every tiny sound was amplified. Something scratched behind the skirting board, and the ceiling creaked like a ship at sea. She lit three of the church candles, but their warm, fragrant glow did little to quell her fear.

She'd lost her faith long ago, even before Papa had been taken so cruelly. There was no sense, in her mind, in a benevolent god who could sanction such barbarity as war. And yet, here in this deserted, abandoned church, she found herself praying.

Dear God, please keep Maman safe. Look after Gilbert, and Doris, and the others, wherever they are. Let me get through this night.

At last, she curled up in the corner, pulling the moth-eaten robes over her. She closed her eyes, willing sleep to come, but her thoughts churned like a weir.

Who was Father André really? She was trusting him with her life, and she didn't even know his real name.

And yet that was how the Resistance network operated, she reminded herself. Identities and connections were mired in secrecy, the whole system like an underground river, with countless hidden tributaries, twisting and turning. It was impossible to follow such a river to any source. Her rational mind told her it was better not to know the identities of the people she was dealing with. The less she knew, the less she could divulge if, God forbid, she was ever caught by the Nazis and tortured.

But despite this, it still unnerved her to think how much her survival depended on the whim of strangers.

16

2018

Ever since her threatening encounter with Leo a fortnight ago, Tali has done everything humanly possible to avoid him. Her efforts have been made easier by his frequent, mysterious absences from Weyside. It's been three days since Tali last set eyes on him, and she has no clue where he is, or if he'll be back for his mother's birthday party tomorrow.

Secretly, guiltily, she hopes he never comes back.

She certainly doesn't need his assistance with Betty's party preparations, even though there is so much to do. She'd rather die than ask Leo for help.

In truth, Tali is glad to be busy. As she clears away the breakfast things, she tries not to think of Betty's son, or what plans he might be concocting. Instead, she lets her mind wander and, as always, her thoughts lead to Jo. The ache in her chest intensifies whenever she recalls the awful incident on the narrowboat, but she can't help herself; it's like a wound she can't stop poking. Tying an apron around her waist, Tali imagines the strings are Jo's arms encircling her.

'Are you making tea, dear?' Betty's voice drifts from the sitting room.

'*Oui*, Madame Betty.'

Tali closes her eyes briefly, fantasising that Jo is here with her in the kitchen, and they're cooking together. Tali pictures herself feeding Jo morsels of *gato france*, and Jo is licking her fingers, smiling that shy smile of hers that flips Tali's heart over.

Stop it. Why does she torture herself with these dreams, when the truth is she's lost Jo for ever? Just like she lost Zezette.

Tali's phone rings, startling her, and she fumbles the mobile from her skirt pocket.

'Natalia?'

At the sound of her father's familiar voice, Tali sags against the counter. 'Papa.'

'Natalia, is that you?'

'Yes, Papa. It's me. How are you?' She wonders if he will detect the false cheer in her voice from so many thousands of miles away.

'Natalia, your mama and I need to talk to you.'

The back of Tali's throat begins to ache. 'Is everything all right?'

'Not really, Natalia. Your mama is very upset. We're both very worried about you.'

Tali closes her eyes. She's waited months to hear this, but it couldn't have come at a worse time.

'I'm fine, Papa.' She has to force the words out. For so long, she's shored her emotions up in her leaking little boat of a heart, but lately her morale has been steadily sinking.

She simply hasn't the strength to weather another of her parents' storms.

The line crackles, and her father's voice fades.

'What was that, Papa? You're breaking up ...' Tali swaps the phone to her other ear.

Her father's voice resumes, '... forgive you, and you can come home ...'

Dizziness swoops.

'Natalia? Are you there?'

'Papa ...' Tali stammers. *I can never come home.*

'Wait ... Mama wants to speak with you ...' Her father fades away, and Tali hears odd clicking sounds on the line, and then her mother's voice is filling her ear.

'Natalia, I've just about had enough! You are being ridiculous ...'

'Maman ...'

'Now just you listen to me, Natalia, this has gone on long enough ...'

Tali hears her father mumbling something in the background.

'It has to be said, Benjamin,' Tali's mother snaps. 'Natalia, are you there?'

Tali's stomach roils. '*Oui*, Maman—'

'Noa's parents have been phoning every day,' Tali's mother interrupts, '*several* times a day, wanting to know when you're coming home. There's so much to organise for the wedding, Natalia, and I can't keep making excuses ...'

Tali dreads to think what excuses her mother has made for her. She holds the phone away from her ear as her mother rants on.

She's only met Noa, her supposed husband-to-be, three times at social gatherings thrown by his parents, and she can barely bring an image of him to mind now. In all this time he hasn't called her or texted her once.

'Are you there, Natalia?'

'*Oui*, Maman.'

'It's embarrassing, Natalia,' her mother forges on. 'When are you coming home, so we can sort out ...' Static reduces her voice to an incomprehensible crackle. '... and then we ... so can you ...'

'I can't hear you, Maman ...'

'So if ... Natalia ...'

It's no good, she can't take any more. Tali cuts her mother off.

She will pay for that later, she knows.

'Is everything all right, dear?' Betty's voice drifts from next door.

Tali takes a deep, shuddery breath, shoving her phone back in her apron pocket. 'Everything is fine, Madame Betty.'

Blessed silence from the sitting room.

Tali just needs a moment to gather herself.

She contemplates the kitchen, every available surface covered in dishes and bowls of food in various stages of preparation. There is so much to do for Betty's birthday party tomorrow, she hardly knows where to start. She rubs her brow. Her temples are throbbing; if it gets any worse, she'll have to raid Betty's stash of painkillers.

'Are you making a pot of tea, Natalia?'

'*Un moment*, Madame Betty.'

Tali opens the back door, admitting a soft, fragrant breeze, and the chatter of sparrows on the bird-feeder. It's a beautiful June morning, and she longs to feel the warmth of the sun on her face, if only for a few seconds. The phone call from her parents has dredged up all the dark thoughts lurking in the murky niches of her mind.

She brings a cup of tea and a plate of biscuits through to the sitting room, to find Betty dozing. Whenever Tali catches Betty asleep in her armchair, her wisp-white head nodding, she's reminded of her Nani so much that her chest aches. As she gently sets the tea and biscuits down on the side table, Betty's eyes snap open.

'I wasn't sleeping,' Betty says with a sniff.

'*Bien sûr que non.*'

Tosca waddles into the room, and sits staring hopefully at the plate of digestives.

'You've been working away in the kitchen all morning, Natalia,' Betty says, as Tali turns to leave. 'Anyone would think you're cooking for an army.'

'I'm making the food for your party, Madame Betty,' Tali replies. *Do you expect your guests to eat air?*

'No one will come.'

'Why do you say that?' Tali asks. 'I've invited everyone from the club, and they have all said they will come.'

Betty takes a slow sip of her tea, meeting Tali's eye. 'Even that lovely Jo?'

Tali can't hold Betty's gaze. She pretends to tidy the sideboard, wiping dust from a framed black-and-white photograph of an unsmiling baby Leo sitting in a huge, old-fashioned pram.

She hadn't had the courage to invite Jo herself. Instead, she'd asked Abeo to tell her about the party. Abeo had reported back that Jo had another engagement.

Lost in her thoughts, it's a moment before Tali realises Betty is talking to her.

'So is Jo coming?'

'I think she's working, Madame Betty.'

'Up a tree, is she? Or perhaps she's off on that boat of hers?'

'I don't know.' Tali can't bear any more questions. 'I have to get on, Madame Betty.'

'Before you go,' Betty says. 'Have you seen Leo?'

Tali shakes her head. She has absolutely no clue where he is. The last time Tali had seen Betty's son, three days ago, he'd told her he was going out to 'see a man about a dog'.

Tali has no idea why he would want another dog. Surely Tosca is enough?

'I wonder where he is?' Betty says.

'I'm sure he'll be back soon,' Tali replies. *Unfortunately*.

Pushing thoughts of Leo and Jo to the back of her mind, Tali continues with the party preparations, ticking things off in her head: there's Betty's mismatched crockery to gather and wash, sufficient cutlery to find, tables and chairs to arrange in the garden.

If Betty's house was bigger, they could perhaps have held the party inside, but the rooms are too cramped with furniture and junk. Tali much prefers the idea of celebrating outside, in the fresh air and sunshine.

The sky this morning is a flawless, hopeful blue, and according to the weather app on her phone the next few days promise to be dry. But Tali knows better than to trust the fickle British climate.

What if it rains tomorrow? She adds another job to the list in her head: look in the cellar for a parasol or gazebo, or even just some plastic she can rig up as an awning.

She's beginning to regret her decision to serve a multicultural feast, including rotis and naan bread, egg-fried rice, potato salad and sesame gajak. Instead of a birthday cake, she's baked a hundred little Neapolitan cookies. The buttery, iced biscuits are a Mauritian delicacy, and Tali is using her Nani's special recipe. But they're fiddly, and take time to decorate. She still has almost half the cookies left to ice.

She hopes everyone from the Century Society will turn up tomorrow, otherwise there'll be an awful lot of food left over. She sets half a dozen eggs to boil on the stove, then begins the painstaking task of icing the letter 'B' on the next twenty biscuits.

'Oh, *tou tou*,' she murmurs to the dog as he pads into the kitchen. 'I wish you could help me today.' Tosca cocks his head quizzically, wags his stump of tail.

At the sound of the front door opening, Tosca's tail sinks. Tali's stomach clenches.

Seconds later, Leo appears in the kitchen doorway. 'What's that smell?'

The piping bag slips in Tali's hand, and she squirts icing over the counter. 'I'm cooking for tomorrow.'

'What's happening tomorrow?'

Tali tries to wipe up the mess, smearing icing everywhere. 'Madame Betty's party,' she answers as calmly as she can. Surely Leo hasn't forgotten his own mother's hundredth birthday?

'You'll have to cancel that. She's got an appointment.'

'Pardon?'

But Leo is already heading into the sitting room.

Tali wipes her hands on a tea towel and follows him, to find him standing over Betty, tugging the newspaper from his mother's grasp.

'Just put the damn crossword down for five minutes, Mother ...'

'Madame Betty?' Tali croaks from the doorway.

Leo turns and fixes Tali with a glare. 'Sorry, did we call you? Did you call her, Mother?'

'Leo—'

'No, we didn't,' Leo interrupts. 'Close the door when you leave, please.'

'Don't speak to Natalia like that.' Betty yanks the newspaper out of her son's hand, tearing the front page. 'Oh, now look what you've done!'

Leo's jaw flexes. 'I'll speak how I like, Mother, in my own home.'

His own home? Tali grips the door frame.

Leo frowns at her. 'Why are you still here?'

'Natalia lives here, Leo, in case you'd forgotten,' Betty sighs. 'She's entitled to come in this room if she pleases.'

'Not if I'm having a private conversation with my mother, she isn't.'

'Oh, is that what we're having? A conversation? It feels more like an interrogation.' Betty flaps the newspaper at her son as if he's a bothersome fly. 'Sit down, I don't know what's the matter with you.'

'There's nothing the matter with me.' Leo perches on the edge of the sofa. 'I just want you to listen.'

'I *am* listening, Leo. What is it you want to say?'

Tali hovers in the doorway. She doesn't want to leave Betty alone with Leo, but can't think of an excuse to stay.

'I've made us an appointment to view a room at Oak Manor tomorrow, Mother,' Leo says.

'Oak Manor?'

'Don't pretend you've forgotten already.'

'I don't know what Oak Manor's got to do with me.'

'We've talked about this, Mother. It's a lovely retirement home by all accounts. And once I've sorted Power of Attorney, we can get this place sold.'

'Power of Attorney? I don't recall agreeing to Power of Attorney ...'

Leo sighs, his fists clenched on his knees. 'This is what I mean, Mother. Your mind is going. And if we don't sort this out now, while you're still relatively *compos mentis*, then it'll cause all sorts of problems when the time comes to sell Weyside ...'

'I am perfectly *compos mentis*, thank you very much. There's nothing wrong with me, is there, Natalia?'

Leo's head snaps round, pinning Tali with his stare. 'I thought I made myself clear. This is a private conversation I'm having with my mother. Please leave us.'

'Stay where you are, Natalia.'

Tali's grip on the door tightens. She waits for Leo to explode, but instead he turns back to face his mother.

'Is it the party you're upset about?' Betty asks. 'Because you knew it was tomorrow. Natalia told you …'

Leo shakes his head slowly. 'The party's not happening, Mother. We're going to Oak Manor tomorrow. I've made an appointment, and they're very busy people.'

'I have no intention of going to Oak Manor tomorrow, Leo.'

A charged silence descends. Leo's cheeks flush, and he breathes through his nose. 'I'm concerned about you, Mother,' he says at last. His eyes slide from Betty to Tali, trapped in the doorway; she forces herself to hold his gaze. 'I only want you to be taken care of.'

'Natalia takes very good care of me,' Betty says, a warning note in her voice.

'I don't doubt it,' Leo murmurs, his eyes pinning Tali. 'But now I'm here, and I can take care of you. I'm sure Natalia agrees with me, don't you?'

Tali's tongue cleaves to the roof of her mouth.

'Natalia is going nowhere.' Betty's voice rises.

'I'm sure she's served you admirably, Mother,' Leo says. 'But you must realise she was never going to stay with you for ever. Oak Manor has dedicated nurses—'

'I don't need nursing.'

'Not yet, perhaps. But one day you will. A lovely little room of your own, Mother, think of it. None of this dusty old clobber tripping you up,' he sweeps an

276

arm around the room. 'No garden to worry about. As soon as you grant me Power of Attorney, like we've discussed, I can take care of everything, and we can all get on with our lives.'

'What on earth has happened to you, Leo?' Betty breathes. 'You're not the son I raised.'

'*You* raised?' Leo emits a snort. 'Let's not open that can of worms, eh, Mother? Not in front of the hired help.'

Tali bites her lip. *Mon Dieu*, she wants so much to punch him.

'If your father was alive now …'

'But he's not, is he?' Leo counters. 'It's just you and me left, Mother. And I just want what's best for you.'

'No, you want what's best for *you*, Leo.'

'How do you know what I want?' Leo surges to his feet. 'We both know you've never been interested in me.'

'Don't talk rot, Leo …'

'Rot?' Leo snorts. 'I think you're the one talking rot, Mother. I suppose the past is all forgotten, isn't it? Water under the bridge?'

Betty closes her eyes briefly, and Tali longs to take her hand.

'I see I've touched a nerve,' Leo says. 'I wasn't going to bring any of this up, but you've pushed me to the limit.'

'Where has this come from?' Betty's voice is faint.

'Where has what come from, Mother? The truth is you've never wanted me, never loved me.'

Betty looks up at Leo. 'I did the best I could.'

'The best wasn't good enough, though, was it?'

In the silence that follows, Tali ventures to speak. 'I think you should leave now, Monsieur Shepherd.'

Leo jerks his head round. 'I'm not going to ask you again,' he says. 'Get out.'

Tali ignores him, an ember of rage smouldering in her chest. She's grown fond of Madame Betty over the months, and she knows Betty likes her too, in her awkward English way. Tali has come to think of them as a pair of lonely conch shells knocking about on the shore. How dare this man destroy their relationship? What right does he have to get rid of her? 'I will only leave when Madame Betty tells me to leave,' Tali says, lifting her chin.

'I don't want you to leave, Natalia.'

Leo sighs through his nose. 'All right, Mother, I can see you're not in the mood to listen to me right now. We'll continue this conversation later. *In private*.'

'There's nothing more to say,' Betty says. 'I've told you I want to stay in my own home with Natalia looking after me.'

'And I've told you,' Leo says, leaning down into his mother's face, 'that's not going to happen.'

He straightens, moves towards Tali in the doorway. She sidesteps swiftly.

'Cancel the bloody party,' Leo snarls at her. He pauses on the threshold, then turns back to his mother. 'I'm going out. I'll be back tomorrow to pick you up. Be ready after lunch.'

The front door slams, and Tali exhales. Tosca emerges from behind a tower of paperbacks in the corner and gives a soft whine.

'Oh, my boy,' Betty sighs, leaning down to stroke the dog with a trembling hand.

'Are you OK, Madame Betty?'

Betty lifts her head, and Tali is shocked to see a tear tracking down her cheek. 'Leo's right. We have to cancel the party,' Betty says, fumbling a tissue from her sleeve and blotting her eyes.

'Oh, Madame Betty.' Tali drops to her knees before the old woman and clasps her cold hands. 'You don't mean that.'

'I can't face anyone, Natalia. And Leo won't give up, I tell you.'

'But you don't want to go to this oak place, and he can't make you.'

'I'm so tired, Natalia. Until you reach my age, you'll never know how tired ...'

'You're strong, Madame Betty.' Tali swallows a sob. 'Please don't give up now.'

Betty shakes her head, blows her nose. 'I'm not giving up, girl.'

'But if you go there with your son ...' Tali can't finish the sentence. She has the awful suspicion that Leo has no intention of bringing Betty home again.

'I'll go with him,' Betty says quietly. 'Let him think I'm interested. But he can't sell the house without my say-so. And I simply won't give it.'

A quiver of fear shivers down Tali's spine. This is not a safe plan.

'Please, Madame Betty,' she tries again. 'We can't cancel the party now. Everyone is coming and I've made all the cookies ...' *A hundred of the things.*

279

'But what happens when Leo comes back? I don't want another fight.'

Tali pulls herself to her feet and gives Betty's hands a final, gentle squeeze. 'The party will be happening, and he can't stop it then, can he?'

Back in the kitchen, Tali stares at her phone. Her hands are shaking. She longs to ring Jo, to hear her voice, talk through the awful events of the past hour. Ask her what the hell she should do. In her mind's eye, Tali conjures the last image she has of Jo, at the Century Society. Jo had looked thinner, if that could be possible, her face pale and drawn.

Tali blinks tears away. Her fingers hover over the blank phone screen, and it flashes to life in its supernatural way, displaying the home-screen photo of Tamarin Bay. She really must delete that picture; it twists her heart every time she sees it.

Who else can she talk to about what's going on? Only Jo would understand. There's Abeo, of course, she could maybe tell him, but she doesn't have his number.

Everyone is due to come to Betty's party tomorrow. There's no way of cancelling at such short notice.

She'll text Jo. Better than phoning her cold. All she wants is to ask her advice about Leo.

Liar, liar, liar.

Hi Jo, she types. I hope you are well?

No, that's no good. She laboriously deletes each word, starts again.

Hi Jo, I know what I did was wrong.

No, she can't write that. *Think.*

Hello Jo,
It's Madame Betty's birthday party tomorrow.
I know you are busy, but there is a problem.
I don't know what to do.
Can I call you?
Tali xx

Her finger hesitates over the Send button. Two kisses – is that too many, or not enough? She fights the overwhelming urge to cover the entire screen with little crosses.

Stop being pathetic. Send it.

What if Jo doesn't answer?

For fuck's sake, just send it.

She presses Send.

17

May 1944

Hidden in the vestry, Elisabeth lay listening to the endless drone and crash of bombs dropping over the city.

Never had she felt so alone.

Eventually she drifted into an exhausted slumber, only to be shocked awake by a huge explosion. The ground shuddered as though rent by an earthquake, and she stifled a cry. Huddled amongst the robes on the floor, she struggled to contain her mounting terror. What if the church took a direct hit? No one knew she was here apart from Father André. If she should be obliterated by a falling bomb, her mother would never know what happened to her only child.

Worse even than that, she'd never see Gilbert again.

If only he was here, enduring this ordeal alongside her. She took her mind back to Arisaig, and one particularly gruelling training exercise on the remote Scottish moors. Every detail of that night was ingrained on her memory. She'd been paired with Gilbert; their task was to be the first team to locate an abandoned bothy in a secluded valley. Together, they'd navigated by map and compass and sheer blind luck, slogging for hours through the freezing darkness, battling the pelting rain and fierce winds.

But they'd made it to their destination.

Sheltering in the bothy, Gilbert had managed to light a meagre fire with some discarded wood. Exhausted, they'd sat close together on the bare stone floor, drenched and shivering, waiting for the other teams to arrive. Elisabeth's feet had ached so much, it had seemed like her soles were burning. A blister had formed on her left heel, the skin chafing through her sodden woollen socks.

'Take them off,' Gilbert had advised. 'They'll dry over the fire.'

'But my feet will freeze.'

'Have my socks, they're pretty dry still.'

Before Elisabeth could protest, Gilbert had slipped his own socks off and she found her feet encased in warm wool.

'How come your feet aren't soaking?' She peered suspiciously at his army-issue boots. They didn't look so different from the walking boots that Stewart had found for her.

'Beeswax.'

'Beeswax?'

'I melted a candle down and rubbed it over the leather. I'll show you how to do it when we get back, if you want.'

'Thank you.' She lapsed into silence, longing to close the gap between them, be held by him until she was warm again. But that would not be professional.

'Can I ask you something?' Gilbert said after a while.

'If you want.' Elisabeth threw another piece of broken wood on the fire, feigning indifference. She thought of her friend Josie, with her four older brothers and a succession of male admirers. She knew precisely what Josie would say if she was here. *Play hard to get, girl.*

'What's the worst part of the war for you?'

Elisabeth glanced at Gilbert, watched him unscrew the lid of his water flask and take a drink. The question surprised her.

'Apart from the Nazis?' She touched her tender heel and winced. 'I hate the blackout.' She thought of Weyside, pictured the thick curtains drawn across the windows, the gloomy low-wattage bulbs that her mother insisted they use. The house had felt like a cave in the winter months, a place of shadows and trip-hazards.

'My father came home really upset from an air-raid patrol one night,' she found herself telling Gilbert. 'He told me about a poor family he'd met who had no curtains at all. So they'd painted their windows completely black.'

It still made Elisabeth shudder to think of the darkness some people were living in. Not like the darkness out here. The storm had finally passed, and through the bothy's doorway she could see the moon and stars blazing from a clear sky, bathing the moor in a silvered light.

'It's the air-raid shelters I dread,' Gilbert had confessed. 'Being trapped underground with a load of strangers, kids screaming and crying, waiting for Hell's symphony to burn itself out up top.'

The wind outside had fallen to a whisper, and the crackle and snap of the fire in the hearth grew loud in the sudden quiet. Elisabeth gazed into the flames, lost in memories of home.

'But if I was with you,' Gilbert said, breaking into her thoughts, 'I'd endure anything.'

They'd shared a smile then, and Elisabeth had no longer felt cold.

As the night wore on, the bombing gradually waned. Elisabeth succumbed to a shallow sleep, and when next she woke, disoriented and dry-mouthed, the oil lamp had burned itself out and daylight was bleeding through the thin curtains. Struggling up from the tangle of robes, she saw by Father André's wristwatch that it was already eight o'clock. She drank some water Father André had left for her, stretching her aching muscles.

Her thoughts turned to the night to come. Would the *cheminot* disguise work? Women were employed on the railways now as conductresses and clerks, but she'd never seen a female train driver or engineer. Could she pass as a man? If she was caught and arrested, who would tell her mother? Would it fall to Lena Watkins? Captain Porter? Officer Stewart?

She mustn't think about it, for fear it might come true.

She took off her skirt and blouse, folding them neatly behind the bureau. She kept her underclothes on, but untied the money-belt from around her waist. That would have to stay here, hidden with the wireless. The photo of her and Gilbert she kept tucked in her bra, along with her good-luck talisman: the lipstick containing the cyanide pill.

Slowly, she dressed in the engineer's overalls. The legs were several inches too long, but once she'd turned up the cuffs and put the work boots on, they didn't look too ridiculous.

An hour later, there came a soft tap on the door, and Father André appeared. Elisabeth's spirits lifted at the sight of him.

'*Bonjour*,' he greeted. 'Did you sleep?'

'Not much,' Elisabeth admitted.

'You must be hungry.' He'd brought some breakfast – more apples and ripe cheese, and some 'off rations' black pudding that was like chewing tasteless rubber, but at least it was something different.

As they ate, they went over the plan again. Father André had sketched a rough map of the station showing the main entrance and various exits, and where the *poste de commandement* was in relation to them. The map included the area immediately surrounding the train station, and a cross to mark the position of the church, to the east.

'You'll gain access through here,' Father André said, indicating on the map one of the station's side entrances, used only by railway personnel. 'There shouldn't be a guard on it.'

Once she'd taken the photographs, Elisabeth was to leave the same way she'd come in, then head straight back to the church. Father André pencilled in the route she should take, a black line twisting through the streets and alleys.

Elisabeth's mind whirred; there was so much to remember, so much that could go wrong. She released a long sigh.

'At times of stress, I often turn to Descartes,' Father André said. 'Have you read any of his work?'

Elisabeth's father had once shown her a book by the philosopher, not that she'd read it herself. 'A little,' she lied.

'Descartes wrote: "We hold nothing entirely within our power except our thoughts."' Father André gave her a steady look.

'Wise words,' Elisabeth had to agree, though the philosopher's wisdom offered scant comfort to her. Father André departed again, leaving Elisabeth with the remains of the food and a tatty pack of cards. Alone, she played hand after hand of solitaire in an effort to distract her mind from the storm of thoughts that swirled and massed and multiplied as the minutes and hours ticked by.

Once, she took out the photo of her and Gilbert, and the illicit visit to the photo booth swam up from the depths of her memory. Her eyes blurred as she stared at their smiling faces, a brief moment of happiness caught on paper.

Where was Gilbert now? Was he safe?

When at last Father André returned, it was almost six o'clock. He had brought more wine back with him, and hot soup in a flask. While they drank, he told Elisabeth about Rouen, how his beloved city had suffered for years under the hands of the German occupying army.

'I remember back in June of '40,' he began, 'a huge fire broke out in the old city, between the cathedral and the Seine. The Boche stopped our firemen from fighting the blaze, and the city burned for two days.'

Elisabeth could only shake her head, finding no words to express her dismay.

'The fire destroyed so many medieval buildings,' Father André went on. 'So much history gone up in smoke.'

He took a long swallow of wine. 'My city was once a beauty. But she's suffered for too long, and now she's on her knees.'

It was the same story across the whole of the country, Elisabeth knew. The Germans had wreaked havoc for years, and France would be suffering the consequences for a long, long time.

'London has suffered so much destruction too,' she said. And the capital wasn't alone. Southampton, Liverpool, Hull, Bristol, Portsmouth, Plymouth, Cardiff, Swansea; all had endured terrible air raids. Even her own home town of Guildford hadn't been spared. The destruction went on and on. 'But the Allies are fighting back. *We* are fighting back.'

'I don't know how much more we can take,' Father André sighed. 'Last night, RAF bombers targeted the Sotteville rail yard.'

'Where's that?'

'South of the city.'

It was a huge risk for the Allies to bomb French targets, Elisabeth didn't need Father André to tell her that. There would be heavy civilian casualties with this strategy.

'The rail yard was destroyed by the first salvos,' Father André went on. 'But the second lot missed, landing in the residential areas of Sotteville. Even the centre of Rouen took some hits.'

So that was what last night had been about, Elisabeth thought. Her own side, trying to bomb her.

'Only last month, our beautiful cathedral was struck by nine bombs, all told,' Father André went on. 'The south side was worst hit, shattering two stained-glass windows, and seriously damaging the spire. Did you know, it was once the tallest building in the world?'

'I didn't know that, no.'

'Not any more.' He dug another bottle of red wine from his satchel, topping up their enamel mugs. 'The heart of Richard the Lionheart is buried in the cathedral,' he said, passing Elisabeth her cup.

Elisabeth swallowed a mouthful of wine, thinking of the centuries of history contained in Father André's city, all at risk of being lost for ever.

'A little while back, bombs fell on the Palais de Justice,' Father André continued. 'The interior was gutted by fire, but the water mains were ruptured, so all we could do was watch it burn. Some reports I've heard put the destruction at over two thousand buildings so far. Countless civilians murdered.'

Elisabeth listened, fascinated and horrified in equal measure, as he described how the recent air raids had destroyed German machinery and equipment, severely obstructing enemy traffic. In addition, the continual bombardment had forced the Germans to man the trains with their own crews, as too many of the French railway workers had now abandoned their posts.

'But despite everything, the Boche are still moving trains and troops and weaponry,' he sighed. 'There's still so much more to do.'

Elisabeth thought of all the brave men and women of the Resistance, risking their lives to help the Allies. So many nameless heroes, but would their numbers be enough to defeat the Nazis?

At last, the time came for them to leave. While Father André packed his satchel, Elisabeth donned the borrowed beret, pulling the felt hat down low over her brow. She tied the neckerchief so that it covered most of her neck and chin, then smeared her cheeks with greasy coal dust scraped from the soles of the work boots.

She strapped her sleeve dagger to her left forearm, hidden beneath the baggy cuff. Her pistol was too bulky for the pockets of the overall, and too risky to carry in case she was caught. She would leave it behind in the vestry and collect it afterwards.

The miniature camera, so crucial to the whole endeavour, she tucked in the deepest of her trouser pockets, along with the skeleton key.

'Let me see,' Father André said, when she'd finished.

Elisabeth stood as tall as she could, turning a slow circle. The overalls puddled at her ankles, she had no needle or thread to hem them, but Father André's brief nod suggested the disguise passed muster. 'Good,' was all he said.

Elisabeth drank some water, then had to visit the pail in the closet. As she crouched, peeing in the dark, her head swam as a wave of tiredness swept over her.

The knowledge that it would be hours until she could sleep again worried her greatly; she must stay sharp and alert until this mission was over.

Suddenly, she remembered the Benzedrine tablets Lena Watkins had given her at Tempsford Airfield a lifetime ago. She'd forgotten all about them. Hurrying back to the vestry, she rummaged in her coat pocket, her fingers closing about the little phial.

'What's that?' Father André asked, sharp brown eyes missing nothing.

'Headache tablets,' she lied.

How many should she take? She decided on two, and washed them down with a mouthful of water.

At half past eleven, they were ready to leave. Elisabeth's tiredness had receded and she felt as though a small electric current was passing through her veins. The tablets must be taking effect.

'Time to go,' Father André said.

It was long past curfew, and Elisabeth knew with a terrifying certainty that if they were caught in the streets by any patrolling German soldiers or French Milice, they would be arrested. Father André kept to the back alleys, leading Elisabeth through the city. The sky was overcast, only the dim glow from Father André's lamp lighting their way, and Elisabeth was forced to employ every trick she could recall from her training to commit the route to memory.

They paused beneath the station's clock tower. The front entrance was deserted except for a single German night guard, sleepily trudging back and forth across the concourse.

Elisabeth glanced at her watch. It was almost midnight. There would be no passenger trains running this late, but she could hear the distant clank and rattle of what must be a freight train leaving the station.

'Your way in is just down there,' Father André whispered, pointing behind them into the darkness. 'Remember on the map I showed you?'

Elisabeth nodded, heart beginning to thud.

'The office will only be empty for five minutes, at most,' he reminded her. 'Get in and out as quickly as you can.'

Elisabeth nodded again.

'*Bonne chance*, Marie.' Father André gave her shoulder a brief squeeze. '*Vive la France!*'

Keeping to the shadows, Elisabeth slipped through the unlocked side entrance reserved for railway workers. She crept along a dark corridor and when, after twenty paces, the passage turned a corner, she paused, listening for any sounds that might suggest a guard was nearby. All she could hear was the distant clanking of metal on metal, and the faint shouts of men somewhere on the platforms below. Pasted on the wall was a large sign that read: *Mort aux saboteurs*. She offered up a silent prayer for the maquisards she hoped would help her in her mission. These men she would never meet were risking their lives tonight, just as she was.

Moving slowly, she followed the map in her head, praying she'd remembered the route correctly. Emerging from the side passage, she realised she'd reached the main section of the station, and was brought up short by a terrifying sight. Perhaps a dozen armed Wehrmacht soldiers were gathered near the front entrance, standing at ease, talking amongst themselves. Elisabeth shrank back into the shadows, pressing herself into the wall, considering her options. It was too dark to see her wristwatch; she could only hope that the soldiers moved on before it was too late.

Her heart beat in her throat, rapid and fluttery, and she tried to take deep breaths. The soldiers erupted in raucous laughter, and Elisabeth stiffened. Seconds later, she heard the muted but distinct sound of an explosion, followed by distant shouting. She watched as the soldiers hurried away, leaving the concourse clear.

She forced herself to move, running on numb legs across the expanse of concrete, the pounding of her boots echoing beneath the vaulted dome of the roof. Her eyes swept the area, at last glimpsing the sign she needed: *Poste de Commandement*. Reaching the office door, she noted a thin strip of light along the bottom, and placed her ear to the wood, but all was silent beyond. With a last glance behind her, she turned the handle and cautiously opened the door. The office was bigger than she'd expected, and mercifully deserted. There were several desks covered in papers, charts and telephones, with three tall cupboards ranged along the far wall. Where on earth to start searching?

Heart hammering now, she hurried over to the nearest cupboard, to find it was unlocked but contained only stationery.

The second cupboard was similarly unlocked, filled with boxes she hadn't the time to investigate.

The third and last cupboard resisted her attempts to open it. She scrabbled in her pocket for the skeleton key.

She was shaking so much, she had to use both hands to guide the wire into the keyhole.

Take it slowly, feel the lock. Mr Smith's voice came to her.

Gently, she twisted the wire, manipulating the simple mechanism just as she had been taught. Moments later she was rewarded with the faint thunk of the lock releasing.

Stacked on shelves inside the cupboard were rolls and rolls of paper.

Elisabeth forgot to breathe, as she desperately seized one roll after another, scanning the dates at the top of each sheet of paper. At last she found the one she needed, and spread it out on the nearest desk, pinning down the curling corners with anything she could grab – a telephone, a dirty mug, a full ashtray.

The schedule of train movements was incomprehensible, a blur of numbers and codes, but she fumbled out her camera and took several shots. She had just closed the cupboard again when she heard the door to the office open. Spinning round, she found herself facing a tall German soldier. He was pointing a rifle at her.

'*Wer bist du?*' Who are you?

She was caught.

The soldier took a step towards her, his gun trained on her, and Elisabeth suddenly saw herself as if from above, her face smeared with grease, the overalls swamping her small frame. Trapped.

From outside on the concourse came shouts and the slap of running footsteps. The soldier lunged at Elisabeth, and she ducked sideways, shoving a desk between them. She was banking on him not firing his weapon; it would destroy this room if he did.

'*Halt!*' the soldier yelled, grabbing Elisabeth's arm as she dived for the door. She twisted from his grasp, her hip colliding painfully with the edge of a table. She was almost at the threshold, when another figure burst through the doorway and she froze. She had only a moment to take in the man's dirty clothes, his soot-blackened cap, before he flashed her a feral grin, and launched himself at the German soldier.

Elisabeth ran.

The journey back to the church was a blur. Father André, true to his word, had left the entrance unlocked. With the last of her strength, Elisabeth made it to the vestry, and barricaded the door with a chair.

As she collapsed on the pile of robes in the corner, her limbs began to shake, the darkness of the vestry pressing down on her chest. The near miss with the soldier had brought back the assault in the wood in all its horror, and all she could do was ride it out.

Despite her exhaustion, the effects of the Benzedrine tablets lingered, a ripple of electric through her veins. For the remainder of the night she lay awake, alert to every sound beyond the vestry door. Morning finally dawned, a pale sun shining through the curtains. Elisabeth sat up wearily. Father André had left her some fresh water, and she drank deeply. Changing out of the overalls, she dressed in her skirt and blouse, tying the money-belt around her waist. She found a rag stuffed in a drawer and used the remaining water to clean her face and hands as best she could.

If only she had a mirror. She hoped she didn't look quite as awful as she felt.

The Benzedrine had finally worn off, and her temples thumped with a dull headache. Digging in her coat pocket, she shook two more tablets from the little glass phial. Returning to Rouen train station would take every ounce of courage and vigilance she possessed.

As she passed through the station entrance, she tried to remind herself that no one was looking for a Frenchwoman in a trench coat and headscarf. Buying a ticket, she made her way towards the platforms, doing her best to avoid eye contact with the German soldiers swarming everywhere, praying they wouldn't notice a small, drab-looking woman hurrying past.

German troop trains and freight took priority over passenger trains, and Elisabeth had to wait an uncomfortably long time on the platform. When at last her train arrived, it was so overcrowded that she was forced to stand in the corridor, sweating with fear, the wireless tucked behind her legs.

To her enormous relief, she survived the journey unchallenged, arriving back in Chounoît shortly before noon. The wireless felt almost too heavy to carry, but somehow she managed to reach Rue Vincent and the flat, slipping through the deserted yard.

She hauled the suitcase up the back stairs, with only one thought in her mind now.

Sleep.

On the landing, she knelt to retrieve the door key she'd hidden in a gap between two floorboards near the wall.

Her fingers met a dusty void.

The key was gone.

Her pulse beat faster, her breaths growing shallower.

Stay calm.

And then she noticed the bay-leaf trap she'd left in the keyhole, lying on the floor.

18

May 1944

With an unsteady hand, Elisabeth reached inside her coat and withdrew her pistol.

Then she placed her ear against the door. Silence. A thought darted into her mind: if Gestapo officers were inside, surely she'd hear them crashing about, destroying the room in their hunt for evidence?

She eased the door open a crack. Through the gap, she could see most of the room; both chairs were neatly tucked under the table, the bowls and plates on the dresser were intact, the pot of water was where she'd left it on the stove. Nothing appeared to have been disturbed.

Gripping the gun, she pushed the door wider, edging over the threshold. Immediately, her eye caught on the bedroom door, standing ajar.

She was certain she'd closed it before she left.

It took all her courage to cross the few steps to the door. The shutters in the bedroom beyond were closed as she'd left them, but there was enough light that she could make out the washstand, her blouse hanging from a hook on the closet door, the trunk at the foot of the bed.

As her eyes swept over the bed itself, she drew in a sharp breath, her fingers instinctively tightening on the gun.

There was someone in her bed.

She moved closer, and now she could see it was a man, asleep, his dark tousled hair on her pillow, the shape of his face so familiar, so longed for, she must surely be dreaming.

It couldn't be him.

It simply couldn't be.

Lowering the gun, she stumbled the last few steps to the bed. At her touch on his shoulder, Gilbert jerked awake with a cry, his arm swinging up reflexively, causing Elisabeth to step back.

'*Mon Dieu!*' she gasped.

'Elisabeth ...' Gilbert exhaled.

Was it really him? His hair was tangled and matted, his face pale. An odour of damp and stale sweat and woodsmoke emanated from him.

Her throat tightened. 'I-I can't believe it's you.' The gun slid from her fingers and thudded on the floor.

'I've found you,' Gilbert breathed. 'Thank God, I've found you.'

He opened his arms to her, and as Elisabeth sank into his embrace, all her stifled fear released in a flood of emotion, and she began to sob. They held each other for several long minutes, until at last Elisabeth's tears subsided enough for her to pull away.

'I've dreamed of this every night,' she sighed. 'I can't believe you're here ...'

Gilbert rubbed his eyes on a grubby shirtsleeve and gave Elisabeth a tired smile. 'Neither can I.'

'Are you thirsty? Hungry?'

'Famished.'

She rose from the bed. 'I'll see what there is ...'

In the main room, she discovered the door to the flat still open, and suffered a moment of paralysing fear. She'd completely forgotten about the wireless out on the landing! To her immense relief, it was where she'd left it. As she dragged the suitcase into the flat, bolting the door behind her, Gilbert emerged from the bedroom and sank down at the table.

'I've eaten nothing but leaves and berries the last two days,' he confessed, when Elisabeth returned from hiding the suitcase in the closet. 'What I wouldn't give for some bacon and eggs and a cup of tea ...'

'All I've got is some stale bread,' Elisabeth apologised.

'No tea?'

She shook her head. 'No coffee either, before you ask. But there's some wine left ...'

Gilbert drank straight from the bottle, before Elisabeth could bring him a cup. She watched him chew the heel of bread with painful care. Had he lost a tooth? There was a livid purple bruise on his jaw and a smear of dried blood down one cheek, more crusted blood on the collar and cuffs of his shirt. Had he been in a fight?

Elisabeth crossed the room to open the shutters wider, let in more light.

'Don't,' Gilbert stopped her. 'Someone might be watching.'

Elisabeth stiffened at his words. 'Who? Were you followed?'

How on earth did you even find me?

Gilbert drained the dregs of wine. 'I shouldn't be here. I've put you in more danger.'

'What do you mean?'

'Sit down,' Gilbert sighed.

Elisabeth sank on to a chair, as Gilbert began to haltingly recount the sequence of events that had brought him to her door.

'I was sent to work for a new circuit,' he told her. 'North of Paris.' He wiped a shaking hand across his mouth. 'Organising drops, radioing London all hours. It was bloody intense.'

The Maquis he was working with were mainly involved in rail sabotage, he went on. He'd messaged London for explosives, and some emery powder, then shown the maquisards how to apply the abrasive grit to the axles of railway trucks. The wheels would seize up way down the line, leaving the engines vulnerable to attack.

'God knows how many trains I've de-railed.'

Elisabeth had a sudden, vivid memory of explosives training in Scotland, detonating lengths of rusting track on the shore. It seemed like a lifetime ago.

Gilbert rolled his shoulders. 'I'd kill for a smoke.'

Elisabeth craved a cigarette too, and fetched her dwindling supply of Gauloises from her case.

'A few days ago,' Gilbert continued, 'I got word that the chief from another circuit wanted to meet me. I agreed to liaise on a train out of Paris.' He closed his eyes, drawing deeply on his cigarette. Dread crawled along Elisabeth's spine at the thought of what he was about to say next.

'It was a trap.' Gilbert's voice broke and he covered his eyes with his hands, the cigarette smouldering in his fingers. 'The Gestapo caught me.'

Elisabeth sat rigid with horror. The dangers they faced here were far beyond anything their SOE training had prepared them for.

'I tried to run,' Gilbert resumed, dropping his hands to the table, scattering ash. 'But there was one German bastard ...' He took a shaky pull on his cigarette.

Elisabeth reached for Gilbert's hand across the table.

'He chased me down, laid into me so fast, I couldn't defend myself.'

Elisabeth gently squeezed his fingers.

'They took my wireless,' Gilbert went on. 'Then they cuffed me and threw me in a cell.'

He pulled his hand free and rubbed his brow, as though trying to erase his memories.

'A guard brought me water.' He gave a grim laugh. 'Threw it in my face, then beat me with a cosh.

'Later – I don't know how much later – I was thrown in the back of a car and driven to a nearby hotel. I don't know which one; they smuggled me in the back way. The Gestapo had commandeered all the rooms on the top floor.' His head dropped, eyes fixed on the table. 'I stuck to my story, Elisabeth.' His voice grew quiet. 'I was beaten, again and again and again. Every time I refused to answer their questions, down I went. They even tried to drown me ...' He faltered, and Elisabeth could find no adequate words of comfort.

'Oh, Gilbert,' she whispered.

'They told me that unless I made radio transmissions to London, they'd torture me to death.'

Elisabeth shuddered.

'So I sent a message. Tried to warn London. Omitted my true check, just like they trained us. Got a message back telling me not to be so bloody careless next time.'

Elisabeth stared at Gilbert in dismay.

'It's just a bloody game to the brass in London,' he whispered.

It was more like the Germans were playing an evil game with them, Elisabeth thought.

'But then they let you go?' she prompted gently.

Gilbert shook his head. 'The hotel was hit in an air raid, and all hell broke loose.' He took a ragged breath. 'In the chaos, someone left the door unlocked and I was able to get out down the service stairs.'

So he'd escaped the Gestapo.

But no one escaped the Gestapo.

'How were you not caught?' she asked. 'With no papers ...?' *How had he found her?*

Gilbert sighed deeply. He looked so tired, Elisabeth hadn't the heart to press him.

*

Elisabeth gathered a flannel and a sliver of soap, filled a bowl with warm water, averting her eyes as Gilbert took off his filthy shirt and wiped the dried blood from his face and neck. The water had to be replaced twice before he was clean. Then Elisabeth did the same for herself.

'I was going out of my mind with loneliness,' Gilbert said, drying his face with Elisabeth's towel. 'Talking to myself like a madman.'

He passed the towel back to Elisabeth, and she couldn't help but notice the wiry outline of his torso beneath his thin vest.

She poured the last of the dirty water away, listening to him talk; it was so good to hear English spoken again. 'I've had no one to talk to either,' she replied.

'You have me, now.'

'I've been so worried, not knowing where you were.' Elisabeth's voice caught.

Gilbert's expression, so tender and sad, caused her eyes to brim again.

'My little sparrow,' Gilbert whispered. 'Even in my darkest moments, I always believed we would be together.'

From somewhere outside came the wheezing notes of an accordion; someone was playing a languid, mournful waltz. To Elisabeth's surprise, Gilbert rose from his chair and reached for her.

She stood, and Gilbert pulled her gently to him. As they swayed together, Elisabeth closed her eyes, feeling the warmth of Gilbert's hand resting lightly on her waist. Slowly, they danced to the tune of the accordion, holding each other, and for a brief, heavenly time, nothing else existed, only their two bodies and the music. The heat from Gilbert's touch radiated through Elisabeth's skin into the very centre of her; a healing force, regenerating her soul.

And then the accordion fell silent, and Gilbert's mouth was seeking hers, and though his lips were rough, Elisabeth craved his kiss. His palpable desire brought her own urge rising, and somehow they found their way to the bed, and Gilbert's hands were stroking her cheek, her neck, the length of her arm, sending tremors through her whole body.

'Are you sure ...?' he murmured, fingers brushing her throat. His eyes were dark as honey.

In answer, she kissed him, felt him shiver.

Gently, he undid the buttons on her blouse and it fell open. Elisabeth took one long breath, her limbs loosening as Gilbert cupped her face. She caught his hand, pressed her fingers to the veins beneath the skin of his wrist, felt his pulse leap.

Their bodies fitted together as one, and she moved beneath him, sliding her hands down his back, lower, lower.

'Elisabeth,' he groaned into her mouth. He gently parted her legs, his touch like a feather. As his fingers dipped inside her, she gasped, her body tensing.

'Is it ...?' he breathed. 'Are you ...?'

Unable to speak, she took him in her hand, guiding him. Slowly, he moved inside her, and she rose to meet him, riding the current of her desire. When the moment of soaring release came, everything, all thought, all pain, all fear faded away, and the world was still.

*

She woke to a warm, amber light streaming through the cracked wooden shutters. Gilbert lay on his side facing her, head resting on one palm. He ran his fingers lightly along Elisabeth's hip, his touch sending a delicious quiver through her. 'You sleep like a baby,' he murmured.

It was the deepest sleep she'd enjoyed for days, she wanted to tell him.

'What time is it?' she yawned.

'Nearly four, I think.'

She'd slept for hours.

Gilbert gently stroked Elisabeth's collarbone, and she flushed. She could hardly believe they were lying together, half naked, his trousers on the floor, her bra crumpled between them. She felt suddenly bewildered and overwhelmed, like she imagined an explorer might feel, discovering new and wholly unknown lands.

The afternoon sun fell in shafts across the bed. They lay facing one another, and in the shifting light Elisabeth watched Gilbert's irises change colour from chestnut to dusky hazel. She could gaze at him for ever.

Eventually, her bladder began to ache. She sat up, reaching for her bra, and as she did so the gold lipstick holder rolled on the bed between them.

'What's this?' Gilbert reached for it. 'Contraband?' His mouth twitched, as Elisabeth snatched the lipstick away.

'Insurance.'

Gilbert grinned. 'Is this insurance too?' He uncurled his fingers, revealing the creased photo of the two of them. 'Do you know these people?' he teased. 'They look a dodgy pair to me.'

A laugh burst from Elisabeth, and she lunged for the photograph, but he whipped it out of her reach. They wrestled gently, playfully, giggling like children, and the release was glorious; it felt like the first time Elisabeth had ever laughed.

At last, she managed to rescue the photograph, clasping it to her bosom.

With tantalising slowness, Gilbert removed her hand, replacing it with his mouth, tracing the curve of her breast with his warm tongue, up to her stiffening nipple, until Elisabeth trembled.

'I never want us to be apart again,' he whispered, lips moving against her skin.

Elisabeth took his head in her hands, drew him up, and kissed him.

*

'Tell me a secret.'

'What?' Gilbert yawned deeply.

'Tell me something you've never told anyone else ever.'

'Why?'

She waited for him to look at her, but his eyes remained closed.

'Because, we've just slept together, and it's my first ... I've never ... I just want to feel closer to you ...'

Slowly, he turned to her. 'And will I hear your darkest secrets too?'

'Maybe,' she whispered.

307

'There's something I do want to tell you,' Gilbert said at last. 'But I can't.'

'Don't tell me you've never done this before either.' Elisabeth gave a short laugh. 'Or are you going to tell me you're married with twins?'

'It's not important.' Gilbert gave another yawn, and slid from the bed. 'I need a drink; do you want one?'

She lay listening to him moving quietly about in the other room, fetching them water. She could still sense the trace of his caresses on her body, like the ghosts of cobwebs. What secrets was he hiding from her?

She sat up, glimpsing her reflection in the mottled mirror above the washstand. Her pale face stared back, and she found herself wishing she had some lipstick. She thought of the tip Josie had once shared with her, how to crumble the old ends of lipsticks into an eggcup, melt them down over a saucepan of hot water, mix in cold cream to make a concoction of rouge.

But Elisabeth had no lipstick, only a suicide pill rattling around in the gold holder that Lena Watkins had given her.

The situation suddenly struck her as so utterly ridiculous, she snorted with laughter.

Gilbert appeared in the doorway, smiling. 'Share the joke?'

'Come back to bed, and I'll tell you a secret ...'

*

Soon, they were both so hungry it was decided that Elisabeth should venture out for food. With no identifying papers on him, it was too much of a risk for Gilbert to go in her stead. He would have to remain hidden in the flat.

'Do you have your ration cards?' he fussed, as Elisabeth gathered together the string shopping bag, the empty wine bottle and a few francs, in case the opportunity arose to purchase something on the black market.

'Yes. I won't be long.' Turning to the door, the room spun and she swayed.

'Elisabeth?' In a heartbeat, Gilbert was at her side.

She set a hand against the wall, waving away his insistence that she come and sit down again. This had happened to her before, and all she could do was breathe deeply until the sensation of dizziness passed. Slow starvation was hollowing her out, and she must draw on her inner strength now, an animal strength.

'Don't worry,' she said, her head clearing. 'I'll be fine.'

As Elisabeth slipped out of the back door and across the yard, she knew that Gilbert's arrival couldn't have gone entirely unnoticed. There were eyes everywhere, even in a backwater town like this. She glanced over the low boundary wall, but there was no sign of Madame Couly hanging out her washing. She raised her eyes to the stark blue sky arcing above, eerily empty of birds. At the very back of her mind, unease lurked.

A pair of German soldiers were patrolling the streets, and Elisabeth kept her head lowered as she hurried to buy bread, cheese, onions, carrots.

At last, having purchased what provisions she could, including a tiny portion of stewing meat, she headed back to the flat. As she hurried along Rue Vincent, she dreaded a hand descending on her shoulder, a German voice in her ear declaring her under arrest. If she was caught, how long could she last? A week? A day? An hour? She could never relax for a single moment.

*

For dinner she cooked a simple stew, and as they ate Gilbert told her stories of the maquisards he'd been involved with, how the young men saw themselves as bandit heroes.

'Bloody amateurs,' he sighed. 'They think they've got a chance against the Boche, but they're hopelessly ill-equipped.' He mopped up the remains of the stew with a hunk of bread. 'All they've got are old rifles from the last war, mostly. And whatever London can send over.'

Elisabeth told him about meeting Father André in the disused church, how scared she'd been infiltrating Rouen Station. 'I need to get the camera back to London urgently,' she said. 'I missed my sked earlier, but I'll send a message now—'

'Wait.' Gilbert took Elisabeth's hand across the table, stroking her knuckles tenderly. 'Do you love me?'

Taken by surprise, Elisabeth couldn't think what to say.

'Because I love you,' Gilbert went on. 'You have to remember that.'

'What do you mean?' His words sounded ominous.

'Marry me, Elisabeth.'

'Wh-what? How can we ...?'

'Marry me.'

A nervous laugh escaped her, and she pulled her hand free. 'Don't tease ...'

'I've never been more serious in my life.' He dropped to his knees before her, fumbling in a pocket, and pulled out a tarnished metal curtain ring. He offered it to her in his open palm. 'Elisabeth Ridley, will you take this *bague d'or* as a symbol of my love?'

Gilbert was looking up at her, his gaze so intense, so desperate, so vulnerable, Elisabeth heard herself say, 'I will.'

Gently, Gilbert slipped the curtain ring on to her finger. Now, she thought ludicrously, what will Edouard say when he discovers his wife is a bigamist?

'I promise never to leave you,' Gilbert said.

He rose from his knees and drew Elisabeth to her feet. They gazed at one another, and Elisabeth could only think that nobody had ever looked at her like this before. It made the candlelight sharper, the flicker of hope in her veins stronger, the throb in her pelvis more intense.

'I love you,' Gilbert whispered.

They kissed, softly at first, Elisabeth's blood tingling as their lips met.

Afterwards, they lay in the narrow bed, limbs entwined. Talk turned to their families, and the discovery that they'd both lost their fathers in the war.

Elisabeth told Gilbert about Florence, how her mother was unable to cope for the first few weeks after Papa's death, until she'd thrown herself into working for the Women's Voluntary Service.

Gilbert described his own mother, a tiny, fierce Irish woman, with a temper as short as her stature. 'She's either beating a carpet to within an inch of its life,' he said, 'or pummelling lumps of bread dough into submission, or wringing the neck of some poor chicken.'

'She sounds terrifying,' Elisabeth said, pulling a face of comical fear. 'And now she's my mother-in-law.'

Gilbert laughed then, and it changed his face entirely. But then his smile faded. 'Mother always said I took too many risks. That I was selfish like that.'

Elisabeth touched his chest, felt the warmth radiating from it. 'I've never thought of you as selfish,' she said. 'Impulsive, perhaps, but not selfish.' Her deepening feelings for him were so swift, so acute, she trembled.

'Being here,' Gilbert gestured at the dingy bedroom, 'is the most unselfish thing I've done in my life, and she has no idea.'

'I know,' Elisabeth agreed. 'The worst thing about all this are the lies we have to tell our loved ones. My mother thinks I'm in London, translating for the War Office.'

'London see us as entirely expendable,' Gilbert said, after a while.

Elisabeth swallowed, tasting the remnants of the red wine they'd drunk earlier, the earthy flavour reminding her somehow of blood. She thought of Lena Watkins, how the officer had shown such concern and care for her at Tempsford, and felt sure she wasn't expendable in the officer's eyes.

When the time came to contact London by wireless, Gilbert insisted it should be him, not Elisabeth, who sent the message. He was quicker at tapping out Morse than her, a fact she couldn't refute.

'But won't London be suspicious?' she worried. Every agent had their own 'fist', and the signals clerks back home were trained to pick up on any aberrations in the messages.

'London will never know the difference,' Gilbert assured her, and Elisabeth had no time to question him.

'Do you have the coordinates of a suitable field?' Gilbert asked.

Elisabeth fetched her crumpled Michelin map, and they studied it by the light of a fresh candle, finally deciding on a meadow close to Raoul's farm.

'I'll work fast,' Gilbert promised her, his voice taut. 'Help me set up, and then keep watch.'

Moving swiftly, they prepared the transmitter and Gilbert began to compose a short cypher message. While he worked, Elisabeth stationed herself at the window, scanning the street below.

But however much she tried to relax, she felt a deep-seated unease pressing down on her.

She glanced over at Gilbert, head bent over her silk coding pad, pencil moving in focused concentration.

Hurry up, hurry up.

She chewed her lip as Gilbert put the headphones on, turned the knobs on the set, then swiftly tapped out Elisabeth's personal call sign, followed by a three-letter code.

QTC – I have a message for you.

Moments later, a shrill piping sound emanated from his headphones. He glanced up. 'They've heard me.'

He began working the Morse key, and Elisabeth wished there was some way the erratic tapping could be muffled, but all she could do was pray Raoul's aunt wouldn't hear it in the shop below.

At last, Gilbert was done. He took off the headphones and leaned back in his chair with a groan. As Elisabeth moved towards him, he straightened, snatching up the coded message, holding the scrap of paper to the candle flame. In seconds, it was reduced to charred dust.

'Can't be too careful,' he muttered.

More than half an hour had passed. While they waited for a response from London, they smoked the last two cigarettes. Gilbert remained at the table, Elisabeth on a chair by the window, her leg jiggling with nerves. She tried not to think about the danger they were in.

A reply from London finally came. Gilbert listened intently to the dits and dahs travelling through the ether into his headphones, scribbling down a stream of nonsensical letters on another scrap of paper.

'It's done,' he said at last. 'They're coming.'

Elisabeth sighed in relief, as Gilbert rose and pulled her to him.

'I won't be parted from you again, my darling,' he said, bringing her hand to his mouth and softly kissing the curtain ring.

19

2018

Tali suffers a restless night full of strange, unnerving dreams. She wakes before her alarm, and immediately checks her phone for messages, but there's no text from Jo.

She sinks back on to her pillow, as the tiny flame of hope she's been nurturing all night snuffs out.

So that's that then.

She longs to pull the covers over her head, stay buried under the blankets all day, but instead she forces herself out of bed. There's too much to do. Betty will be expecting her breakfast soon, and she can hear Tosca whining downstairs to be let out.

She hurriedly dresses in her brightest clothes: a long cerise skirt and a lemon-yellow blouse. The waistband of the skirt feels alarmingly tight since she last wore it. As she tugs a brush through her hair, she tries to ignore the queasy churning in her guts. She's never hosted a hundredth birthday party before, never mind in a foreign country with guests she hardly knows. The unpredictable British weather doesn't help; it might be sunshine now, but in the space of an hour it could change to rain, and all her plans for an outdoor celebration would be ruined. And on top of all that, she has no idea if or when Betty's arsehole of a son might make an appearance.

Somehow, she must find the strength to get through today.

Downstairs, Tali unbolts the kitchen door and lets Tosca out. She stands on the step, allowing herself a moment to bask in the early-morning sunshine. The river sparkles at the bottom of the garden, the rippling water sprinkled with diamonds. Tali looks up at the birds soaring across the blue sky, and feels her spirits lift with them.

Sometimes, England was beautiful.

Having a garden party today was the right decision.

She heads back into the kitchen to prepare Betty's breakfast of sardines on toast and a cup of tea. She adds the birthday card and present she's bought Betty to the tray, along with the envelope addressed to *Mrs Elisabeth Shepherd* that arrived yesterday. With its gold-embossed seal, it looks like a very posh birthday card, and Tali is intrigued to find out who it's from.

Whoever's sent it, Tali is grateful to them. Apart from hers, it's the only other card Betty has received.

She carries everything through to the front room, nudging the door open with her foot. The thick curtains are closed, the room lit by the glow from Betty's Anglepoise lamp. Betty is sitting up in bed, peering at something in her hands, and doesn't react when Tali comes in.

'*Joyeux anniversaire*, Madame Betty!'

Betty's head jerks up, and she clasps her hands to her concave chest. 'Oh, Natalia, you gave me a fright.'

Tali hovers with the tray, trying to see what it is that Betty is clutching. 'Happy hundredth birthday,' she tries again.

'Is it today?'

'All day,' Tali smiles. Surely she hadn't forgotten? 'Are you looking forward to your party this afternoon?' She sets the tray down on Betty's lap, glimpsing a flash of gold between the old woman's fingers.

'What is that you have?' Tali asks. Was it the lipstick she'd found the other day when she was tidying Betty's bedroom?

'Nothing,' Betty mutters, burying the mystery item under the tray.

'I can make you up,' Tali offers. 'Put some nice rouge on your cheeks, little bit of lipstick ...'

'Waste of time.'

As Betty reaches for her false teeth on the bedside table, Tali is shocked to see how thin her arm is. Betty seems to be shrinking; she probably weighs little more than a feather-full of sparrows, Tali thinks, contemplating her own burgeoning waistline.

'What's this?' Betty inspects the wrapped present on the tray.

'I hope you like it, Madame Betty.'

'You shouldn't have, Natalia.' Betty slowly unpicks the pink satin ribbon that Tali had found in a drawer, peeling back the floral wrapping paper to reveal a pot of lavender-scented talcum powder.

'Your powder is empty,' Tali explains.

'So thoughtful,' Betty smiles. 'Thank you, Natalia.'

'The card will make you laugh,' Tali says, perching on the end of the bed.

Betty's fingers fumble with the envelope. On the front of the birthday card is a picture of a Scottie dog wearing a party hat, and the words: *Look Who's 100 – it's time to paw-ty!*

'It's Tosca, isn't it?' Tali smiles. As if on cue, the dog noses his way into the room.

'Ah boy, there you are,' Betty says. She looks so sad all of a sudden, Tali longs to give her a hug.

'He likes you,' Betty says.

'Who?'

'Tosca.'

'We're friends now, *oui*,' Tali agrees, bending to scratch Tosca under his chin. The dog's eyes close in brief ecstasy, one back leg twitching.

'He knows which side his bread is buttered,' Betty says.

Is that why the dog is so fat? Tali wonders. Because Betty feeds him sandwiches? She'll have to talk to her about that, but not today. 'Don't forget your other card, Madame Betty.'

Betty sighs. 'You open it, dear.'

Tali breaks the seal on the envelope and draws out a thick ivory card decorated with a coat of arms on the front. She reads aloud the message printed inside:

Dear Elisabeth

I was pleased to learn that you are celebrating your one hundredth birthday on 10 June. My best wishes to you on such a remarkable achievement.

Elizabeth R

'Elizabeth R?' Tali breathes. *'Mon Dieu!* The queen has sent you a birthday card!'

Betty makes no reply, staring at a spot beyond Tali, as though in a trance.

'Madame Betty?'

Betty's eyes refocus on Tali. 'That's nice, dear.' She pokes at the sardine with her fork.

Tali rises, not wanting to distract Betty from her breakfast. She eats little enough as it is. 'I'll put your cards here, Madame Betty, where you can see them.' Tali arranges the two contrasting birthday cards next to each other on the bedside table. 'I'll be back soon.'

Betty doesn't look up as Tali leaves the room, Tosca at her heels.

Back in the kitchen, Tali is pouring a bowl of cereal, when something makes her pause. The strangest of sensations passes through her, a shiver of foreboding down her spine. She finds herself back at Betty's partly open door.

Through the gap, she sees Betty pull a small object from beneath her tray.

Tali's eyes widen. She was right, it's the gold lipstick holder. As she watches, Betty unscrews the holder, and tips what looks like a large vitamin tablet into her palm. Is she crying?

'Madame Betty?'

'Oh, Natalia.' Betty blinks back tears as Tali approaches the bed. 'I can't do it.'

'Can't do what?' Tali asks, eyeing the strange pill in Betty's hand. 'What is that you have?'

To Tali's surprise, Betty relinquishes the tablet, and Tali examines it in her palm. The capsule is encased in what appears to be a thin skin of rubber. It resembles no headache pill Tali's ever seen before.

She meets Betty's eye, and a terrible thought occurs to her. This is no painkiller, but something much more sinister.

'I'm sorry, Natalia,' Betty whispers, closing her eyes.

'Are you all right, Madame Betty?' A stupid question, but she has to ask it. Of course Betty isn't all right. She's a hundred years old, with a son who wants her gone, no friends left alive, and a very limited future.

Betty sighs. 'Please leave me, Natalia.'

'If you're sure, Madame Betty?'

Betty nods.

'OK,' Tali frowns. She drops the capsule in her apron pocket, and lifts Betty's tray from her lap. The breakfast has barely been touched. 'I'll come back soon.'

*

Tali leaves Betty to rest for an hour, and when she returns to check on her, she's relieved to find Betty awake and in a happier mood. Tali makes no mention of the pill, still in her apron pocket, and Betty doesn't ask her what she's done with it.

'The river is looking so beautiful today,' Tali chatters on, as she helps Betty to the lavatory. 'As if it knows it's your special day.'

'You do say some funny things, Natalia.'

'I try to make you smile, Madame Betty.'

'I don't deserve you ...'

'That's not true. Now, I thought you could wear these today.'

Tali has chosen Betty's birthday outfit with care: a pastel-blue blouse and navy trousers, with a matching navy cashmere cardigan that she recently discovered at the back of Betty's wardrobe.

Once Betty's dressed, Tali settles her at the table in the sitting room and gives her the job of folding linen napkins into triangles. 'Even birthday girls have to work, Madame Betty.'

'My mother used to love organising an event,' Betty remarks, causing Tali to pause on her way out. 'She was surprisingly good at persuading ladies with too much time on their hands and men with too much money to help her.'

'She would be very useful today,' Tali smiles wryly. She retrieves the two birthday cards from the bedroom, and sets them on the mantelpiece, pondering whether to take a photograph of the queen's card on her phone and text it to Rozo. Her family would think Madame Betty was a personal friend of the Queen of England.

'VE Day: now that was something I'll never forget,' Betty continues, as Tali hovers in the doorway. 'Maman hung red, white and blue bunting everywhere, tables and chairs were set out all down the street, church bells were ringing all over town. And the food! More than anyone had seen in years. Leo tasted a banana for the first time, I remember.' Betty's mouth curls into a smile. 'Spat it out on Fred's sleeve.' She laughs to herself, staring off through the window.

Bunting, Tali thinks. That's what she's forgotten. What English party is complete without little flags on string? But where can she get some?

'The entire royal family remained in London all through the war,' Betty continues, as Tali turns to go. 'Bombs were raining down all over the city, but they stayed put.' She folds another napkin, pressing the crease flat.

Tali thinks of the suitcase from the cellar, stuffed with old documents, tucked away under her bed. 'Do you wish you could go back in time?' she hears herself ask. 'Back to the war?'

Betty stares through the window, her face so wan and drawn that Tali worries afresh if the party will be too much for her.

'*On ne se baigne jamais deux fois dans le même fleuve,*' Betty mutters.

You can never swim in the same river twice.

*

She can't help it. She has to check her phone again, just in case.

No text from Jo.

Forget about her, Tali tells herself sternly. She heads out into the garden to organise the furniture. She'll set the table and chairs on the lower lawn, she decides, down by the willow tree.

Brandishing a torch, Tali braves the dank, creepy cellar, unearthing four camping chairs, a rusty but intact two-seater metal bench, and a couple of mildewed deckchairs. She dusts the cobwebs off a small wooden table, lugs it down to the river bank and covers it with an oilcloth. Last, she puts up an old green parasol, the fabric speckled with white patches. Hopefully, no one will notice the mould.

What has she forgotten?

She dredges her memory for anything she has ever seen or read about English garden parties, but the only thing she can think of is *Alice in Wonderland* and the Mad Hatter's tea-party. She pictures a china tea set, dainty cups and saucers and fairy cakes on wire stands.

Thinking of *Alice in Wonderland* brings Jo to mind again.

As she makes her way back up the garden path, she's startled by a woman's strident voice calling through the trellis from next door.

'I say!' Betty's neighbour calls, her tight silvery perm bobbing above the fence. Tali tenses. Betty had warned her to be wary around Mrs Voller. 'She'll wheedle information out of you, that one,' Betty had said. 'Like the Gestapo.'

'*Bonjour*, Madame Voller.' Tali forces a smile.

'Good morning, yes,' Mrs Voller replies. 'Can you help me with something, dear? Timothy's gone out golfing, and I wanted to paint the shed, but I can't get this damn lid off.' She passes the tin of paint over the trellis.

'You have a screwdriver, Madame Voller?'

'Here you are ... I'm afraid I've bent the rim ...'

Tali kneels on the path and tries to prise up the lid on the can of paint.

'Got visitors coming, have you?'

'*Pardon?*' Tali pants, arms trembling as she leans on the screwdriver.

'All the furniture you're dragging about ...'

Tali frowns at the thought of being observed. 'It's Madame Betty's hundredth birthday today,' she answers shortly. The paint lid creaks but remains stuck.

'A hundred?' Mrs Voller exclaims. 'I had no idea Mrs Shepherd was that ancient.'

With a grunt, Tali wrenches the screwdriver up and the lid finally pops free. 'The party is at two o'clock,' she says, handing the paint back over the trellis.

'Oh how wonderful,' Mrs Voller beams. 'I haven't been to a garden party in ages.'

Tali can't think what to say. Has Mrs Voller just invited herself? How did that happen?

'Can I bring anything?' Mrs Voller asks.

Tali's mind clicks. 'Do you have any bunting?'

*

She's lugging a rickety stepladder out of the cellar, wondering where to hang Mrs Voller's little triangular flags up, when Violet and Abeo arrive, an hour early. Abeo had misread the invitation, he apologises, but by the time he realised his mistake, they were in the taxi and it was too late to turn back and go home again.

'It's no problem,' Tali assures him, as they settle Betty and Violet beneath the parasol on the lower lawn. 'An extra pair of hands will be helpful.'

Abeo heads into the house to make a pot of tea, while Tali finishes stringing up Mrs Voller's red, white and blue bunting around the garden. Then she and

Abeo ferry the plates of food from the kitchen down the garden and arrange everything on the table.

'You've made so many delicious things, Tali,' Abeo says. 'This must have taken you days.'

Tali waves away his praises. 'I wish I could have done more, but time ran away ...'

'Where is Mrs Shepherd's son?' Abeo asks, as they return to the kitchen to collect bottles of elderflower cordial and Prosecco. 'Didn't you say he was living here now?'

'He is,' Tali says. Just the thought of Leo makes her crave a slug of rum. 'But he's seeing a man about a dog.'

Abeo shoots her a questioning look, but further interrogation is prevented by the arrival of the rest of the guests. Tali welcomes everyone, and leads them down the garden to Betty. Robert has brought along his new Zimmer frame. He proudly shows off a number plate attached to the basket that reads 'BOB 100'. Duncan laughs, and Hilda tells him off.

'Mrs Shepherd has such a pretty garden,' Juliana remarks to Tali, as together they shunt Margaret in her wheelchair along the brick path. 'You are so lucky, living by the river.'

With Abeo's help, Tali pours drinks, fetches more plates of food, wipes up spillages, all the while keeping half an eye on Betty. The birthday girl seems happy enough, chatting with Hilda and Olive. Violet has already dropped off to sleep in her deckchair, a plate of untouched food balanced precariously on her blanketed knees.

Tali returns from another trip to the kitchen to find Alfred making his way across the lawn, Robert and his frame close behind. They're heading for the dilapidated greenhouse, and alarm shivers through Tali. She hurries to intercept the two men. 'Don't open the door,' she warns them. 'The glass, it's loose.'

It's a death-trap, really, but Betty won't hear of it being taken down.

'Don't fret,' Alfred tells her. 'We're just stretching our legs.'

'Nice grub,' Duncan compliments Tali, as she returns to the table and collects up some empty plates. She can't believe how fast the food is disappearing. She suspects Duncan to be the main culprit, but is surprised to see Olive's plate is also piled high with gajak, rice and naan bread dripping with melted butter. For someone who resembles a little guinea pig, Hilda's carer has the appetite of a wild boar, Tali smiles to herself.

With everyone taken care of, she feels her shoulders begin to relax, lifting her face to the sun.

The only thing that would make this party perfect was if Jo was here.

'You must eat something too,' Abeo says, appearing at her side and making her start. 'All this work, you must be hungry ...'

But for once, Tali can't face eating anything; the faint hope she'd had that Jo would come today has withered, taking her appetite with it.

She gives herself a mental shake, and realises what the party is missing: music. She hurries back inside the house, to the gramophone on the sideboard in the sitting room. Earlier in the week she'd discovered a stash of vintage vinyls in the cupboard under the stairs, and now she selects one at random and cranks the handle. Setting the needle down gently on the disc, Tali smiles as crackly music issues from the gramophone's horn. She opens the sitting room windows wide, releasing Glenn Miller's band music into the garden.

The party is going so well, Tali thinks, as she makes her way back outside.

'Does Betty have a birthday cake?' Abeo asks her, pouring a glass of cordial.

'She didn't want one,' Tali replies. 'So instead I made a hundred Neapolitan cookies.' Secretly, she's glad Betty refused a cake. The last time Tali had baked one, it was for Zezette's thirty-first birthday party. She'd made a pineapple and cinnamon upside-down cake, a labour of love that had taken her hours.

She doubts Zezette's new boyfriend even knows how to turn the oven on.

'Wonderful!' Abeo raises his glass. 'We must sing "Happy Birthday" to Betty now.'

With Abeo helping, Tali conveys the plates of iced birthday biscuits down to the guests. She's also dug out an old, slightly melted beeswax candle she found in one of Betty's kitchen drawers, and Abeo lights the wick, shielding the flame with his large hand.

'Time to sing!' he cries.

Tali hovers with the candle at Betty's side, catching Abeo's eye, and with his baritone leading, the gathering launches into a halting, slightly out-of-tune rendition of 'Happy Birthday'. Betty smiles bashfully from her chair, as the song reaches its rousing conclusion.

'Make a wish,' Hilda commands, and Tali bends down to bring the candle closer to Betty. She screws up her eyes, and Tali wonders if she's wishing for her son to come home, or return to Australia. Or something else entirely. Her face, as usual, gives little away.

Betty takes a breath and lets it out, extinguishing the flame in one decisive puff. A wobbly cheer goes up, and Betty grins and gives a clap, her eyes shining, and for a fleeting moment Tali glimpses the young woman she once was.

'Speech!' Abeo cries.

Betty's smile falters. 'No one wants to hear me rattling on ...'

'Just a few words, on this momentous occasion,' Abeo cajoles. 'Otherwise, I will have to treat you all to my a-capella version of "Over the Rainbow"—'

'Bloody hell, spare us,' Duncan interrupts loudly. Abeo's face falls, and Hilda slaps Duncan's arm.

'Thank you all for coming today,' Betty begins, blinking up at the group gathered around her. 'To be with friends on my birthday is ... is ...' She falls silent, and Tali has the sudden, horrible suspicion that this is the first time in many, many years that Betty has celebrated her birthday with company.

'Wonderful,' Betty continues, reaching for Tali's hand. 'You've worked so hard, Natalia, to make this day special. No one has ever done more for me. Your friendship has beamed sunshine into my wintery soul, and I want to thank you from the bottom of my heart.' She squeezes Tali's fingers in her bony, tenacious grip.

Tali gazes down at Betty, swallowing tears. It is the kindest thing Betty has ever said to her.

'Mother? What's going on?'

A familiar voice drifts down the garden path.

Tali's heart plummets.

Merde.

Leo is back.

20

May 1944

A Lysander was due to collect them at the start of the next moon period, in six days' time. The urgency of London's response brought home to Elisabeth how important the contents of the camera film were.

'We'll have to stay hidden,' she fretted. What if the landlady became suspicious? What if Gilbert was discovered? What if Nazi Direction Finders tracked their wireless signals down?

'I'm a ghost,' Gilbert assured her. 'No one knows I'm here.'

Elisabeth wished she felt as confident. Time passed agonisingly slowly. Only when their food ran out did Elisabeth venture outside, her nerves raw as she hurried to buy supplies.

At last, the time came for them to leave the flat.

It was unwise to tell the landlady she was going, Elisabeth knew, though it felt wrong to just vanish. To compensate, she counted out an extra month's rent from her emergency fund, tucking the francs under a jug on the dresser for Raoul's aunt to find later.

She dressed in her trousers and blouse, then tied the money-belt tight around her waist, determined not to let the camera out of her sight until she reached London. Then she packed her suitcase, and stowed her loaded pistol in the hidden pocket inside her coat.

'I'll take the wireless,' Gilbert said. 'Can you manage the other case?'

'Yes.' She'd brought both cases here on her own, she wanted to remind him.

'We'll leave at ten,' Gilbert decided. Curfew would be well under way by then, and there shouldn't be anyone on the streets.

They agreed the safest route would be to head straight for Raoul's farm, cutting through fields and woods on the way. Once there, they would hide in the barn until the pick-up the following night.

At ten o'clock, Elisabeth closed the door of the flat for the final time, and followed Gilbert down the back stairs. They hurried through the moonlit streets, the scuff of their shoes echoing on the cobblestones. Gilbert moved fast, despite the bulky wireless, and Elisabeth struggled to keep up with him. She could feel the slickness of sweat beneath her arms, across her back. Her coat was too heavy, too warm, but she couldn't discard it.

Every shadow in every doorway was a Gestapo agent poised to shoot; the image of Mausers trained on her head urged Elisabeth on. They reached the edge of town, and Gilbert knelt by a ditch to tie a loose shoelace. Elisabeth willed him to hurry. They were horribly conspicuous, travelling illegally after curfew. If they should be caught by the Gestapo, interrogation and torture would be inevitable. There would be no explaining away the wireless or the pistol in her coat or the micro-camera or Gilbert's lack of papers. Their lives would be over, she had no doubt.

Suddenly, they heard the growl of an engine in the distance. Elisabeth tensed, the sound growing steadily louder as a pair of muted headlights swung into view. A car was coming along the road towards them.

Elisabeth felt the blood drain from her head. She couldn't move.

Gilbert seized her arm. 'Get down!' He dragged her into the ditch, their feet sliding in the mud, brambles tearing at their legs.

The car was almost upon them, headlights sweeping along the edge of the ditch. Squatting ankle-deep in sludge, Elisabeth ceased to breathe. What would they do if the car stopped? She closed her eyes, a childish thought careening through her head ... if she couldn't see the car, then the driver couldn't see her.

'If they stop, let me do the talking,' Gilbert whispered.

The vehicle's engine rumbled as it slowed to a crawl, and Elisabeth's hand closed over her pistol. Just as she was about to draw her weapon, the throb of the engine began to recede. The car was moving on.

Gradually, the sound of the motor dwindled, and the quiet of the night flooded back.

'Christ, that was close,' Gilbert exhaled.

They had to get off the road before the car returned.

Elisabeth sucked in a ragged breath, then dragged her suitcase back out of the ditch. After a brief check of the map, they set off again, soon reaching a track that skirted the edge of a cornfield. The track narrowed to a footpath as it plunged into a wood, the route so dark beneath the canopy of trees that Elisabeth could barely see her sodden feet. Gilbert took her hand and they walked in silence, Elisabeth praying they were going in the right direction. She thought fleetingly of the treks they'd endured together across the bleak Scottish moors. Those navigational training exercises were paying dividends now.

The eye of the moon tracked their ever-slowing progress, but at last they came to a broken gate that Elisabeth recognised, beyond which sprawled Raoul's farm.

They'd made it.

They crept across the dark, deserted yard, the muddy ground muffling their footsteps, and slipped inside the barn. The familiar stench of cow manure and hay assailed Elisabeth, and for one surreal moment time seemed to contract, and it was as though she was arriving in France all over again.

With the last of her strength, she crawled up after Gilbert into the hayloft.

'All right?' Gilbert whispered, as they lay side by side in a recess between bales of hay. Elisabeth stared up into the dark rafters, her mind churning.

'Will London broadcast *un message personnel*?' she asked.

She turned to Gilbert, but his slow breaths told her he'd already fallen asleep. Exhaustion swept through her, yet her mind continued to twist and turn. What if Raoul didn't have a radio? How would they know the rescue flight was actually on if they couldn't hear the BBC's secret coded messages?

The strengthening breeze whistled through gaps in the barn roof. Gilbert snored gently, and Elisabeth envied him his ability to sleep. The long, yawning expanse of night stretched ahead of her.

*

She woke at dawn. Without disturbing Gilbert, she slipped down the ladder and hurried across the yard to the farmhouse. She could see a light burning in the kitchen window.

She knocked on the door.

Moments later, she heard shuffling footsteps approaching, and then a rasp as the bolt was drawn back. Raoul's wife stared out at her.

'I need your help, *madame*.' Elisabeth's voice was barely a whisper.

The Frenchwoman wrapped her shawl tighter, and for a second Elisabeth was sure the woman would tell her to go away. But instead, Mathilde opened the door and gestured for Elisabeth to come in.

Later, hidden in the hayloft again, it seemed to Elisabeth, that time had slowed to a standstill. She picked at the bread and cheese Mathilde had given her, as Gilbert drank milk from a jug. At last, dusk fell, but still they had to wait.

Though he said little, Elisabeth could tell from Gilbert's restlessness that he was just as anxious as her.

'Can I ask you something?' she said. 'Why did you join the SOE?'

Gilbert shifted in the hay, trying to get comfortable. 'You know why.'

'I know your boss at work told the War Office about you. But why did you join?'

Gilbert rolled over to face her. 'The truth? I didn't want to go into the bloody army. I wanted to be my own master.'

Don't we all, Elisabeth thought.

'I don't know why men willingly sign up to die for their country,' Gilbert sighed, shifting on to his back again. 'I hate the thought of being ordered about by some bastard in an office. I joined the SOE because I want to be in charge of my own fate. Old Churchill might give the order to set Europe ablaze, but it's down to me when and how I light the fire.'

'What will you do,' Elisabeth ventured, 'when we get back to London?'

Gilbert was silent for a moment. 'I haven't thought about it.'

'What do you mean?'

'Just that, really. I'll decide when the war's over.'

'How did you find me?' She had to know.

Gilbert took a long pause, then pushed himself up to sitting. Obscured by shadow, his expression was impossible to read. 'When I escaped the Gestapo,' he said, his voice low, 'I knew I had to get out of France. One of the maquisards had told me about a farmer who smuggled people out.'

'Raoul?'

Gilbert nodded.

'You walked here?'

'Mostly,' he sighed. 'Hitched a ride on a cart once.'

'But how did you find me?' Elisabeth pressed.

'Raoul's wife let slip they'd had an English girl here, a "bird from the sky", as she put it. From her description, it had to be you.'

Elisabeth listened in stunned silence. The fact that their paths had crossed still felt utterly incredible.

At quarter past five in the evening, Gilbert crept from the barn to listen to the BBC World Service on Raoul's illegal wireless. Radio Londres broadcast the *messages personnels* after the news every evening, and Elisabeth thought of the many messages transmitted through the ether, the nonsense sentences holding meaning for someone, somewhere. All being well, the secret message Gilbert had arranged with London would be broadcast twice this evening, once at half past five, and again at a quarter past seven.

Elisabeth waited for Gilbert's return, trying to distract herself by cleaning the Colt of hay dust, checking the camera was safe in her money-belt, going over in her head the pick-up procedure she'd been taught at Ringway. She pictured Gilbert and Raoul hunched over the radio in the farmhouse, listening to the opening bars of Beethoven's Fifth Symphony which preceded the messages.

Dit, Dit, Dit, Dah.

In Morse, the notes translated to 'V'.

V for Victory.

Was the choice of music intentional, Elisabeth wondered, or just a lucky coincidence?

At last, Gilbert climbed back up to the hayloft. 'Radio interference is intense,' he said. 'The Boche are jamming the frequencies. Could hardly hear the messages.'

'But you heard our message?' Hope and dread burned in Elisabeth's chest, an unpleasant alchemy.

When Gilbert answered that he had, and she mustn't worry, Elisabeth tried to relax, but it was impossible.

*

Night deepened, and Gilbert told Elisabeth to rest, that he would wake her when the time came to leave. She slumbered for an hour or so, but then something woke her, and when she reached for Gilbert, her hand met empty air. She sat up, thinking perhaps he'd slipped outside to relieve himself. The cows below her shifted in their stalls. It must have been their movements that had roused her.

Minutes ticked by, and she began to grow worried by Gilbert's absence. What if he'd tripped and hit his head on his way around the barn?

Checking her gun in her coat pocket, she crept down the ladder and inched open the barn door just wide enough to slip through. The night sky was awash with stars, and the almost full moon beamed down, bathing the yard in its ethereal light. She needed no lantern to see her way, but having completed a circuit of the barn, there was no sign of Gilbert at all.

Maybe he was in the farmhouse, talking with Raoul? But all the lights were out, the place in darkness.

With no notion what else to do, she made her way back up into the loft. A short while later she heard the scrape of the barn door opening. She lay tense, gun ready, as footsteps scuffed through the straw. The ladder creaked, and Gilbert's face appeared. 'Elisabeth?'

She lowered the gun, arm shaking. 'Where have you been? I was sick with worry!'

Gilbert collapsed on the hay, chest heaving, as though he'd run miles. 'I went to ask Raoul something,' he said between gasps. 'But he got the wine out, and we lost track of time.'

'What did you have to ask him?'

Gilbert wiped sweat from his brow with a shirt-sleeve. 'If he could lend us some torches for the pick-up.'

Elisabeth thought of the pitch-black farmhouse.

'Sorry I worried you,' Gilbert sighed, pulling her to him and kissing her. 'We have to go soon.'

In a box on the farmhouse step, they found two bicycle lamps and a pocket torch, along with a round of cheese sandwiches wrapped in newspaper, two apples, a chunk of seed cake and a bottle of red wine.

Elisabeth wished she could thank Raoul and Mathilde for all their help, but there was no time.

The moon rode the heavens, as they made their way to the pick-up field, a couple of hectares of ploughed mud bordered on all sides by hedges and woodland. Elisabeth was worried the mud might prove too thick for the Lysander's wheels, that they should have chosen a different place instead. But it was too late now to search for a better location.

They waited next to a fallen oak at the edge of the field. Elisabeth crouched on the ground, her back resting against the fissured trunk, but Gilbert remained on his feet, restlessly scanning their surroundings.

'Tell me again what's going to happen,' Elisabeth said.

'We'll hear the plane before we see it,' Gilbert told her. He sank down on his haunches alongside her and patiently went over the plan, although they'd discussed it at length already.

Elisabeth listened, but though she tried not to think about what could go wrong, her mind teemed with worries.

What if the Germans saw the plane? She wanted to believe Gilbert when he told her that the vast size of France – half a million square kilometres – was too much for the Germans to patrol effectively, that a blacked-out little aircraft like their Lysander would go unnoticed, even on a moonlit night like this. 'Remember what they told us at Ringway?' he said. 'Lysanders can't be heard from more than about five miles away.'

She listened to him in silence, not caring about any of the facts or figures, only that the plane landed safely, though how it would ever find them, two tiny figures, in this pocket-handkerchief-sized field, in the middle of France, in the dead of night, she had no idea. She tried to recall what she'd been taught about Lysanders in training: the compact three-man aircraft had a range of several hundred miles, but carried no guns. They had no radio link, and no navigation system either.

The pilot relied purely on landmarks, the plane's compass, and the light of the moon to steer his course by.

The minutes dragged past. Each one felt to Elisabeth like a year.

She could hardly believe she was in a field again, waiting to go home. Such a short time had passed, and yet so much had happened.

The night was dry, the wind light, which was something at least. They ate a slice of Mathilde's seed cake, drank a little of the wine, and waited.

The moon shone down, casting its mother-of-pearl glow over the furrowed soil. It was eerily peaceful, and Elisabeth found herself gazing up at the stars, trying to remember the names of the constellations Papa had once so patiently taught her.

Ursa Major, Orion, Gemini.

She reached for Gilbert, feeling his warm, strong fingers fold around her own colder hand.

'We'll be home soon, won't we?' she whispered.

Gilbert squeezed her fingers gently, but made no reply.

*

Zero hour approached.

A rustling in the nearby undergrowth made them both stiffen. But it was only a fox, its white-tipped tail melting into the blackness of the woods.

'Time to go,' Gilbert whispered at last. He rose and ventured a few steps into the field, throwing a handful of dried leaves in the air to determine the direction of the prevailing wind. They set off, Elisabeth lugging her suitcase and the torches, while Gilbert took the heavier wireless case and three long, sturdy sticks he'd collected. Quickly and silently, they paced out two hundred metres from the downwind end of the prospective landing strip. At the end, Gilbert drove a stick into the ground, and Elisabeth passed him a torch which he deftly tied to the top of the stick with a strip of rag.

They trudged on, one hundred and fifty more paces, and Gilbert thrust another stick into the ground, upwind of the first. Another torch was attached.

The third and last stick was set fifty metres square to the right of the second stick, and Elisabeth's pocket torch was affixed to this.

Gilbert checked his watch. 'Fifteen minutes,' he whispered. 'We need to split up now. You know what to do.'

Elisabeth nodded, turning away, but Gilbert gently pulled her back. 'Whatever happens tonight, I'll always love you.'

They held each other, and Elisabeth rested her head on his shoulder. 'I love you too.'

After a moment, Gilbert pulled away. He switched on the first lamp.

Elisabeth made her way back across the field, and took her place by the second stick. She fumbled with the lamp, managing at last to turn it on.

She could just about make out the dark shape of Gilbert, squatting by the first stick. His torch had a light that shone all around, whereas Elisabeth's bicycle lamp, and the one fifty metres away, were angled so that their lights shone towards Gilbert. He had Raoul's torch in his hand, ready for signalling to the plane.

It occurred to her that if they survived tonight, only Gilbert would ever fully understand the ordeal they'd been through, the constant fear and danger they'd faced here.

They waited. The moon floated above, a dispassionate witness to whatever would unfold. Suddenly, the stillness of the night was broken by the faint, dull thrum of an approaching aircraft. The low growl of its engine grew steadily louder. Peering up into the night sky, Elisabeth made out the small, dark shape of a plane coming slowly closer. The Lysander descended inch by inch, the moonlight reflecting off its black painted flanks, its long, narrow wings reminding her of a dragonfly.

Across the field, Gilbert flashed his recognition signal: 'F'.

Dit, Dit, Dah, Dit.

Had the pilot seen it? Elisabeth's eyes strained to glimpse an answering flash from the plane. Seconds ticked by, the little aircraft continuing on its journey across the sky.

She tracked its progress with growing alarm.

It hadn't seen their signal!

Gilbert flashed his torch again.

Dit, Dit, Dah, Dit.

And suddenly, there it was, the lamp under the plane's fuselage flashing an answering signal:

Dit, Dah, Dit, Dit.

'L' for London.

But instead of slowing, the plane passed on overhead, vanishing beyond the far trees.

Elisabeth stared into the empty, gaping darkness, hope disappearing fast. She counted the seconds in her head, and when a minute had passed and the plane did not reappear, she began to feel really frightened. Then, there it was again, that familiar thrumming sound, and a movement above the trees caught her eye.

The plane had come back!

Adrenalin surged in her as she watched it come down to land across the field, propeller whirring. She seized up her suitcase, and was about to run when she noticed two dark figures hurrying from the trees opposite, heading towards Gilbert. He stood facing them, showing no signs of alarm.

Elisabeth ran to Gilbert over the rutted, claggy ground, pulling her pistol from her pocket. As she reached him, he grabbed her arm, pushing the gun down.

'I'm so sorry,' he said, his eyes fixed on the approaching men, a hundred metres away and gaining.

'What do you mean?' Elisabeth tried to wrest her arm free.

'Halt!' the nearest man shouted, and the unmistakable German voice sent ice through Elisabeth's veins.

'You have to believe me, my love, I had no choice!' Gilbert's face was ashen, his eyes wild. 'They let me go, in exchange for the plane.' His grip on her arm was hurting now.

She stared at him, trying to understand what he was saying.

And then the truth dawned.

Oh God, no.

This was a trap.

Gilbert had known these Germans would come.

He'd lied to her about everything.

'What have you done?' she cried.

'We're never going to win, Elisabeth!' He was desperate now, stuttering his words out. 'It's all over, don't you see? But not for us if we give them what they want.'

Elisabeth's mind raced: if she surrendered, did what Gilbert said, their lives might be spared, but her whole mission in Rouen would be a failure. The Lysander pilot and passenger – for there was surely an incoming agent on the plane – would be killed. Raoul, Louis, Mathilde, Father André, the whole Resistance network in the area would be put at enormous risk. She would never see her home or her mother again.

Another shout made her jerk. The Germans were almost on them. Elisabeth could see now that they were dressed in the uniform of the Gestapo, and one of them held a gun.

'Just do as they say,' Gilbert hissed. 'Trust me!'

But how could she trust him ever again?

From the corner of her eye, she saw the plane begin to move, and a freezing hand clamped around her heart as she realised it was preparing to take off again.

For a moment she stood paralysed, and then, deep in the kernel of her brain, her training kicked in. Her mind blazed, as she realised exactly what she had to do. The only thing she could do.

She reached for Gilbert, pulling his head down to hers, and kissed him. In that brief, liminal moment of united breath, she brought her gun between their bellies, the short barrel angled up towards Gilbert's heart.

Without breaking the kiss, she pulled the trigger.

Once, twice.

One to maim, two to kill.

Gilbert staggered back, a hand to his stomach, blood spilling through his fingers. He coughed, and Elisabeth recoiled as his blood sprayed her face. He wiped at his nose and mouth with a shaking wrist, blood smearing across his cheek, and Elisabeth could hear a strange keening sound. It took her a second to realise it was her.

Oh God, oh God, oh God.

Gilbert moaned, his legs giving way, and he slumped to the ground.

'Beweg dich nicht!' A shot rang out.

Through a haze of terror, Elisabeth backed away from Gilbert's motionless body.

'Run!' she heard a man scream. *'Fucking run!'*

She lurched around, stumbling towards the Lysander. She couldn't feel her legs.

'Halt!' Gunfire burst behind her, clods of earth erupting at her heels. Somehow she reached the plane's short ladder, and hands reached down to haul her up. She found herself in the tiny plane, a man crouching in front of her, his voice coming to her as if from far away.

'She's in! Go!'

The pistol shook in Elisabeth's hand and the man took it from her, shoving it into her coat pocket.

Elisabeth's mind split. Half of her was aware she was in the Lysander, jolting along the ground, gaining speed, the other half was down in the field still. The image of Gilbert's body, slumped in the mud, swam before her eyes.

Bullets peppered the body of the plane, and the agent swore.

'Go!' he yelled at the pilot. 'For fuck's sake, go!'

Elisabeth flinched, as another volley of bullets ricocheted off the fuselage, and then the plane was rising, juddering into the air.

With each beat of Elisabeth's heart, the carnage below fell further and further away, until at last there was only the night sky, the cold distant stars and the all-seeing moon.

21

2018

'What's going on?'

Leo is striding down the garden path, and Tali's spine stiffens as he comes to a halt before Betty.

'The wanderer returns at last,' Betty says. 'You're just in time for a birthday biscuit ...'

Leo glares around at the group, his eyes coming to rest on Tali. 'I thought I told you to cancel the party.'

Tali's veins fizz, but before she can respond, Betty speaks.

'Everyone, please meet my son, Leo.'

'Good afternoon, sir,' Abeo beams, stepping forward. 'My name is Abeo, and I just want to say how lovely it is of your dear mother to share her birthday celebrations with us,' he gestures round at the rest of the guests, 'her friends from the Century Society.'

Leo gives a snort, and a faint waft of beer comes to Tali on the breeze. 'So this is the famous Century Society.' Leo surveys the small gathering, taking in Duncan, stuffing a naan in his mouth, Olive alongside him, blinking like a rabbit, on to Alfred and Robert with the Zimmer frame between them. Juliana is busy tucking a napkin into Margaret's collar, but Hilda returns Leo's glare with an equally glacial stare. The silence is broken by Violet's gentle snores.

'I don't think we've met,' Mrs Voller pipes up. 'I don't actually belong to the Century Society, I'm your mother's neighbour ...'

Leo runs a hand through his dishevelled hair, and Tali notices his eyes are bloodshot, his unshaven cheeks stippled with grey. Today he looks even older than his mother, Tali thinks.

'Now you are here, Mr Shepherd,' Abeo says, exchanging a glance with Tali, 'perhaps you would like something to eat ... Tali has made some delicious food – her Neapolitan cookies will simply melt in your mouth.'

'I don't have time to eat,' Leo snaps. He turns to Betty. 'We have to go, Mother. We're late.'

'I don't want to,' Betty says.

Another awkward silence falls, as mother and son regard each other.

'Would you like a drink, Mr Shepherd?' Abeo ventures. 'We have Prosecco, or cordial, or tea ...' Tali wants to hug Abeo for his efforts. She can hardly bear to be near Leo, let alone find the strength in herself to offer the man refreshments.

'I don't want a drink,' Leo replies, his tone so aggressively cold that Tali's fists clench at her sides. Abeo, a head taller, several stones heavier and decades younger than Leo, merely blinks.

'OK,' Abeo says smoothly.

'Come along, Mother.' Leo reaches down to Betty, but she snatches her arm away.

'She doesn't want to go, Monsieur Shepherd.' The words are out before Tali can stop them.

'Excuse me?' Leo lunges towards Tali, forcing her to step back. 'I don't know who you think you are, but my mother is coming with me.'

'I'm not going anywhere, Leo,' Betty says firmly.

Sudden flapping and splashing sounds cause everyone to turn to the river. A pair of swans are taking off, their huge wings smacking the water. Tali envies them their freedom, as she watches them fly away. Gradually, attention returns to Betty and Leo.

'I think Betty's made her wishes very clear,' Hilda remarks.

'Very clear,' Mrs Voller echoes. Tali has no doubt this scene will be replayed later in the Voller household, and throughout the street.

Leo's lips are compressed in a weird smile, and Tali can't read his expression.

'The party's over, people.' Leo claps his hands once, twice, like a pre-school teacher commanding the attention of toddlers. 'Time to go home. Mother and I have some things we need to discuss.'

'Don't be ridiculous, Leo,' Betty says. 'Nobody's going home. You may not appreciate what she's done, but Natalia has gone to an awful lot of bother.'

Leo's sallow face blanches. 'Nothing changes, does it, Mother?' He sways, and for a second Tali fears he might collapse, but Abeo is there, a practised hand on his elbow, steadying him. Leo jerks his arm away.

'I don't know what you're talking about, Leo.' Betty gives a bone-deep sigh. 'But I do wish you'd stop making such a scene.'

'A scene?' Leo replies. 'It's you who's making a scene, Mother.'

'I think it's best if you leave, Leo.' Betty reaches for Tali's hand. 'There's no need to worry about me.'

'No, Mother, I'm not leaving.' Leo's eyes flick to Tali, and his gaze narrows. 'But your *friends* are.'

Before Tali can think of a response, Alfred totters forward. 'Well, Betty, Tali, it's been a wonderful afternoon,' he says. 'But I think it's time I headed home now. Duncan, are you ready?'

'Whenever you are, boss.' Duncan shoves a couple of extra cookies in his pocket, and gives Tali a thumbs-up. 'Top tucker.'

'You don't have to leave,' Betty says, as Alfred stoops to kiss her cheek.

'Never outstay your welcome, that's what my old mum used to tell me,' Alfred says. 'Take care of yourself, Betty, and we'll see you at the next club.'

'Thanks for coming,' Leo calls with undisguised sarcasm, as Duncan escorts Alfred away.

Tali feels a tap on her shoulder.

'Are you OK?' Juliana whispers urgently. 'Mr Shepherd, he seems angry?'

'It's OK,' Tali says, forcing a smile. The two women watch Leo pour himself a glass of Prosecco at the table. 'Thank you for coming today. It's meant so much to Madame Betty and me ...'

351

'If you are sure,' Juliana murmurs, releasing the brake on Margaret's wheelchair. 'He looks angry to me.'

Mrs Voller pats Tali on the arm. 'Would you like me to stay, dear? I can help you wash up?'

'Thank you, but I'll be fine,' Tali replies. Her cheeks are beginning to ache with the effort of maintaining a smile. 'There isn't much to tidy.'

'If you say so,' Mrs Voller frowns, eyeing the table littered with plates and half-eaten food. 'If you need anything, you know where I am.' She winks, her heavily mascaraed eyelashes reminding Tali of a spider. 'Bad penny, that one,' Mrs Voller stage-whispers, nodding towards Leo, now talking on his phone.

Faintly alarmed by the wink, Tali thanks Mrs Voller again and turns her attention back to Betty. It's heartbreaking to witness the slump in Betty's shoulders as she watches her friends depart.

'Come along then, Mother,' Leo says, pocketing his phone. 'There's still time to make that appointment.'

'Madame Betty needs to rest,' Tali protests.

'She can rest in the taxi, can't you, Mother?'

Tali looks to Betty, waiting for her to refuse, to tell her son to go away. But to Tali's bewildered dismay, Betty gives a resigned dip of her head.

*

By six o'clock, Leo and Betty have still not returned from Oak Manor. Tali has spent the intervening hours trying unsuccessfully to distract herself. She's cleared away the sad remains of the party, walked Tosca down the road and back, and prepared chicken stew for dinner.

Unable to sit still for even a minute, her nervous energy has worked itself into an unsettling anger. How dare Leo Shepherd force his mother out of her own home? What gives the bastard the right to kick Tali out on the street?

There must be something she can do to stop him.

Her hand steals to her apron pocket, and she pulls out the strange little capsule. The incident this morning with Betty seems like it happened years ago.

She turns the capsule over in her palm. What was inside? A powder? A liquid? Another, smaller, pill? The rubber-encased capsule could be a drug from the last century.

It looks sinister, whatever it is.

Her thoughts darken, as she pictures herself stirring its unknown contents into Leo's evening whisky, or crumbling it into his morning coffee.

Would the capsule kill him? How long would it take for him to die? Would he writhe on the floor, frothing at the mouth, before collapsing of a heart attack?

She shudders, dropping the capsule back into her pocket.

Much as she hates the bastard, much as she wants him gone, she can't do this.

She might be a loser, a liar, a coward.

But she isn't a murderer.

At last, she hears a car draw up outside. Leo and Betty have returned.

In the hall, Tali gently helps Betty out of her coat, alarmed at how frail and exhausted she looks.

Betty musters a weak smile. 'Something smells delicious, Natalia.'

'*Daube de poulet* – your favourite, Madame Betty.'

Leo hovers on the doorstep, but Tali pointedly ignores him.

'You'll soon be enjoying three-course feasts at Oak Manor, Mother,' Leo says, backing down the steps. 'I'll see you later.' Without another word, he returns to the taxi and is gone.

Tali shuts the door, and Betty slumps against her arm. 'Oh, Natalia, I'm so tired.'

'You're home now,' Tali soothes.

Once Betty is settled in her armchair with a bowl of chicken stew, Tali tries to find out what happened at Oak Manor. Betty tells her that Leo has reserved her a room there.

'They were very pushy,' Betty sighs. 'In the end, I let them all think I was interested, just to get out of there. The whole place gave me the willies.'

Tali doesn't like to ask Betty what exactly she means by this, but by the look on her face it isn't nice. Sometimes, the English language is so bizarre, it makes Tali's head hurt.

'It wasn't until we were back in the taxi that Leo told me what he'd done,' Betty says. 'I don't know why he can't just wait until I'm gone. He can do what he likes then.'

Gone? Tali stares at Betty, words failing her.

Betty reaches for her hand and gives it a squeeze. 'At least I have you, Natalia,' she says.

The clock on the mantelpiece has barely chimed eight o'clock, when Betty declares she wants to go to bed.

'It has been a long day,' Tali concedes. 'Shall I make you a little cup of *chocolat chaud*?'

'Not tonight, dear.' Betty shuffles to her bedroom, clinging to Tali's arm. It's chilly in the front room, despite the warmth of the day. Tali draws the thick curtains, disturbing a large, grey, papery moth that flutters to the carpet. It looks like the ghost of a butterfly, Tali thinks, as she gently scoops it up and sets it on the windowsill.

'Do you think Leo will be back tonight?' Betty asks, as Tali helps her into her nightdress.

'I don't know,' Tali replies. *I hope not.*

'I'm so sorry, Natalia.'

'Why are you sorry?'

'You went to so much trouble today.'

'But the party was good, *non?*'

'It was the best hundredth birthday party I've ever had,' Betty smiles. 'And I have you to thank for that.'

Once Betty is settled in bed, Tali fetches her an extra blanket from the airing cupboard. By the time she returns with it, Betty's eyes are already flickering closed.

'Sleep well,' Tali whispers, shutting the door softly behind her.

Alone in the kitchen, Tali's mind turns over and over, as she tries to process the events of the day. The party had been going so well, and then Leo had come along and ruined everything. Where had he disappeared off to? She has a sudden, terrifying image of Leo back at Oak Manor, signing the paperwork to have his mother admitted. But he can't do that without her consent, can he? And he'd have to sell Weyside first, and surely Madame Betty won't let him do that?

Tali craves a drink. On the side sits an unopened bottle of whisky Leo had brought back a few days ago – a gift for his mother, apparently. Tali has no doubt Betty won't see a drop.

She's pouring herself a double measure, when she's startled by a knock at the front door. Her hand jerks, the glass slipping from her grip, cracking on the edge of the countertop.

Is Leo back already? But he has his own key.

She glances down to find the glass has broken, and a puddle of whisky is spreading over the counter. Blood is trickling from a cut in her right thumb pad, but for some reason she can't feel any pain.

Merde.

She grabs a tea towel to mop up the spillage, and jumps at a second knock on the door.

Wrapping the tea towel round her hand, she hurries from the kitchen. Tosca gives a low bark from the landing, but doesn't bother coming downstairs.

'Great guard dog you are,' Tali mutters, as she unlocks the front door.

Jo is standing on the doorstep, clutching a small parcel wrapped in sparkly blue paper. Tali stares down at her, momentarily unable to think or speak.

'Hi,' Jo says. She visibly swallows. 'I got your text.'

Tali's senses flicker into life. 'You came,' she whispers.

'I'm sorry I didn't ring before, it was just that …' Jo hesitates. 'Well, I've got Betty a little something.'

Tali steps back to admit Jo into the hallway, and they face each other in the cramped space. Never has Tali been more grateful to see someone in her life.

'It's nothing much,' Jo says, offering Tali the gift. 'I hope Betty likes home-made fudge.'

It's Tali's turn to swallow. 'She loves anything sweet.' The tea towel slips as she takes the box, smearing blood on the paper.

'Oh,' Jo says, 'have you hurt yourself?'

'It's nothing,' Tali stammers, wrapping the cloth tighter around her thumb, almost dropping the present. 'I broke a glass.'

'There's no glass left in the cut, is there?'

'I don't think so ...' Tali realises she has no idea.

'Will you let me check?' Jo says. 'I'm an expert at extracting splinters of wood, so I should be able to find a piece of glass.'

Tali forces herself to meet Jo's eye. Something passes between them, and just as swiftly is gone.

In the bright light of the kitchen, Jo takes Tali's hand in a firm yet gentle grip and inspects the wound. 'It's not a deep cut,' she pronounces. 'If I press on it, does it hurt?' She lightly squeezes Tali's thumb, and Tali's heart pulsates at her touch.

'It doesn't hurt, *non.*'

'I don't think there's anything in it,' Jo says. She gives Tali's thumb one last check, her warm breath making Tali's skin tingle. 'Do you have any plasters?'

A brief search of the dresser drawers unearths a roll of ancient, yellowing surgical tape. Jo rinses the blood from Tali's thumb, dabs the skin dry with a piece of kitchen towel, and deftly binds it.

All the while, Tali can do nothing but stand and breathe in Jo's complex, intoxicating scent of strawberries and woodsmoke and the faintest hint of oil. 'There,' Jo says when she's finished. 'I always wanted to be a nurse.'

'You would make a wonderful nurse,' Tali finds herself saying, and instantly feels the heat of a blush.

They part, and Jo retreats to the kitchen doorway, leaning against the door frame, hands in the back pockets of her jeans. 'Did the party go OK?'

Tali's nod turns into a head shake, and she's appalled to feel the prickle of tears.

'Oh.' Jo's brow creases, and she takes her hands from her pockets again. 'What happened? Is Betty all right?'

'A lot has happened today.'

'Do you want to tell me about it?' Jo's voice is soft.

Tali nods, gratefully. 'I could make us a *chocolat chaud*?'

'I'd love one,' Jo says and smiles.

The chocolate made, Tali lights an old oil lantern she'd found in the cellar, and they head down the garden path. They sit on the bench beneath the willow, encompassed by long, trailing branches. A fragile eggshell moon hovers over the inky water.

'Dusk's the most enchanting hour,' Jo says. 'I love to sit up on deck in the evenings and watch the first stars emerging, one by one.'

'*La nuit est belle,*' Tali agrees.

They sip their chocolates in quiet contemplation for a time.

'Do you want to tell me about today?' Jo asks.

Tali's hand slides into her apron pocket. She's desperate to show the capsule to Jo. She can't bear all these secrets any more.

'It started with this.' Tali reveals the sinister pellet. 'I think Madame Betty tried to kill herself.'

'Oh my God.'

'I stopped her, just before she swallowed it.'

'I've seen something like this before,' Jo says, peering at the capsule in the dim glow of the lamp. 'In a military museum. It looks like a suicide pill they used to give pilots and spies in the war, in case they were captured by the enemy.'

Tali shivers. She thinks of Betty's handbag in the wardrobe, full of bizarre things like the knife in its cracked leather scabbard, and the strange wire key Betty had shown her. What had Betty called it? A skeleton key?

And then there was the gun ...

What had Madame Betty done in the war?

'But the party?' Jo presses. 'Did you still have the party?'

'*Oui.*' Tali briefly describes how it had all been going so smoothly, and Betty had just given a speech, when Leo had turned up. 'He sent everyone home, and then took Madame Betty away to Oak Manor.'

'The old people's home?'

Tali nods. 'He brought Madame Betty back later, but he went away again.' Tali takes a gulp of her chocolate. 'I hope he never comes back.'

Jo rests her mug on her lap, clears her throat. Tali risks a glance at her, but she's staring out over the moon-silvered water.

'Poor Betty,' Jo says. She turns and meets Tali's eye. 'I wish I'd been here to help you.'

Tali takes a breath of the cool evening air, the familiar tang of the river calming her jumping heart. 'But you're here now.'

Jo twists round on the bench, her bony knee making contact with Tali's. Her touch sends a ribbon of heat along Tali's leg.

'I'm so sorry,' Jo says. Her voice frays and she falls silent, staring at her lap, rubbing a hand through her hair. Tali longs to smooth it.

'I've been doing a lot of thinking,' Jo says quietly. 'For years all I've done is deny my feelings. It's become a habit, like brushing my teeth every day. I wake up, I get dressed, I brush my teeth, and I tell myself I want to be alone. That I'm happy on my own.' She takes a deep breath, looks up, fixes Tali with a clear-eyed gaze. 'But everything changed when I met you.'

'Oh …'

'I've never felt like this about anyone before. You're the kindest, sweetest woman I've ever met. You care for Betty like she's your own grandmother. You have a heart of gold, Tali.' Jo clasps her hands together. 'And you've made me see the truth.'

'The truth?' An image flits across Tali's mind of the gun, arcing over the water. She closes her eyes, and opens them again as Jo continues. 'I think I'm falling in love with you.'

'Oh ...'

'I know I should've been braver, on the boat, when you ...' Jo falters, wipes her eyes with the heel of her hand. 'But I was scared.'

'It's OK to be scared,' Tali hears herself say. 'I'm scared too.'

'You are?'

Fearing she might cry if she says any more, Tali can only nod.

'Can you forgive me?' Jo says, searching Tali's face.

Tali swallows. For some reason she's finding it hard to get enough air in her lungs. Jo sets a gentle hand on her wrist, fingers resting on Tali's pulse.

'Tali?' Jo holds her with an intense gaze. 'Are you all right?'

'I have to tell you something ...'

'What?'

'I found a gun.' There, she's confessed it.

'A gun? A real one?'

Tali nods. 'In a suitcase, in the cellar.' She gestures behind her in the vague direction of the house. 'When Madame Betty found out, she got very upset and made me throw it in the river.'

They both look towards the water.

'Have you told anyone else about this?' Jo asks.

Tali shakes her head, her body trembling now, bones aching with the effort of holding herself together. 'Only you.'

'Oh, Tali.' Jo reaches for her, drawing Tali's head down to rest on her shoulder. Jo's arms are all-encompassing, strong and secure as tree roots.

It's the loveliest hug of Tali's life.

'It's all right,' Jo whispers. 'It's all right.'

After a while, Tali lifts her head. Jo's face remains close, eyes shining.

Tali leans forward, closing the gap between them. Their mouths meet, and Jo's lips are warm and soft and taste of chocolate.

22

May 1944

Afterwards, Elisabeth would recall only fragments of the journey home. She was numb to her core and, as the plane flew over the Channel, her limbs began to shake uncontrollably.

The agent whose name she didn't know grabbed her wrists, said something to her. She couldn't hear him. He thrust a flask of coffee laced with rum into her hands, but when she tried to drink, most of the liquid ended up spilled in her lap. The few mouthfuls she managed to swallow barely revived her enough to feel the agent's hand squeezing hers.

Below them flickered the faint lights of Tangmere Airfield at last.

To Elisabeth, they looked like stars in a sky turned upside down.

She was escorted straight from the plane to an operations room. In the warm, smoke-fugged office, a FANY nurse with kind eyes sat Elisabeth down and gave her a glass of water. RAF officers bustled in and out of the room, tense voices thrumming in Elisabeth's head.

'Are you injured?' The nurse was forced to repeat her question before Elisabeth understood her. She shook her head, and the movement brought a hot surge rising in her gullet. She only just made it to the waste-paper bin in time.

Slowly, the nausea passed, and the nurse brought her fresh water. The room gradually emptied, and Elisabeth found herself alone. Her head felt too heavy for her neck, and she closed her eyes. There came a knock at the door, and she jerked up to see a face she recognised: Lena Watkins.

Even through a haze of fatigue, Elisabeth was shocked by how much the officer had changed in such a short time. She remembered a brisk, somewhat intimidating woman, not this person with troubled eyes and deep worry lines etched into her brow.

'How are you?' Watkins asked, drawing a chair close.

Elisabeth tucked her trembling hands under her thighs. She was still wearing her coat, stained with coffee and blood.

Gilbert's blood.

The numbing cloud of shock had begun to dissipate, exposing the tangled mass of fear in her mind. Here in this room, alone and safe with Lena Watkins, the door open, she wanted only to run away.

An orderly tapped on the door. 'Car's ready, ma'am.'

'Thank you,' Watkins said. She rose and helped Elisabeth to her feet.

'Am I going home?' Elisabeth croaked.

'Soon,' Watkins said, her voice low. 'After your debriefing.' She snatched up a cushion from a chair in the corner. 'You can sleep in the car.'

Elisabeth slept all the way to London, waking to find herself back outside the bleak façade of the SOE offices. Groggy and still nauseous, she followed Lena Watkins up to an empty room. After visiting a bathroom down the corridor, she stumbled back to Watkins to find a WAAF orderly delivering a tray of tea and sandwiches. Sitting in a corner of the room was a pale man in a creased suit, a briefcase open on his lap.

'This is Mr Lenten,' Lena Watkins said, gesturing at Elisabeth to take a seat.

Mr Lenten barely acknowledged Elisabeth as he extracted a pad and pencil from his battered briefcase.

'Mr Lenten is here to record our debriefing,' Watkins explained, pouring out three cups of tea. 'I'll make this as quick and painless as possible.'

Elisabeth clasped her hands in her lap, twisting the curtain ring Gilbert had given her round and round on her finger.

Elisabeth Ridley, will you take this bague d'or *as a symbol of my love?*

'Before we begin,' Lena Watkins said, passing Elisabeth a cup of sweetened tea, 'I want to apologise for putting you through this now, but as I'm sure you can appreciate, time is of the essence.'

Elisabeth took a swallow of tea, looking up to meet Watkins's steady gaze.

'I should have asked you this at Tangmere,' Watkins said, glancing at Mr Lenten in the corner. 'Do you have the camera?'

Elisabeth nodded, and her cup tipped, spilling tea. Lena Watkins came around the desk and gently took the cup from her, and Elisabeth managed to tug the money-belt free. She handed it over and Watkins passed the camera straight to Mr Lenten.

After making a note on his pad, he left the room.

Now Elisabeth was alone with Lena Watkins she felt the sudden threat of tears, and dug her fingernails into her palms. The officer's voice came to her as though from afar.

'I know you've been through the worst ordeal ...'

The blood was draining from Elisabeth's head, and she dug her nails deeper.

'What you did was beyond brave,' Lena Watkins said. 'Your actions in France have saved so many lives ...'

Elisabeth focused on a tea-stain on the desk, willing herself not to black out.

'You went above and beyond, and for that we are immensely grateful.'

The door opened and Mr Lenten came back into the room.

Elisabeth's throat tightened.

'When was the last time you ate, Elisabeth?' Lena Watkins asked.

'I'm not hungry.'

'At least have some more tea.'

Elisabeth dutifully drank.

Lena Watkins rested her chin on her fingertips as she leaned forward on the desk. 'Tell me everything, from the start.'

Haltingly, Elisabeth told the officer about Raoul's farm, and his aunt's flat in Chounoît. She briefly described her train journeys to Rouen, the café and the meeting with Father André. A sense of shame stopped her from mentioning the attack by the soldier at the checkpoint. What good would it do to admit that grave, almost fatal mistake?

'Tell me about Operation Moonlight,' Lena Watkins pressed.

Elisabeth closed her eyes briefly, summoning the mission to mind.

'So,' Officer Watkins said, when Elisabeth had finished, 'you left Rouen that final time and returned to Chounoît?'

Elisabeth nodded.

'And then what happened?'

The moment she'd dreaded had come. What she chose to divulge from here on would determine the path she took, now and for ever. She tried to think. When Gilbert had sent the request for a pick-up, he can't have mentioned himself, otherwise questions of his whereabouts would already have been asked. Only Elisabeth was witness to Gilbert's appearance at the flat. No one but her knew he'd escaped the Gestapo. No one but her knew of his subsequent treachery. As far as SOE were aware, Gilbert was still a prisoner of the Nazis.

If she told Lena Watkins the truth about Gilbert's betrayal and death, his name would be sullied for ever, and Elisabeth would stand trial for his murder. If she kept quiet, Gilbert would remain a war hero, sacrificing his life for the SOE. And she would remain free.

Her spiralling thoughts turned to the pilot and the agent in the plane. What had they seen?

'Take your time ...' Lena Watkins's voice brought her back. 'Tell me what happened at the pick-up.'

'The Germans came.' Elisabeth forced the words out. 'They were going to take the plane. They had guns.'

She closed her eyes, felt again Gilbert's warm mouth on hers, the terrible spray of his blood on her face. 'I tried ...' She faltered, began again. 'I shot ...' Her voice trembled and a tear escaped her eye, tracking down her filthy cheek.

'It's all right,' Lena Watkins said, giving her a look of such pity it made Elisabeth want to sob. 'The pilot has told us what happened, as he saw it.'

Elisabeth wiped her nose on her coat sleeve. 'He has?'

'He's spoken of your bravery,' Watkins said. 'How you single-handedly fought off three Gestapo agents.'

A faint ringing sound came to Elisabeth's ears, and her vision blurred.

'I know how terrifying it must have been,' Lena Watkins said, her voice summoning Elisabeth back to the airless room. 'You were so brave ...'

Elisabeth shook her head. It wasn't true.

From the corner of her eye, she saw that Mr Lenten was writing down everything that was said, every single word that came out of her mouth. She felt a surge of hysteria rising up in her chest, and she bit down hard. She must not lose control here. Not now. Later she could collapse, but not now, not in front of these people.

A silence fell. Elisabeth's mind contracted, narrowing to a single thought: *Gilbert was dead*.

What future could there be without him?

She realised Lena Watkins was talking, and dragged her attention back.

'You'll need to sign an official statement,' Watkins said. 'Is it ready, Mr Lenten?'

'Almost, ma'am.'

An official statement. As if the dreadful events of the previous night could ever be put down in words.

Mr Lenten spread out various papers on the desk, and Elisabeth was asked to sign not only a record of her account, but also a declaration that she wouldn't disclose anything she knew about the SOE or its work.

She would happily have signed her soul away if it meant she could escape the room.

'Let's get you home now,' Lena Watkins said gently. 'You've been through enough.'

*

Elisabeth was driven back to Guildford, and no time seemed to pass before she was stumbling up the steps of Weyside, into her mother's arms.

'*Mon Dieu*,' Florence breathed, as she helped Elisabeth up to her bedroom. 'What has happened, *ma chère*?'

369

Elisabeth caught sight of her reflection in her dressing-table mirror, and hardly recognised herself. Her face was gaunt and streaked with dried blood. Shadows bruised her eyes.

Florence disappeared, returning with a steaming bowl of water and a towel. *'Ma pauvre chérie,'* she said, stroking Elisabeth's brow. *'Tu as l'air fatiguée.'*

'I'm so thirsty, Maman.'

'Un moment.' Florence dashed off to fetch water.

Left alone, Elisabeth shed her coat, the pockets heavy with her gun, and the money-belt Lena Watkins had returned to her. Elisabeth kicked the coat beneath her bed, out of sight, and slowly undressed to her underclothes. She washed her face and hands, longing for a bath, with scalding hot water and real soap.

She sank down on to her bed, pulled the blankets around her and closed her eyes. Images circled her mind: the Lysander emerging from the night sky; the two Germans running across the field; Gilbert's look of stunned disbelief as his blood soaked into the mud.

And above it all the eye of the moon, floating clear and stark, a witness to all she had done.

She was interrupted by a knock at the bedroom door, and Frederick appeared.

'Your mother asked me to bring you some water,' he said shyly, proffering a glass. 'She's fetching you something to eat.'

'Tell her not to worry,' Elisabeth said, closing her eyes again. 'I just need to sleep.'

Much later, when Florence had finally left her alone and gone to her own bed, Elisabeth lay listening to the bones of the house creak and settle. She'd taken some of her mother's Luminal, but the sedative barely had any effect.

In her mind she churned over the meeting with Watkins, and all that she hadn't told the officer.

Don't think about it, don't think about it.

She imagined herself in her father's old rowing boat on the river.

Don't think, don't think.

Each chant was an oar stroke pulling her further and further from the bank.

Don't think, don't think.

With each pull, her mind began to sink into blessed oblivion, until a sudden rattle of gunfire made her lurch awake, heart clamouring as though she'd raced ten miles. She must have cried out, because Florence appeared at her bedside.

'Elisabeth?' Her mother's voice came to her through the darkness, a transmission of calm from the ether.

'I-I heard guns ...'

Florence stroked her hand. *'C'est juste un mauvais rêve,'* she soothed.

Just a bad dream.

If only that were true.

She woke in the early hours, tugged from a deep sleep. She struggled up, the darkness pressing all around her, and felt the faintest whisper of breath on her cheek. A blend of scents filled her nose: strong French tobacco, sandalwood spice, the coppery, mineral smell of blood and earth.

Gilbert.

Shadows yawned, and another cold breath came, brushing her cheek like a cobweb. She searched the darkness, but nothing stirred. She closed her eyes, tried to drift off again, but all she could see was Gilbert's face, and it flayed her heart anew.

He'd betrayed her.

A sob escaped her, and she gripped her tear-dampened pillow.

She'd killed him.
She'd killed him.
She'd killed him.

*

The following morning Elisabeth woke with a headache, her limbs leaden, as though her body was succumbing to a bout of flu. Dimly, she was aware of her mother and Frederick talking out on the landing, but she couldn't bring herself to move. She remembered when Papa died, how grief had blunted her, how she'd stayed in her room for a week barely speaking to anyone, unable to concentrate on anything. Her mind felt unmoored again now, the days stretching ahead of her, infinite and meaningless.

The voices grew fainter, footsteps retreating.

With an effort of will she forced herself out of bed, pulling on an old skirt and blouse. Shuffling slowly down the stairs, she noticed a Church Army shelter booklet lying on the hall table. Aimlessly, she flicked it open, and a line jumped out at her:

Let not your heart be troubled, neither let it be afraid. God is with you.

She threw the booklet back down again. She'd long since lost her faith in God or heaven. But she'd made her own hell, and now would suffer in it for ever more.

She found her mother in the sitting room, tidying away breakfast things.

'Oh Elisabeth,' Florence said. 'I thought you were sleeping still ...'

Elisabeth swayed on her feet, light-headed suddenly.

'Come, sit down,' Florence led her to a chair. 'Tea and toast and honey, that's what you need.' She bustled away.

Alone, Elisabeth stared through the window, down the long narrow garden to the glint of river at the bottom. Fred was mowing the grass in slow, methodical stripes.

She was home.

She listened to the tick of the carriage clock on the mantelpiece, the sound of Florence moving about in the kitchen next door, the faint rasp of the lawnmower.

They could never know the truth. They could never find out she had killed. She must bury what happened in France in the depths of her mind; a stone, sunk without trace in the river.

Two can keep a secret, if one of them is dead.

*

Over the following days, Elisabeth's sleep gradually improved, and her appetite began to return, but she found it difficult to settle to anything. Even reading, which had always relaxed her in the past, took too much concentration. Her jagged nerves kept her prisoner, and she barely left the house. The moment she stepped outside the front door, she sensed danger around every corner, potential attackers lurking in the shadows.

Only the river calmed her, and she spent many hours beneath the willow, staring into the rippling depths.

A few days after her return, Elisabeth found herself alone in the house. She dragged her bloodstained coat from beneath her bed, intending to get rid of it before her mother came back, and the pistol fell out of the pocket. Sinking to the floor, she stared at the gun for a long time. At last, she forced herself to pick it up, shoving the weapon and the money-belt and its contents into an empty suitcase. Unable to think what else to do, she hid the suitcase at the back of the cellar.

One morning in early June, Elisabeth was woken by a strange droning noise coming from beyond her bedroom window. She slipped downstairs, unbolting the kitchen door. The dawn sky was a glorious wash of pink. High over the water meadows a stream of aircraft headed south, like a huge flock of mechanical birds.

Elisabeth found herself padding barefoot down the garden path to the river's edge, watching as plane after plane flew past overhead.

Lena Watkins's voice came to her.

Your actions in France have saved so many lives.

What she'd risked, what she'd sacrificed, meant the men in those planes had a chance.

After breakfast, Fred turned the radio on, and they listened to a special bulletin. As the newsreader's calm, authoritative voice announced, *'D-Day has come,'* Elisabeth shivered. Florence put her arm around her.

'Early this morning, the Allies began the assault on the north-western face of Hitler's European fortress,' the newsreader's voice went on. *'Under the command of General Eisenhower, Allied naval forces, supported by strong air forces, began landing Allied armies this morning on the northern coast of France ...'*

Elisabeth closed her eyes, as images swarmed her mind: grey figures looming, the Lysander swooping, swooping.

'Mon Dieu,' Florence whispered. Fred reached across the table and took Elisabeth's hand.

'The Allied commander-in-chief, General Eisenhower, has issued an Order of the Day addressed to each individual of the Allied Expeditionary Force. "Your task will not be an easy one. Your enemy is well trained, well equipped and battle-hardened. He will fight savagely ..."'

Elisabeth struggled to breathe, as Gilbert's face swam behind her eyes. She barely heard the newsreader's voice.

'"... But this is the year 1944. The tide has turned. The free men of the world are marching together to victory ..."'

All that she had been through, all that she had suffered, the fear and pain, the grief and guilt, it had all been for this moment: the return, at long last, of Allied forces on French soil.

'Are you all right?' Fred's voice brought Elisabeth back. She looked up, mustered a smile. This was such good news, and yet she felt nothing.

'I must know,' Florence said, turning to her. 'Were you in France?'

The radio droned on in the background.

'*Oui*,' Elisabeth whispered.

Please don't ask me any more.

Florence regarded her with the ghost of a smile, and though she said nothing, Elisabeth sensed pride in her mother's gaze.

*

Over the following days, Elisabeth pored over the daily papers, hungry for news of the Allied offensive. Her birthday arrived, and Florence baked a barely edible sponge cake, made with powdered egg. Elisabeth tried her best to enjoy the day, to bury the memories of France beneath a façade of normality. When Fred asked her if she was all right, she blamed her melancholy mood on tiredness.

'*Mrs Miniver* is showing at the Odeon tonight,' he said. 'Fancy a trip into town?'

'I'd like that,' Elisabeth said, and almost meant it. At least in the darkness of the cinema she might be able to forget everything, if only for an hour or two. And it was her birthday, after all.

That evening, as she walked arm in arm with Frederick along the quiet, unlit streets into town, a black saloon car, its footboards and mudguards edged with white paint, emerged from the darkness.

For one teetering moment, panic gripped Elisabeth's heart.

'What's the matter?' Fred asked, as she tugged him back against a hedge.

Elisabeth fought for breath, as the car disappeared into the night. 'I'm sorry,' she stammered. 'I don't know what came over me.'

'Are you sure you're all right?'

'Yes, I'm fine, truly. I'm just ... I thought it was going to hit us.'

Fred tucked Elisabeth's arm back through his. 'You're safe with me.'

They carried on walking, and Elisabeth was grateful for the darkness hiding the tears that now welled in her eyes.

She didn't deserve Fred's kindness.

*

When her monthlies didn't come at the end of July, Elisabeth wasn't surprised or much concerned. Stress had whittled any spare fat from her body, and with rationing so tight still, she'd remained underweight. Her appetite suffered most, and her spirits dipped lowest on those nights when the moon was at its fullest. Sleep became even more elusive, and her right ankle would ache, the pain unalleviated by the aspirin or Luminal she took.

The summer days stretched interminably, and she spent hours wandering along the river. She found the play of sunlight on the tranquil water helped sweep her mind clear, at least for a short while.

When she wasn't walking alone, she joined Fred in the garden, tending to the vegetable patch and helping him construct a couple of cedarwood hives. He hoped to catch a bee swarm, and then they could eat honey to their heart's content.

'But do you know how to keep bees?' Elisabeth asked.

'Not a clue,' Fred admitted. 'But I'm sure I can learn.'

His optimism made her smile.

It was only when September came, and her period still hadn't arrived, that Elisabeth began to suspect. Lately, her skirts had felt tighter, her breasts tender.

'Your cheeks,' Florence remarked one evening, as the two of them sat at the sitting room table, Elisabeth reading a novel, Florence darning soldiers' socks. 'They are blooming like your Papa's roses.'

'The sun has been hot today, Maman.'

'You are filling out a little, too.'

Elisabeth met her mother's eye, and a silent acknowledgement passed between them.

Could she be pregnant?

The thought she might be carrying Gilbert's child made Elisabeth want to weep and sing.

*

September passed, and Elisabeth's waistline continued to expand. Florence was busier than ever, working as a billeting officer for the WVS, and was rarely at home, but Elisabeth knew she couldn't deny the truth of her pregnancy much longer.

One evening, as Elisabeth and Fred were clearing away the dinner things, the air-raid siren went off.

'It's probably a false alarm,' Elisabeth said, pouring hot water from the kettle into the washing-up bowl. But the siren's haunting wail went on and on.

'I don't think it is this time,' Fred said, after a while. 'We should shelter.'

Elisabeth thought of the life growing inside her, and relented.

Florence was out delivering food parcels to refugees, so Elisabeth left the front door on the latch in case her mother returned home, then followed Fred down to the cellar. It had been some time since she'd last been down there. Fred had erected a couple of camp beds, piling them with blankets, set up the gramophone on a little table, and dug out Elisabeth's father's old Tilley lamp.

Elisabeth sat on one of the camp beds, pulling a blanket round her, trying not to think of the suitcase hidden in the shadows.

Fred lit the lamp, its glow warming the blue distempered walls.

'You know I donated blood at the hospital yesterday,' he said, sitting next to her on the camp bed. 'Well, the nurse asked me if I was a conscientious objector.'

Elisabeth made a sympathetic noise.

'I told her I wasn't,' Fred continued. '"I'm an invalid," I said, "hadn't you noticed my limp?" And do you know what she said?'

Elisabeth shook her head.

'She said, "Good,"' Fred replied. '"Else I'd take eight pints and drain you dry."'

Elisabeth smiled. She felt a quickening sensation in her belly, not unlike hunger pangs. The hunger she'd endured in France haunted her still, even though she was never far from a source of food now, if only an apple from the garden, or a handful of tomatoes.

But the feeling in her belly this evening was different. There was a new life growing inside her, and nothing would ever be the same again.

They were quiet for a time, listening to the whine and thud of bombs dropping over Guildford.

As Elisabeth's eyes adjusted to the gloom, she saw her father's old Ross rifle propped in the corner, and above it, hanging from a nail, his greatcoat that still reeked of the battlefields. Would they ever be free of war?

'Shall we have some music?' Fred asked.

He rose and cranked the handle of the gramophone, and a woman's crackly voice filled the cellar. It was 'They Can't Black Out the Moon', a song she loved.

As the melody played out, Elisabeth bit back tears. She couldn't stop thinking about the baby, and how it would never know its father.

'Glenn Miller's band is playing at the Castle Inn tomorrow,' Frederick said, his voice drawing her back. 'Would you like to go?'

She turned to him, and his smile was so hopeful, so sweet.

'I'm pregnant.' The words came of their own accord, and she could no longer hold back the tears.

Fred took her in his arms. 'I know,' he said. 'I'm here, and I'll always be here.'

23

2018

The kiss lasts not nearly long enough. Tali sinks into Jo's embrace and for a brief, blissful time the world ceases to exist.

Eventually they pull apart, and Tali draws in a deep breath.

Jo's smile is shy, and she bites her lower lip. 'I've never ...' She blinks. 'Oh God ... you're so beautiful.'

Their second kiss lasts longer than the first, and stars are bursting behind Tali's eyelids by the time they come up for air again. The evening breeze is a cool balm on her hot cheeks.

'Can you stay?' Tali hears herself ask.

'There's nowhere else I'd rather be.'

A gust of wind sets the willow tree shivering. 'It's getting cold ...' Tali says.

'I don't really feel the cold.' Jo plucks at her thin blue shirt, and Tali suspects she's wearing nothing but a bra underneath. 'I seem to have this internal furnace that keeps me warm.' Jo places her palm flat on her breastbone. 'And whenever I look at you, it's like an inferno burning in my chest.'

Tali can't help but grin. No one has said anything like that to her before.

'But we can go inside if you're getting chilly,' Jo says.

Inside. Tali pictures her room, the dishevelled bed, the discarded clothes, the empty doughnut packets scattered everywhere. She's been so busy today she hasn't had a chance to tidy up her own mess. Her romantic fantasies of being alone with Jo have only ever involved them kissing on the deck of *Thyme*, or taking long, tranquil walks along the river. She's never envisaged Jo in her actual bedroom, and for a moment she can't think.

'You can show me the suitcase you found, maybe,' Jo says. 'There might be something in it that explains the gun ... But you don't have to, if you don't want to ...'

'I want to.'

Jo smiles, and Tali's heart soars.

As they tiptoe past the front room, careful not to wake Betty, Tosca barrels down the stairs, jumping up at Jo, tail wagging.

'Shh, *tou tou*,' Tali whispers, as she leads Jo upstairs. The dog follows behind them. While Jo visits the bathroom, Tali quickly tidies her room, shoving stray underwear and empty cake wrappers in the wardrobe, straightening the bedsheets, lighting a scented candle and a few tea-lights. Tosca hoovers up crumbs from the carpet.

'Looks like we have a chaperone,' Jo laughs, as she comes back into the bedroom.

Tali gently herds Tosca out on to the landing, where he curls up in the corner and falls back to sleep. She closes the bedroom door softly. 'He is *trop curieux*.'

Tali pulls a face, and Jo's laugh sends a shiver of delight through her.

For a moment, Tali can think of nothing but the fact that Jo is here, in her room. It feels like a dream.

'Tali?' Jo's voice jolts her back to earth. 'You were going to show me the suitcase ...'

'*Oui, oui,*' Tali says quickly. She kneels and drags the case out from under the bed, manipulating the stiff catch with practised ease. The lid creaks open, revealing the muddled heap of papers inside.

'Have you looked at all this?' Jo asks, kneeling next to her.

Tali shakes her head, as Jo tentatively lifts out a bundle of postcards tied with a faded pink ribbon. 'I want to show Madame Betty, but after I showed her the gun ...'

Jo peers at a postcard. 'Canadian stamp,' she remarks. She squints at the signature. 'From someone called Dominique ...'

Tali extracts a small burgundy leather notebook, 1944 embossed in gold on its cracked cover. It's a diary written entirely in French. The handwriting is tiny, the letters looping neatly, as though a spider has inscribed the words. Tali has read a few pages already, enough for her to deduce that it's Betty's mother's diary. She offers it to Jo, who peers at the dense script, her brow furrowed.

'What does it say?'

'Madame Betty's mother is writing about how Elisabeth, that's Madame Betty, has gone away, but she doesn't know where.'

'1944 ... the war,' Jo muses. 'I wish I could read French.'

'There are more,' Tali says, and slowly she begins emptying everything from the suitcase on to the bed. There are five more pocket-sized diaries spanning the years 1939 to 1945.

'Perhaps it says in one of these about the gun?' Jo wonders aloud, flicking through the brittle pages filled entirely with neat black ink.

Tali shows Jo a birth certificate for *Elisabeth Marie Ridley*, and they both agree it must be Madame Betty's as the date of birth inked on it, 10 June 1918, is the same as the old lady's.

In amongst a plethora of letters are two death certificates, one for *Thomas Arthur Ridley* and the other for *Florence Amélie Ridley*. The same names are inked in beautiful copperplate handwriting on a yellowing marriage certificate dated 1917. 'Madame Betty's parents,' Tali says.

'It's kind of weird to think we're touching things that are over a hundred years old,' Jo says.

For a while, Tali loses all track of time, as she and Jo pore over the letters and receipts and scraps of paper. Jo finds a 1940s cake recipe torn from a magazine.

'*Honey pound cake*,' she reads aloud. '*You can keep your sugar tin tight shut, when you make this tempting, delicious cake. Not even a pinch of sugar goes into it, only delectable honey instead.*'

'I found some old jars of honey in Madame Betty's kitchen cupboard,' Tali replies. 'I don't know how long they've been in there, but Madame Betty said honey never goes bad.'

'It lasts for ages,' Jo confirms. 'They've dug up Egyptian mummies who were buried with jars of the stuff, and it's still been edible.'

Tali pulls a face of disgust, making Jo laugh again.

'What's this?' Jo says, unearthing a small rectangular parcel wrapped in wax-coated brown paper, crumbling with age, the words '24-hour Ration (F) – instructions within' printed on one side in faded lettering.

'I've never seen that,' Tali breathes. How had she missed it?

Jo carefully peels back a corner of the waxed paper, revealing the edge of a tin beneath. 'Shall I open it?'

Tali nods. It resembles one of Betty's sardine tins.

Jo removes the rest of the wrapping and then, with strong fingers, she prises the lid open. Folded on top of the contents is a note.

Read before you feed. Do not open the waterproof packets until necessary.

Jo unpacks the contents, laying them out on the bed.

'It looks like army food,' she remarks. 'I've seen these sorts of tins before, when I went to that army museum I told you about.'

Tali is astonished at how much has been packed into the tiny container. There are two bars of chocolate, the faded wrappers clearly decades old; two packets of milk powder; three thin cracker-shaped packets labelled 'Biscuits, savoury'; a couple of little packets of tea; a paper sachet of salt; two larger sachets labelled 'Sugar'; and a box of matches.

'Twenty-four-hour army rations,' Jo muses. 'Maybe Betty's husband was a soldier?'

'I think he was.' Tali continues sifting through the suitcase.

'I wonder what the chocolate tastes like ...'

'You can't eat it, Jo!'

'But I'm starving.' Jo pretends to unwrap one of the bars.

'Well, you should have come to the party,' Tali mock-scolds her. 'Plenty of food there.'

Tucked down the side of the suitcase is an old-fashioned money-belt, the mildewed cotton bulging with mysterious contents; Tali pulls out a wad of French francs, a stub of pencil, and a strange pocket-sized notepad made of silk, each sheet printed with lines of individual letters.

'Some sort of code,' Jo muses.

'Look at this,' Tali says, handing Jo the letter from Captain Porter at the War Office.

Jo shakes her head, mystified. 'The gun,' she says, 'it was just under all this stuff?'

Tali nods.

'That must have given you a shock,' Jo murmurs. 'What sort of gun was it, do you know?'

'Like a gangster gun,' Tali shrugs. 'It was black, about this big.' She indicates with her hands.

'And when you showed it to Betty, she lost it?'

Tali shakes her head. '*Non*, I found it.'

'No,' Jo gives a gentle laugh. 'What I mean is, Betty was upset when you showed her the gun.'

'*Oui*,' Tali replies. 'Very upset.'

'Well,' Jo says, taking a deep breath, 'I think it's very interesting. Does Betty's son know about this suitcase?'

Tali stiffens at Jo's mention of Leo. 'I haven't shown him.'

'So he doesn't know about the gun?'

Tali shakes her head. She glances back at the pile of stuff on the bed. On the top is a creased, black-and-white passport-sized photograph of a young man and woman. Tali picks it up for a closer look. On the back is written, in faded ink, *Southampton 1944.* The young woman is smiling into the camera lens, and her eyes, her nose, her smile all look vaguely familiar.

'I think this is Madame Betty, many years ago,' Tali says, showing Jo. 'I don't know who the man is. Maybe her husband?' There is something about the shape of the man's eyes, the angle of his jaw, that makes Tali wonder if she's seen this man before. But she can't have done, the photo had been taken nearly seventy-five years ago. The man must surely be dead.

'There's a hole here ...' Jo is peering at the inside of the suitcase lid. The fabric is spotted with mould, the stitching slightly torn along one edge. 'I can feel something behind the cloth.'

Tali fetches her tiny pair of nail scissors from her bedside table, and carefully snips the seam open further. Jo reaches in and extracts a folded sheet of paper, covered in nonsensical lines of letters. 'Another code?' She passes it to Tali.

'I wonder what it says ...' Tali muses.

'Do you know what I think?'

Tali looks up, shakes her head.

'I think Betty was a spy.'

*

The repacked suitcase sits on the floor, forgotten for the moment.

They lie together on the narrow mattress, surrounded by pillows, and Tali suffers a second of self-consciousness, wishing her body didn't take up quite so much space. But her concerns are soon swept away, as Jo begins to press butterfly kisses along her jawline, setting Tali's skin alight wherever her mouth touches. Their lips brush, mouths parting, tongues tasting, and Tali's blood sings. Jo must have done this sort of thing before?

Jo pulls back slightly, and Tali wonders if she somehow spoke the words aloud. She can hear Tosca snoring out on the landing, and Jo smiles as she plays with Tali's blouse buttons.

'I can't believe we're doing this,' Jo murmurs, her warm breath tickling Tali's throat. 'I can't believe I'm here with you.'

Hand trembling, Jo fumbles a button free, and Tali's skin tingles at the brush of Jo's fingers. She can hear nothing but the rhythmic, frantic swoosh of her heartbeat. Another button is eased through its eyelet, then another, until at last Tali's blouse is undone.

'Oh,' Jo murmurs.

Tali's breasts, encased in their substantial, lacy cream bra, rise like two small mountains between them. Jo deftly shucks off her own shirt revealing, just as Tali suspected, a plain black sports bra. The slight rise of Jo's chest, the defined sweep of her collarbone, leaves Tali breathless.

She feels a flicker of reticence; she hasn't been this intimate with anyone since—

She slams the door shut on that memory.

They gaze at each other, and Tali's habitual insecurity gradually ebbs away, to be replaced by a warmth that suffuses her whole body.

'Have you …?' Jo blinks. 'You know … been with a woman before?'

Mon Dieu. This is her first time too?

'Not really,' Tali admits, stroking her fingers down Jo's toned arm.

'Oh, thank God,' Jo breathes. 'I was worried you were … you know …'

What? Tali wonders.

'You're so gorgeous,' Jo whispers. 'Totally gorgeous.'

Tali flushes; nobody has ever called her gorgeous or attractive before. Zezette was the beauty, Tali the brains, and even in that regard Tali often felt deficient. All thought ceases, as Jo dips her head and trails kisses down Tali's neck, sending shivers through Tali's entire body.

She closes her eyes. *'Fraîche est ta beauté, doux est ton parfum …'*

After a moment, Jo lifts her head. 'What's that?' she says softly.

Tali opens her eyes. 'Our national anthem,' she whispers. Tali's eyes close again as she resumes her mumbling chant. It's the only way she can cope with Jo's caresses, and the devastating sensations her touch is generating.

'I have no idea what you're saying,' Jo murmurs. 'But French is so sexy …'

Tali's breath catches, as Jo's mouth moves lower, her lips skimming the slope of Tali's breasts, straining from her bra. *'N-nous voici tout debout, en un seul p-peuple ...'*

Jo's hot breath tickles, and Tali can no longer speak. Jo pauses, seeking silent consent to continue.

Don't stop. Don't stop.

Jo dips her head once more, and Tali is lost.

*

A crashing sound jerks Tali from slumber.

What was that?

She struggles up in the bed. Had she just heard the front door slam? She nudges Jo.

'Mmm?' Jo stirs.

'Listen,' Tali whispers.

Heavy footsteps are coming up the stairs, and out on the landing Tosca starts barking. Tali seizes Jo's arm. 'Who is it?'

Instantly alert, Jo slides out of bed, grabbing up a can of Tali's spray deodorant. She cracks open the bedroom door cautiously.

From out on the landing, Leo's slurring voice is heard to say: 'Fucking dog, get outta my way ...'

A muffled thump, and Tosca yelps.

Tali leaps from the bed, as Tosca sets up a frantic barking. There comes a strangled cry from Leo, followed by the unmistakable sound of something heavy falling down the stairs.

Jo wrenches the door open fully and stumbles out on to the landing, snapping the light on. 'Quick, Tali!'

But Tali is already tugging on her blouse, hurrying to join Jo. They stand together, staring down the stairs.

Lying in the shadows at the bottom is a dark, unmoving shape.

Leo.

Tosca is whining and barking from down in the hallway.

'Merde!' Tali staggers down the stairs, Jo a step behind her. Leo's body lies twisted at an unnatural angle, his eyes half closed, his head resting on the bottom step.

'Is he dead?' Tali whispers. She can't bring herself to touch him.

'No,' Jo exhales. 'He's breathing, look.'

They both stare at Leo.

'Monsieur Shepherd?' Tali reaches down to touch his shoulder.

'Don't move him,' Jo says quickly. 'His back might be broken.'

Leo remains motionless, the only sign of life the shuddery rise and fall of his chest.

'I'll call an ambulance.' Jo hurries back upstairs for her phone, leaving Tali crouched on the floor. She starts, as the door to Betty's bedroom opens.

'Natalia?' Betty emerges. 'Is that you?'

Tali scrambles to her feet. 'Oh, Madame Betty, don't ...'

But it's too late.

Betty sways, a hand flying to her mouth.

'We just found him, Madame Betty.'

'Leo?' Betty's voice cracks, as she sinks down beside her son.

'Ambulance, please,' Tali hears Jo's voice from upstairs. 'Yes, I need an ambulance, now. There's been an accident ...'

'What happened?' Betty says, so quietly Tali almost misses it.

'I was sleeping,' Tali stammers. 'A noise woke me. I came out and found Monsieur Shepherd ...' She tails off.

A moment later, Jo hurries down the stairs. She's thrown her shirt and jeans on, Tali is relieved to see.

'Oh, Mrs Shepherd,' Jo says, manoeuvring past Leo's body and coming to crouch on the other side of Betty. 'You shouldn't be here.'

Betty doesn't seem to hear her. She stares at Leo, stroking his cheek.

'Is the ambulance coming?' Tali asks.

'They'll be as quick as they can,' Jo says. 'But apparently there's been an incident in town, and all the units in the area are dealing with that.'

Betty clasps Leo's hand, and Tali wants to tell her not to touch him, not to move him at all, but she can't bring herself to say this.

'We should keep him warm,' Jo says. 'Do you have any spare blankets?'

'Upstairs in the cupboard,' Tali says, grateful beyond words for Jo's calming, practical presence.

Jo hops over Leo's prone body again, and disappears upstairs in a few bounds.

Tali can hear Tosca whining from the kitchen, wanting to be let out into the garden. She can't believe the direction the evening has taken. A few minutes ago she was lying in a heavenly dream with Jo, the next she's in some unfolding nightmare.

She returns from the kitchen, to find Jo stumbling back down the stairs, arms laden with blankets.

'Where is the ambulance?' Betty asks, her voice brittle.

'It's coming, Madame Betty,' Tali tries to comfort her. Leo lies silent between them.

'Is he drunk?' Tali mouths at Jo. There's a whiff of stale beer in the air. Jo nods.

'What happened?' Betty asks again.

Tali has no answer for her.

'Oh Leo,' Betty says, beginning to cry. 'You were always getting yourself into scrapes ...'

'What sort of scrapes, Madame Betty?' Tali asks gently.

'He nearly drowned once, when he was a boy,' Betty says. 'He'd built a raft out of barrels and old planks.'

'Like Tom Sawyer,' Jo offers.

'The barrels had holes in,' Betty says. 'The raft sank, nearly taking Leo down with it. Fred had to dive in and rescue him. Fred would have done anything for Leo, loved him like his own, even though he wasn't ...'

Tali exchanges a look of surprise with Jo. This is the first Tali has heard of Leo's father not being the hallowed Fred.

'Fred wasn't Leo's father?' Tali asks without thinking. Jo shoots her a look, as if to say, *Should you be asking this of Betty right now?*

'We never lied to Leo,' Betty murmurs, as though speaking only to herself. 'It was never a secret that Fred wasn't his father. But Leo refused to forgive me.'

'Forgive you for what?' Tali finds herself asking.

'For not telling him who his real father was,' Betty says. 'I couldn't tell him.' Tears slide down Betty's cheeks, dripping from her chin.

Tali offers her a tissue. 'It's nothing to be ashamed of, Madame Betty,' she says, as Betty removes her glasses to wipe her eyes. 'Lots of people don't know their fathers. But Leo had Fred.'

'I couldn't tell him the truth.' Betty gives a shaky sigh, her misty eyes magnified through the smudged lenses of her glasses. Jo passes Tali a spare blanket and Tali wraps it around Betty's shoulders.

'Don't upset yourself, Madame Betty,' she says uselessly.

'Oh, my son,' Betty whispers, gripping Leo's hand. 'You deserve to know the truth.'

'Mrs Shepherd, you really shouldn't be here, cold and uncomfortable,' Jo says. 'Why don't you come into the sitting room? I can put the fire on ...'

Betty shakes her head. 'I'm not leaving you,' she says to Leo. 'I should have told you the truth a long time ago.'

Tali exchanges a glance with Jo. Should they insist Betty go back to bed? But Betty is talking on. 'No one who has lived as long as I have can escape regrets, Leo. And I have many. But I never regretted having you, despite what you may believe.'

Tosca is scratching at the kitchen door, and Jo goes to let him back in. Tali hears her fill the kettle, and a wave of gratitude sweeps over her again.

'You deserved to know who your real father was,' Betty says, 'and I longed to tell you. But the memories were too painful.'

Tali thinks of the suitcase upstairs in her bedroom, a case full of memories.

'Your father's death haunts me,' Betty tells her son. 'Every full moon, I'm reminded of that night. Of what I did.'

Betty pauses and Tali holds her breath. She can hear Jo moving about in the kitchen.

'It's time you knew the truth, Leo,' Betty resumes. 'Your father was a man called Gilbert Donoghue. I met him in the war. We both worked for an organisation called Special Operations Executive.'

Jo brings tea through from the kitchen, and Tali accepts a mug gratefully.

'Gilbert was a trained wireless operator,' Betty continues. 'The most dangerous job in the SOE. He was sent to France to work for the Resistance. I was sent out too, but to work for a different circuit. I told everyone at home I was in London translating for the War Office.

'They made us sign the Official Secrets Act,' Betty goes on. 'We were ordered never to tell.' She pauses, her watery eyes meeting Tali's briefly. 'We risked our lives to fulfil our missions. And then one day the Nazis caught Gilbert. They tortured him almost to death.'

Tali reaches for Jo's hand, no longer sure she wants to hear this.

'During his terrible ordeal, he made a decision he believed was right.' Betty's eyes are streaming, but she makes no move to wipe them. 'It was a fatal mistake, a betrayal of everything – France, freedom, our love.'

From out on the street comes the blare of a siren. A flashing blue light pulsates through the frosted glass of the front door, and Jo leaps to her feet.

'Your father put all our lives at risk,' Betty whispers, lifting Leo's slack hand to her mouth and kissing it. Betty's voice is so quiet now, Tali strains to hear her. 'I had no choice but to kill him.'

24

November 1944–February 1945

They were married at Guildford Register Office on a crisp, cold morning in November. Theirs was the third of twenty weddings that day. Elisabeth wore a dark blue tailored woollen dress, donated by one of Florence's wealthier WVS colleagues, and altered to accommodate Elisabeth's growing bump. Fred wore his army uniform, his shoes polished to a shine, hair Brylcreemed to his scalp.

The wedding was inevitably a modest affair. Only Florence, Frederick's brother James, on home leave from the Navy, and Elisabeth's friend Josie were present as witnesses.

Elisabeth managed to hold herself together through the mercifully brief proceedings, right up until the moment she was required to speak her vows.

'Repeat after me,' the registrar hurriedly intoned, 'I, Elisabeth Ridley ...'

'I, Elisabeth Ridley,' she echoed, her voice barely above a whisper, 'take thee, Frederick Shepherd, to be my wedded husband ...' She stumbled over the words so badly, the registrar was obliged to ask her to repeat them.

All the while Elisabeth could sense Fred's affectionate gaze, but she couldn't meet his eye.

They exchanged no rings, on Elisabeth's insistence. She'd buried Gilbert's curtain ring in the old suitcase in the cellar, along with the gold lipstick and the money-belt and everything else from France. She never wanted to see any of it ever again.

At last, the registrar announced they were man and wife.

The deed was done, the papers signed, and Elisabeth found herself outside again, gulping in the chill fresh air.

Due to the shortage of camera film, the wedding photographer was only allowed to take two pictures. One would be of the bride and groom on the lawn in front of the register office, seated in a little rose arbour decorated with paper roses at this time of year. The second would be a small group shot on the steps.

'At least it's not raining,' Josie whispered in Elisabeth's ear as they waited their turn before the photographer. 'Are you all right? You look awfully pale.'

Elisabeth had barely seen Josie since her return from France. On the couple of times her friend had called round to Weyside, asking if she wanted to come out for a quick half at the Royal Oak with the girls, Elisabeth had pretended to be too tired. The truth was, she couldn't face anyone, even her best friend.

She'd only ventured into town once since her return, a few weeks ago, when Florence had insisted she accompany her on a shopping trip. Elisabeth had clung to her mother's arm as they made their way up the cobbled High Street, the sandbagged shopfronts, blacked-out windows and shuffling crowds reminding Elisabeth disturbingly of Rouen. American troops mingled amongst the Guildfordians, the tanned young men looking bored and terribly out of place, but Elisabeth had barely noticed them. Passing the offices of Lawson and Farr Solicitors, she'd thought fleetingly of Josie and the other girls hunched over their typewriters. She missed her friends, but she was a different person now. She couldn't imagine herself ever working in an office again.

Elisabeth had trailed after her mother from shop to shop, until finally they had reached the public library in North Street which, by some miracle, was still open. Desperate to escape the bustle and chaos of the streets, Elisabeth had persuaded her mother to let her wait in the library. For a blissful half-hour while Florence finished her shopping, Elisabeth had browsed the shelves, losing herself amongst the rows of books.

Now, here at her wedding, Elisabeth found herself tongue-tied, unable to think of anything to say to her best friend. 'I'm fine,' she lied, mustering a smile. 'Just tired.'

She longed to tell Josie everything, unburden herself of the slew of emotions that weighted her bones and robbed her of sleep, but she knew she couldn't, Josie would never understand. Their conversation remained polite and stilted, as Josie told Elisabeth about old Mr Farr and the girls in the office, how they kept asking after her.

'I don't half miss you too, old bean,' Josie said, as they posed on the steps for the group commemorative photo.

A lump formed in Elisabeth's throat. 'I miss you too,' she said.

More than you can ever know.

It was the first truth she'd uttered all day.

They took a taxi from the register office back to Weyside, where Florence had organised a very small wedding tea. The cake, a fruit sponge, had been made by a friend of Florence's in the baking trade. To supply him with the necessary ingredients, Florence, Frederick and Elisabeth had all given up their food rationing coupons for the month. Decorating the cake was not possible, of course, and so the baker had devised an ingenious cardboard cover, printed to resemble white swirling icing.

At least everyone had something to eat and drink, Elisabeth thought; a slice of cake and a glass of her father's home-made rhubarb wine to toast. Fred gave a short speech, blushing as pink as the wine. 'I can't believe my luck,' he said, taking Elisabeth's hand. 'You are the most beautiful girl in all of England.'

It was Elisabeth's turn to blush then.

As a token of his love, Frederick gave Elisabeth a chicken house he'd built from scrap wood, and half a dozen scrawny hens. It was such a thoughtful gift, typical of Fred to give her something useful.

In return, Elisabeth gave Fred a book – *The Practical Bee Guide.*

'Will you be going away for a few days?' Josie asked Elisabeth, catching her alone in the kitchen as she was drinking a glass of water. 'I wish I could escape like you, you lucky thing.'

'No,' Elisabeth replied. 'We'll be staying here.' She and Fred hadn't even discussed a honeymoon; a trip abroad was liable to end in an enemy prison camp, and all the seaside resorts in Britain had beaches covered in barbed wire and mines.

But none of it mattered. Elisabeth had no desire to leave Weyside.

'I wish I could find a chap as sweet as Fred,' Josie said.

Elisabeth felt an unaccustomed pang of pity for her friend. She'd had countless boyfriends, but none of them were of the staying kind. Josie had a warm heart and the knack of making light of the worst situation, and she would make a terrific wife and mother, Elisabeth had no doubt. It should be Josie's wedding today, not hers.

'The perfect chap's out there, waiting for you,' Elisabeth said. 'I know it.'

'Well, I wish they'd make themselves known,' Josie said. 'I'm not getting any younger.'

'You're twenty-four!'

'Exactly,' Josie sighed. 'Practically a spinster.'

At last, the wedding tea was over and the few guests departed. Elisabeth and Frederick found themselves alone, as Florence had tactfully opted to stay at a friend's overnight.

'You must be exhausted,' Fred said, gently rubbing Elisabeth's back as they sat together in the quiet sitting room.

'Will you come down to the river with me?' Elisabeth said.

'Now? It's getting dark.'

'Just for a little while. I need some fresh air.' She couldn't explain why she had such a sudden yearning to be by the river, and was grateful when Fred agreed. They wrapped up warmly and walked together down the garden path to the willow at the river's edge. The evening sky was clear, the first stars emerging. The only sounds were the trickle of water and the occasional distant hoot of an owl, hunting somewhere over the water meadows.

'Sometimes I could almost forget there's a war on,' Fred murmured. He found Elisabeth's hand and clasped it in both of his. 'I'm so lucky to be here, with you.'

Elisabeth was glad of the darkness, for once. She'd known Fred for less than a year, and yet here she was, married to him. It wasn't unusual, she told herself. There were wartime weddings all the time. These days, a woman had to take her chance at happiness, and maybe even love, wherever she could find it.

But no matter how much she cared for Fred, she could never tell him the truth, that she was a trained agent with blood on her hands. She was a wife now, soon to be a mother, and must put her past life behind her.

The worst of it was, there was no one to share the burden of what had happened in France. No one to share her secrets.

She suddenly craved a cigarette.

Fred put his arm around her shoulders. 'Penny for your thoughts, Mrs Shepherd?'

I don't deserve your kindness or your love, she wanted to cry. *I'm not the woman you think I am.*

Instead, she turned and took his face in her hands, and kissed him.

*

November was followed by a freezing December and January. Each day was marked by bitter frosts and wintry showers, punctuated by the occasional snowfall. A national coal shortage and continued rationing took its inevitable toll, but little changed for Elisabeth at Weyside. For two months, she barely went further than the end of the garden, spending her days keeping house for Frederick and her mother. In an attempt to distract her mind from morbid thoughts, she steadily read her way through her father's modest collection of classics. Descartes she left on the shelf.

At night, lying next to Fred as he gently snored, she would rest a hand on her stomach, feeling the baby's increasingly strong kicks pummel her insides. Whenever she thought about the actual process of birthing, of which she knew frighteningly little, her mind shut down with terror. It was at times like this, deep in the night when she couldn't sleep, that she was at her most vulnerable to dark thoughts. Her mind would churn over the events of that night in France, unanswered questions tormenting her. Why had Gilbert betrayed her? Why had he relinquished all hope, when the tide of war was on the turn, and there was everything to fight for? How could he have thought she would agree? Was there anything different she could have done?

Whenever she closed her eyes, images of Gilbert lying alone in the field in France flickered through her mind, and her pillow grew damp with half-stifled tears of muted rage and grief.

*

One morning, at the end of January, Elisabeth answered a knock at the front door, and found herself staring at a familiar face. Shock rendered her speechless.

The woman looking up at her from the step seemed similarly lost for words.

Elisabeth swallowed, tried to gather herself. 'Doris?' Her friend had changed drastically; already slim, Doris's figure was now gaunt, her shoulders stooped, cheekbones angular. It was as though Elisabeth was looking at a much older version of the woman she remembered from only a few months ago.

'I tracked you down at last, Elise.' Doris smiled, but her eyes flicked to the street and back to Elisabeth, unable to settle.

'Come in, out of the cold.' Elisabeth led Doris through to the sitting room, where a fire was burning in the hearth. The wood Fred had cut recently was still damp, and the fire barely warmed the room.

Doris kept her long coat on, but peeled off her gloves, and Elisabeth caught a glimpse of crooked fingers and red raw nail-beds. Her stomach lurched, and for a terrible moment she thought she might be sick.

'Tea?' she managed to ask.

'Anything,' Doris said. 'I'm parched.'

'Please,' Elisabeth gestured, 'have a seat. I'll put the kettle on.'

She escaped to the kitchen, grateful for a moment to compose herself. How on earth had Doris found her? What had happened to her friend? What did she want?

'Have you come from far?' she asked, carrying a tea tray through to the sitting room. Doris was standing before the fire, fumbling with a packet of cigarettes.

'London,' she said. 'Do you mind if I smoke?'

Elisabeth shook her head, though she knew if Fred or her mother were here they would be thoroughly disapproving. Thankfully, Florence was out all day with her WVS duties, and Fred was at the allotments, not due back until teatime.

Elisabeth wished she had something, anything, to offer her friend to eat. But there was precious little in the larder. As it was, she was going to have to perform a miracle with the two meagre chops for their tea tonight.

'It's so good to see you,' she said. It was the truth, she realised, despite the undercurrent of unease that pervaded the room.

Doris offered the cigarettes, and Elisabeth found herself taking one. She had hardly smoked at all since France, but now all she wanted was the harsh smoke in her lungs. Doris passed her a book of Canadian Air Force matches.

'Where'd you get these?' Elisabeth asked. Matches were rarer than hen's teeth at the moment.

'Met a chap,' Doris said, her smile fleeting. 'Matt's from Canada.' Her eyes drifted to Elisabeth's swelling stomach. 'When are you due?'

'Next month,' Elisabeth answered, busying herself pouring the tea. She was powerless to prevent the teapot spout from rattling against the cups.

Fetching her father's old glass ashtray from the sideboard, Elisabeth lit her cigarette. She took a long draw, the smoke hitting the back of her throat and almost making her cough. The unaccustomed nicotine instantly made her head swim. She took another drag, and felt a little sick.

Doris was staring at Elisabeth's belly, smoke curling from her nostrils, and Elisabeth knew with a cold certainty that her friend was calculating the months of the pregnancy, working backwards to the last time they'd seen each other at Beaulieu.

'I'm glad you found me,' Elisabeth said at last. 'I've thought of you so much, wondering ...'

Doris smoked like an automaton. 'Me too.'

'Where did they send you?' Elisabeth's voice was hoarse, but not just from the cigarette.

'Paris.' Smoke sighed from Doris's thin lips. 'What about you?'

'Near Rouen.' Elisabeth's own cigarette smouldered in the ashtray. To her surprise, she found she no longer wanted it. 'I thought of you often, wondering where you might be. And you weren't that far from me, in the end.'

'You wouldn't have recognised me, if we'd met in the street,' Doris said quietly. Her haunted eyes met Elisabeth's briefly, and all at once Elisabeth knew her friend too had suffered some terrible ordeal.

An oppressive silence filled the room, like an unwelcome guest.

'What happened?' Elisabeth whispered. The urge to confess her own story was crowding her tongue, and she bit her lip.

'I've told no one,' Doris said eventually. 'Not even Matt.' Hand trembling as she tapped ash, Doris began to speak. 'I was sent out as a courier for the Magician circuit.' She paused, eyes flicking to the door. 'Are we alone?'

Elisabeth nodded.

'Magician were waiting for a new wireless operator, and a day or so after I arrived, Gilbert turned up.'

'Gilbert?' Elisabeth could barely say his name.

'London's plans for me changed after he came,' Doris went on. 'My new mission was to infiltrate a local underground brothel serving German officers.'

'A brothel?' Elisabeth's eyes widened.

'You mustn't breathe a word,' Doris said. Haltingly, she told of her mercifully brief time as a *fille de joie*, spiking German officers' drinks, rifling their pockets, and reporting back to London anything important the men disclosed in an unguarded moment.

All was going well, until Gilbert was arrested. 'He'd had one too many drinks,' Doris told Elisabeth. 'Was caught out after curfew.'

Elisabeth couldn't think how to respond. Gilbert had said nothing to her about working with Doris. Agents were expected to be discreet, she knew this, but his omission somehow felt like the worst deceit.

'The very next night,' Doris went on, her voice low, 'we were raided. Someone had tipped off the Gestapo that the Madam was working with the Resistance. All the girls, me included, were arrested.'

Silence fell again, as Doris lit another cigarette. Elisabeth tried not to stare at her friend's missing fingernails, as a chilling thought occurred to her.

Gilbert had betrayed Doris and her network too.

Gradually, she realised Doris was asking her a question. 'What about you?'

A sound from the hall made both of them start. The front door clunked shut and Fred's cheery voice called out: 'I'm back!'

Elisabeth locked eyes with Doris, and an unspoken understanding passed between them.

Fred appeared in the doorway, carrying a basket of winter cabbages, big as muddy footballs. 'Oh hello, I didn't know we had guests.' He smiled at Doris, his cheeks flushed from the cold.

'Freddie, this is Doris,' Elisabeth said, rising. 'An old friend from school.'

'Nice to meet you,' Doris said quickly.

'Would you like a cabbage?' Fred offered. 'Old Davey's given us half a dozen. We'll be eating cabbage till midsummer.'

'That's kind of you, but no thank you,' Doris smiled. She drained her teacup. 'I really must be going.'

'So soon?' Elisabeth felt a flutter in her chest as the chance to share her secret with Doris faded.

'There's a lot to do before we sail,' Doris said.

'Sail?'

'I'm moving to Canada with Matt. We're going to get married out there.'

'Oh.' For a second, Elisabeth could think of nothing to say. 'That's lovely,' she managed at last.

'What part of Canada?' Fred asked, as if he knew anything about the country at all.

'Edmonton,' Doris replied. 'It's the capital city of Alberta.'

Elisabeth nodded and smiled, none the wiser. The baby gave a sharp kick, and she gasped.

Fred set down the basket, moving to Elisabeth's side. 'All right, love?'

'I'm fine,' she snapped, and instantly regretted her tone.

'I must be going,' Doris said, rising and pulling on her gloves. 'Nice to meet you, Fred.'

'You too,' Fred replied politely. He picked up his basket and headed off to wash his hands.

Elisabeth turned to Doris. 'Do you really have to go?' she said. But already Doris was across the room.

In the hallway they awkwardly embraced. Elisabeth was shocked at how insubstantial Doris felt beneath her coat. Her own jutting belly made her feel enormous in comparison.

'Take care of yourself.' Doris reached out and stroked Elisabeth's stomach gently. 'And the little one.'

'Please write. You will write?'

'Of course I'll write.' Doris winked, and Elisabeth glimpsed a shadow of her old friend. 'In code, so no one else can read it.'

'Oh Lord, not Morse again,' Elisabeth joked weakly. 'I couldn't bear more of that torture.' The moment the words left her mouth, Elisabeth wished them back, as Doris's face drained of colour.

'Well, I'd better go, or else Matt will think I've eloped without him,' Doris said, backing down the steps. 'I'll write, I promise.'

She blew Elisabeth a kiss, and was gone.

*

February arrived and the months of freezing weather changed almost overnight, as though someone had flicked a switch. Tropical maritime air flooded north-eastwards, heralding the mildest February most people could recall in a long time.

An air of expectancy hung over the country, the newspapers full of Hitler's defences crumbling. As Britain waited for the final act, Elisabeth's pregnancy was nearing its conclusion.

Towards the middle of February, she began to suffer pangs that Florence termed *'fausses contractions'*. The pains felt terrifyingly real to Elisabeth. She couldn't get comfortable in bed, and in the end moved herself into the little spare bedroom, so that Fred could at least get a decent night's sleep.

The prospect of her impending labour frightened Elisabeth almost as much as the parachute jump over France had. Sometimes, in the small hours, when her weak bladder and the false contractions kept her awake, she wished she could jump again instead of endure this living nightmare.

Rising exhausted in the morning, she tried to keep her fears buried, busying herself with housework and eking out the ever-dwindling rations. In the evenings she would try and read, while Florence knitted baby clothes by the fire, and Fred hammered nails into wood upstairs, building a cot.

And then, one evening at the end of February, Elisabeth was making a pot of tea in the kitchen when she felt an intense, urgent pain radiate across her stomach and down her legs, sending her staggering against the stove with a cry.

Florence called out from the sitting room. '*Qu'y a t-il?*'

'I don't know,' Elisabeth gasped, as wetness gushed between her legs, soaking her skirt.

Her mother appeared. 'Your waters have broken,' Florence asserted. 'The baby, it comes.'

Somehow, Elisabeth made it upstairs to her bed. The pain was rapidly growing in strength, and the hot-water bottle and aspirin Florence brought did nothing to relieve the pulsing waves of agony.

Fred returned from locking in the chickens for the night, drawn to the bedroom by Elisabeth's cries.

'My love,' he choked at the sight of her, his face blanching.

Florence quickly despatched him to fetch one of her colleagues from the WVS, a midwife, and soon a broad woman with a ruddy, kind face appeared at Elisabeth's bedside.

'I need hot water, towels, sheets,' the midwife instructed, and Florence hurried from the room.

'All right now, my love.' The midwife loomed over Elisabeth. 'Let's take a look, shall we?'

The woman smelled of rusty coins and carbolic, but her fingers were deft and sure, and Elisabeth surrendered to her probings.

'Well, this one's keen,' the midwife remarked, unable to quite disguise the tension in her voice. Florence returned with water and towels, and Elisabeth suddenly felt a deep pull between her legs, a pain of such intensity her back arched and she cried out.

'The baby's crowning,' the midwife said, glancing up. 'Deep breaths now, my love. Nice and slow ...'

Elisabeth clutched her mother's hand as another contraction eviscerated her, a cold knife of pain tearing through her stomach.

'Breathe, Elisabeth,' she heard her mother urge. 'Breathe ...'

She sucked in air as though she were drowning.

Gradually the pain eased, only to build again seconds later.

'I'm frightened, Maman,' she whimpered, in a brief lull between waves of agony.

'*Je sais, ma chérie,*' her mother said. 'But you have to be brave now.'

Another wave of pain swept through her, and she was overcome by an urge to bear down. She tried to rise, but the midwife pressed her down again. 'Relax, my love, save your strength.' The midwife's meaty arms forced Elisabeth gently back into the pillows.

Sweat dripped down her forehead, stinging her eyes. The agonising ache between her legs was unbearable, it felt as though her body was being ripped apart, and she began to pant and moan and writhe.

Florence held a damp flannel to her brow, murmuring encouragement, but Elisabeth's torment had reached such an intensity that she barely registered her surroundings any more. Her fevered mind began to drift, down to the dappled shade beneath the willow tree, where the river flowed on and on and on.

She was going to die.

She was certain of it.

Florence held her, crying with her.

'Push,' the midwife said. 'Push now!'

The baby's skin was a mottled blue, the umbilical cord wrapped around his neck. Dazed with exhaustion, Elisabeth could only look on as the midwife unhooked the pulsing cord with swift, bloodied fingers, turning the baby face down along her strong forearm. She rubbed his tiny, wrinkled back, and after a moment he gave a mewl, like a kitten.

'*Dieu merci!*' Florence cried. She held her grandson while the midwife cut the cord.

'It's a tough one,' the midwife grunted, but at last the bond between baby and mother was severed. The baby was wrapped in a blanket and placed in Elisabeth's arms. She gazed down at her child, Gilbert's son, and a flood of love and grief rolled over her, deep and profound.

25

2019

The taxi drops Tali and Jo at the gates of Guildford Crematorium. As they step from the car, the clouds part and a shaft of early spring sunshine warms Tali's face. Oh, Madame Betty, she thinks. You're here.

They've arrived early, and Jo suggests they take a short walk around the grounds of the crematorium while they wait for everyone else to arrive. Tali finds herself holding Jo's hand, something she'd never be brave enough to do in public back home. As they follow the neatly tended paths that wend around the chapel, Tali thanks Jo for her support.

Jo squeezes Tali's hand. 'Betty would have loved this place, wouldn't she?'

Tali gazes at the flower borders swathed in bright yellow daffodils and delicate lilac crocuses, and the colours cheer her. Yes, Madame Betty would have loved this place.

Soon, other cars begin to arrive, and Tali and Jo make their way back to the chapel. Abeo helps Violet out of a taxi, and Tali hugs them both. Abeo is resplendent in a kingfisher-blue agbada, and looks to Tali like African royalty. Violet is clutching a posy of pink carnations. 'For remembrance,' she tells Tali.

'Thank you so much for coming,' Tali says.

'It is a pleasure,' Abeo replies, and envelops Tali in another warm hug.

A Volvo estate draws up, and Robert and his Zimmer frame are deposited on the path by a middle-aged woman, who drives off before Tali can speak to her.

'My daughter's late for her yoga class,' Robert apologises. Jo tucks his arm in hers.

Robert's arrival is closely followed by that of Alfred, Duncan, Hilda and Olive, who have shared a car. Juliana pushes Margaret in her wheelchair up the path, having travelled to the crematorium by bus.

Last to arrive are Jo's boss Choppy Ayling and his wife, Bridie. Tali smiles to see the couple. She's come to know them well over the last few months, often enjoying dinner at their house with Jo. Bridie, thin and frail following her illness, is dressed in a padded jacket and thermal boots, despite the mild weather. She is enthusiastically greeted by the members of the Century Society.

'It's so good to see you all,' Bridie says. 'And what a glorious day!'

'You bearing up, lass?' Choppy asks Tali, patting her on the shoulder. He's wearing his customary outfit of jeans, checked shirt and leather Stetson, silvery hair tied back in a ponytail. He looks like some line-dancing nut, but it suits him, Tali thinks.

'*Oui, merci,*' she smiles.

Choppy nods. 'We're all here for you,' he says.

'*Merci ...*' Tali hardly knows how to respond to this. She glances over at Jo, talking with Robert and Alfred.

'I just want to say, lass.' Choppy leans closer and Tali catches his scent of wood shavings and motor oil. 'I don't know what your plans are, now that Betty's gone, but Jo loves you hard, lass. I hope you know that.'

'I know that,' Tali smiles.

'Good lass.' Choppy pats her arm again. 'Life's too short to run away.'

I'm never running away again, Tali thinks.

A woman appears at the door of the chapel and catches Tali's eye. It's the humanist minister Tali has hired to oversee the service, as Betty had expressed in her will a desire for a non-religious funeral.

As everyone files into the chapel, Tali thinks of the only other person who should be here. She'd last visited Leo at Oak Manor the day after Betty had died. The nurse on duty had warned Tali that Leo's mental and physical health were deteriorating rapidly. 'But it's good you come and see him,' the nurse had said. 'No one else does.'

Tali had sat by Leo's bed, and told him how his mother had passed away peacefully in her sleep. Leo had stared at the ceiling, a fleck of saliva in the corner of his gaping mouth. He'd made no sign that he'd heard Tali, but she hadn't really been expecting a response. Leo had never recovered from his fall down the stairs, existing in a state of semi-comatose confusion. The first and only time Tali had taken Betty to see her son in the home, it had upset Betty so much she hadn't gone again.

The chapel, though small, is furnished in pine, sunlight flooding through the high windows, a pleasant floral scent permeating the air. Tali takes her place at the front, Jo on one side of her, Bridie on the other.

Before her, on a raised plinth, lies Betty's casket.

While everyone takes their seats, and the minister organises her notes on the lectern, Tali finds herself comparing Betty's small, intimate funeral with her old friend Doris's flamboyant affair. A few days ago, whilst sorting through the last of Betty's paperwork, Tali had come across Doris's obituary, cut from *The Times*.

Mrs DORIS BONE née WATERS, 101, died peacefully following a short illness on 27 January at her home in Oxford.

Doris was born on 3 May 1916, in Tring, Hertfordshire, but spent her childhood in France. Bilingual in French and English, Doris returned to Britain in 1938 and began her career in the hospitality industry. In 1944, a chance encounter resulted in her being selected to work for Special Operations Executive. Sent to France as a courier to work with the Resistance, Doris was instrumental in maintaining communication with London, despite her circuit's penetration by the Nazis. She was awarded the George Medal for her bravery.

Doris married Matthew Bone in 1945. They settled in Canada after the war, where they brought up their only daughter, Elise.

When she'd first read the obituary, Tali hadn't realised the significance of the name 'Elise'. But since then, she'd discovered a letter in Betty's suitcase. It was postmarked from the War Office, and addressed to 'Elise' – Betty's code name in the war, Tali now knew.

As Tali gradually pieces together Betty's extraordinary exploits during the war, she finds the letters from Doris particularly poignant to read.

She thinks of the suitcase of memories safely stowed on the narrowboat, along with Tosca. Tali hopes the dog isn't scratching Jo's cushions in protest.

'Good morning, everyone,' the minister begins, bringing Tali back to the present moment. 'My name is Alice and I'd like to welcome you to a celebration of Betty Shepherd's life ...'

*

Tali couldn't have hoped for a better service. She thanks the minister, as everyone files back outside. Tali's eyes are red from crying, and she blinks in the bright sunshine. It's a day for walking along the river with Jo, she thinks. Perhaps later they will.

'That was a lovely service,' Hilda pronounces. 'Well done, Tali.'

'Thank you.'

Someone has laid out Betty's wreaths. Tali reads a label – it's from Mr and Mrs Voller – and has a sudden flashback to Betty's party and hanging Mrs Voller's flag bunting all over the garden.

'I'm so glad you could all come,' Tali says. 'It would have meant so much to Madame Betty.'

Taxis are beginning to arrive, and one by one the members of the Century Society head off. As she hugs each person goodbye, Tali suffers a moment of plunging sadness; she'll probably never see them again. She'll miss them. The Century Society had been fun, and both she and Betty had come to appreciate it, each in her own way.

Jo comes to stand next to Tali, and takes her hand. 'The minister told me we can collect Betty's ashes tomorrow,' Jo says.

Tali nods, not trusting her voice, as she watches the last of the cars disappear through the entrance gates.

*

A week later, and the urn of ashes sits atop the chain-locker on *Thyme*'s front deck. Every time Tali looks at it, she hears the crematorium clerk's heart-breaking words.

So many urns are never claimed. Hundreds every year.

Tali can't imagine why anyone would abandon their loved one's remains. At the same time, she finds it almost impossible to believe that Madame Betty is inside the little bamboo-wood urn. It doesn't seem possible for a person she once knew and cared for to be reduced to a few handfuls of dust.

Tosca climbs the steps to join Tali on the deck, and gives the urn a wary sniff.

'You won't believe what's in there, *tou tou*,' Tali says, scratching Tosca's ears. He wags his tail, then hops, rather nimbly for a dog of his age and girth, on to the bank.

Does he miss Madame Betty? Tali wonders as she heads back inside the narrowboat to begin preparing dinner. Tosca has taken to life on the river like a duck to water, as Betty would have said. He doesn't seem to miss Weyside at all. Tali wishes she'd thought to ask Betty how she'd come to get Tosca in the first place.

Tali's mind drifts to Weyside. It's taken her and Jo a long time, but the house is finally empty of Betty's furniture and belongings. It's been on the market for a week, and there have been several viewings already. It's a very sought-after property, the officious estate agent keeps saying. Tali has taken an instant dislike to the woman's cheap black suits and sniffy manner. The estate agent's job, Tali knows, is to sell houses. But Weyside is more than a house, it's a repository of history, a museum of memories. Tali doesn't want to know about Weyside's 'potential', how easy it would be to rip the old kitchen out, and build an extension at the back, and pave the messy little front garden over.

Madame Betty's house deserves a family, Tali reminds herself. A lovely family with children who will appreciate the garden and the river.

Tali still can't quite believe that Madame Betty left her the house in her will.

'But she loved you, didn't she?' Jo continually reminds Tali. 'Like a granddaughter. And besides, who else did she have in her life but you?'

Only her son.

Tali can hardly bear to think about Leo, after all the awful things she's wished on him, before his dreadful, tragic fall. When she recalls that night, discovering his broken body at the bottom of the stairs, it still makes her shudder.

She opens the fridge, takes out two chicken legs, bastes them in butter and chopped garlic and pops them in the tiny oven.

The only consolation is that Leo is now being well cared for. Tali had agreed to accept the terms of Betty's will with one proviso: the solicitor would split the proceeds from the sale of Weyside, and pay half to Oak Manor for Leo's ongoing care. The other half Tali will use to fund a year of travelling the waterways with Jo.

Their plan excites Tali beyond words. To spend time with Jo in their little floating nest, visiting places Tali has only ever imagined, is a dream come true. It's still hard to believe how her fortunes have changed, as unexpectedly and miraculously as the sudden reversal of the river's flow. And it's all thanks to Madame Betty.

There's one other thing Tali needs to do.

She thinks of the suitcase, currently residing under the bench seat at the stern. It's practically the only thing Tali salvaged from Weyside, apart from Betty's old leather handbag and its weird contents, and some useful kitchen utensils. Over the past few days, Tali has been systematically sorting through the contents of the suitcase, carefully re-reading all the letters and postcards and official documents. A history of Betty's life has slowly emerged, and Tali is starting to wonder if she could write Betty's biography. Jo's suspicion that Betty was a spy is looking increasingly likely, the more Tali discovers.

She's rinsing tomatoes in the galley sink, when she feels the boat rock beneath her feet. Jo's face appears in the hatchway, and Tali's heart gives its customary flip.

'I'm back!' Jo jumps lightly down the steps. Her jeans are streaked with mud, her work boots caked in the stuff.

'Take them off!' Tali cries. 'You make dirt everywhere.'

'All right, all right, keep your hair on.' Jo grins, tugging off her boots. 'What's for dinner?'

Tali smiles to herself. She'd been expecting this question. Jo is permanently hungry, though where she puts all the food is a mystery to Tali, who only has to look at a potato to gain half a stone.

Tali dries her hands on a tea towel. 'Salad,' she says sweetly.

Jo pulls a face.

'Salad is good for you.'

'But I'm starving.' Jo pulls off her jumper, and Tali catches her lover's familiar blend of scents. She has a sudden mental image of Jo wielding a chainsaw, and feels a thrum of desire in her loins.

'Choppy tried to get me up the ropes again today,' Jo sighs. 'He keeps saying if I try it every day, I should eventually get used to working at height. But I don't know … it just makes me feel sick.'

'Have you told him how scared you are?' Tali asks. 'Have you been honest with him, Jo?'

'Gotta clean up …' Jo disappears into the bathroom.

'When are you going to tell him?' Tali persists, when Jo emerges again.

'I will, I've just got to time it right …'

Tali wants to shake her, until she's reminded of a saying Betty had used a lot, about the pot calling the kettle black. Tali still hasn't phoned her family to tell them about Betty's death, or the sale of Weyside. Or Jo.

Jo comes towards her, a glint of lust in her eyes. She spots the tomatoes in the sink. '*Pommes d'amour*,' she whispers, lifting Tali's thick curls and kissing the nape of her neck. 'Are we really only having salad?'

'And chicken and rice,' Tali breathes, a delicious shiver running through her, 'if you let me get on with it.'

'I want to eat *you*,' Jo murmurs, gently pulling Tali round to face her. The gangway is so narrow, their bodies are pressed together.

'What part of me first?' Tali laughs, her breasts rising like bread dough between them. Jo grins, but as her hungry gaze lowers, Tali's mobile phone rings.

'Shit,' Jo mutters, as Tali fumbles to answer it.

'Hello?'

'Tali? Is that you?'

Her brother's familiar voice seizes Tali's heart and for a second she can't think. 'Rozo,' she stammers.

'You sound faint, Tali ... can you hear me?'

Tali glances at Jo, who returns her look with a worried frown. 'I can hear you, Rozo.' She presses the speaker-phone button.

There's a glitch in communication, a few empty seconds before Rozo's voice issues from the phone. 'Good,' he says at last. Tali thinks she hears children's voices in the background. She pictures her older brother in his garden, full of hibiscus and jacaranda trees, surrounded by his four daughters – her nieces – and feels a sudden tug of homesickness.

'Is everything OK, Rozo?'

'Yeah, yeah. All cool.'

Tali's shoulders drop slightly. 'How's everyone?'

'When are you coming home?'

Rozo's question comes from nowhere, sending Tali's mind into free-fall.

'I'm not.' The words escape her mouth before she can stop them. Jo's eyes widen.

'What did you say?' Her brother sounds confused, and Tali pictures the frown line deepening between Rozo's thick black eyebrows, as it always did when he struggled to understand something.

'My plans have changed,' Tali says quickly before she loses her nerve. 'I'm staying here.'

Jo pumps the air with her fist and silently mouths *at last*.

'What do you mean, you're not coming home?' Rozo's distant voice sounds angry now. 'Mum and Dad have come round, Tali. It's taken months of persuasion, but they're ready to listen. And everyone's hoping you'll be here for Jaime's birthday. Your niece is going to be five in a couple of weeks, in case you'd forgotten …?'

Merde! She had forgotten.

Tali closes her eyes. 'I'm sorry,' she says. Jo rubs her arm.

'You there, Tali?'

'*Oui.*' She raises her voice a notch. 'I'm here.'

'So what's going on?'

She has to tell Rozo the truth, she owes it to him at least, but still she has to force the words out. 'I've met someone,' she says at last.

'Met someone? Who? What's his name?'

Tali looks at Jo, and they both smile.

'Her name's Joanna,' Tali says.

*

The darkening sky is pinpricked with a scattering of stars, and a full moon rises over the water meadows.

Earlier in the day, Jo had strung solar-powered fairy lights all over *Thyme*'s long roof, and as Tali sits on deck waiting for her, the tiny coloured bulbs begin to wink into life. She glimpses Jo through the hatch, buttoning up her shirt, and feels a pleasurable stab of love in her chest. What would she have done without Jo? It doesn't bear thinking about, and she turns her mind back to Betty's urn, waiting on the anchor locker.

Tali is ready. She's done her research, googled 'scattering human ashes' on her phone, checked it was permitted to do what she planned to do. Apparently, it's perfectly legal to dispose of someone's cremated remains in the river, as long as various strict guidelines are adhered to. Tali has ticked all the boxes.

The evening is unusually warm for April, the air still.

'Muggy,' Jo says, flapping the hem of her shirt as she climbs up to join Tali on deck.

Tali can't help but smile. She's heard Jo use this word before. The English definition of muggy bears no comparison with the hot, steamy Mauritian nights she once lived through.

But instead of correcting Jo, she reaches for her hand and pulls her closer.

'Betty would have liked *Thyme*, wouldn't she?' Jo says. 'I wish we could have taken her for a trip down the river.'

'She would have loved *Thyme*.' Tali lifts her eyes to the moon, stitched like a pearl to the deep navy velvet of the sky.

The river's true nature is heightened in the dusk, as the energy of the day dissipates. Curious nocturnal sounds are beginning to emerge from the shadows, and the green, fecund smell of the water drifts on the faint breeze, the air alive with dark, flickering shapes.

A bat flits so close, Tali feels the whisper of its wings against her face. She turns to Jo. 'I still can't believe Madame Betty has gone.'

'I know,' Jo says.

Tali feels the hot prickle of tears, yet Betty would not have wanted her to cry.

'But she'll never be forgotten.'

No, Tali thinks, she won't forget Madame Betty.

Tali rises and takes up the pot of ashes. It's time to bid Madame Betty adieu.

They climb on to the bank, moving a little way from *Thyme*, to an empty berth. Tali kneels at the water's edge, and Jo sinks down next to her on the grass. Tosca appears, sniffing around them, as if he knows what they are about to do.

Tali carefully unscrews the lid of the urn. The moon's luminescence shines down, and a soft breeze ripples the silvered water.

'*Bon voyage*,' Tali whispers. Leaning forward, she slowly tips the ashes into the river. They float for a moment, before melting away beneath the surface.

She sets the empty urn down on the grass, and Jo's warm hand finds hers.

'All right?' Jo murmurs.

Tali nods, then rests her head on Jo's firm shoulder.

The night is deepening, shadows dissolving into darkness.

Tali thinks of the dawn to come.

Author's Note

The genesis of Operation Moonlight was a conversation I had with a friend back in 2018. She told me about a super-centenarian she knew, a 110-year-old woman who was still going strong, determined to become the oldest person in Britain. This woman's stalwart attitude reminded me of my own late maternal grandmother, who, if she'd still been alive, would have been the same age. My gran died soon after my twins were born, but her long life was inspirational to me.

Born illegitimately in 1908, Gran grew up in poverty in the north of England. Despite her harsh upbringing, she survived two world wars, the 1918 influenza epidemic, breast cancer, and a bigamist first husband. Her slight, five-foot frame belied an inner strength that even as a child I admired, and now as a grown woman I seek to emulate. My gran was the main inspiration for the character of Elisabeth. But Elisabeth is also an amalgamation of thirty-nine other women whose stories I discovered while researching tales of women in the past, and whose extraordinary achievements have been largely forgotten.

These women became instrumental during World War Two, when Winston Churchill set up a clandestine organisation known as Special Operations Executive. The SOE trained secret agents – mostly men – but also a small group of women of various ages and backgrounds. These French-speaking wives, mothers and daughters endured the same training as their male counterparts, and were then parachuted, alone and at night, into Nazi-occupied France to aid the Resistance. Elisabeth's gruelling paramilitary training in Scotland, her terrifying parachute jump on a moonlit night, and her perilous mission in Rouen are all drawn from the real experiences of these women.

Of the thirty-nine female SOE agents, twelve were executed following their capture by the Nazis, while one died of meningitis during her mission. The remainder survived the war. Most of these women have fallen into shadowy obscurity over the years, and I wanted to bring their awe-inspiring stories back into the light.

As much as possible I have stayed true to the historical fact, but at times I have used creative licence. For instance, I've changed the names of real people involved with SOE, I've placed the Rouen church Elisabeth shelters inside in the same general area as Eglise Saint-Joseph but otherwise it bears no resemblance to that church, and the town of Chounoît is entirely fictitious.

Acknowledgements

I would like to extend my heartfelt gratitude to the following people:

Thank you to Luigi and Alison Bonomi, who saw the potential in my first pages – you are the most encouraging and supportive agents I could ever have wished for.

A huge thank you to Selina Walker, whose patient mentoring and expert editorial guidance has been an absolute privilege to experience.

Thanks also to Sophie Whitehead – it's been such a comfort to have your astute editorial eye on my work.

Thank you also to Penny Isaac, Isabelle Ralphs, Laurie Ip Fung Chun, and all the Century team, working invisibly behind the scenes.

Thank you to my writing friends, Lisa Koning and Scott Goldie, for your early reading of my book and helpful comments. Thanks also to Julie Ma, for the little insights that have shone a light for me.

Thank you to Georgi Fancett, for your friendship, humour and moral support.

Thank you to the debut 2022 bunch, for the online camaraderie.

Thank you to PS – for your military advice and 'talking me down' from that plane.

I would like to pay homage to the late Bob Weighton, the oldest man in Britain at the time I was drafting this novel, who gave me an invaluable, first-hand insight into the war years.

Thank you to all the staff at Alton Library, especially Susan, Michelle, Kevin and Hilary, for the many book reservations over the years. I couldn't have done my research without you.

Thank you to Henrik and Nicky, for your incredible generosity, comprehensive SOE knowledge, and for showing me the beauty of Scotland.

Thank you to Dr Kate Vigurs, historian and author of *Mission France*, who fact-checked my manuscript (any remaining mistakes are all my own).

Thank you to Veronique and Bridie, for your French and German guidance.

Thank you to the Hampshire Writers' Society, whose talks and competitions were so hugely encouraging in my early writing days.

Thank you to the Faber Academy, for giving me the initial courage to share my work with strangers.

Thank you to all my family, especially Mum and Dad, and my children Andrew, William and Ellen. You've had to put up with a lot of distracted mothering over the years, but I love you.

And last, but definitely not least, thank you to Darren. With you by my side on this journey, I won't get lost.

Further Reading

If you are interested in learning more about the SOE and women in the war, I found the following books to be excellent sources of information:

Collyer, Graham, *Guildford: The War Years*, Breedon Books (1999)

Fairburn, Captain W. F., *All-In Fighting*, Naval and Military Press (2020)

Foot, M. R. D., *SOE: Special Operations Executive, 1940–1945*, Bodley Head (2014)

Helm, Sarah, *A Life in Secrets: The Story of Vera Atkins and the Lost Agents of SOE*, Abacus (2006)

Longmate, Norman, *How We Lived Then: A History of Everyday Life during the Second World War*, Pimlico (2002)

MacKenzie, William, *The Secret History of SOE, Special Operations Executive 1940–1945*, St Ermin's Press (reprinted 2000)

Miles, Constance, *Mrs Miles's Diary: The Wartime Journal of a Housewife on the Home Front*, Simon & Schuster (2013)

O'Connor, Bernard, *Agent Rose: The True Spy Story of Eileen Nearne, Britain's Forgotten Wartime Heroine*, Amberley Publishing (2014)

Pattinson, Juliette, *Behind Enemy Lines: Gender, Passing and the Special Operations Executive in the Second World War*, Manchester University Press (2011)

Rée, Jonathan, ed., *A Schoolmaster's War: Harry Rée, British Agent in the French Resistance*, Yale University Press (2021)

Rigden, Denis, *How To Be a Spy: The World War II SOE Training Manual*, Dundurn Group (2004)

Special Operations Executive Manual: How To Be an Agent in Occupied Europe, William Collins (2014)

Vigurs, Kate, *Mission France: The True History of the Women of SOE*, Yale University Press (2021)

Walker, Robyn, *The Women Who Spied for Britain: Female Secret Agents of the Second World War*, Amberley Publishing (2014)

About the Author

Louise Morrish is a librarian, whose debut novel won the 2019 Penguin Random House First Novel Competition. She finds inspiration for her stories in the real-life adventures of women in the past, whom history has forgotten. She lives in Hampshire with her family.